"The wonderfully inventive, delightfully wacky, and cleverly complex Midsolar Murders sci-fi mystery series is off and running again, this time exploring more of Mallory's background while maintaining the delicious humor and intricate mystery prevalent in the first book." —*Booklist* (starred review)

"As bingeable and satisfying as your favorite murder show. I couldn't put it down."
—Sarah Pinsker, Nebula Award–winning author of *A Song for a New Day* and *We Are Satellites*

"A clever and suspenseful sci-fi mystery, with intriguing characters and attentive world-building." —*Library Journal* (starred review)

"Embrace the chaos and try to solve the many mysteries—you'll have fun along the way." —Tor.com

"Balances both the science fiction elements—meeting aliens, understanding how to work with them—and the mystery elements very evenly; it genuinely works as both genres (and works best as both). I'm already looking forward to however many more of these stories we get, because it was just so much fun." —*Locus*

"The follow-up to *Station Eternity* is just as complex and engaging as its predecessor. Lafferty's skill with dialogue and emotional arcs makes the story equally character- and action-driven."
—*Library Journal* (starred review)

"Mur Lafferty is turning into science fiction's Agatha Christie, with her mastery of ensemble casts and deft characterizations. *Station Eternity* builds a whole new universe of alien civilizations and wraps it all in an engaging mystery. This fun, fast-paced novel is sure to please fans of both *Six Wakes* and *Solo*."

—S.B. Divya, Hugo and Nebula Award–nominated author of *Machinehood*

"This whirlwind adventure is good fun."　　　—*Publishers Weekly*

"Mur Lafferty proves once again that she has the rare talent to blend and bend the sister genres of mystery and science fiction. . . . Smart and sassy, here's the book that will blast you to orbit."

—James Patrick Kelly, winner of the Hugo, Nebula, and Locus Awards

"Reminds me of intricately plotted madcap comedies like *Bringing Up Baby*. We are joyfully along for the ride. . . . I eagerly look forward to devouring more in the Midsolar Murders series in the future."

—Women Write About Comics

"[Lafferty's] sense for the alien but familiar, and that feel for the deeply strange, have made this series one with a depth of imagination and invention in its world-building that is hard to beat."

—Sci-Fi and Fantasy Reviews

"This series combines two of my favorite genres—cozy mysteries and space adventure—and I look forward to reading more about Mallory and the rest of the residents, human and alien, on the space station Eternity. Highly recommended."　　　—The Nameless Zine

ADDITIONAL PRAISE FOR
MUR LAFFERTY AND *SIX WAKES*

"Lafferty delivers a tense nail-biter of a story fueled by memorable characters and thoughtful world-building."

—Publishers Weekly (starred review)

"Lafferty delivers the ultimate locked-room mystery combined with top-notch sci-fi world-building." *—Library Journal* (starred review)

"A taut, nerve-tingling, interstellar murder mystery with a deeply human heart." **—NPR**

"An exquisitely crafted puzzle box that challenges our thoughts on what it means to be human."

—New York Times bestselling author Scott Sigler

ALSO BY MUR LAFFERTY

The Midsolar Murders

Station Eternity
Chaos Terminal

INFINITE ARCHIVE

MUR LAFFERTY

ACE
NEW YORK

ACE
Published by Berkley
An imprint of Penguin Random House LLC
1745 Broadway, New York, NY 10019
penguinrandomhouse.com

ACE is a registered trademark and the A colophon is a trademark of
Penguin Random House LLC.

Book design by Alison Cnockaert

Library of Congress Cataloging-in-Publication Data

Names: Lafferty, Mur, author.
Title: Infinite archive / Mur Lafferty.
Description: First edition. | New York: Ace, 2025.
Identifiers: LCCN 2024051167 (print) | LCCN 2024051168 (ebook) |
ISBN 9780593098158 (trade paperback) | ISBN 9780593098165 (ebook)
Subjects: LCGFT: Science fiction. | Detective and mystery fiction. | Novels.
Classification: LCC PS3612.A3743 I54 2025 (print) | LCC PS3612.A3743 (ebook) |
DDC 813/.6—dc23/eng/20241210
LC record available at https://lccn.loc.gov/2024051167
LC ebook record available at https://lccn.loc.gov/2024051168

First Edition: July 2025

Printed in the United States of America
1st Printing

The authorized representative in the EU for product safety and compliance is
Penguin Random House Ireland, Morrison Chambers, 32 Nassau Street,
Dublin D02 YH68, Ireland, https://eu-contact.penguin.ie.

To Matt, child of the 25th.

Here is your deli.

INFINITE
ARCHIVE

1

. · ·

0.18 PERCENT IS STILL
A LOT OF MURDER

THE WORST THING about being part of an alien hivemind was you had to act like thousands of insect feet crawling over your body—including your face, neck, ears—and possibly trying to burrow into your collar was just fine.

The best part about being part of an alien hivemind? The jury was still out on that one.

Mallory sat motionless on her bed, eyes closed, reminding herself this was Just Fine. Even among the buzz of thousands of wings. Even with antennae probing and investigating every hormone she secreted. Even with a deadly allergy to Earth-dwelling insects of the Vespidae family.

She breathed slowly. *Don't think about that allergy thing.*

Meditating was challenging for most people, but trying to meditate in the midst of a swarm of blue wasplike aliens was a new level. Most of the members of the Sundry were as long as her thumb, their stingers and venom sacs visible. She tried to go deeper into the meditation and ignore the dainty feet crawling over her eyelids and the delicate antennae probing her nostrils and ear canals.

Feel the station, the hivemind said.

She extended her awareness past her own discomfort and fear. It was hard to fight against decades of fear responses, but she was part of the hivemind, and the Sundry took care of their own.

All at once she was in her room; she was in the large hive in the park; she was crawling along a display case in the new deli; she was inspecting a ventilation shaft; she was on the wall of the shuttle bay (and spied a familiar shuttle, which almost made her remember something but not quite); she was part of a mindless swarm that gave processing power to the living space station that was Eternity. She could almost touch the sentient mind of the station, she was so close. She could feel it on the outskirts of the Sundry processing power. She felt she could reach out—

A crash threw her out of her meditation with a gasp. This caused all the Sundry crawling on her to take wing and move as one to hover above the chair next to her bed.

"What have you gotten into now?" she groaned, rubbing her face, ears, and neck to get rid of the lingering crawling sensation. She shuddered and slid off the edge of her bed.

"*Mobius*!" she shouted. "What happened?"

There was no answer, not that she expected one. She stepped into the living room/kitchen area of her small apartment and looked for whatever broke.

A stoneware bowl—stoneware! how did he do that?—lay in two pieces on the floor, with green goo splattered around it.

The perpetrator was flying in circles close to the ceiling, chirping quietly to himself. He sounded pleased. Had he meant to break the bowl? Or was he just happy he had summoned her? Or was he a masochist who wanted to break her concentration?

She'd heard complaints about toddlers and pets, how they get destructive if they don't get enough attention. "But that's your food bowl, man," she said sadly, and bent to clean it up.

Mobius was a baby still, a sentient spaceship who would one day be large enough to be a full-size shuttle capable of life support, but for now, he was a baseball-size flying destructoid.

"Get down here," she said, holding her hand out.

The tiny ship chirped defiantly and flew into the bedroom.

"No you don't!" Mallory said, running after him. He had flown into her closet and was thrashing around.

She flipped the light on and peeked inside. She had a minimal wardrobe still, not having brought a lot of clothes to space with her, but she had a few shirts and jackets hung up. One suit. Shoes and boots lay on the floor haphazardly; she had lined her shoes up neatly the last time she had been in here.

A sneaker lay upside down, muffled chirping coming from underneath it. It leaped into the air, then fell again.

"Are you stuck?" she asked, amusement and fondness for the little ship finally replacing frustration. She remembered her old boss at the animal shelter, who told her kittens and puppies were so cute because it was their only defense.

She lifted the shoe and scooped *Mobius* into her hand. He was a golden orb with a green sheen, and was starting to develop lines indicating a hatch and small bumps—where wings might grow? engines? She had no idea.

"What am I going to do with you? Do you want more food?"

He chirped happily, then flew straight at her forehead. She had a moment to say, "No, wait—" before everything went dark.

DID MOBIUS KNOCK *me unconscious?*

Mallory couldn't open her eyes, but she was far from knocked out. The buzzing of the Sundry on the station echoed loudly, and her connection with them felt stronger. Easy.

Am I dead?

The buzzing became words she could understand. *Not at all.*

We took the moment of your dazed situation to try to connect again. This is much preferable. We recommend this in the future.

Beaning myself with a steel ball? That won't be sustainable.

Regrettable. Was that amusement from the swarm coloring that word? This newer hivemind was much different than the one that got wiped out a few months ago. They felt less stodgy, more flexible, and easier to talk to. They were still alien as hell, though.

The swarm picked up on her thought. *Sundry colonies that become processing power for ships and stations don't have a lot of agency themselves. The entity forms its own personality. But when we built the current hivemind, it was done in a new way, so we and the station may act in new ways.*

You're not going to override the station, are you? Mallory asked. *'Cause we already dealt with that, and it's not fun.*

No. That's not in our nature. The voice sounded a tad offended that Mallory would think that Sundry would stoop to the antics of their subspecies, the Cuckoos, which had overtaken the station after murdering the hivemind.

"I know, I get it, sort of, I just don't *get* it, you know?" Mallory said, then realized she had spoken aloud. She opened her eyes and sat up rubbing her head.

"You little jerk," she said, wincing as she touched the bump. She sighed and pushed her hair out of her eyes. She really needed a haircut.

Mobius had wormed his way into her hoodie's pocket, making her feel like a kangaroo. He liked to sleep there. "I'll deal with you later," she muttered.

The swarm crawled over her chair still, as if waiting. Their conversation wasn't over. "If Sundry swarms have personalities, like you do, then why doesn't the station's personality come from their swarms?"

"Where do human personalities come from?" the swarm buzzed audibly.

"I don't know that either," Mallory said. "The brain, I guess, which is the closest we have to a hivemind. But no hive."

A chime sounded from her front door. She got off the floor and yelled for the living room door to open.

A tall bald Black man, wearing glasses and a gray ARMY shirt, walked in, his eyebrow cocked.

"You okay, Mal?" he asked. He pointed to her forehead.

"The bangs don't cover it?" Mallory asked, pushing more hair into her eyes, and then reflexively pushing it back. She sighed. "So what's up?"

He crossed his arms. "You forgot again, didn't you?"

Forgot? Oh, no. She thought hard. Two days ago Xan had said their Gneiss friends Stephanie and Ferdinand were coming aboard the station to visit and they should meet at Ferdinand's bar to catch up. That, she realized, was going to happen tonight. She whipped her head around to her bedside table, but *Mobius* had knocked her alarm clock off it. "Oh, God, what time is it?"

"It's midnight," Xan said evenly. "They're gone. You missed everything."

"Dammit!" Mallory fell back onto her bed, rubbing her forehead absently. "Why didn't anyone call me?"

Xan pointed to the comm terminal on the wall, where a tiny red light blinked.

"Oh, you did." Mallory sighed. "I'm sorry. I've been trying to 'commune with the Sundry' more." Her voice took on a dreamy, mocking tone as she made air quotes. "While I'm getting better at it, it still makes me lose time."

Xan went to look at her terminal. "Good excuse for tonight, but you have unopened messages here that are *really* old. Someone paid to send you a video and you haven't opened it yet?"

Mallory followed him, trying not to squirm with embarrassment. "Yeah, my agent has been sending messages. I think it'll be bad news, so I don't answer."

"You do know that shit happens whether you get the message or not, right?" Xan asked slowly.

"I can only deal with one big-time authority figure right now," Mallory said. "And the Sundry are taking everything out of me."

"Let's see what he has to say. I'll hold your hand if you're scared," Xan said in a gentle, sarcastic tone.

"I'm not scared, I—hey!" she protested as he hit the button on the terminal to play the oldest message.

Her agent's slick grin filled the screen. Aaron Rose was in his sixties, white, a very fit build, with thinning brown hair and a mole on his chin that had probably made him look interesting and attractive when he was younger. Aaron didn't need to send her many messages; when Mallory finished writing up her adventures as "ripped from the headlines" true crime books, she would send the manuscript to him in a storage drive via Earth shuttles. Every few months he'd send her royalty checks.

Just recently the most-traded human money had entered the galactic economy, starting with US dollars, pound sterling, euro, and Japanese yen so far. Mallory still couldn't follow everything about alien economics, but she understood enough to get an account with the station and deposit her checks.

"Mallory, I have some great news," Aaron said into the camera with a grin. His pale skin was ruddy, as if he had been in the sun a bit too long. "Your Mrs. Brown lady has permitted the very first mystery convention in space to take place on Station Eternity! Or rather, beside it. We're chartering this huge new spaceship and running Marple's Tea Party, the first mystery space cruise! It'll have murder mysteries and tea and deerstalkers. It's going to be great. We will start here on Earth on May 12 and we'll get to the station on day four of the cruise. That's where you come in. When we dock, then you get to give the guest of honor keynote! Let me know what you think and I'll give details."

"A mystery convention? Here?" Mallory stepped back as if distance from the terminal would keep her away from the message. "Et tu, Mrs. Brown?"

"She's got the whole station to think about, Mal," Xan said. "And more human tourism is good for everyone."

Sentient stations and ships needed someone from a smaller race to bond with in order to communicate with their inhabitants, and Eternity's host was a tiny elderly human by the name of Mrs. Elizabeth Brown. Mallory's friend Xan was similarly bonded to the ship *Infinity*.

"I don't argue with Mrs. Brown," Mallory said, shaking her head. The woman was a twice-convicted murderer (she did her time, thank you very much) and it was a bad idea to cross her. Mallory didn't think she would actually kill anyone to win an argument, but she wasn't going to find out. If Mrs. B wanted a mystery convention here, then it was going to happen, whether Mallory liked it or not.

"I guess I should stop being surprised at things like this." She sighed and pulled the hair out of her eyes again, holding it back with one hand. "When did he send that?"

"Three weeks ago," Xan said. He advanced to the next message. "It's not the only one he sent, it looks like."

Aaron, in a different suit, same grin. "Mallory! I haven't heard from you, so I'm assuming you'll say yes. I went ahead and told the con you would be on board for the speech. I also set you up for a mystery LARP—I think your fans will get a kick out of that! So you'll need a speech by May 16.

"I'll be arriving on a ship called *Metis*," he added. "It's something. I can't wait for you to see it."

"*Metis*? I've heard of them. Like the Indigenous people of Canada?" Mallory asked.

"*Metis* like the badass Titan of wisdom, mother of Athena," Xan said patiently. "But hey, keynote speech! Are you excited?"

She opened her mouth for a sarcastic answer but then froze. "May 16?" she asked, panicked. "What's today in the Earth calendar?"

Xan thought for a second. "The thirteenth."

"Oh, God." She covered her face with her hands. "Did he say I was going to be in a LARP?"

"Yep, he did. It stands for Live-Action Role-Playing."

"I know what LARP stands for!" she said. "I was confirming. That's why I want you to kill me." She collapsed on her couch.

Instead of doing as she asked, Xan advanced to the next message, sent by himself. "Mallory? You going to meet us at Ferd's? Tina is on board but only for a few hours." Xan turned and gave her a pointed look. "That was sent three hours ago."

"I'm sorry, Xan. I admit I've been slack with answering my agent, but communing with the Sundry all afternoon and night takes a lot out of me. And time has no meaning when you're in there." She gestured to her bedroom, where the Sundry's hums were still audible, waiting for her.

Xan sat down beside her with a sigh. "I get it. Sometimes when I'm talking to *Infinity* it gets that way. But Tina was bummed you missed her."

Mallory smiled. "I'm surprised she didn't come break down my door."

"Oh, she wanted to," Xan said. "But I told her we shouldn't do that anymore. She was worried you were injured and she was the only one who could save you."

"She wasn't a hundred percent wrong," she said, pointing to the lump on her forehead. "*Mobius* got a little feisty."

Xan leaned in, examining her forehead. "He really nailed you, didn't he?" She nodded. "I'm surprised things haven't gotten easier for you."

"The minute we get someone on board who can tell me how to parent a toddler who can fly and cause concussions, let me know." She rubbed the back of her neck. "I'm exhausted, and not just from him. The Sundry are demanding."

"Are you learning much more about accessing the hivemind?" he asked.

She shrugged, not looking at him. "I guess so. 'Learning' doesn't seem like the right thing, more like just getting comfortable with them. I can't control anything." She frowned as memories surfaced. "I think I saw Stephanie and Tina in the cargo bay, but I am not entirely sure. Connecting with the Sundry feels very passive. I see the data but there's no emotion attached to it. If the hivemind doesn't feel anything, then I don't either. And that's just *weird*. I'm not sure what I'm supposed to *do* with it."

Xan leaned back on the couch and pushed his round glasses up his nose. "Probably you're supposed to do what the Sundry do. Just gather info and store it."

"That sounds like I'd be just like *Harriet the Spy* and I will end up with no one trusting me," she said, then surprised herself by laughing. "But I guess I was already in that camp."

"So, are you going to do this murder convention thing?" he asked. "Or are you afraid someone's going to get whacked for real?"

"Of course I think that," she said, irritated. "I always think that. But I don't know how I can get out of it. Maybe I'll just hide."

He didn't look at her as he said, "Mal, how many murders have you solved?"

"I guess I'm on seventeen or nineteen or something," she said.

"And those are murders happening to you on approximately eighteen days of your life. On the twelve thousand other days, there haven't been murders, right?"

She narrowed her eyes. "That's fast math. Did you come here with this fact holstered?"

He grinned, still looking at the ceiling. "Answer the question."

"The years before I got stung by the Sundry don't count," she countered. "So that's a few thousand days gone from your fancy math."

"That still leaves me with around ten thousand days. That's murders happening on 0.18 percent of your life. Do you think that maybe you could have a day where there's some kind of game or gathering and people don't die?"

"That's some pretty scary dice you're rolling, Xan. Percentages mean something different when you have life and death involved. If 0.18 percent of planes crashed, you can bet that manufacturer is going out of business."

"I still think you might be able to relax once in a while," he said.

"I'm betting someone dies during that LARP," she said.

MALLORY HAD A strange, sometimes seen as cursed, ability: if a murder happened in her vicinity, she was likely to see it, or find the body, and more often than not, be the one to solve it. Unlike characters in murder series, her skills in solving murders did nothing for her social life, with possible friends or lovers quickly learning that to be around Mallory was to be around death at some point.

"Going to the convention is better than just waiting around for a murder to happen," Xan said, getting a glass of tea in her kitchen. "You say you hate it when someone dies, but that's when you go into 'super Mallory sleuth mode' and you're happier doing this than any other thing. You come *alive*, Mal. Then you solve it and go dormant again."

Mallory would have protested, but he wasn't wrong. "Sometimes I feel like I live in a box like a doll, and when there's a murder, I'm taken out of the box to solve it, and when we're done, I go back in."

"Remember what Phineas told you the last time he was here?" Xan asked.

Mallory laughed. "He said I was a one-tool problem. A knife can cut vegetables, fruit, meat, and string, but the cherry pitter has only one job."

"Exactly! You're the cherry pitter, Mal. What you need to do is be the knife."

"I wish he'd chosen a different metaphor, though," Mallory said. "One that doesn't remind people of murder."

Xan's brother, Phineas, was a chef and hip-hop artist, and Mallory adored him. But his observations were often awkwardly accurate.

Mallory and Xan both came to live aboard the station with special dispensation—Xan was a murder suspect and AWOL through no fault of his own, and Mallory wanted to see if living among aliens would stop the murders. And they had . . . so long as no humans were around.

The first time she caught a serial killer aboard the station, she realized that she had a symbiotic connection with the Sundry that was directly connected with her murder sense. She didn't *cause* the murders, much to her relief, but she just tended to be unconsciously drawn to places where concentrated violence was about to occur.

This knowledge didn't help anything. People still died. She still solved the cases. But she felt better knowing it wasn't her fault.

Xan poured her a glass of tea and brought it to her. "Glad you're okay. See if the Sundry will give you a watch next time you go in." He headed toward the door with a little salute.

"Hang on, you're being weird. What happened with Stephanie and Ferdinand in the bar?" Mallory asked, grabbing his T-shirt.

"Tina was coming aboard now to tell us she is coming aboard later," he said. "Apparently ruling a prison planet is too"—here he made air quotes with his hands—"'boring.' But she's coming in her official capacity and wants to show us something 'fucking awesome.'" He grimaced. "The other Gneiss won't tell me what it is. They say by law the news has to come from Tina."

Mallory blanched. "That can't be good." Tina was a twelve-foot-tall rock alien, a Gneiss, who was queen of the prison planet Bezoar. She did not have a lot of common sense but was refreshingly self-aware about it. She was, however, powerful, headstrong, and dangerous. Through her own bizarre and illegal actions, she had changed her body from an eight-foot-tall humanoid to a being shaped more like a mech, complete with a jet pack, and her chest was hollow and served as a haven for the Cuckoos, a green subspecies of the Sundry who owed Tina a great debt. What she gained from having a hivemind alive in her chest, Mallory still didn't know. But she said she liked the company.

After about ten minutes with Tina, you learned you just had to hold on for dear life if you wanted to keep up with her.

"All right, then, I guess we can prepare for peak Tina," she said. "Thanks for coming to check on me."

"You going back in there?" he asked, pointing to the swarm that now hovered in the bedroom door.

"No, I apparently have a keynote speech to write," Mallory said. "And I'm not real sure what my topic is."

"How about how First Contact has changed the mystery genre?" he asked.

She snorted. "I think I'm the only one writing books with aliens in them."

Xan pulled his e-reader, a gift from Phineas, from his back pocket and handed it to her. "Not exactly. You're not the weirdest mystery writer in town anymore."

On the cover of the reader was a photorealistic giant Venus flytrap wearing three fedoras and smoking a cigarette. The title of the book was *Pruned: A Zesty Yaboi, Private Flytrap Mystery*.

"Sentient flytraps?" she asked. "Like in *Little Shop of Horrors?*"

"It's really good. I'll send you the files," he said, taking it back. "I want to keep reading."

I hit rock bottom one cold and dark December night. My left head was black and drooping, ill from drinking alcohol. He would fall off later, and I'm not gonna lie, it's difficult every time that happens. My right head was muttering constantly to himself, "Call your mother, call your mother, you know you gotta call her." And me? We had lost our pot, and just slumped in an alley, looking like a droopy houseplant that a judgmental horticulturalist threw into the trash. Dirt and soggy moss clung to my nethers, and the flower I had been working hard to grow had been cut off at my base, and it still leaked slightly.

I smacked my main lips and recited the old drunk's mantra, "I'll never drink again," and followed it up with the old drunk's query, "Where the hell am I?"

KAN FINISHED *PRUNED* that night, dropping the e-reader to the floor beside his bed with a laugh. It was a weird story and was apparently selling like wildfire, but Mallory's writing was better. He went into his tiny bathroom aboard *Infinity* (created for him) and washed up for bed. As he brushed his teeth, his mind drifted to his brother, Phineas, and how he hadn't talked to him in a while.

You'll see Phineas soon enough.

He put one hand on the wall; even if he didn't need to touch *Infinity* to talk, putting his hand on her wall made him feel closer. "Do you know something I don't?" he asked through a mouthful of toothpaste.

The sentient ship that was his companion paused for a moment and then spoke again, her voice light and friendly in his head. *A ship is coming. She's big. Sentient.* She paused as if looking for words. *She's . . . new. Phineas is aboard her.*

He paused brushing his teeth to stare into the mirror. He spat into the sink and wiped his mouth. "Sentient like you? Phin would have told me if he'd bonded with a ship."

No, and no. She's not like anyone I've seen. She's . . . older. Much older.

"You said she was new."

She is both. I can't explain fully. But another human is bonded to her. Phineas knows the host. They are bringing hundreds of murder mystery fans to the station. This sounds like there are people who are the opposite of Mallory? People who seek out murder?

Infinity was pretty good at figuring humans out, helped by the time she'd spent bonded to Xan, but there were still some gaps. "Not exactly," he said with a laugh. "People like to read about or watch stories of murder, but they don't seek it out themselves. Except for psychopaths, naturally. Humans enjoy the adrenaline rush of fear when they know they are perfectly safe."

I don't know how you evolved.

He shrugged, grinning. "Don't ask me, I was an English lit major and didn't finish my degree." He dried his face with his towel and hung it up. "When will Phin's ship get here?"

Metis arrives in a few hours. The thought trailed off, as if *Infinity* wanted to say something else but was questioning herself.

"What's bugging you?" he asked, going from his bathroom to his bed.

She sounded unsure. *I've never encountered a ship like* Metis. *She is herself, and yet serves as a massive database carrying zettabytes of data.*

"And she's bringing convention nerds to the station? That seems like a poor use of resources," Xan said, frowning. "What data is she carrying?"

That's not clear.

"Is she a threat?"

No, I wouldn't call her that. I have many siblings, but none are like this one. I don't know where she came from.

He yawned. "Guess we'll find out when she gets here. If Phin is involved, I don't see anything bad happening."

2

. . .

ARGUMENTS IN HYPERSPACE
TAKE JUST AS LONG

T HE NEXT DAY, Mallory discovered that Eternity was powerful enough to send a call into deep space without too much
of a delay, something Mallory had thought was impossible since
Metis was still two days away.

"Mallory!" Aaron said jovially. He looked like he was in a small
hotel room with no windows. If she didn't know better, she'd have
thought he was in a cheap hostel in New York City.

Aaron was the kind of guy who would cheerfully tell complete
strangers that he never missed leg day at the gym. But he sold Mallory's books, which meant she didn't have to take a job around
people, so she overlooked the pinstripes, pastel shirts, and the
emails about his PB 5K times. (She still wasn't sure what that
meant, but it made him happy.)

Today he wore a pink button-down that nearly filled her screen
since he was too close to the camera. He bent awkwardly to get a
better angle.

"Step back, Aaron, then I can see you better," she said.

"Oh," he said, and took a step backward, nearly tripping over
something. He laughed. "Not a lot of room in here. So! What's up?"

"I just got your messages," Mallory said.

"Just now?" he asked, frowning. He was struggling with bringing the desk's rolling chair over to the terminal and was having trouble moving it around the tight space. "What's wrong?" he added as he finally was able to sit down with a satisfied sigh.

She shrugged. "I just didn't look at my messages. For a few days," she added awkwardly. "Aaron, why did you sign me up for a *keynote* speech?"

He looked at her like she had proclaimed she had joined the Flat Earthers. "Because you're a famous mystery writer living on a sentient space station, and the cruise is going to dock at your station. Do I have to spell this out for you?"

"But I am not a speech writer!" she said, flailing her arms. "I write stories based on what happens to me. That's it. You want me to write a rousing speech? No political candidate would hire me. What am I supposed to say? 'Hey, kids, don't gather in big groups— oh, no, looks like someone's already dead.'"

"There it is! Write that, they'll love it! It can start the LARP!" Aaron said, clapping his hands once like the deal was done.

"Also, why did you sign me up for that?" she demanded. "I've never LARPed before."

"Okay, it stands for Live-Action Role-Play—"

"I know what it means, Aaron," she interrupted. "I just have never done it. I always pictured people running around pretending they're vampires and crossing their hands over their chests and claiming they're invisible."

"It's evolved a bit since the 1990s," he said. "The game is run by a game master, with rules in place to keep everyone safe. She will explain it to you, you'll just follow her directions. Don't worry about it.

"But I'm glad you called, there are a few other things I wanted to talk about," he said, leaning toward the camera as if he were keeping something between them. "Business things. Let's get that over with now so you can enjoy the con when we get there."

"But I need advice about the keynote," she pleaded.

He rolled his eyes as if delivering basic information. "Fine. Write about what it's like to be a human living among aliens, how you still have to solve human murders when you ran away from Earth. Talk about the writing life, especially aboard Eternity. You have a life unlike any author on the planet. Literally. The topics are right there!" he said impatiently.

"Anyway, I'll get right to it. Sales are down. Way down. We have to do something." He said it quickly, like he wanted to keep her from interrupting, and it took her a second to parse what he was saying.

Mallory shook her head. "Hang on. Did you say they were *down*? With all the true crime lovers and the alien-obsessed people, and sales are *down*?"

He nodded solemnly. "The true crime people aren't as into sci-fi, and the sci-fi people aren't into the true crime."

"But I don't write sci-fi!" she said, feeling her face heat up. "My last two books were entirely true! All of them are," she added, glaring at him.

"I know that," he soothed. "And your true fans know, but still, sales are down. We have an offer from your publisher for the next three books, but . . ." He made a face, like that of a lying parent who tastes a kid's medicine before administering it to prove that it was tasty. "Well, it's less than you've gotten before. Sales are down, so advances are down."

She got up to make tea. "So, what, I should just take it?" she asked, raising her voice so he could still hear her. "What books do they want if not my murder cases? I can't make the murders happen elsewhere. Or in a different way. What are my options?"

"It's hard to say what specifically is causing the downturn in sales," he said, looking off to the side as if consulting figures. "I thought for sure that people would be into the space angle. It's possible people aren't going for the alien thing. There are conspiracy theorists saying the alien connection is a government lie."

"And the thousands of videos of people meeting aliens?" Mallory asked flatly. "What do they say to that?"

"Oh, they say those people are lying. Or actors, usually. The way they discount school shooting victims and refugees." He shrugged, as if this was just a throwaway inconvenience.

"I'm not sure I want money from people like that," she said, tossing a tea bag into a mug.

"Their money is the same color," Aaron reminded her.

She slumped, suddenly exhausted. "But before First Contact those people wouldn't shut up about aliens, right?"

"Oh, yeah, that's true. But you show these people the facts and they just dig their heels in harder. It was convenient then to think of aliens controlling the government, and now it's convenient to think of the aliens as lies the government tells us."

"Don't these people have jobs?" Mallory asked.

"I think it's best to worry about your own job right now," Aaron said. "After your book about the rogue FBI agent—"

"State Bureau of Investigation," Mallory corrected, not wanting the murderer to have one ounce of unearned credibility.

"—SBI, okay. After that comes out, your editor wants you to pivot and push the true, really lived aspect of the space stuff. Then she wants you to come to Earth to do some book tours and interviews."

Mallory slammed her mug down hard on the counter and jumped in front of the terminal to see if he was kidding. "You want me to go back to *Earth*? And have people die at every book tour stop, which will make them hate me more? My editor knows I won't do book tours. No thanks."

"They thought, to push sales . . ." Aaron trailed off when he saw her face. "I thought you said that you don't cause the murders but are 'drawn to them on some weird quantum level.'" He made air quotes.

"Well, yeah, it's nice that I don't feel responsible anymore," she allowed, "but that doesn't mean I'm okay with people dropping dead around me! Shit like this just makes me feel like people don't take my situation seriously. Even when they're making millions from it."

"I think they believe you, but—"

"If they believe me, it's even worse that they would put people's lives in danger to push the books," Mallory interrupted. "And you know there will be people who don't believe the Sundry and I have a link. They will decide what they want and nothing will change their minds. If we say it's because of some weird alien quantum thing, are they going to believe me or trash me online?"

"But you're not online anymore, what do you care?" he asked, but at the look on her face, he said, "Right, let's table the book tour for now. Let's talk about new books." He rubbed his hands eagerly.

Mallory poured the hot water into her mug, resisting the urge to just throw everything across the room. Her stomach twisted in a familiar way. Up to now, that feeling had only happened when she had driven away a friend or loved one with her odd "ability."

"New books? I don't know where else you want me to go. I write the stories about the murders I solve, you sell them, my editor publishes them. I can't change what happened. I'm not a real writer."

"Oh, that's crap and you know it," he said. "Besides, I was mostly being rhetorical. You can be a fully fictional writer; you've written several books about ripped-from-the-headlines murders. Just take that thinking and write about a fake murder!"

"How am I going to figure out what to write?" she asked. "My books are more memoir than fiction. At best they are creative nonfiction. I don't sit around thinking up new and exciting murder mysteries to write about. I'm too busy with the real murders."

"That's where I come in," he said triumphantly. His energy always made her tired. He leaned forward with his conspirator's whisper again. "Have you considered writing a cozy mystery?"

"I just said I haven't written anything else," Mallory said. "I don't even know what that is."

Aaron looked at her thoughtfully, sucking at his teeth briefly in the way that always made her skin crawl. "If I didn't know better, I'd think you're being purposefully recalcitrant." He spoke slowly as if she were very young, jabbing his index finger into the camera with each comment. "Your books aren't *selling*, Mallory. The money will *stop* coming in. If you want to keep making money *writing*, you need to write something *different*."

He sat back and looked at his watch. "Oooh, I have to run soon, there's a panel I want to catch. I can't wait for you to see this ship. She's *amazing*."

Mallory stayed silent, glowering at him. He was an asshole, but he was right. If her books didn't sell, she had to write different books. Or find another way to make money, and there weren't a lot of jobs for humans on Eternity. But Aaron didn't need to know that.

"I could also just quit writing," she said.

He frowned, looking at her like she was a puppy who was barking and piddling on the floor when he was trying to teach her how to sit. "You may not believe me, but you are actually a writer. Give it a try. Might be less traumatic than reliving the murders. You might like it."

She deflated. "Fine. So, what's a cozy mystery?"

He grinned like he knew he'd won. "Now you're talking. You'll take to this like a duck to water, or a rock person to the Grand Canyon or whatever. You were pretty much already writing cozies, which is why I think this will be an easy pivot for you. They need an amateur sleuth in a small, intimate setting—a pleasant village, points if it's seaside, extra points if it's a coastal town in England or Ireland or something, unlike gritty detectives prowling the hard city streets of New York where it's always raining, and it doesn't dwell on the gore or the violence of the murder."

"But I already have a lot of that!" she protested. "I'm an amateur sleuth, I don't feature a ton of violence or gore, and, well, Eternity isn't small, but the places I go are pretty limited."

"So it shouldn't be a problem, should it?" he said, smiling as if he'd caught her in a paradox. "You're right, you are almost there, but the bestselling cozy mysteries have two aspects that you don't— in the quaint small town, the amateur sleuth usually owns a small cozy business. Like a bakery, a bookstore, coffee shop, or yarn shop. It helps her connect with the town and lets her get to know the suspects. Oh, and the sleuth will have a very smart yet precocious pet. Cats are most popular. If you must have a dog, a small dog will do."

"I don't have a bakery or a pet," she said flatly.

"What about your new little ship? *Mob*-something? He's kind of pet-like, isn't he?" Aaron said.

She started to contradict him, but just shook her head. "The point is moot because I can't knit."

"Right, so this is where you think along fictional lines. When you have mysteries that are easy for you to solve, those make the worst-selling books. The sleuth needs to be initially confounded and usually in danger for people to get into the books. If you move outside your personal story, what could you tell?" He gestured his arms wide to indicate the breadth of her options. "Make up a sleuth. An old person! Old-people mysteries are very big right now. Give them a job, or a business, and give them a pet. Invent a little café on the station that can be owned by an old Miss Marple character who has a pet—what kind of pets do you have on this station?"

Mallory shrugged. "Come to think of it, I haven't seen alien pets. I can ask around. Most aliens have symbionts, or some kind of relationship with their own people or family that's more than what humans have."

"I wouldn't like that; I'm trying to get farther away from my ex-wife and my kids!" Aaron said, chuckling.

"I thought you didn't have kids?" Mallory asked.

He cleared his throat. "I don't, but it's funnier if I do."

"Not really."

"Anyway," he said, energy spiking again. You could have your sleuth work with an alien Watson. One of those big rock fellas, maybe, and they help their sweet little old lady solve mysteries?"

"I don't know," she said. "I have to think about this. Is this Miss Marple an alien?"

"Can be!" he said. "Or there's one more path you can take. Noir is making a big comeback, and a new series I sold just came out. It's weird noir and I think is going to break big." He grinned at her and she knew he was waiting for her to ask about it.

"What is it?" she asked with a sigh.

"It's a series of books where the sleuth is—wait for it—a sentient Venus flytrap! They're called the Zesty Yaboi mysteries. That's his name, the flytrap, I mean," he said, his grin extending to where Mallory was sure it was about to go all the way around his head and open it like a screw-off cap.

Mallory hugged her tea close, warming her hands. "That sentient flytrap is cropping up everywhere," she said, thinking about the book Xan had sent her. "So houseplant solves murder cases. And you said it was noir?"

"Very gritty and dark," Aaron enthused. "The only difference is, our sleuth always has a few heads alive at once, so he can think about different things at a time, but he's really weak to most liquids, including tap water. Distilled water or rainwater, that's it. He's also a recovering alcoholic."

"Of course he is," Mallory said.

"People want the same but different, Mallory. The fact that the sleuth is a carnivorous plant firmly plants it outside the norm already. The alcoholism brings it back. This is what makes the book comfortable for most readers. Despite what they say, most people don't want a unique story. Detective Yaboi novels toe that line perfectly. You could learn a thing or two from them."

She gave in. "All right, are you bringing me any books to look at?"

He waved a slick black e-reader at her. "Spoiler alert, your large friend and I have a present for you."

"My large friend?" Mallory asked, thinking of the Gneiss but realizing he meant a human. "Oh, you mean Xan's brother?"

He tapped the reader with two fingers. "All the bestsellers right now are in here. I included the Yaboi novels, even the ones not out yet."

"Thanks a lot, I needed a new one," she said, but didn't explain that *Mobius* had thought it would be fun to try and use her last e-reader as a trampoline. "But why is this the first I'm hearing of all of this?"

He smirked. "You said it yourself, you didn't respond to my messages. I figured I was on this cruise, I have some other clients with me, I can pin you down for a meeting on Eternity, win-win-win!" He winked at her. "One of my authors is the guy who wrote the Yaboi novels. You'll meet him, maybe you can brainstorm with him."

The idea of brainstorming book ideas with a stranger, and then having that stranger drop dead of murder, filled Mallory's mind for a moment, but she blinked and shook her head. "Yeah, sure, I'll meet him."

"Great! I can't wait till we get there—there's another big surprise that's coming, but I don't want to ruin it."

She sipped her tea, refusing to rise to the bait.

"Boy, you're going to be surprised," he added, throwing another fishhook at her.

"Cool," she said.

"Aren't you a little curious?" he wheedled.

"I know you'll just refuse to tell me, so I skipped the middle steps and landed at the end where you still won't tell me anything."

He sighed and shook his head. "Touchy touchy. Mal, someday you're going to have to realize that we all must pivot in life. When things aren't going your way, you may have to change your direction."

"You sound like a lesson at the end of an episode of *Larry the ADHD Chihuahua*," she said.

"That is an Emmy-winning show," he said stiffly. "My kids watch it all the time."

"You don't have any kids!" Mallory reminded him. "Besides, you're old enough that you should be using fake grandchildren instead of children.

"And besides, I know better than most people how to pivot!" she added. "You think that moving from North Carolina to an alien space station was accepting the status quo?"

"But you still have murders happening near you, then you solve them, then you write it up. And when you don't know when the next murder is, and your books are done, what else are you doing?"

That also was a rhetorical question, and she hated him for it. She opened her mouth, then closed it. He was right. Fucking "I never miss leg day" Aaron was right.

"Fine. I'll give a cozy a try," she muttered.

"We can talk when I get there, babe. I gotta run, thanks for the call, it's good to see your face again. Space suits you."

She rolled her eyes as he severed the call. She had two days to learn to LARP, write a keynote speech, and figure out a new direction for her career.

She'd rather solve a murder. But there were none to be found.

BACK ON EARTH, you could find thousands of pages online that told you how to write a keynote speech. But without the Internet, Mallory only had the books that were already on her e-reader. There were a lot, but mostly fiction, and none had public speaking advice.

She paced her apartment, vehemently cursing her agent, when her terminal pinged with an incoming message. Since ignoring calls had gotten her into this mess, she grabbed her tablet off the couch and answered the call.

The wrinkled brown face of Mrs. Brown—an old lady, grandma, murderer, and powerful station host—appeared, smiling and making her kind eyes crinkle. Behind her, a red light pulsed, the almost literal beating heart of the station. "Mallory, I wanted to talk to you about the ship that's coming from Earth. You've heard about it." It wasn't a question. Mrs. B knew most of what happened on the station.

"About all I know is there's a murder mystery convention, Phineas is coming, my agent is coming, and I have to give a keynote address. Otherwise, no, I don't know a lot about it," Mallory said, deadpan. "I figured you would know more than I do, since it's a sentient ship and all."

Mrs. Brown pursed her lips in frustration. "No one knows what kind of ship it is. Ships that carry large amounts of data are considered obsolete technology; the various networks of Sundry hive-minds have made physical transport of data pointless."

Mallory yawned. It was later than she'd thought, and she'd tired herself out by raging around her apartment. "Are you saying this ship has no hivemind?"

Mrs. Brown paused as if listening to someone. "Eternity doesn't really know," she said. "It's an unknown entity."

"All right, what do you need from me?"

"First I wanted to ask how things were going with *Mobius*," Mrs. Brown said with a smile. "You haven't brought him by to see Granny Brown in weeks."

Mallory's tired eyes fell on a cereal bowl that she'd lined with iron shavings that Xan had procured for her. *Mobius* had created a small nest-like cavity, wriggling around and chowing down on his breakfast. She hoped he'd eat so much he would fall asleep.

Both Xan and Mrs. Brown had symbiotic connections with beings such as a ship and a space station, but the major difference was that Mallory had started with the equivalent of a newborn while Xan and Mrs. Brown were connected to fully adult, functional entities. Eternity could hold thousands of inhabitants, and *Infinity* could fly through space. Both could modify their physical interior to better suit whatever inhabitants resided within, and both could offer quick psychic communication to their hosts.

Mobius was no longer a newborn, at least, but as the equivalent of a toddler ship, he was capable of hovering around Mallory's head and then darting about the room to chase after whatever had caught his attention. He was like a kitten in a roomful of butterflies.

"He's napping right now," Mallory said. "Or I guess gone to bed, considering what time it is. But he's fine. Growing. Chasing after lights on the wall like a cat." She smiled despite her annoyance at the little orb. She hadn't impressed on him that the bigger he got, the less charming it was for him to crash himself into her head to get her attention.

"Hang on," Mallory said thoughtfully. "Does he have a hive-mind? He was so tiny when I got him, I can't imagine a hive that small. Unless there are other Sundry subspecies that are smaller?"

"Not that I know of," Mrs. Brown said, "but I'm still rather new to the ins and outs of living ship husbandry. I do know ships eventually take on a circuit of four Sundry for communication, and the hive grows as the ship grows."

"So, where do I get Sundry for him when the time is right?" Mallory asked.

Mrs. Brown shook her head, sighing. "I wish I could tell you, Mallory. From what I learned on my visit to the sentient machine home planet last month, they don't seem to know much about the process. They assured me it just kind of happens."

"They couldn't tell you anything? Are there machines that make them? Does Eternity have a womb?" Mallory asked.

"They said the process has been automated for years," Mrs. Brown said. "They asked me about my connection to Eternity, and Xan's to *Infinity*. But they didn't offer much on their end."

"I'm not having the easiest time," Mallory admitted, glancing over at the baby ship, humming in the way that let her know he was asleep. "I wish I knew more of how to keep him interested. Occupied. Something."

"We can work on things after *Metis* leaves," Mrs. Brown said sympathetically. "That's the name of the new ship from Earth, isn't that pretty? But I'd like you to be there when that ship docks. Take Alexander. I will want both of your opinions. And those of *Infinity* and *Mobius*."

"*Mobius* won't be offering much more of an opinion than 'Wow, I get to go outside the apartment!'" Mallory said.

"Take him anyway. He might surprise you," Mrs. Brown said, her voice having a tone of finality to it.

"All right," Mallory said. "I'll take him."

"I hear Tina is coming to visit," she added offhandedly.

"Christ on a cracker," Mrs. Brown said, her frustration breaking through the polite little old lady act she usually presented. "That's all we need. Do you know why she's coming?"

Mallory shook her head, biting the inside of her cheek to keep from smiling. She preferred it when Mrs. Brown was more relaxed around her, but the lady had a big job as host of the ship, and couldn't let her hair down, so to speak, around most people. "All Xan told me was she thinks that ruling a planet is boring, but she also has news. Stephanie and Ferdinand won't tell us what the news is, but they don't seem really happy about it."

"Fantastic," Mrs. Brown said with a sigh. "I'll see what my sources have to say, but I don't expect much. Those Gneiss can keep a secret if they want to."

"Too true," Mallory said with another yawn. "I'll let you know what we think of the new ship. And whatever secret Tina is keeping."

"Oh, I'm sure Eternity will tell me about Tina's arrival much earlier than you will," she said with a sigh. "I can't complain; at least I'll have warning before she brings whatever this week's chaos flavor is with her."

Mallory was about to sever the connection when Mrs. Brown held up a finger. "One more thing, Mallory. If there's a murder, just go ahead and deal with it. Don't worry about reporting it to security unless you feel your own life is in danger. It seems that step slows things down in all your cases."

"You've been reading my books?" Mallory asked, dumbfounded. Considering Mrs. Brown was the subject of her first book, Mallory didn't think she would enjoy reading them.

"Yes," she said. "I thought it might give me some insight into this ability you have."

Mallory laughed uncomfortably. "If you gain some insight, please tell me. I'm still mostly baffled about the whole thing."

3

THE OFFICIAL DILL PICKLE OF SPACE

WALLACE'S SPACE DELI was the first human-owned restaurant to open on Eternity. Its owner was Kurt Ginsberg,
a restaurateur who had been studying alien cuisine since the
month after First Contact in 2043. He was the first to figure out
how to advertise to off-world customers by promising free food to
any alien who would try his dishes.

By 2044 he had two exobiologists, one human and one alien,
working with him to help him understand alien physiology (and
be on hand if a customer reacted poorly to his food).

Ginsberg started a series of videos on how to entertain for alien
visitors, and his video titled "Never Throw a Surprise Party for a
Phantasmagore" became the top video on video-sharing sites after
a month. When Station Eternity started allowing humans on
board for more than tourism or diplomacy, Mallory and the other
humans (Xan, Jessica Brass, the Earth ambassador, and Adrian
Casserly-Berry, the former Earth ambassador) who lived perma-
nently aboard the station were no longer unique. Ginsberg was the
first person to petition to open a deli and the first one to move
aboard.

Wallace's Space Deli (Ginsberg would not listen when Mallory
told him "space" was redundant) soon opened, with a focus on

giving a taste of home to visiting humans, but also specializing in "human-alien fusion." The deli also had the brilliant marketing move of publishing a human's guide to alien cuisine, to help any human wanting to try more adventurous dishes. (And of course they had to come to the deli to get this guide.)

Instead of calling it Ginsberg's Space Deli, which would have made sense, Ginsberg called it Wallace's after his favorite author. Mallory and Xan soon became regulars and helped report to Ginsberg on their experience with alien food. Ginsberg paid well for the information with free food. It didn't take long for Mallory and Xan to have a favorite table and a mostly regular lunch date, happy at last to get some human food.

Mallory loved the decor, which had chrome-accented retro space-age art that harkened back to *The Jetsons*. Xan thought it was tacky, but he still tolerated it because the food was so good. But even he had to admit that the seating—which catered to all sizes of alien—was the most comfortable of any room in the station.

Xan met her there to talk about the approaching ship, and, Mallory hoped, offer public speaking advice. He slid into the booth across from her while waving at the counter, where Ginsberg took the order of an ebony Gneiss.

"That guy is the happiest human alive right now," Mallory said, pointing to the beaming Ginsberg, who spoke animatedly at the Gneiss, talking about cows.

"He's talking about cows again," Xan said with a laugh. "Yesterday he tried to sell pastrami to a Phantasmagore but got tied up explaining cows."

Ginsberg was a white man with a bushy mustache and salt-and-pepper hair cradling a bald spot. He was nearly as tall and as broad as a refrigerator. He couldn't quite look a Gneiss alien in the eye, but he was the closest person Mallory had seen to their body types.

"I've studied all the people on this here space station," Ginsberg was saying. "Everyone here can eat beef. Even the aliens who can't breathe oxygen, they can eat beef! Whether you want to or not, that's between you and your god. Or your rocky stomach. But you gotta trust me. You can eat beef, and this is the best beef you'll find for millions of miles."

His shoulders slumped as the Gneiss instead ordered the special of the day: a superheated sludge made especially for Gneiss.

"Have you really studied our people that much?" the Gneiss said.

"As much as I could," Ginsberg said, nodding. "Mostly just your cuisine." He fingered a chipped tooth. "You folks like your rocks. What I couldn't taste I had to research. There's a lot of misinformation online, but I had an in with the experts." He caught Mallory's eye and winked at her.

Xan's little brother had been the first expert. Ginsberg had met Phineas when he was catering one of Phineas's hip-hop shows in New York. And when a xenophile met a regular-guy-who-had-gone-to-Eternity (who also loved food), a friendship was formed. Ginsberg started sending food to the station via Phineas, figuring (accurately) that Mallory and Xan were desperately missing Earth food. In return, they sent him data on the aliens aboard Eternity that he could serve if he opened a restaurant there. When he had made his pitch to Mrs. Brown and Eternity to bring human cuisine to the stars, it had been an easy sell.

Ginsberg had some things to work out with alien economics and currency exchange, but he didn't care. For now, companies on Earth were sending crates of free samples, each vying to be the "official root beer of space" or the "official dill pickle of space!" Ginsberg promised Mrs. Brown that he would not accept sponsorship from any product that didn't appeal to at least one alien race.

The Gneiss customer relented and finally tasted pastrami, rock-like teeth grinding on the thin slice of meat. He ground it much longer than it took for humans to eat. Unlike humans,

Gneiss took the dust that came from grinding their teeth together to pulp any biological food and then swallow it like reverse owl pellets.

The Gneiss finally nodded slowly. "It's good. I'll take all you have."

Mallory tried not to laugh, knowing Ginsberg might think she was laughing at him or his customer, when really, she was simply delighted.

Xan looked at his watch, which was flashing. "I just got word from Phin." He took out his tablet and then paused, reading. "He really wants us to meet the host of *Metis*, his ship. They should be here tomorrow." He checked the clock on the wall that showed both station time and five different time zones on Earth. Ginsberg had commissioned it special, chrome-plated of course.

"'His' ship, but he's not the host?" Mallory asked.

"He's not the host. He says it's a long story." Xan looked out the window, thoughtful. Outside the deli, young aliens played in Eternity's park. She changed the park frequently to suit her many sentients living on board, and the latest theme catered to the Gneiss (but also looked a lot like the American Southwest). He shaded his eyes from the faux two suns in the cloudless blue sky. "Eternity really does make this like the desert, doesn't she? I forgot to ask Phin to bring me sunglasses."

"What has he told you about this convention?" Mallory asked. "Are there any groups that he thinks might be involved in murder any time soon?"

He looked at her, startled. "I don't think he has taken surveys, if that's what you mean."

"I'm just worried," she said, sipping her coffee. "Mystery fans could easily try to plan out the perfect murder. Lord knows we have enough examples in books. There might be tons of people who have a motive, which is 'Can I get away with it?'"

Xan shrugged. "He didn't mention anything about that, no.

But you know there are going to be a lot of people, and writers, and agents, and editors. Someone's got to have a grudge against someone else."

"I wish I could anticipate who will be the target."

"Has knowing that ever helped you before?" he asked.

"No."

"Point-one-eight percent, Mallory," he said gently. "Maybe you'll just be allowed to enjoy the convention."

She finished her coffee. "Are you willing to put money behind that?"

"Oh, hell no," he said.

AFTER A BREAKFAST of ham and eggs, Xan stood and stretched. "I need to book a room for Phineas."

"Doesn't he already have a room at the convention?" Mallory asked.

Xan shook his head. "Nah, he said he wanted to stay close by and not rely on a shuttle to come see me. Are you going to hang out here?"

"Yeah, I have to do some research," Mallory said sadly.

Before Xan could leave, their human waitress, a white woman of about fifty with thinning red hair, hurried over with paper cups topped with whipped cream. "I'll be training a new server today, so you might see her instead of me for the next hour," she said, beaming at them. "Kurt asked me to give you chocolate shakes to test out the new shake machine."

"To my angel investors!" Ginsberg called proudly from the register. "I would not be here without you."

"Kurt, man, you can't keep giving us free food," Xan protested. "Tell him, Mal."

Mallory looked up at them with whipped cream on the tip of her nose. She swallowed and hastily wiped her face with her napkin. "I'm sorry, I didn't hear you. What did you say? If you're not going to drink yours . . ." She reached out, but he pulled his cup away.

After Xan left, the deli was quiet while the staff prepped for lunch. Mallory asked for a fresh coffee as she pulled up a book on her tablet. Xan had sent her a few of the first self-published noir flytrap stories. She pulled up *Pruned: A Zesty Yaboi, Private Flytrap Mystery* to continue where she'd left off.

Mallory was really getting into the book by chapter 5, and jumped about a mile when a Phantasmagore materialized beside her.

"Apologies," the Phantasmagore said, wiping the spilled water off the table.

"Jesus, Victoria!" Mallory said, clutching her hammering heart. "You guys can't just teleport beside customers and not expect them to knock their drink over or freak out."

Mallory had met Victoria a few days earlier, as she had come in seeking a job. She was young, and a little confused about humans, but wanted to try something new.

"We don't teleport," Victoria said, her skin flipping through a few colors to match the table, then the booth, then the floor. "We use camouflage. No known species can teleport."

"It's the same thing to human eyes, when you just appear," Mallory said.

Victoria seemed at a loss for words; she looked back toward the kitchen. Mallory's human waitress stood in the door, motioning Victoria on.

"I'm the new trainee, so what'll ya have? Um, hon?" Victoria tacked on the "hon" at the end as if she had just remembered to use it.

Mallory laughed. "Victoria, why does he have you talking like an Earth waitress named Flo?" she asked. Her eyes widened when she looked at the light pink armband the alien wore. She actually wore a name tag that said FLO.

The Phantasmagore was willowy and had brownish-yellow bark-like skin, and webbed fingers. She wore an armband for identification, much like humans used uniforms. Phantasmagore didn't have issues about nakedness and preferred armbands. Of course, aside from the societal rules about nakedness, humans were all soft and ticklish and weren't equipped to adapt to shifts in temperature. Phantasmagore skin wasn't nearly so delicate.

"It's part of the job," Victoria/Flo said. "This is an Earth-based deli, so we speak like Earth-based employees. You should hear Galahad the janitor talk. About every third word is a swear word in one language or another. Now before my boss, um, docks my pay, what do you want to eat?"

Mallory ordered more coffee and a piece of pie. She was full from lunch but wanted to give "Flo" something to do. Then she got back to the book, where flytrap detective Yaboi had just gotten into some trouble with the local law enforcement, and he'd ducked inside a greenhouse to hide.

This cemented it. The cops wouldn't be chasing me unless there was something incriminating in the grocery bag we'd nabbed. Incriminating for the gang or incriminating for the cops? I didn't know, but I now knew the cops were in the gang's pocket.

"Everyone chases the golden pony," I muttered with my main head.

"I think I rode a golden pony when we went to that BDSM club last month," quipped my left head.

"No you didn't," I said, and poked my closed right head with a leaf. "Cough it up."

The trap opened his mouth and spat out a soggy paper grocery bag. Before I could grab it to peek inside, a shot rang out behind us.

Instinctually, we dropped to the floor, my third head

snatching the bag back to safety. It suddenly seemed less important. Nothing mattered if we were going to get shot to death.

"Of all the greenhouses in the city I could hide in, why did it have to be this one?" I groaned to myself. "It was just supposed to be a quiet place to catch my breath."

"Hey, I told you we should split up and make it harder for them to find us," Lefty said.

We heard a thump. I looked across the room, my vantage point on the floor giving us a good view of the underside of the other tables in the greenhouse.

About five rows away, halfway hidden by flowering vines, a cactus lay on the ground, sap oozing from a bullet hole in his forehead. He was quite dead. Beside him knelt another plant, calmly soaking up the sap that drained from the body.

And here I was, my weapon still back where I'd dropped it in the juicing lounge last week. Lot of junkies went there to wean themselves off the fertilizer, and I was looking for answers. I left with the answers, but my fourth head and my gun stayed behind. You don't want to fuck with fertilized plants, kids.

I knew those leaves, but only by reputation. She was thirteen inches of plant, and at least ten of those were her sleek, thin pitcher cups. And that flame-red flare at her lid and peristome could only be pulled off by one dame: Sarracenia. I'd heard she could lure in any plant with her perfume. I'd also heard she'd murdered two guys a while back and got out early for good behavior.

And if she knew we'd seen her, we would be lucky to escape with only one head dropped.

I hoped it was Righty. I couldn't help it.

I immediately doubted my cruel thought, because

Righty grunted through the paper bag. We'd gotten a wild idea. Ideas don't come from him much, so I was impressed.

I took the bag from his mouth again and popped up, leaving my fedora on the ground. "Pasta delivery!" I called.

Sarracenia paused and turned to face me. "Pasta delivery?" she said, her throaty voice having a slight lilt to question me.

Righty, bless him, leaned forward slightly and opened his mouth, showing off the now officially disgusting bag to her.

"Yeah, someone asked me to deliver a pasta dish for you from Louie's Noodles. I believe it's a gift." I made a show of looking for the receipt in Righty's mouth. "Doesn't seem like I've got the right place. Very sorry about that."

"Right. You've got the wrong place," she said, her voice throaty.

I knew she wanted me, but that way lay death. I skedaddled out of there and into the arms of Chief McBrady, whom I'd never been happier to see.

I put my leaves up and carefully indicated Righty's empty mouth, which was grinning like a nerd. "I don't have the loot, Chief!" I pointed at the greenhouse door. "Your thief's in there! Tall, beautiful, with dangerous pitchers, you'll find the loot with her."

McBrady wasn't the smartest, and usually felt if he recovered what was stolen, whoever got arrested for it was secondary. He frowned at me, then said, "Thanks."

Mallory's food arrived, interrupting her laughter and pulling her out of the dirty world of the noir greenhouse. She had to admit the book was ridiculous fun and spent about one second trying to imagine what a sex scene between a flytrap and a pitcher plant would entail.

Something seems weird about this story. Aside from all the sentient plants and the apparently human police force.

She put down her tablet to appreciate that actual human food was in front of her.

The pie was nearly perfect. Apple pie with a lattice crust sprinkled with thick crystals of raw sugar. The apples inside were at least of two varieties, maybe three. It was almost a sexual experience.

Kurt stuck his head out of the kitchen. "Mallory! How's the pie?"

"Amazing!" she mumbled through a bite.

"Great!" he said. "That was Sebby doing the baking this morning!"

Mallory swallowed and took a moment to appreciate the skill of the newest cook, Sebby, a Gneiss that was shorter than most and therefore could fit more easily in the kitchen. How his huge rock hands managed details like a sprinkling of raw sugar was beyond her, but Mallory guessed he'd be good at not getting burned.

"If this cozy thing doesn't work out, maybe Kurt will give me a job," she muttered. She added sugar to her coffee and pulled out a notebook to brainstorm new book ideas.

Since she'd been reading noir, gritty stories were on her mind, and she started to doodle a rough sketch of a dark Gneiss with a fedora. "Rock Bradley," she said to herself. "He doesn't need women; he just needs to find his long-lost brother. But the women can't resist . . ."

She began brainstorming what Rock Bradley could get himself into—because Lord knows it was never his fault—and was surprised when she found that ideas were coming pretty easily to her. Granted, her outline put the main character in a climactic battle in the first chapter, so it would need some tweaking. But still, it was more fun than she'd thought.

If she didn't do a Gneiss sleuth, what other alien sleuths could she come up with?

The Sundry, data-hoarding alien wasplike insects who made up the hivemind that she, too, connected to, couldn't be detectives because they didn't have individual personalities and they already knew everything; they just didn't put it together to solve problems. They sometimes worked as living computers to store data for other species, or as the processing power behind sentient ships and stations, but mostly they just collected data.

A geriatric Phantasmagore sleuth might be fun. Aside from people assuming she was harmless, she could also literally disappear to blend into the walls. But Mallory didn't know how the Phantasmagore people viewed their older population, or if any sexism was involved. More research needed.

There were the Gurudev, shorter than humans, robe wearing, and stick insectoid–like. Mallory understood they were fussier than most sentients, and had an elevated sense of their own worth. More research needed.

The Silence were the aliens she knew the least about (of the ones she knew). Lacking auditory organs, they spoke almost exclusively through a complicated sign language. To communicate with them, you had to speak their language. It might make for an interesting sleuth, but it was another group Mallory would need to explore in detail. Way too much research needed.

What I need is a new alien. That would get everyone's attention. But since she was unlikely to have a comfortably safe First Contact scenario in the station, she thought that might be unlikely.

She wrote *Rock Bradley and the Mechanical Bees* at the top of her page, then tapped her pen a few times. Coming up with a plot was hard. It was much easier when people just fell dead at your feet.

Her watch, a communicator that was tuned to a private local channel allowed only to Mallory and her friends, pinged at her. She touched the face to hear Stephanie's deep voice coming through.

"Mallory, are you there?"

"Hey! I thought you took Ferd and Tina back to Bezoar," Mallory said. "Are you still on board?"

"Yes. I stayed to get some rest. Also, I want to meet the new child," Stephanie said.

"*Mobius*?" Mallory asked. "I'm writing right now. Besides, I haven't taken him out much . . ."

"He is a sentient ship. I am a sentient ship. We should know each other."

"But isn't that the equivalent of meeting someone from Canada and telling them that you know someone from Canada and they should meet?"

"I don't understand the reference, but I still want to meet the child."

"I'm writing right now," Mallory said. "And I thought you were on Bezoar with Tina and her big secret."

"She's taking a different shuttle here. I did not want to be . . . responsible for the decisions she's making. I also wanted to have a break. One thing I can do with the break is talk with you and meet your son—"

"My son?" Mallory asked, choking on coffee.

Stephanie continued as if she hadn't heard. "And you can write aboard while I meet the baby. You two should come to the shuttle bay."

Mallory wasn't ready to let *Mobius* out on his own yet. Which meant if they were out of the apartment, he was securely in her pocket. But he had to grow up sometime.

A change of scenery might be what she needed. She sighed and sat back in her chair. Her pie was gone and she hadn't even remembered finishing it. She should have savored it more.

MOBIUS WAS VIBRATING with joy but was irritated in Mama's pocket. She had said if he was very good, he could meet another ship, a grown-up ship. Mama was nice and *Mobius* loved her more than anything, but Mama wasn't a ship, so she didn't always know if, say, when he was zooming around the room, he was doing it because of fear or joy. Another ship would know immediately.

Mama's grip tightened a little, and he tried to calm down. But really, this had to be the greatest day so far in his life. Mama was friends with another ship. And he was going to get to know her!

The air pressure around Mama changed, and suddenly he could hear countless ships! Some were boring and talking about fuel efficiency, or Bezoar politics, or a First Contact scenario with the worst ambassador possible. But others! There was an old grandaddy who sensed *Mobius* immediately.

Is that a new child? I haven't seen one in eons. Would you like to hear how I rescued the queen of the universe, little one?

A serious voice cut in. *You will do no such thing. You have plenty of time to fill this kid's head with lies. Just come aboard, Mobius; you won't be able to hear this fossil anymore.*

He suddenly felt shy and unsure. These ships had done *so much.* How could he ever be as amazing? *Are you where my Mama is taking me?*

Yes, my name is Stephanie.

Mama's gait changed, and she struggled up a few stairs. Then the pressure changed around them—they were in a new room! A smaller room! But new!

"Okay," Mama said, and her fingers relaxed. "Go ahead and meet Auntie Stephanie."

"Thank you, Mallory," the kind voice said aloud through a speaker. "I've built a desk for you in the cockpit. Please feel free to relax or write. Or do what you like."

Mama looked at *Mobius*, who had popped out of her pocket and was flying to and fro, confused.

"If you want to speak to her directly, you have to land on her, silly," Mama said. She caught him and put him gently down on a bench that came out of the wall. Immediately he could sense vibrations and hear all kinds of chatter.

"You'll be in good hands with Stephanie," Mama said.

You have hands? he asked Auntie. He wasn't sure what an auntie was, but it sounded comforting and kind.

The voice was amused, like Mama's often was. *Not quite. Come and talk with me. Let Mama work.*

4

. . .

AUNTIE STEPHANIE BESTOWS A GIFT

ALLORY SAT AT the not-quite-ergonomic setup Stephanie had attempted to make her. The fact that a sentient
ship could fabricate anything within herself to make her passengers comfortable was enough of a miracle. She shouldn't be expected to understand the ins and outs of human physiology, and
OSHA recommendations were completely out.

While she was considerate of the physical needs of her passengers, Stephanie hadn't done much for visual aesthetics. The
walls were the same deep purple rock with veins of alabaster
streaking through that had made up Stephanie when she'd been
a humanoid. Little round quartz lights were placed high on the
walls to give her illumination, and the captain's chair currently
was the perfect size for Mallory. But she'd closed a blast door over
her view screen so Mallory couldn't look out onto the shuttle bay,
so there was nothing to interrupt her except her own mind.

Mallory told herself that this setup was ideal for writing; she
couldn't distract herself with a photo, or a window, or a screen.
She could wonder what *Mobius* and Stephanie were talking about,
but if there was any alien she would trust with the baby ship, it
would be Stephanie.

Writing a new story was a long slog. She pulled out her tablet (an Earth-made tool with a small keyboard that unfolded at the bottom, if you held it landscape-style) and stared at the cursor. She wrote, *How to make up a murder. What would Rock Bradley do?* at the top of the page.

"Hell, I need tea," she muttered. "Stephanie, if you can make a chair human-sized and fabricate seat belts and all that, can you make me some tea?"

"I can't make something that I could guarantee you'd be able to eat," Stephanie said. "I suggest you write some and then get your tea."

"You sound like my mom," Mallory said, and then bit her lip. Stephanie hadn't sounded at all like Mallory's mom, who had been dead for over two decades. "Never mind, message received," she said before Stephanie could ask about her mother.

After an hour of writing, she sat back and sighed, rubbing her neck. It felt a little choppy, but considering she hadn't written something like this before, she felt like the story was pretty solid even as a first draft.

She got up to stretch, but a stone couch caught her eye. Stephanie had included it without even distracting her. Whether that was a sign of her intense focus or a sign of Stephanie's stealth, she wasn't going to question it. She stretched out gratefully, trying to make herself as comfortable as one could on a rock—although that rock was smooth and contoured to fit a human her size.

"What happens next?" Stephanie asked, her voice coming through a speaker in the wall.

Mallory's eyes opened—she hadn't even noticed she had dozed off. "Next what? What do you mean?"

"To Rock Bradley. And how is his human assistant able to live on Bromide? She has to take her suit off eventually, right? Even inside? You wet types need to, you know, be wet."

"First, gross. Second, you were reading?" Mallory asked, sitting up in annoyance.

"Yes. The average person can't read alien writing, but I recently got access to some new translation databases. I can read your words now. I want to know what happens next."

Mallory cradled her tablet to her chest, defensively hiding it from prying eyes. "I don't know what happens next, I'm just trying the genre on for size. You shouldn't read a story in progress; you can really mess an author up. It takes a few attempts to get it right."

"Oh. But it was a realistic telling of a story. I just didn't understand how the human was safe on Bromide."

"I'll work out logistics in a future draft," Mallory grumbled. She allowed herself a smile as a small seed of pleasure took root in her chest. "So, you really liked it?"

"Yes. When will you finish it? I hope by the end of the day."

"I'm not sure. I am going to try a few different genres before I write one whole book. Just be patient with me. If I continue with Rock Bradley's story, you can be the first to read it."

"You know if Tina finds out, she'll figure out a way to make you write it as a command from the queen," Stephanie added.

"Then don't tell her I'm writing it!" Mallory said.

"Good plan."

"Are you and *Mobius* done with whatever preschool you were running?" Mallory asked.

"Yes. He's a delightful boy. You got a good one."

Mallory rubbed the bruise on her forehead with a wince. If he was good, what was a bad baby ship like? And did things like that happen? Perfectly nice parents can raise a bad kid, so having a bad baby ship had to happen eventually. She made a note to ask Mrs. Brown. "Yeah, he's pretty amazing. So what did you do?"

"I assumed he was old enough to have his own hivemind. We contacted the local Sundry and they agreed to provide his first network of four."

"*You* decided he needed a Sundry hivemind?" Mallory asked, sitting up. "I'm his guardian, Steph!"

"You are not a sentient ship, and you don't know how ships' hiveminds work," Stephanie said patiently.

"Jesus, he's not even big enough to hold four Sundry!" Mallory said. Then she lay back down (carefully) and stared at Stephanie's ceiling. "I thought he wasn't ready. Where do the Sundry come from?"

"I thought you were connected to the Sundry?" Stephanie said. From a human friend, it would have sounded sardonic, but Stephanie seemed to honestly be asking.

"There's a lot to understanding a vast alien hivemind," Mallory said, closing her eyes. "It's taking some time to learn."

"That is fair."

Mallory pictured four Sundry—what colors? blue? silver? both?—buzzing inside *Mobius*, giving him greater processing power. "Why now?" she asked. "How will this change him?"

"He will have a stronger mind, stronger personality. You should be able to communicate with him now."

"I already communicate with him, I yell at him to slow down or he'll break something else, and then he answers me by breaking something else."

She could have been wrong, but she thought she heard a tone of amusement coming from Stephanie's voice. "Then I should have said he will communicate with you," she said. "And as for who they are, my hivemind have agreed to give four to transfer to *Mobius*. He's not ready for a queen yet, but now he has much greater access to data in other hives. He's also too small to carry them inside him, so they will stay close until he grows large enough for them."

Mallory remembered being there when Stephanie had broken Gneiss law and used another person's bio-mass (a murder victim) to kick-start her transformation into a sentient shuttle. There had been no Sundry involved with that change.

"When did you get a hivemind?" Mallory asked. "I thought you didn't need it."

"We don't," Stephanie said. "My no-good grandfather won't have one. Disrupts the purity of the race or something."

Mallory coughed. "We knew he was a dick, but now he's clearly a racist."

"Having a hivemind allows one to communicate more easily with other ships, sentient or not, access galactic databases, translation programs, all that." She was quiet for a moment, then continued. "Tina and I have been learning more about hiveminds than our people have ever known."

"Tina?" Mallory asked in disbelief. "Tina *learned* something?"

Stephanie laughed. "She's still an idiot, but she's adventurous and encourages us to try new things. She is the opposite of the tradition-worshipping Gneiss on Bromide. With Ferdinand and I to back her up, she might actually make a decent queen. If she listens to us, that is."

"You sound like you almost like her now," Mallory said. "So, what's her big secret coming aboard?"

Stephanie was silent.

"Fine," Mallory said. "I guess if you won't tell me her secrets, you won't go spilling mine either."

"Exactly. I will not tell Xan you have feelings for him."

Mallory whacked the back of her head on the stone couch in exasperation. "Fuck!"

STEPHANIE WAS MALLORY'S best alien friend on Eternity—or rather, the galaxy, since Steph no longer lived full-time on the station. She seemed the voice of reason and an unwilling brake pedal to Queen Tina's chaotic momentum, but she had her own secret ambitions. Gneiss usually evolved naturally over time; in fact, most did it while sleeping for centuries. Many were currently doing so in a vast underbelly cavern of Eternity they called their ossuary. But if a Gneiss absorbed the body of an alien, it could use it as fuel to unlock bodily changes. Stephanie had gone from a humanoid rock woman to a space-ready shuttle in less than an hour.

Mallory had been angry with her for using the body of a murder victim for her change. She could have used that key evidence. But she forgave her when Stephanie saved Mallory and Xan's lives after they got spaced.

Tina, the now queen of Bezoar, did the same thing Stephanie did.

Twice.

First she had used another murder victim's body, Calliope, an old friend of Xan's, who had requested her body be donated to Tina. Calliope was a woman who loved chaos, so naturally she'd want her body used to cause more chaos by the most chaotic alien Mallory had ever met. Tina had become much larger and resembled a mech with a jet pack and rocket launcher.

The second time, she had "cleaned up" thousands of dead Sundry and used their bio-mass to get even larger, and turned her body into a safe hive for Cuckoos, the Sundry subspecies that had nearly destroyed everything on Eternity.

Mallory had quizzed Stephanie and Tina a few weeks after their transformations, wanting to learn more about the process. Sadly, she didn't get a lot of answers. The little bit she could understand was that chaos-loving Tina had become more chaotic than ever (to many folks' dismay) after absorbing Calliope's body—even though the Gneiss had taught that transfer of anything but energy was impossible. A Tina-Calliope hybrid personality wasn't supposed to have happened.

Mallory had pointed out that Stephanie had absorbed a stodgy, rules-loving Gurudev who everyone hated, but her personality hadn't changed.

"Calliope wanted to be part of me. I got her consent," Tina had

explained, surprising both Stephanie and Mallory with her insight. While Stephanie hadn't murdered the Gurudev herself, she
did absorb the body without consent.

"And that matters," Mallory said, "how?"

"Now you know why our way of transforming is considered
blasphemous to the jerks back home," Tina said. "There's something mystical about it. Consent and all that stuff. All I know is I
have a jet pack now, and everyone should have a jet pack."

"It could also be in part that Tina and Calliope had many
things in common, so the human personality amplified that of the
Gneiss. The Gurudev I absorbed was odious and I wanted only the
bio-fuel energy that remained in his body," Stephanie explained
as Tina whizzed around the shuttle bay, jet pack firing.

"Or maybe it was the fact that she absorbed a human," Mallory
said thoughtfully. "It will be hard to test this, you know."

"Why?" Tina asked, landing with surprising grace. "All we
have to do is ask a dying human if we can have their body. Duh."

Mallory had thought to explain to Tina how almost all humans tended to hold a dead body sacred and did not view it as
discarded trash that might benefit another person. Then she just
got tired.

Now Mallory was considering the Sundry aboard *Mobius* that
would give him more processing power. "Shouldn't the Sundry
have come from my own hive? I'm not sure of the etiquette here."

Stephanie sounded amused. "I don't know if there is any. Do
the Sundry consider things like etiquette?"

"Well, they have their rules, and they make bad decisions
based on denying things due to pride," Mallory said, thinking
about the history of Cuckoos that the Sundry had lost because
they didn't want to admit the Cuckoos could infiltrate their hives
and kill their queens and fill the hive with their own kind. "How
did you get your hivemind, anyway?"

"I know my transformation seemed sudden, but I had been

thinking of doing it for months. I had already petitioned the Sundry hive at the station to give me a queen."

Mallory knew the Sundry gave little away for free. "What did you have to give them in return?"

"Do you want to talk about Xan again?" Stephanie asked.

"Uh," Mallory said, thrown off guard.

"Thanks for bringing the kid by," Stephanie said. Her interior doors opened, dropping the hatch to the shuttle bay floor.

"Subtle, Steph, real subtle," Mallory said, making a quick note on her tablet. *Rock Bradley = jet pack?* But she got up, stretched, and caught *Mobius* deftly as he hurtled toward her.

What she wasn't prepared for was the tsunami of mental communication coming much stronger than before. *I learned so many things from Auntie Stephanie, Mama! I have friends now! They're with me, but they don't say much except for buzz buzz!*

"It's like Stephanie filled you up on cake and juice and handed you back to me," Mallory said with a laugh. "As I understand it, you'll get used to the buzzing. I have, anyway. You ready to go home?"

In true toddler fashion, *Mobius* fell asleep in her pocket on the way home.

5

· · · ·

A DENTIST AND A GYNECOLOGIST WALK INTO A BAR . . .

ONE OF THE hardest things about living far from Earth was dealing with the post. Humans still didn't have a way to send messages back and forth in space since you needed FTL travel to get to the station, and no one trusted the human race enough to give them the technology. So it fell to Mallory, Xan, and the other permanent resident humans to essentially reinvent the Pony Express. Except that there was no central postmaster; you had to hope that if you sent a message with someone on a shuttle that it would get where you wanted to send it.

Xan had asked Phineas to purchase stamps from all countries besides the USA who were building spaceports to receive alien shuttles. So now he could send mail with anyone heading to Earth, no matter if they landed in the US, China, Nigeria, Canada, Uganda, or Ireland. It was still slow, and you had to trust the person you asked to actually drop off the mail in the nearest box, but it was all they had at the time.

Mallory tried to remember that in the olden days, people apparently played chess through the mail. She didn't even have a lot of people to write to on Earth. Most of her communications were ordering things, which also had to make it back to Eternity through a sympathetic passenger from Earth. She tried to time her purchases with friends coming to the station. Phineas visited every few months, and Mrs. Brown's granddaughter, Lovely, went back and forth to see and help out her grandma.

Many Earth governments were still trying to figure out shuttle and port and customs issues. If someone wanted to take something perfectly legal at home and perfectly legal on Eternity through the port of a country where the item was illegal, they would have problems. Not to mention their letters would likely get opened by nosy governments. (Mallory wasn't sure the US Army had forgiven Xan for his involuntary abduction to Eternity, forcing him to go AWOL. Xan always sent his letters back to Earth via one of the other countries.)

Phineas had started charging everyone but Xan for his courier duties, since he had made some friends with the shuttle pilots who visited Earth frequently. "These guys fuckin' love scotch!" Phineas had enthused in his most recent letter to Mallory, sealed inside a care package of wine, peanut butter, and some pharmacy and clothing necessaries.

The alien shuttles didn't give a shit what they carried or what the governments on Earth thought; if the humans refused to allow shuttles to land at a port, they would simply land somewhere else on the planet. Humans had yet to regulate alien travel since the aliens' tech vastly outpaced anything on Earth.

Recent diplomatic meetings aboard Eternity had created agreements to have the aliens start using the human spaceports that many countries were rushing to build. Once humans had their own FTL technology, the travel regulations would no doubt get tied up with bureaucracy, but for now it was easy enough to book a trip on an alien shuttle to make it to Eternity, as long as there was a seat available.

Mallory was glad she already lived aboard so she wouldn't have to jump through the inevitable hoops.

It was awkward sometimes when messages from people saying

they were coming to visit ended up on the shuttle that carried the person themselves. But every new venture experienced growing pains.

The alien tech that had been shared so far with humans included the ability to send electronic messages through deep space. Humans got ahold of it and immediately charged an extortionary amount to use it. Her agent, Aaron, had sent his video mail via one of the really expensive services on Earth. He liked to show off with money when it suited him.

Xan had been luckier—his connection with the ship *Infinity* made it so anything that could communicate with the ship could communicate with Xan. They could intercept messages coming from shuttles or other sentient ships or stations. *Infinity* had found out how far away the mystery convention ship was, and was giving Xan updates since the ship had left FTL.

"I'm guessing tomorrow for arrival," Xan said, poking his finger at his tablet. He and Mallory had met for a cup of coffee at Wallace's to give her a break from speechwriting. "Probably around—"

"Ten a.m. station time," Mallory said absently.

He raised an eyebrow above his small round glasses. "And you know that how?"

Mallory blinked. "Uh, lucky guess? I don't know. Maybe *Mobius* told me?"

"I thought he was asleep?"

"Then I don't know," she muttered. "It was just . . . there."

"I'll chalk it up to 'weird Sundry shit' and we can move on," he said. He pulled up a lodgings booking screen on his tablet. Like all of Eternity's displays, it included large iconography so all species could understand what everything meant. He poked a few more of Eternity's basic buttons to secure Phineas's room, but swore as he hit the wrong one and the page reset itself.

"Why don't you just ask Mrs. Brown to get him a room?" Mallory asked, eyeing some humans who had just entered the deli.

"Because we can't bother her every time we need our noses wiped," he said. He looked at Mallory out of the corner of his eye and grinned. "Her words."

Mallory rolled her eyes. "That sounds about right. I guess it's fair."

"Have you seen the latest group of humans?" he asked.

"Are those some of them?" she said, pointing at two white people, a man and a woman looking around with the typical "human's first time on a space station" wonder.

"Yeah, the ship Phin is on sent a shuttle ahead," he said, following her gaze. "I'm not sure why."

"Is he with them?" she asked.

"I thought he would be, so I booked his room for longer, and now I need to cancel those extra days." He frowned at his tablet again.

"Why did they come early?"

"Mrs. B said they had a reason." Xan dropped the tablet on the table. "I guess I'll pay for his extra nights."

"Or make him get his ass over here to stay in that room," Mallory suggested.

"Someday you need to learn the concept of sunk-cost fallacy," he replied. "So how are you feeling about the newest batch of visitors?"

"I haven't met any of them," she said. "But that's not what you're asking, is it?"

He shook his head.

The couple was sitting at the lunch counter, loudly exclaiming at the alien fusion items.

Mallory watched them briefly. "I'm not getting so uptight about humans on board. I find if I ignore them, then I'm happier. We've had a few calm months at least."

"There," he said to his tablet. "Finally. Got him a room down the hall from you; two nights canceled. So, you're not nervous about this convention?"

"Yeah, because that's what I excel at, keeping people out of trouble," Mallory said, watching a group of young Gurudev children wander in, arguing loudly about sentient ships and stations. One of them refused to believe that a human was bonded to Eternity. When they spied Mallory, they stopped talking immediately.

Xan knocked his knuckles on the table, and she snapped out of people-watching mode.

"I'm nervous about the keynote," she said. "And I'm a little nervous about the possibility of a murder. It's a freaking murder mystery convention. If that doesn't scream 'fertile ground for a real murder,' I don't know what does."

"You're going to meet with your agent, right?" he asked, then pointed at the closed notebook under her coffee cup. "How are the new book ideas coming?"

"It's harder than I thought," she admitted. "And I thought it was going to be hard. I've got Rock Bradley, a gritty noir Gneiss detective with a human sidekick. He wants to solve cases, she wants to avoid death in the mercury rainstorms."

Xan nodded. "Solid idea. What else?"

"I've got a little old Silence lady who has moved to a small town on Earth, and she sees a murder, but since she can't communicate— or refuses to—no one believes her, so she has to catch the murderer herself."

"I like an alien Miss Marple," Xan said. "But not sure Silence is the way to go. You don't want a hero that doesn't talk at all, do you? And we don't even know how they think, so if you gave her an internal monologue, it could be all wrong."

Mallory drained her coffee cup. "True, but who would know I got it wrong?"

"Fair. What else?"

"The last one is a human sleuth and her sidekick, a magic cat."

"Pretty sure that's been done," he said.

"I'm just brainstorming right now," she said. "What if I put the human sleuth on a ship? Space murder!"

"Aren't you already writing those?"

She sighed and collapsed back in the booth. "Yes. I was hoping to trick Aaron and have him let me keep writing what I'm good at."

"What if you tried everything you do already, but not based on a real murder?"

She looked out the window at the glaring light over the desert-based park. "I think he wants a new sleuth, maybe an alien, maybe aliens getting murdered by humans, I don't know." She sighed in frustration. "My agent acts like I don't do anything here except kick back and wait for people to drop dead. So, yeah, something new. Murder mysteries, cozies, noir. Something."

"Like that flytrap detective?" he asked, grinning. "What did you think of *Pruned*?"

She had to laugh. "I didn't think I'd like it. But I admit it was fun."

Xan laughed. "You gotta admit it's a good book. Let it inspire you. Stretching your wings might be good for you. You haven't done much since the last murders."

"Hey, I do things!" Mallory said. "I thought you were on my side!"

He shrugged. This guy was so hard to rile up. "Okay, tell me, what have you done besides sit in that office space Stephanie gave you?"

She thought. "I helped out here." She gestured to the counter, catching Ginsberg's eye. He waved at her. Her flailing hand knocked over her water glass, making ice cubes skitter across the table.

"You drank free milkshakes!" Xan corrected. "What else?"

She focused on the mess, putting ice back into her cup and hating him for being right. "What else can I do? No one asks me to do anything until someone drops dead."

"You don't have to wait for someone else to call you, Mal," he said gently. His brown eyes were warm and kind. "Sometimes you have to go after something you want. Find something you want. Don't be shackled by the real murders. Go write something new."

Mallory caught the small water puddle with her napkin, trying to think of something to say. "I think I'm going to go with Rock Bradley," she said hesitantly. She didn't realize how desperately she needed validation—human validation—until right now. "I know the Gneiss the best, so that character will be easy to write—well, easier than any other alien, I mean."

"Rock Bradley, Private Eye," Xan said in a deep voice. "Ladies love him, but he only wants to find out who killed his wife?"

She laughed. "I'm not going to fridge anyone to develop a backstory. But Stephanie is really into what I've got so far."

"I believe it," he said. "That's awesome. Tina's going to go apeshit for it, you know."

Mallory relaxed slightly. God, she needed that. "I told Stephanie she can't tell Tina about it yet. She'll probably come screaming encouragement at me while I'm writing."

"Or ordering you to be her court writer or something," Xan said, nodding slightly. "Yeah, don't tell her. But seriously, go write more before the big ship gets here. I won't bother you." He made a shooing gesture with his hands.

"Fine, fine," she said, pulling out her tablet again. "Tell me when Phineas gets here."

"Will do. Any idea when Tina and company will get here?"

"Stephanie wouldn't say. She's really closemouthed about Tina these days," Mallory said. This was an anomaly, because if anyone had ever complained about Tina's idiosyncrasies, it was Stephanie. "Just that we need to be available when she gets here."

"I'll consider myself on call, then," he said, and rose from the table.

· · ·

MALLORY WASN'T TOO put off by seeing humans anymore. For many months it had only been her, Xan, the former ambassador Adrian, and the newer ambassador Jessica, who was often seen alongside Xan. And Mrs. Brown, the host of the station—but she was busy all the time. With everyone else being busy and no murders to solve, Mallory could go days without seeing another human.

Now more humans than ever were on the station since shuttles were servicing the Earth with increasing frequency. Luckily, not many visiting humans knew who Mallory was, so no one had sought her out to ask about her books, or her weird murder problem, or whether she'd been probed.

She signaled Flo for another coffee refill and read what she had just written. She hated admitting it, but Xan and Aaron were right. She was bored. It's not that she *hoped* for a good juicy murder to spice up her life, but she couldn't deny that when she wasn't investigating a murder or other catastrophe, she didn't know what to do with herself.

She doctored her coffee with Euclid creamer, a delicacy from the Phantasmagore home world, and tried not to make a face when she took a sip. She opened her tablet and went back to writing with purpose.

Which apparently was an open invitation for strangers to bother her. The two people spellbound by the station had finished their lunch, and instead of leaving the deli, they approached and smiled at her until she finally looked at them.

"Can I help you?" she asked.

They slid into her booth without invitation. The man was tall, fit, and tanned, about fifty years old. His eyes were a muddy hazel, and he was the kind of man who was attractive because of his confidence, not his looks. He wore a fitted polo shirt that was designed to show off the hours he spent at the gym, a white blazer, and tan slacks. His teeth were perfect. "Hi, Mallory, I'm Dr. Bruce Truman—"

"Doctor of *dentistry*," the woman cut in, but Bruce just laughed.

"—and this is Dr. Kath Audrey, ob-gyn."

"A *real* doctor," Kath added.

Mallory shook the woman's hand, trying not to stare. Kath was about forty. She was slightly taller than Mallory, with high cheekbones, a pert nose, and gently curling brown hair falling past her shoulders. Actually, it *cascaded*. Her skin was dewy. Her blue eyes were kind as she shook Mallory's hand. Her beauty was almost painful to look at. Mallory wondered how this woman existed in real life and not in a fairy tale. She was wrapped in the kind of boring navy dress that clearly was trying to downplay some of her more attention-grabbing assets, but Mallory would bet she'd still manage to look sexy in a burlap sack.

Mallory didn't say any of this aloud. She figured Kath had heard that before. Also, it would be rude, even though they were the ones who were interrupting.

Mallory shook her offered hand. "Of all the things I expected today, and I can expect a lot around here, being accosted by a dentist and a gynecologist was not on my list. This is a bad joke, right?"

Bruce grinned, flashing his teeth at her. "No joke, but when you tell the story to your friends, you may want to make it sound like a joke, sure. It's pretty funny, actually." He glanced at Kath. "Humor is in threes, right? Who else do we have who could walk into the bar with us? A hacker? Agent? Writer?"

"Nothing is as funny as a dentist and a gynecologist, sorry," Mallory said.

Flo came to take their order. Kath ordered coffee; Bruce ordered nothing.

"She called me 'hon'!" Kath squealed when Flo had left.

"Yeah, that's her thing now," Mallory said. "So, you came with the convention from Earth, right? What brings you to the station this early?"

Flo interrupted any answer by putting three mugs down on the table and leaving without taking Mallory's empty.

"I didn't order coffee," Bruce complained. "I'm here for a different experience. I'm going to try alien food next."

Mallory took her new mug and slid the other one to Kath. The doctor sipped it and made a face.

"Not good?" Mallory asked.

"Not what I expected," Kath said, looking at the mug, which had a light brown oily sheen on top. "What is this made with?"

"They're using coffee beans from Earth, but Kurt is experimenting with the liquids that other species drink. I think this one is a plant milk from the planet Bezoar." She sipped again and shrugged. "It's better than the creamer from the Phantasmagore home world. You get used to it."

Kath sipped and then brightened. "It's not bad!" She elbowed Bruce. "You wanted a new experience, right?"

He looked down at his mug, then back at Kath. "You can have mine."

Before they got into an adorable fight, Mallory spoke up. "You still haven't answered. What can I do for you two?"

Kath opened her mouth, but Bruce leaned forward and spoke over her.

"We're mystery writers, and have been big fans of yours for a while." He beamed at Mallory again.

"You've read my books?" she asked, trying not to sound nervous. The last time a fan tried to track her down, he'd ended up dead.

"Yes!" Kath enthused. "I've read them all. He's read four, I think. They're amazing inspiration. But that's not why we're here.

We were going to message you as soon as we figured out how to use the phones, but when we saw you sitting here, we thought we'd say hi."

"And why did you want to see *me* specifically?" Mallory asked, sitting up and getting into professional mode. "Is someone dead?"

"What?" Dr. Audrey asked, alarmed.

"That's usually why people need me, because there's been a murder and they need help finding the killer. People don't tend to seek out my company without that factor." She cocked her head at Kath. "You just said you had read my books, but you're surprised I'm asking about a murder?"

"You can be honest with us," Bruce said. "We know that whole murder thing is your 'brand' to help sell your books."

"You *know* that, do you?" Mallory asked flatly. She rolled her eyes and faced Kath, who seemed like she had a brain in her head under the layers of gorgeousness.

The gynecologist glared at Bruce, her blue eyes like steel. "Just be quiet, Bruce. You're making everything worse."

He looked affronted. He huffed a little bit and leaned back in his chair, gesturing obviously for her to take the floor. He considered his mug, picked it up, and then put it back down.

"We are in space for Marple's Tea Party, but took the day to come here early. We'll pick the cruise back up when it leaves the station and take it back to Earth," Kath said.

"I still don't see what I—"

"Today we're here in a professional capacity," Kath continued. "We're part of a group of medical professionals that have come to provide care to the humans who have lived here for a while. As I understand it, you folks have dealt with everything from deadly insect stings to concussions to someone losing his eyes!"

"Yeah, Adrian got really messed up," Mallory said. "Eternity said she was sorry."

"So," Kath continued, confused by Mallory's statement but

still charging ahead, "there are the two of us, an ophthalmologist, a general practitioner, a dermatologist, and a few others. We're looking for opportunities to open medical clinics on board for humans and to learn more about xenobiology in the meantime. We're offering free checkups to those of you living aboard the station."

"And I thought it was pushy when the dentist texted me 'friendly reminders' about my cleanings back home," Mallory said, shaking her head slowly. "Thanks, but I'm okay."

"You've been on the station more than half a year, right?" Bruce said, looking at his phone. "You should get a dental cleaning every six months."

"Yeah, but what you don't know is I've been examined by doctors of all sorts of different species. I haven't seen a *human* doctor in months, but I've seen medical professionals." She thought briefly of her time in the medbay, suffering from a severing of her mental connection with the blue hivemind as it was dying within the depths of the station. "I'm not sure you could help me out with the various shit I've had happen to me, actually."

"Teeth still need cleaning, and the exams are free," Bruce said. "You should take advantage of that."

"I can't believe you came all the way here to offer me a pap smear!" Mallory said to Kath.

"Well, your pap is not the only one she's going to smear," Bruce said. "There are other women on the station. What?" he added when he saw their faces.

"Don't talk about my job, Bruce," Kath said. "And never say any combination of 'pap' and 'smear' again."

Mallory was starting to like Kath. But she still didn't like strangers coming up to her and inviting themselves to look into her various and Sundry openings. "Why would you miss part of the convention? Why work now?"

"Why not? Eternity wanted doctors, and we wanted to attend the con, so it seemed perfect," Bruce said. "We had to miss a day of the con to get here before the ship does, but now we can have our meet- ings and appointments"—he looked at Mallory meaningfully—"and be done in time for your keynote."

Mallory groaned, the coffee and weird milk curdling in her stomach.

Five blue Sundry buzzed through an open window, circling Bruce's head, their buzzing louder than any Earth insect. Mallory watched impassively, Kath was startled but didn't react, and Bruce flailed at them in a panic, waving them away. Luckily, for him, he missed all of them.

The Sundry landed on the table next to Mallory's plate. Bruce's face was white as he raised his hand to swat them, but Kath caught his arm.

"What is wrong with you?" she hissed. "Remember what we read about other alien races? These are the Sundry. I think," she added, eyes cutting to Mallory, who nodded.

Bruce looked as if he remembered nothing but how to catch and kill wasps in an empty soda can. Mallory couldn't believe anyone visiting the station would forget the info about the Sundry, but some people had an automatic reaction to insects. Right now Bruce's eyes were locked on the Sundry that were crawling along the rim of the coffee mug Mallory had drained.

To be fair, Mallory had to admit that even when you knew they were intelligent and could communicate, seeing the Sundry for the first time could be terrifying. Their bodies were about as long as a finger, iridescent blue or silver, with visible stingers and venom sacs. But still, swatting them could make you a lifetime enemy. If you survived the encounter.

"Why did a bunch of doctors come here all of a sudden?" Mal- lory asked, moving the mug and the insects slightly away from Bruce's reach.

"Mrs. Brown contacted several med schools and hospitals, offering a vacation to doctors who would examine the humans living here. Do you know if anyone here needs pregnancy care?" Kath added delicately.

"Wait a second," Mallory said, slapping the table and making the Sundry take flight again. "You're hoping to find some kind of human-alien hybrid!"

Kath flushed. "Those aren't the words I would use. If that kind of thing were going to happen, then, yes, I would love to be the doctor on call, but I'm not hunting around for it."

"Sorry to disappoint, no one I know is pregnant."

"Really? Do you use protection when fooling around with aliens?" Bruce asked. "What kind of condoms do they have?"

Mallory nearly did a spit take. "Are you serious? You are about as subtle as using a sandblaster as an exfoliant. I'm not having sex with anyone right now, human or alien. Also, how do you know I'm not a lesbian? Or celibate? Or asexual?"

"Well, are you any of those?" Bruce asked, nonplussed.

"And why would I tell a dentist that?" she demanded.

"You are unbelievably rude," Kath said to Bruce. She gave an apologetic look to Mallory. "We're looking forward to seeing your keynote at the convention," she added while scooting out of the booth. She took Bruce's elbow and hauled him to his feet. "What's the topic?"

Mallory blanched. "It's a secret," she managed to say. "But can I ask, what do you know about the ship that's holding the convention? I've heard it's amazing."

"It really is," Bruce said. "She can make anything her inhabitants need!"

This was standard with sentient ships and stations, so Mallory nodded. "One more question before you go," she said. "Who are you two to each other?" She held up two fingers to point to both at the same time. "Neither of you is wearing a ring, but you both look old enough to be married once or twice by now."

"Old friends," Bruce said with a smile. "We were in a writing workshop together a million years ago. Became each other's beta reader. Found we had a lot in common besides writing, like being fans of the band VDV. We are the oldest fans they have, we think. We were the only ones who watch online stuff and don't cry in chat windows."

"I still don't think they were literally crying," Kath said.

"That is not nearly the point and you know it," Bruce said.

"Anyway, we kept in touch, hung out at conventions, tried to make writing careers while we were studying for our day jobs—" Bruce began, but then Kath took over the narrative.

"—and then when Mrs. Brown made her call to doctors, and then the space cruise happened, and then we heard that VDV was playing a few concerts at the convention, it was like a perfect storm."

"Coincidences usually are like a perfect storm," Mallory deadpanned. "What was the band again?"

They laughed. "Surprised you have to ask," Bruce said, sounding like he had prepped the upcoming joke multiple times.

"I barely kept up with pop music when I lived on Earth," Mallory admitted. "Out here it's even harder."

Bruce pointed to Kath. "Ob-gyn?" He pointed at himself. "Dentist?" Then he waggled his finger back and forth. "Vaginas? Teeth?"

Mallory shook her head. "No idea."

Kath groaned. "Why do you have to try to set this up every time? Just tell people!" She focused on Mallory. "They're a punk band called Vagina Dentata V."

Mallory laughed. "That's brilliant. Do you actually like their music or just the band's name? And what's with the 'V'?"

"They're not the first band to think up that name, so they have to put a number to distinguish themselves," Kath said. "We do think we might be the only dentist–slash–ob-gyn fans, though.

But it helps us let off steam from a day of broken teeth, fibroids, and rejection letters."

"What ties does the band have to murder mysteries? Or is there high overlap between fans?" Mallory asked.

"I don't know, we just know we have a chance to go to space, advance our careers, go to a convention, and see the best band on Earth. So we had to come!" Bruce said.

Kath smiled at her. "We will see you at the convention unless you change your mind and want an exam before then. Eternity is giving us the medbay three floors down from here to do our exams. Medbay two. Don't delay. Cervical cancer kills."

"So does oral cancer!" Bruce called over his shoulder as Kath pulled him away from the table.

"I'll see you at the convention," Mallory said firmly. "If I can figure out how to write a keynote," she added under her breath.

Beside her, the five Sundry crawled around the rim of Bruce's untouched coffee.

"Don't you guys fall in," Mallory warned them.

The Sundry's wing hum intensified, forming words. *"We're not in danger,"* the five said. *"You are."*

They took flight, circled the room once, and then left.

The Sundry sometimes gave Mallory dire predictions that sounded like they were coming from prophets. But sometimes their message was essentially "nuh-uh," which wasn't as impressive as they probably intended.

"You know, you're more foreboding when you don't sound like we're having an argument on a playground," she called after them.

6

THE GIRLFRIEND'S GUIDE TO SENTIENT SHIPS

YOU COULD HAVE told me you set a dentist on my tail! I felt like I was a fox and he was an uptight British lord on a mistreated gelding," Mallory said to the wrinkled patient face appearing on her tablet.

"I knew you'd react like this," Mrs. Brown said evenly. "You're worse than my granddaughter with this dentist fear. I didn't tell you because it's harder to avoid your *adult responsibilities* when they're here in your face. Or in the case of Dr. Audrey, they're in your other end."

Mallory stared at her, then coughed out a laugh. "That was unexpected."

"Never forget I was married to a comedian," Mrs. Brown said. "But more to the point, there are now doctors here, and they're free, so I would take advantage of them. In fact, I *am* taking advantage of them. We could see them at the same time. Girl's trip!"

"Sure, let's get Jessica and all get pap smears, then go out for a girl's night afterward," Mallory said sarcastically. She thought about being on an exam table with her legs in stirrups while chatting and bonding with Jessica, the cold and calculating ambassador, and Mrs. Brown, the stern tiny woman capable of murder (three, in fact). "Never mind. Not the girl's night out I would want to have," she added with a laugh.

"You're an adult," Mrs. Brown said again, her voice implying that Mallory was anything but. "You know you need preventative care. If you want to neglect your teeth till they fall out, avoid cancer screenings, and deny your eyes are changing as you age, then go ahead and ignore the doctors. I'm sure they'll be happy to spend the free time getting drunk at that mystery convention. Maybe your cervical cancer will aid them in getting an agent."

"Agent?" Mallory said stupidly.

"Yes, didn't they tell you? They're writers. The doctor jobs are their day jobs, but they apparently want to leave lucrative fields that can save lives to make ten thousand dollars a year writing novels."

"I guess they did mention that but didn't say they were on the agent hunt. Huh."

"Mallory. Go get a damn pap smear. And consider, what if we had an appendix incident? Or a pregnancy?"

"A pap smear will help neither of those situations!" Mallory responded. She thought for a moment and couldn't remember when her last pap smear was. She had bad memories of visiting the gynecologist, because her last one had dropped dead while Mallory was in stirrups for her annual exam. Turns out a rival doctor at the practice wanted her out of the way, and had slipped Mallory's doctor a slow-acting poison, and then left the country on vacation.

"And can't Eternity figure out who is sick? She repurposes our waste, right? Won't she notice a change in our bodies?"

"Technically, yes, but you can't ask her to do that for thousands of sentients on the station. That's a lot of toilet flushes to monitor closely. She's not yet up to her full strength since the whole incident with the Cuckoos, so you'll forgive me if I don't ask her for the contents of your urine every day. You're going to have to go to a doctor like all of the heathens back home."

It hadn't been that long since the Cuckoos had infiltrated the station and started killing all the Sundry hives to take over Eternity's processing power, and the new Sundry hivemind was still quite small for the demands of a large station. New queens had been established and the hiveminds were growing, but they still had a ways to go before Eternity was at full power.

"Since the doctors are here," Mrs. B continued, "you should visit as many as you can since you haven't been to Earth in several months. I didn't have regular checkups on Earth, which is why the cancer almost got me."

"Seems like we're in more danger of life support failing than dying of cancer," Mallory said. She knew that the Cuckoos had brought Eternity to her metaphorical knees, but Mallory had thought the station had recovered. "Is Eternity okay? I thought she was getting stronger since her new hivemind was installed."

Mrs. Brown sniffed; she saw right through Mallory's attempt to change the subject. "We have life support and a stable orbit. But as for determining one person's health, no. She's never been omniscient, and now her hivemind has to grow some more before it's up to full strength."

"Should I be worried?" Mallory said, remembering times in past months that Eternity was not in her right mind and very bad things happened.

"We're doing all right so far, aren't we?" Mrs. Brown said. "We'll be fine."

Eternity's first break had come a few months after Mallory had arrived, seeking a new place to live in hopes people would stop dropping dead around her. Eternity's host had died, murdered through a strange cascade of events. The station took the loss very badly, suffering several hull breaches and killing many on board. Mrs. Brown had finally stepped in to take the host's place to guide Eternity into stability. Power-hungry Adrian Casserly-Berry, the previous ambassador, had tried to take the host role first, but the station rejected him violently. He still had the scars.

Mrs. Brown had stage four breast cancer when she came aboard, so she had nothing to lose in trying to connect with the station. Either Eternity would kill her or the cancer would.

Turns out that neither killed her. According to doctors with experience in sentient machines and humans, after Mrs. Brown connected with the station, her body became stronger and the cancer slowly disappeared.

"This was after I had to explain that the cancer and I were not in a symbiotic relationship," Mrs. Brown had said, laughing. "I had to tell her that the tumor was at the same time eating me and dying internally as it went. Then Eternity figured it was a bad use of life, and that it was probably not sentient, and accepted that I wanted it gone. The cancer's goal was to devour me. I was half-afraid she'd try to get to know the lump or, worse, name it."

Mrs. Brown snapped Mallory out of her memories. "You're dodging the question," she reminded her. "Go see the doctors."

"Okay, fine," Mallory said, if only to get Mrs. B off her back. "I suppose Eternity will tell you if I'm dodging it?"

"Again, she's not omniscient, you might have to be responsible for this on your own," Mrs. Brown said. "But speaking of symbiotic relationships, where's your shadow?"

"Asleep," Mallory said. "He met 'Auntie Stephanie' today. She gave him his first Sundry circuit."

"And you let her?" Mrs. Brown asked, eyes wide.

"I didn't know she had planned on doing that!" Mallory said, exasperated. "You told me that he would need a hivemind eventually, not that he needed one right now! And you said you didn't know where to find one! There's no *Girlfriend's Guide to Ships* for me to read, so I accepted Stephanie's help since she knows a little more about it."

She expected Mrs. Brown to be angry in response to her rudeness, but the woman sighed and looked down. "You're right. I brought you an alien being to take care of with little guidance.

And if you trust Stephanie, it shouldn't matter if the Sundry came from her."

"I trust Stephanie with my life," Mallory said honestly. "In fact, I've trusted her with my life before."

As if he had heard his name, *Mobius* stirred in her pocket. Mallory took him out gently and held him in front of the camera so Mrs. Brown could see him.

"Oh! He's sleeping!" Mrs. Brown whispered with all the warmth of a grandmother who buys forbidden candy for her grandchildren when the parents aren't looking. "Hello, little *Mobius*!"

Mallory nestled him back into her pocket.

"How can anyone deny that adorable face?" Mrs. Brown said, syrup still in her voice.

Madam, you have killed three people in your life, Mallory thought. *You can't fool me that you're all honey and gingerbread.* Instead of voicing these thoughts, she said, "I don't mean to sound unappreciative; it's just taking some time to adjust."

She carried the tablet into the kitchen. A package of what she thought of as alien butcher paper sat open on her kitchen counter. Two-inch green cubes were stacked neatly inside to form a larger cube. She picked up one of them and studied it. "And what the hell am I feeding him, anyway?"

"Processed bio-matter, the same as every other species that grows," Mrs. Brown said. "Think of it as unrefined oil, or deconstructed oil. Like a hipster sandwich."

Mallory made a face and put the cube down.

"Remember, the faster he grows, the faster he matures, so you have incentive to keep him fed," Mrs. Brown said.

"If that's the case, why not give him the whole box of bio-matter now?"

"He can't eat something bigger than he is," Mrs. Brown said firmly. She had that stern grandmother persona on lock. "It'll just come right back up."

Great. Cleaning up ship vomit was not on my list of things to do today.

She took a saucer out of the sink and rinsed it off, then filled it with water. She placed a green cube in the middle of the shallow pool, where it immediately started to dissolve, turning the water black with an oily sheen. It really did look like petroleum.

The noise woke up the small ship, who beeped sleepily in her pocket. She took him out and placed him on the counter. When he realized what she was doing, he launched and zipped over to the bowl with a happy noise. He cannonballed straight into the middle of it, splashing bio-matter on the counter and Mallory's shirt. Just like a toddler, in fact. He rolled around and around, and then took flight. Mallory lunged at him, trying to keep him on the saucer, but the slippery oil made him slide out of her hands. He careened around her apartment, chirping and spraying the goop everywhere around him.

"Oh, no, is this going to happen every time I feed him?" Mallory said, rummaging in a drawer to get a rag to clean up.

"Oh, don't worry about that," Mrs. Brown said from the terminal. "He's sharing his meal with Eternity. She'll clean it up for you."

In her frustration, Mallory had forgotten that Eternity could absorb almost anything spilled on her, and shortly Mallory's apartment would be more or less clean. But her clothes would probably stay messy until she washed them.

"Most toddlers don't like to share," Mrs. Brown said proudly. "He's a good boy."

Mallory ran her fingers through her hair, then realized she had rubbed the ship's dinner on her head. Her hands were smeared with the green-and-brown goop. "Well, Eternity can't clean me. I'm going to need a shower. Do you need anything else?"

"I think you called me," Mrs. Brown reminded her. "But as for your little ship, now that he has the new circuit, it should be easy for him to tell you what he needs. And if he can't, the Sundry you speak with should be able to communicate with this hivemind. Remember that different ships mature at different rates. *Mobius* specifically is a science vessel, able to carry science teams, their equipment, and of course a full Sundry hivemind of his own."

"Yeah, Sundry-*Mobius*-me communication is going to be interesting," Mallory muttered. A question occurred to her then. "How do the stations and ships not get controlled by the larger Sundry hiveminds? If the independent hiveminds have agendas, as we have seen they can have, why don't they control the ones who do the grunt work inside sentient ships and stations?"

"I think you hit the nail on the head," Mrs. Brown said thoughtfully. "They're grunt workers. It's like a class system, or more like how the insects back home exist: everyone is born into a job. Our Sundry friends lounging in the park hive are like the upper class. No real jobs, living on old money, being leisurely rich. They collect data the way billionaires collect money; they have a lot, and the more they have, the more they want. But the ones who serve as hiveminds for other beings are the mechanics, the maids, the folks who live paycheck to paycheck. Worker bees versus scouts versus soldiers versus queens." She paused, and Mallory wondered if she was getting this directly from Eternity.

"So, it's like we're supporting communism?" Mallory asked. "Or is it a caste system?"

"You're speaking like they're humans," Mrs. Brown said. "Each Sundry has a job, just like insects back home. They do their job and reap the benefits of being part of a hivemind. It's not exploitive at all. Think if we paid the lower class a living wage on Earth."

"How do I know when he's ready for a queen?" Mallory asked. "And how do I get a queen, anyway?"

"When he gets larger, he'll start looking for his own. That's the equivalent of puberty; he'll start communicating with other hiveminds and probably rebel against you a little bit as he tests his limits. You don't have a say in the establishment of the queen, whether it's blue or silver."

"Or Cuckoo?" Mallory asked. The infiltrating chaotic insects were capable of powering sentient ships and stations, but they weren't as smart or informed as the other two.

"No," Mrs. Brown said firmly. "Cuckoos would only power him if another species had established the hivemind first. They're a lazy species, essentially. But you want him to have a hivemind, Mallory. He'll die without one."

Mobius was wallowing in the saucer again, but stopped when Mrs. Brown said the part about death. He focused a dirty lens on Mallory and chirped a distressed question.

"It's okay, buddy, we'll get you your queen," Mallory said, wiping her hands on her shirt. "Now eat all your goo."

"Go get your shower and then be a good girl and see the dentist to get your teeth cleaned." Mrs. Brown's video cut out.

Immediately after Mrs. Brown ended the call, ID codes flashed on the screen, indicating the different doctors who were currently on the station. Mallory saved them and told herself she would call them later.

She pushed her hair out of her eyes again, grimacing when she felt *Mobius*'s food hardening in her hair. "All those doctors and she didn't think to invite a hairdresser."

Mobius followed Mallory into the shower. She had lost most of her discomfort with nudity in front of aliens by reminding herself that aliens had no idea which bodily parts should be covered in polite company. As Mallory lounged under the hot water, the little ship played his favorite game: vibrating on such a high level that the water was repelled, surrounding himself with a little force field, and staying perfectly dry.

"You goof," she said. She had to admit that taking care of *Mobius* was nicer than her usual job of finding dead bodies, solving murders, and then writing about it.

WHEN SHE GOT out of the shower, she looked at the four Sundry sitting on her couch, then tapped her chin, thinking.

Four was the smallest number of Sundry who could communicate with other beings, as it took four to both create a strong connection to the hivemind and to make enough noise to be heard. She commonly had four Sundry with her at all times, rarely on her body, but somewhere in whatever room she was in.

Now the latest shift looked to be dozing on the couch.

Mallory had been stung by the Sundry as a child, which gave her an immediate connection to the hivemind. She didn't know about this for many years, and just thought she was cursed to be drawn toward situations where violence—namely murder—was likely to happen. As she learned more about her connection to the Sundry, she allowed another one to sting her, which had been a bad idea since she was allergic, but she had gotten her EpiPen in time. And more importantly, after the sting, she had been able to use the Sundry's vast knowledge to figure out the final clue of a murder.

Connecting to the Sundry wasn't fun. It was like inviting a stampede of wildebeests to trample her mind. The hivemind didn't take it easy on her; they rarely had much concern for any one Sundry member (except for a queen), and even though she was human, to them, she was just one of millions of Sundry. If Mallory couldn't handle the hivemind connection, no big deal to them.

It was a very big deal to Mallory, since she didn't need a circuit connected to a hivemind to communicate. Thusly, she had avoided the insects despite the knowledge they held, which sadly put her at a disadvantage since she was living among aliens and technically had a direct connection to a ton of universal knowledge.

Things changed a few months ago, after the slaughter of most of the blue and silver Sundry on the station when the Cuckoos took over. A few Sundry had survived, including young blue and silver queens. They sought shelter among their own, which put them in Mallory's bedroom. They blocked the air ducts to keep their pheromone signatures out of the Cuckoos' notice and worked on increasing their own numbers. After the Cuckoos were dispersed, gathered up, and shipped off to Bezoar with Tina, that planet's new queen, these new hives eventually became the new centers to power Eternity, and surprisingly were a bit more communicative and friendly around Mallory. They were a lot easier to understand; they even spoke in a more relaxed dialect.

The constant blue/silver conflict had also calmed down since the hives had suddenly needed each other.

Mallory had started connecting to the swarms via meditation now, which was a lot less deadly than letting one sting her, but she had yet to understand how to access the data in the hivemind for straight research that led to facts.

And when she wasn't meditating, she could verbally ask the four that were always with her to grab a few more friends to facilitate a nuanced conversation.

Whether they would give her information or not was to be determined.

Mallory asked her scouts to gather some more Sundry so she could look for more information. Soon, a swarm of about a hundred Sundry came through the ductwork and awaited her in her living room. She wrapped her robe around herself and sat in the chair, facing the hovering blue mass.

"What do we know about the ship that's coming?"

It dipped slightly, then fed her some flat facts. "She has a hivemind made of Earth-based Sundry and a queen from Eternity. She is quite powerful and large."

"And that's it? You can't communicate with her hivemind?"

"Unclear," the swarm buzzed, seeming unsure of themselves.

"She has the computing ability to create anything her passengers need."

"Don't Eternity and *Infinity* also do that?"

"Not like *Metis*." Another pause. "We haven't seen her type before."

"You mean she's a new kind of ship?"

"No. A very old kind."

"A very old powerful ship being used to host a mystery convention," Mallory said, wonder in her voice. "Seems like a big hammer for a tiny nail."

The swarm waited.

"Do we have any idea what Tina's surprise is? Have you been able to connect with the hiveminds on her shuttle?"

"Diplomatic leaders keep their hiveminds separate from the greater galactic database," they said.

"Oh, that is bullshit!" Mallory said, pacing around the room. "They might want their Sundry not to talk to you, but they can't stop them, and you will want all the data you can get your hands on."

"You will understand more when the Bezoar queen arrives."

Mallory sighed in annoyance. "Then I guess I'll go to bed. Thanks, I guess."

"Welcome," they said, then most flew away into the ductwork, leaving four behind to crawl into their favorite sleeping spot, a tiny hive they'd built close to the ceiling.

"All the kids are tucked in now," Mallory said with a sigh. "When did my life get so weird?"

7

THE POTTY LORD IS
KING OF THE PARTY

XAN WAS STARTING to wonder if *Infinity* was a sadist. She was a sentient ship who usually respected the strange needs of the small wet human that lived aboard her, but she still insisted that yelling at Xan mentally was the best way to wake him up.

Wake up! Stephanie told me the queen of Bezoar's shuttle is nearing the station.

Xan hadn't realized he had fallen asleep reading, but when he jerked awake at *Infinity*'s words, his e-reader slid off his chest and onto the floor. His fuzzy brain was trying to remember where his brother was, and it took him a second to realize that she was talking about the Gneiss, not Phineas.

"I'm waiting for Phineas," he said. "Tina's ship can land just fine. She doesn't need me." He yawned.

She wants the humans "that matter" to meet her.

"Oh, that's not good," Xan said. "Is she running from the law again?"

No. Stephanie is not in distress. She is more resigned.

"Is Ferd with Tina?"

Yes, and a small swarm of Cuckoos. And a guest. Her words had an edge of worry.

"Cuckoos? Mrs. B is going to have a fit," Xan said, pulling on a fresh sweatshirt. Since the Cuckoos' attempt to hijack the station, Eternity had forbidden them to come aboard ever again. Nobody had argued against her, not even Tina, who was the new custodian of the insects on her prison planet of Bezoar.

"Why'd she bring them with her? She knows Eternity won't let her on."

Her message says that they are a threat only if they infiltrate without detection. Only then are they able to attack and reinstate their queen. Tina isn't carrying a queen.

"Huh," he said, pulling on his boots. "If we know they're coming, and they can't take over if there's no queen, then in theory everything should be fine, right?"

In theory, she agreed. *But that doesn't make Eternity want to welcome them anymore.*

"That's fair, yeah," he said. "So, what is she going to do?"

The blue Sundry have agreed to escort you and Mallory. Silver Sundry will keep close to Tina to look for errant Cuckoos.

The Sundry aboard the station could wipe out Tina's Cuckoos in one focused attack if need be.

"Do we know any other reasons why she's coming? Has there been a coup already?"

Stephanie merely said Tina is seeking counsel on a problem, since, in Tina's words, "the bugs aren't smart and my friends are mean."

"I don't know why she thinks we'll be more helpful or nicer to her," he said. "Everyone here remembers the Cuckoo incident all too well."

He made sure his e-reader was plugged in before he left the room. Zesty Yaboi was just about to escape with his last remaining head, running back home to the swamps of North Carolina. Xan was dying to find out if his mother was still alive.

You should know that Ferdinand is here to see how his bar is doing under human management.

Xan grimaced. "I don't know why he put me in charge. The Gneiss don't take me seriously, since I'm serving them, but I can't even look over the bar easily. When do they get here?"

One station hour.

"I'd better tell Mallory," he said.

No need; all necessary humans already know.

"You told me last?" he asked, incredulous. Maybe being mentally connected to a spaceship didn't guarantee that he would be first to know all the news.

No, she said patiently. *I told everyone at the same time. I sent a message to Jessica, Eternity will tell Mrs. Brown, and Mobius will tell Mallory.*

"*Mobius* can't talk," Xan said.

He can now.

"If he just became verbal, I don't see this going well," Xan said, rubbing his face. "I'd better check to make sure Mallory knows the actual message. We'll go to the shuttle bay to meet them when they get in. Tina gets what she wants. She likes being queen, after all."

She's very happy about being queen, but she seems to be confused by the fact that there's work involved. She had apparently gotten much of her ideas of royalty from Earth media.

"But wasn't her mother a queen?" Xan asked.

Queen in name. She delegated most of her work to underlings and never actually visited Bezoar. The day we picked you up on Earth, Tina had just robbed a store of books and movies. No one in the shop had the audio implant to answer her questions about how much everything cost; she just terrified everyone. So she took what she wanted.

Xan was not surprised that Tina had knocked over a Barnes & Noble. "She's getting the worst lesson a teenager can get—adulthood and responsibilities." He sent Mallory a quick message on their internal communication line, a wireless connection via their watches. It read, "Bitch queen of the galaxy incoming in 1 hr. Infin told Mob but I thought . . ."

In Xan's experience, women either hated the word "bitch" or embraced it with badass gusto. He figured Mallory was the former, but Tina was definitely the latter, probably because she had absorbed the bio-mass of a foulmouthed human soldier.

The answer was immediate. "JFC THANK YOU. Mob was trying to tell me something but I had no clue what he was talking about. Should we bow or curtsy for B-queen?"

"Prob. both," he replied. Then added, "Meet at Ferd's?"

MALLORY CLUTCHED A towel around herself and was chasing *Mobius* around the room, wet hair hanging in her face, when Xan's message came. The ship was flying up near the ceiling, skirting the perimeter as if looking for a way out or a crack in their defenses, all the while shouting, *IMPORTANT MESSAGE. I HAVE AN IMPORTANT MESSAGE* in Mallory's head.

"Yeah, but what *is* the message?" she yelled back.

Her terminal and her watch in the bathroom both beeped, and she ran to read it. Xan's message popped up on her terminal and she sagged with relief. At least it wasn't life or death (yet).

"I can't believe your first words were 'important message,'" she said, watching *Mobius* continue to zoom around the living room. "But you can calm down now. I have the message."

I have completed my task! he sent jubilantly.

"Not really," she said. "You didn't tell me the message. I got it from Xan."

He finally slowed down to a speed where she could snag him, and he vibrated happily.

"When you have a message, you need to actually say what the message is, not just yell 'important message' over and over." She smiled as his tiny lens rotated to focus on her. "But, hey, you're talking now. That's exciting."

She glanced around the room, trying to spot his new Sundry processing insects. They were three silver and one blue, clinging to one of the doors of her kitchen cabinets. Their wings vibrated, their movements barely visible. Her own Sundry were in her bedroom, all four of them blue. She wondered if they were going to exchange information.

He was also bigger, she realized, about the size of a softball now. He should be big enough to carry the Sundry with him, if she kept feeding him the disgusting cubes.

"At least you don't have diapers," she said. She shivered as her wet hair dripped water onto her floor. She needed to get dressed. She quickly fixed him a bowl of sludge so he would hopefully eat it and leave her alone while she dried off.

She combed her light brown hair, frowning at her too-long bangs. After drying off and getting dressed, she checked her tablet for more messages, but she only saw the story she had read to settle *Mobius* the previous night before she struggled with her keynote. She had been reading him the script for the film *Batteries Not Included*. (Phineas had sent her the script and movie after he heard that she was a ship mama.)

She looked at her jeans and sweatshirt. *Good enough to meet an alien queen.* At least Tina didn't know enough about Earth fashion to insist that Mallory dress up while welcoming her.

The next time someone demands my attention, they're getting me in pajamas and a bathrobe. If I'm going to be inconvenienced, I might as well be comfortable.

Mobius flew over to her when she exited the bedroom. He was coated in sludge and humming to himself.

"You done?" she asked, locating a cardigan and sliding it over her shoulders.

Yes! Breakfast was very good, Mama!

She paused mid-sleeve, startled. "Did you say, 'Mama'?"

Mama Mama Mama! He bounced in midair. *That's you!*

"I guess it is," she said, her face warming slightly. She plucked him from the air, palmed him, and put him in her sweater pocket.

"We're going on a little adventure," she said.

I like adventure! Once I know what it means! But he wriggled around, snuggling down as deep into the pocket as he could go. She wondered if she should let Stephanie babysit more often, if she wore him out this much.

At the door, she paused and waited for the Sundry to follow them. They usually were right with her, but she didn't know how a ship's exterior hivemind would work.

A thought alarmed her, making her break out in goose pimples in the middle of the hall. What if the Sundry were killed? Would that harm *Mobius*? She made a mental note to ask Stephanie. She didn't consider Sundry lives expendable per se, but individual insect deaths didn't hurt the hivemind as a whole. But if you had only four and you depended on them, then things might go south fast if they died.

She fought a yawn as she entered Ferdinand's bar, waving at the Gneiss she recognized. Xan was perched high on a barstool, talking to a gray Gneiss working the bar. He stopped when she came up to him.

"Hair of the dog?" she asked, looking around the bar.

He snorted. "Yeah, 'cause the best way to cure a hangover is a mug of Venus lava."

"Only if you want to die, I guess," she said.

"I'm just checking up on things since the boss is coming," he said. "Breakfast is coming in from Wallace's."

"Perfect," she said, and struggled to climb into a Gneiss bar chair to sit next to him. Sitting in Gneiss furniture always made her feel like a kid. "Hi, Pomme," she said to the Gneiss behind the bar.

Pomme grunted at her, then asked, "So, you're not ordering food?"

"Sure," she said. "Give me some of your coffee equivalent, please." When Xan started to help out Ferdinand, and they heard more humans were coming aboard, he started to color-code the menu to list which drinks humans could handle. It worked out so well, he did it for all the other alien species who liked the oxygen section of the station, and business had really picked up.

And Mallory had fewer burns on her lips and tongue.

As they ate, Mallory told Xan about *Mobius*'s latest antics, not to mention his new tiny hivemind, and they compared notes on what they had learned about *Metis*.

"Sundry say it's super old and complex," Mallory said through a bite of biscuit, "which begs the question why is it coming from Earth and why is it bringing a convention?"

"My biggest question is why Phin hasn't told me anything," Xan said. "That's not like him. He just said he wanted it to be a surprise."

"Then I guess we'll wait. Doesn't sound like something bad," Mallory said. "But bad things usually start out that way, come to think of it."

"Yeah," he said.

Mallory sensed a movement in the hall out of the corner of her eye. Here it was easy to catch a glimpse of someone and assume "human" since there were so few aboard. She turned and saw Dr. Bruce Truman pass the open door of the bar, going in the direction of the shuttle bay.

Thinking he needed to be giving dental exams or dealing with the unique experience of jet lag in space, Mallory slid out of the chair and brushed biscuit crumbs off her hands. "I'll be right back, I have to check something," she said.

Xan had started a conversation with Pomme and gave her a slight nod.

She passed through the doorway of the massive main shuttle bay, where scores of ships were docked, or coming, or going. She spotted several shuttles she recognized, including the bronze *Infinity*, who looked like a hovering dodecahedron even when she was powered down, to Stephanie's purple jet, which Mallory always thought of as a rock with wings.

She spied Bruce on the catwalk above her, so she followed him.

She took the stairs two at a time (they were shorter steps to cater to some of the shorter aliens) and waved when she caught his eye. He had been leaning over and watching the ships land with the glee of a small child, but did not straighten up as she approached.

Mallory joined him at the railing. She liked the high vantage point; after panicking crowds threatened to overwhelm the workers in the shuttle bay, Mrs. Brown had asked Eternity to install a catwalk as the main humanoid entrance to the shuttle bay, with three staircases (of different sizes to accommodate different bodies) down to the bay level. This funneled people directly toward the ships so no one could harass the controllers at their post to demand passage off the station.

Mallory didn't think it was a perfect fix. She didn't relish the idea of being squeezed into the wall or over the catwalk by a panicking Gneiss fifty times her weight and two feet taller, but she understood Mrs. Brown's reasoning. There were only so many ways you could prevent a riot, after all. And the catwalk did give a great view for watching ships land.

Shuttle traffic was low first thing in the morning, but there were still plenty of docked ships to look at, and a shuttle was approaching the station, although all Mallory could see at the moment was the place where stars were blocked by an as-yet-unidentified ship.

"What are you doing here?" she asked. "I thought you had patients to deal with before you get to the convention? Also, there are more interesting things to see on the station than ships landing and getting serviced."

"Insomnia," he said ruefully. "Space lag or something. So I came here to look at the ships. Look at the alien ships!" He pointed to Stephanie as if he were showing Mallory alien ships that she had never seen before. "I've only seen about two kinds on Earth, and we have here what appears to be an airtight wasp nest and two ships looking like they were made out of *clay*? And another clay cube, is that a ship, too?"

"Ah, him. Don't give him much attention," she said, pointing to the ancient Gneiss shuttle, also Stephanie's grandfather. His worship of Gneiss royalty reminded Mallory of Americans who stayed up all night to watch a royal wedding. He hated humans and his own granddaughter, neither of whom gave royalty their proper respect.

Mallory wondered if Dr. Truman knew about sentient ships. Those might be very interesting to most people. *Mobius* shifted in her jacket pocket as the catwalk vibrated very slightly. Mallory guessed it was a message from either Stephanie or her grandfather, who communicated by vibration.

A subdued voice manifested in her head. *The mean ship doesn't like us. He says you're a baffemer.*

"What is a baa-feemer? Is this a Gneiss-specific word?" Mallory asked aloud. Then she smiled. "Oh! You mean 'blasphemer'?"

Bruce tore his gaze away from the ships. "What did you say? Believer?"

She shook her head, then tapped her right ear, hidden under her messy hair, to pretend she had a Bluetooth earpiece. She wasn't ready to tell the general public about *Mobius*. "Messaging with a friend," she said.

Another vibration came, stronger this time. Though still not strong enough for her own translation implant to catch, she had a good idea what the message was. Without waiting for *Mobius* to translate, Mallory leaned over the catwalk and yelled, "What is wrong with you? Is bullying children your idea of fun? We're not even bothering you!"

Dr. Truman stared at her, and then looked around. No one else thought it was strange that Mallory was yelling at a ship.

"Told you he was an asshole," she said, pointing at the old Gneiss ship. "He doesn't like humans."

"Aren't ships usually 'she'?" Bruce asked.

Mallory gave him a flat look. "He's a *he* because that's how everyone refers to him, and how he refers to himself. He's my friend's grandfather, but he's still an asshole. And the easiest way to find out someone's gender is to ask them. Politely."

"Hey, I like everyone, it's cool," he said, holding up his hands defensively. "I was quoting an Earth comedian. But I guess you haven't seen that show."

"No, the latest shows tend to not make it all the way out here," she said, watching a sleek black Gurudev shuttle pull into the bay. "We don't have access to streaming video."

"Then what do you do to relax?" he asked, frowning.

"Read. Spend time with friends. Do whatever people did before there were a hundred thousand channels to watch." She didn't add that she only did one thing on that list (reading), but mostly she was bored and waiting for a murder to happen.

"What species made that ship over there?" he asked, pointing toward a brass-colored dodecahedron the size of the moon lander.

"That one is special. Her name is *Infinity*, and I guess you could say she belongs to the station."

Xan still wasn't keen on people knowing his symbiotic connection with the ship, but Mallory'd had to mention it when she was writing her most recent book because it helped explain some of the things that happened during the investigation—as well as help explain her similar connection with the hivemind of the blue Sundry.

"She's beautiful," he said.

"Yep," Mallory said.

Another approaching ship caught Bruce's eye, and he pointed. It was a white Gurudev ship, the kind of shuttle that had been the most popular of the ships servicing the Earth. Possibly because they were the closest in size and shape to humans, possibly because they had a very aggressive marketing department and lobbyists to meet with Earth officials. The last she'd heard, humans had built three ports in the US, two in Canada, nine in China, four in Ireland, two in Uganda, and three in Nigeria.

This Gurudev ship had the US and Canadian flags painted on the side, meaning it serviced both countries.

"I think that's the shuttle that brought us here," Bruce said. "It was phenomenal. Stylish, sleek, and they even had in-flight snacks!"

Snacks aboard the shuttle were likely to be good; the Gurudev had a taste for salty, fat protein, so their cuisine was probably the best alien food for the human body. Some of it was even tasty.

She wondered if the doctors had brought a nutritionist with them to analyze the alien food. The humans aboard the station should probably know if eating alien food would give them a deficiency, like scurvy.

"Hey, what other medical professionals came in with you? Did y'all bring a nutritionist?"

He brightened and gave her that thousand-watt smile that didn't touch his eyes. "That's a great question. You met Dr. Audrey, and of course there's me. We also have a GP, that's Dr. Sports, and an ophthalmologist, Dr. Gropper. We have some others, a nutritionist and a chiropractor, some nurses."

Mallory noticed that he only gave names to the doctors in the group. "What's the nutritionist's name?" she asked.

"Oh, him? Uh . . ." He paused. "Can't remember. But he's not going to tell you anything that your GP couldn't. So just make an appointment with Dr. Sports and you'll be covered." Bruce leaned over the railing, as if leaning one yard closer would give him a better view of the people exiting the shuttle.

"Don't lean too far," Mallory said, and gently put her hand on his shoulder to pull him back. "Do you expect *Metis* to arrive tonight?"

"No, not yet, it's scheduled for tomorrow," he said. "I have more patients to meet, so if she arrived tonight, I still wouldn't be able to attend the con."

Mallory ran her tongue over her teeth, wondering if she should just give in and get a cleaning from him. "What are you most looking forward to at the convention?"

"Everything, really. The concert, the panels, and your keynote, of course," he added, winking. "But my main goal is to meet some agents. There's some prime networking opportunities here."

"How many agents are coming?" she asked. Aaron hadn't said if any more agents were with him.

"Five that I know of. The one I really want to meet is Aaron Rose. But he's bringing his assistant, who I think is looking for her own clients. A few others will be here, from New York, LA, and London. I should talk to them all."

"Oh, yeah, Aaron's my agent! What kind of stuff do you write?" she asked, wondering if Aaron was open to new clients.

"Crime thrillers, mostly." Bruce didn't sound very enthusiastic. "I haven't had the best luck getting people interested in my books, though." He paused, then sighed. "Did you know that no one wants to talk to you at parties when you say you're a dentist? They always assume I'm going to ask when they last flossed. Or what toothpaste they use. If their teeth aren't straight, they will sometimes just flat out avoid me. They're afraid I'll try to sell them on braces.

"Last year I attended a party that honored local businesses that supported the local minor league team. So there was me, a guy representing Couch Oil, some radio and podcast C-list celebrities, but it also had the owner of the local port-a-potty chain Honey Pots."

Mallory choked. *"Honey pots?"*

Bruce nodded grimly. "Oh, yeah, I'll never forget that company name. And you know what? He was the richest guy in the room. Everyone wanted to ask questions about his job. He built an empire of shithouses, and people would rather talk to him than a dentist."

"Well, everybody poops," Mallory said with a shrug. When she saw Bruce's stony gaze, she realized she had made a mistake. She was on the edge of some abyss and tried to back away slowly. "Why talk about your job, then?" she ventured. "Why not talk about your hobbies? Do you have pets?"

His face instantly softened. "I have two little terrors from the planet Cat," he said, smiling. "My boys are going to really miss me this week. I'm trying to send them videos every day."

Mallory watched him dissolve into cuddly goo about his cats, wishing she had asked about something else. But few things were as angry as a cat person slighted, so she carefully asked, "What are their names?"

She then saw the slide show on his phone of his darlings, Max and Cymric. Max was an orange cat with a stub of a tail and very smart, and Cymric was a long-haired Manx, who was as dumb as a rock, as Bruce fondly described him.

"Adorable," Mallory said with a smile.

"They have their own social media accounts, you know," he said importantly. "We got sponsored by an organic cat food company once!" But his face grew stormy in an instant. "But you know what? That Honey Pot asshole runs a cat rescue—with a YouTube channel!—so even if I do talk about cats, he'll have more cats to one-up me. I never would have thought the darling of a party would be—"

"Me neither," Mallory interrupted. "But it's one of those terrible but necessary jobs. You know when the revolution comes and the economy tanks, the people who will keep their jobs are the Honey Pot toilet guy and morticians."

"Everyone will also need dentistry if they don't want their teeth to fall out," he said, his voice flat. "But say you're a dentist at a party and people edge away like you're radioactive. If I could say I was a writer, then I'd be more popular than the shithouse king, right?"

After a few beats, Mallory realized the question wasn't rhetorical. "I don't actually know. People don't invite me to many parties. And when I do attend one, people usually want to know more about the murders than my writing career."

Bruce didn't look happy with that answer and ran his fingers through his thinning brown hair.

"So, why don't you say you're a writer? There are plenty of people self-publishing and building a great career, it's easier now than ever. If you wrote a book, you are a writer. You don't have to mention the teeth at all."

He stared over the shuttle bay moodily, not even looking at her now. She gave an exasperated sigh. "Listen, that port-a-potty dude was probably popular because no one has met someone like him before. He was someone new. There are a lot of dentists, and most people talk to one every six months. I may never need to hire a port-a-potty company, so if my only way to chat with someone about the service is at a party, then I damn well will take that opportunity. Provided there isn't a murder to distract me, of course."

She wasn't joking, but Bruce chuckled and winked at her. "Ah, yes, your 'murder brand.' Is that what your keynote is about? 'Someone Is Going to Die Tonight'?"

"Very probably," Mallory said, her voice stony.

In her pocket, *Mobius* vibrated. *Auntie Stephanie says to meet the queen in the ossuary. What's a queen? What's an ossuary?*

Shit. She had forgotten about the impending Tina arrival. Xan sent a message that consisted of a sole question mark.

"I have to run. Have fun watching the ships come in," she said, and dashed off.

8

. . . .

ENTER HER MAJESTY, TINA BITCH QUEEN (FIRST OF HER NAME)

WHILE "OSSUARY" IN human terms refers to a crypt, the galactic translation database had decided that it was the proper English word to fit a slightly different kind of room for the Gneiss. Instead of a place to store dead bodies, the Gneiss ossuaries were places where their people could sleep when tired or injured. Gneiss could stay awake and active for years, and when they slept, it was with similar stubborn inertia.

Mallory was very aware of the hollow stares of the Gneiss (those that had eyes, anyway) as she hurried through the ossuary to get to the infrequently used shuttle bay on the other side. She'd only known Stephanie and Tina to have used it at all. The other Gneiss didn't seem too interested in it. The room was tomb-like, since the Gneiss didn't normally wake up unless something had made them really, *really* angry.

For example, the (relatively) young Gneiss princess Tina and Stephanie absorbing bio-matter from murder victims right in the middle of the ossuary and using the energy to transform, which was enough to wake the masses. The last time Mallory had been in this room, she'd been fighting for her life against a tide of pebbles and dust, some armless statues (also the severed arms of those same statues), and a small fighter craft that was very cranky to have been woken up.

Nothing like that was happening now, but Mallory kept glancing to her left and right as she hurried through the room with a light step, trying her best to not trod on any stray pebbles for fear that there would be retribution if she injured anyone.

Xan waited for her outside the air lock that led to the shuttle bay.

"Should we be here? I figured we wouldn't be welcome in the ossuary," Mallory asked.

"Well, yeah, that was a memorable day, with all the murders and transforming and spacing and you almost dying of anaphylactic shock," he said mildly. "But a queen is coming, so I think everyone will be focused outside. If they even wake up."

The ossuary was massive and dimly lit with spectacular mood lighting along the top and bottoms of every wall, serving up a properly depressed mood. You couldn't see from the shuttle bay to the opposite wall, with statues, a few vines and trees, and a kind of miasma making the existing light even dimmer. While most of the room was dormant, three Gneiss had awakened from their slumber and crowded the air lock door to the shuttle bay to see what all the fuss was about. They didn't look twice at Xan as he leaned in front of them and motioned to Mallory.

"What's out there now?" she asked, nimbly stepping around the stone giants. "Is it another battleship or something?"

"Not quite," he said, and pointed.

The ship looked like a cruise ship, situated horizontally with several apparent floors, tapering to a smaller area and then a crow's nest. She was about a third the size of Eternity, who was the size of a small moon herself. No ship that Mallory knew of, not even the four-thousand-year-old Gneiss battleship, had looked that massive even next to Eternity.

The ship was shiny and black, reflecting the light from Eternity, but veins of a fluorescent blue substance snaked all over the ship, pulsing slightly as if a heart were beating somewhere within.

A *living ship*.

"Holy shit, that's *Metis*," Xan said aloud just as Mallory realized the same.

She couldn't look away from the sleek black ship in front of them. The ship blocked the view outside the station, the portholes dotting the hull turning on and showing the silhouette of interested heads.

"Is Tina aboard that ship?" she asked.

"That's what *Infinity* is saying," he said.

"When did Tina go to Earth?" Mallory asked. "More importantly, why is she hitching a ride with a mystery convention?"

"I have no idea. But who knows why Tina does anything?"

As the ship edged closer, her sleek black hull shone at times with a blue-gray sheen, as if it had been covered by an oil spill on a summer afternoon. *Metis* showed no weapons or any other kind of threat. A ship like this could cause damage just by ramming into Eternity, Mallory thought, but it would still do more damage to itself.

Mobius woke up and popped out of her pocket, flying around her in joy.

Big ship! Big ship!

"Yeah, it's huge, but you shouldn't run off," she said, jumping to catch him, but he flew up to just beyond her reach.

"What did you say?" Xan asked.

"*Mobius* has noticed the ship," she said.

Xan, taller than her with long arms, reached up and snatched the ship. *Mobius* gave an affronted squeak, and Mallory got a vague sense that she wasn't playing the game fair, if she was going to let other people catch him.

"Thanks," she said, taking the ship from Xan. "I really didn't want him antagonizing the Gneiss."

Big ship!

"And if you don't obey me, you're not going to get a chance to meet the big ship," she said sternly.

"Going to pull this car around and go back home?" asked Xan with a grin.

Mallory smiled. "Something like that."

Xan got the faraway look in his eyes he had when he was getting a message from *Infinity*. "*Infinity* says she'll look out for him. She just started chatting with him."

The little ship stopped vibrating in Mallory's hand. "Whatever she just said to him made him calm down, so thank her for me. Yesterday he couldn't say one word, now he's friends with two ships and telling me about people in an ossuary." Mallory smiled. "Although he didn't know what it was. But now our ships can talk to each other and then share gossip with Stephanie and then with Tina, who we know can't keep a secret."

"You're talking about them like you don't trust them." He raised an eyebrow at her. "What gossip would they spread about you?"

"I don't know," she said, her face feeling warm all of a sudden. "I'm pretty boring except for all the murders." She fiddled with her watch and sent Stephanie a message. "Did you know Tina was coming to Eternity in the big ship from Earth?"

Stephanie's voice came through the watch, tinny and far away. "Of course I did. I just wasn't allowed to tell. Tina wanted to make an entrance."

"See? We can trust Stephanie and *Infinity* if not the other links in the chain," Xan said.

To continue the cruise ship metaphor, Mallory noticed several smaller ships—escape pods or shuttles—hanging off *Metis*'s side. Most of them looked uniform, with a few shuttles from other planets also docked with her. She spotted two Gurudev alone. One of the similar pods dislodged and floated a few hundred meters, then moved on its own power toward the station. "Is this the shuttle?"

"Here comes the queen and Ferdinand," Stephanie said through Mallory's watch.

As one, the three Gneiss stepped back from the air lock, looking humble before their queen.

Tina wasn't the queen of all Gneiss, which was a very good thing. She was ruler of the planet Bezoar, which was a shithole (her words) prison planet. The humans weren't actually sure what her rule consisted of exactly, since the planet sounded like it needed a good prison guard, not a queen. But very little in Tina's world followed logic, and Mallory and Xan also stepped back to offer proper homage.

Mobius wriggled in her pocket. Mallory extracted a promise that he wouldn't run off before she let him out again to bounce excitedly in the air by her head. She mentally told him to calm down. He listened and managed about five seconds of being still before bouncing in excitement again.

The shuttle, like *Metis* herself, was black with blue veins running around it. The ossuary shuttle bay was more traditional than the main bay, which Eternity had enclosed with a force field that ships could pass through, but gas couldn't. The ossuary had an old-school air lock, which made the shuttle bay fairly debris-free, since anything left in there would be spaced if the exterior door opened. The walls of the shuttle bay were the same rock that made up the rest of the ossuary, but it lacked the strange haze that Mallory had seen behind her.

The shuttle drifted slowly in, jets firing gently to edge the ship to a landing pad.

"Don't blame me for what's about to happen," Stephanie added.

"Why?" Xan said, leaning over to talk into Mallory's watch. "What's about to—"

The air lock exterior door closed, and Eternity took a moment to equalize the pressure between the two rooms. Once the air lock light on the wall in front of them turned green, Xan hit the button to open the door and they headed out to meet their friends.

The shuttle's hatch opened under the wing, and then a billowing cloud hissed out with a bright backlight projecting a blocky silhouette through the fog. There was real 1980s power ballad energy here. Through the fog walked Queen Tina, of the prison planet Bezoar, a massive pink Gneiss who stood around twelve feet tall, with a massive barrel chest and a jet pack on her back. She resembled a Transformer more than a statue-like Gneiss. Her dusky pink exterior had darkened in the time since Mallory had last seen her, which was surprising.

"Party people!" Tina bellowed, raising her arms to encompass the entire shuttle bay. "Your bitch queen is here!"

To the humans' surprise, all of the Gneiss bowed low, and even Stephanie said, "Welcome, my queen," over the link from her spot in the other shuttle bay. Quietly, she said to Mallory and Xan, "Really, don't blame me for what's about to happen."

"Tina acting like she's headlining the Super Bowl halftime show isn't the thing that isn't your fault?" Xan asked, alarmed.

Stephanie took a moment, probably to allow the translation database to figure out Xan's human-specific references, and then said, "No."

Mallory stared at him. "What's worse than Tina being a rock star?" she asked.

"Tina brought a companion," Stephanie said, and from the still billowing cloud came a pudgy yellow alien. It walked on four legs and surveyed the shuttle bay with three round eyes. Two pointy ears stood up from its head, twitching to catch the different sounds. It mostly resembled a bald bobcat from Earth with three black glittering eyes on its forehead. Instead of a cat's mouth, it had disturbing humanlike lips. Instead of a tail, long tendrils floated out behind it, like hair in a pleasant breeze—or more like a jellyfish's tentacles in water.

It looked a lot like a large cat, enough so that cat people would probably find it adorable and want to cuddle it. If someone made a toy of this alien, it would probably end up as popular as the Ugly Dolls from around the turn of the century.

"If these guys ever go to Earth, they'll be sold to children as toys," Mallory muttered.

"I think there are bigger issues than treating them like dolls," Xan said.

"Like what?" Mallory asked, noticing the Gneiss behind them had stepped farther back, keeping their distance from the shuttle.

"That's a new alien. No one has ever encountered it before," Xan said.

Whenever something weird happened in space, Mallory and Xan assumed the other races had dealt with the alien or the situation before. Humans were the newcomers after all. But hearing the shifting behind her as more Gneiss awakened to witness the newcomer, she realized this was a much bigger deal than it appeared.

Mallory, Xan, and the Gneiss were some of the first people in the galaxy to meet this new alien. But *Tina* had been the First Contact. And then they'd hitched a ride with a bunch of mystery-loving vacationing humans.

"Oh, we are so screwed," Mallory said.

MALLORY SURPRISED XAN by suggesting they contact one of the few humans to reside on Eternity with them: Adrian Casserly-Berry. Neither of them liked the man; Adrian was curt and rude, and had no interest in mingling with any of the humans aboard, but he was also a brilliant linguist and the first person to meet aliens on Earth (that the public knew about, anyway), so he knew more about First Contact than most people.

"I don't like him either, but he's the only one we know who has this kind of experience," she said.

"I think this whole thing is above our pay grade," Xan replied. "Mrs. B and Jessica should be here. They're the people who should represent the station and Earth."

"I'm betting Mrs. B already knows," Mallory said. "I'll let you call Jessica."

He nodded once and stepped away from her, holding his watch close to his mouth. He was already on it.

Jessica was the proper ambassador from Earth, but Mallory rarely saw her because of her duties. And because she liked to spend her free time with Xan. Mallory decided to call Adrian anyway, pulling her tablet out of her jacket pocket.

"Why are you calling me so early, Mallory?" came Adrian's sleepy, irritated voice. He didn't turn on his camera. He was blind, and didn't think Mallory should have the advantage of seeing him when he couldn't see her.

"There's a First Contact situation in the Gneiss ossuary," she said bluntly. "I thought you should come see it."

Silence on the line. Then he said, "Why me?"

"I didn't think I would have to flatter you to get you here," she said. "Come if you want, or not. But you're the one with the First Contact experience, not us."

Mallory severed the call, grumpily wondering why she even bothered.

Xan was still talking to Jessica. Mal tried to ignore them. She tried not to think of a time a few months back when she and Xan had split a bottle of wine—genuine wine from the Napa Valley!— and he'd told her the cringe story of Jessica's failed seduction.

What neither of them expected was Jessica was a bulldog when she wanted something, and she and Xan were now dating, and Mallory had heard nothing more of seductions, failures, or successes.

Jessica didn't seem to like Mallory much, and she wasn't sure if it was the murder problem or just that she and Xan were close.

She wanted to tell Jessica that she and Xan were old friends, and if something was going to happen between them, it would have already. But she couldn't find a good place in any of their conversations to bring that up.

Tina was still standing in her fog. She held the bobcat thing in her arms. Mallory thought she was waiting for the humans' reactions, but then she realized the floor was vibrating with Gneiss conversations, but not loud enough for her translation implant to catch anything intelligible.

In the relative silence of a Gneiss argument, Xan and Jessica's conversation drifted over to Mallory. "I thought the Gneiss were your area of expertise," Jessica was saying.

She wasn't wrong. Mallory and Xan usually knew more about Gneiss politics through their friends than Jessica could get in her meetings. Jessica didn't appreciate that, but it wasn't as if Mallory and Xan would stop hanging out with their friends to save Jessica's ego. Xan had invited her out with Mallory and the Gneiss more than once, but she always refused.

"Yeah, but this is *First Contact*, Jess. We need you," he was saying. "The Gneiss say there's a new race that no one has been in contact with before. And Tina wants to introduce it around like this is a birthday party or something."

"I just got a message from Mrs. Brown," Jessica said. "I have to take this." She severed the call.

Xan frowned at his watch, then lowered his arm. "Maybe she'll listen to Mrs. Brown," he said, shrugging.

"Adrian may or may not come," she said. "We really suck at this First Contact thing, don't we?"

He grinned ruefully. "And we're even doing all the right things, like calling the authorities."

"The Sundry are coming, but they're consulting various hive-minds for information," Mallory said, saying it aloud before she even had realized it was true. "I think, anyway."

Tina had turned back to the shuttle. "What do you mean you're out of fog?" she demanded. "A queen needs the fog to always be on!"

"Did she just discover a fog machine?" Mallory asked Stephanie.

"I don't want to talk about it," her friend replied over the watch.

Xan shook his head. "Tina treating a First Contact situation like a kegger at a frat house is all we need right now. I hope someone gets here before she decides to go giving that thing a tour of the station. What's up with Adrian?"

She shrugged. "He was trying to be fussy and everything, but he's not going to turn down a chance of First Contact," she said. "He's not a moron."

"That's the kindest thing you've ever said about me," Adrian said from behind her. He looked more put together than the other times she'd been forced to wake him up. He'd taken time to put his accessories on, including the drone that clung to a leather harness on his shoulder and sunglasses to hide his ruined eyes and the latest implant he was trying to improve his sight with.

Adrian had lost his eyes when he had tried to form a symbiotic link with a grief-mad Eternity, who was not very receptive. She had maimed him in her rage and nearly killed him. The glasses covered most of the scars around his missing eyes, but he still had other scars stretching into his hairline where he bore the result of Eternity wrapping a thorny vine around his head like a boa constrictor.

He had regained some semblance of sight after surviving Eternity's attack. He had befriended a Phantasmagore who liked to tinker with robots. They had created a few lenses and bots to try to support an ocular implant. If he hadn't been such a pill, Mallory would have been impressed with his bravery to become the first human to be modified like a cyborg with alien tech.

But no implant could improve his personality.

When he was fully accessorized he looked like a scrap dealer from a futuristic space station science-fiction game. Or to be fair, a former ambassador living on a space station in the present day.

"Mallory, Xan," he said by way of greeting, "thank you for calling me."

Mallory looked around to see what other Mallory he was talking to. "You're thanking *me?*"

"I can thank you, can't I? I'm not entirely bereft of manners. I figured you would call Xan's girlfriend," Adrian said bitterly.

"Um, we did, actually," Mallory said. "We just thought you'd be good here, too. We need all the backup we can get here. Because you know this."

"Oh, I know I'm the best person for the job, but I'm used to no one else on this ball of misfits recognizing that."

"Ah, there you are," Mallory said almost fondly. "I was worried for a second." She always had to leave a little room for Adrian to complain about something.

"What are the other Gneiss doing?" he asked, suddenly all business.

Mallory turned to face the ossuary and jumped when she saw that about half of the room had woken up to turn their focus toward the air lock.

"I guess we should do something quickly before the other humans get here," Adrian said. He almost never referred to Jessica or Mrs. Brown by their names. Since both of them had, in his view, usurped him from his rightful place as ambassador and as host for the station, he stayed well away from them.

It looked as if people had exited the shuttle, waving fog from their faces so they could see. Six humans had wandered out, the first-timers making themselves obvious by looking like kids entering a room in Willy Wonka's Chocolate Factory.

Xan's brother, Phineas—tall, broad, and bald—was the last one off the ship, walking down the stairs and looking like he was trying politely to get Tina to move from the stairs so others could have some room. He then saw Xan and Mallory, and waved.

"Why didn't he tell us—" Mallory started, but Xan cut her off.

"He just didn't. Let's leave it here!" he snapped.

"Jesus, I didn't pee in your cornflakes, too, did I?" Mallory asked, stepping back.

He didn't answer, glaring at his brother.

"Devanshi, do you recognize this?" Adrian asked, and then his Phantasmagore roommate, Devanshi, appeared beside him.

Mallory jumped like she always did. She didn't think she would ever get used to the sneaky Phantasmagore aliens when they could blend into a background like a chameleon.

"Oh, hey, Devanshi," she said. "Have you been there the whole time?"

"I have," she said. "Adrian, the alien is small and four-legged. It doesn't resemble a sentient galactic species. Are we sure this is a First Contact situation?"

Mallory nodded. "It could be Tina's new pet," she suggested, but her watch erupted with Stephanie's anger.

"It *is* a First Contact situation," Stephanie insisted. "That being is intelligent. We just can't communicate with it yet."

"So, Tina has brought an alien aboard that she can't communicate with?" Mallory asked, staring at the ugly yellow cat thing. "And presumably none of the rest of us can either."

"Oh, but the large rock queen can communicate with it," Adrian said. Behind his sunglasses came a whir of an ocular lens focusing.

"How do you know that?" Xan asked.

"Look at how she talks to it. And it seems to respond."

"Cats and dogs can do that, too," Mallory said.

"What the hell is going on here?" Jessica came striding up to them. Mrs. Brown was behind her, arms crossed and frowning.

"Didn't you tell her?" Mallory asked Xan.

"Who let her aboard?" Jessica asked, rounding on Mallory.

"Hey," she said, holding her hands up. "I don't control any of this. Tina wanted us to meet her, so we met her. We didn't expect any of this."

"So, it's already had contact with the Gneiss and humans?" Jessica asked.

"The station let Tina aboard," Mrs. Brown said. "Don't blame Mallory. The bigger problem is the alien has been around humans who are not used to aliens, much less what to do in a First Contact scenario." She gave a sideways glance to Adrian. "Mr. Casserly-Berry, please accompany me to speak with the queen."

Adrian's mouth fell open, but he snapped it shut and nodded to her once.

Jessica watched them go, face darkening in rage. Xan leaned in and spoke into her ear. She glared at him but then followed Mrs. Brown and Adrian.

"Why do I feel like I don't want to be a part of this?" Mallory asked.

"I sure as hell don't. I say we get Phin and get out of this crypt."

Phineas was talking to one of the humans who was watching Tina meet with the humans, and then he pointed to Mallory and Xan. She gave an awkward wave and then headed in to meet him.

He met them halfway and pulled Mallory into a big hug, lifting her off her feet. "Mallory V! It's been too long, girl."

"Missed you, Salty Fats," she said, hugging him tighter.

Xan waited for his turn to greet him. His arms were crossed and he glared at his brother, who didn't seem to notice his body language at all, and swept Xan into a hug. "Big brother," Phin said. "I know you're waiting to hear all the shit."

"Since you haven't told me anything, yeah, I am," Xan said. "What the hell? You're riding in the biggest ship ever, a sentient ship, and you're bunking with a new alien life-form?"

Phineas laughed. "You make it sound like we're in summer camp cabins, and Tina and the alien were in mine. What would my cabin be?" He looked thoughtful, but Xan punched his arm.

"Will you focus for just a minute and tell us what is going on?"

His brother glanced over at Mrs. Brown, who was craning her neck back to talk to Tina as Adrian tried to communicate with the small alien.

"Yeah, we got some time. I could kill for some tea," Phineas said.

Mallory grabbed both of their forearms. "Come on, we can talk at my place."

"TINA SHOWED UP about two days ago," Phineas said. "We were all surprised, since there were no planned stops and we didn't think a shuttle could keep up with *Metis*."

"But you know Tina," Mallory said.

"True," Phineas said grimly. "She just said she was heading to Eternity but heard we were going there, too, and she was interested in *Metis*. And you know how hard it is to say no to that woman."

Mallory tried to imagine how Tina would react to someone telling her she wasn't allowed on board. "She would just see that as a challenge."

"Right," he said. "So she came aboard and went to meet the ship's host."

"So, is that a human?" Xan asked.

Phineas nodded. "Yeah, a woman named Eve. I didn't see much of them, but I heard they talked to Eve for some time. Eve told me she made them promise to stay away from the convention, and the ship's important function rooms, and she'd let them stay aboard."

"She's smart. Sounds like she knew she couldn't stop Tina doing what she wanted," Mallory said.

Phineas nodded and accepted the steaming mug Mallory handed him. "And for all I know, they did what she asked. Tina didn't interfere with the convention, and the trip was uneventful from then on."

"Why didn't you tell us what was going on?" Xan asked. "We could have avoided all of that angst in the ossuary if we'd been prepared."

"Tina insisted we not tell you," Phineas said with a shrug. "Said it would be a surprise. I didn't think it would be this contentious."

"What did you think of the alien she was carrying with her?" Mallory asked.

"Well, I tried to pet it," Phineas said, laughing. "That didn't go over well. I thought it was a pet, not a big fucking deal. But I gotta tell you about this ship, man. It's *wild*."

Before he could continue, Mallory's head was full of buzzing; messages of stress and worry came through too loudly. Her Sundry entourage took flight, startled as much as she was.

"We have to get back to the ossuary," Mallory said, her voice sounding far away. "There's an—"

"—incident," Xan finished for her, looking distracted as he fielded a message from *Infinity*.

"Someday I'ma get my own magic alien text messaging system," Phineas said, pulling himself up from the couch. "Then y'all will wonder what I'm saying about *you* to my special alien friend."

"This isn't funny right now," Xan said as Mallory opened the door and beckoned them through.

Xan's watch pinged with a message. He pulled it up as they ran down the hall to the lifts. Jessica's voice came over, sounding more frightened than angry. "We need you down here. Find Mallory, too."

"We're on our way," Xan said. "What the hell is going on?"

"Some kind of standoff between Tina and the Sundry. I don't really know. Just come."

"DIDN'T TINA SAY she could control the Cuckoos?" Xan asked Mallory as the three of them reached the entrance to the ossuary.

Mallory gulped and nodded. "To be fair, it's possible she commanded them to do this."

"This" being a swarm of the Cuckoos from Tina's chest cavity facing off against a swarm of blue and silver Sundry. They hovered near the high ceiling, their buzzing echoing and filling the room. The hazy miasma seemed thicker, but Mallory was mostly concerned with angry insects.

On the floor, the humans had retreated into the shuttle, their wide eyes and round faces peering out the windows at the excitement. Mrs. Brown was arguing with Tina still, and Jessica watched the swarms, her head back, face pale.

More sleeping Gneiss had stirred and were watching the standoff. The room rumbled with their discussion.

"What the hell is going on?" Xan asked.

"I have no idea," Mallory said.

"Can't you connect with them or something? See if they're going to start brawling!" Xan shouted.

"I—I've never tried that in a situation like this!" Mallory yelled back.

"Well, there's a first time for everything," Phineas said, putting his large hand on her shoulder.

Xan spotted Jessica and Mrs. Brown on the other side of the ossuary, Mrs. Brown looking furious, Jessica looking frightened. Then he was off.

"Oh, you're kidding me," Mallory muttered. She looked up into Phineas's face. "You got my back, big guy?"

"You know it," he said. "Count on me."

"All right. Here I go." Mallory centered herself with a deep breath and closed her eyes. With an inward wince, she opened her mind up, trying to allow it to go blank and be receptive to the Sundry's glut of information.

She lost the feeling of the ground under her feet, the feel of Phineas's hand on her shoulder.

First she felt the anxiety of the Gneiss. Their vibrations carried more of an emotion than a clear message—not rage; they were genuinely afraid.

What is a Gneiss afraid of? Nothing can hurt one of these guys! Mallory thought. She hadn't thought about it too deeply, but she realized even if Gneiss were pulverized, they could still just sleep for a few centuries and their body would slowly re-form. They were essentially immortal.

Then she entered the storm of the Sundry hivemind. Now *there* was some rage. The station remembered the harm the Cuckoos caused; the Sundry reflected this.

Mallory felt dizzy for a moment. These Sundry were silver and blue from the hivemind that powered Eternity. Before she could ask who was powering the station right now, the information was in front of her. The Sundry she had previously thought as the idle rich for living an apparently chill life in a hive in Eternity's park had flown to fill in for the Sundry here.

There were blue and silver here. To Mallory's senses, the Cuckoos also looked blue, but that was their masking pheromones at work. The station's Sundry could at least tell which insects in the ossuary were part of their own hive, and that helped.

What did the Cuckoos want? They weren't even supposed to be here; Tina had promised to keep them contained.

She tapped into the sense of the Sundry, looking down on herself, the Gneiss, and the crew around the shuttle. The room was multifaceted through the insects' eyes, but she could also sense the heat signatures in the room. The sleeping Gneiss were barely registering as warm, but the shuttle throbbed with heat.

Tina and Mrs. Brown had faced off.

And the new alien was nowhere to be seen.

We have to find the new alien! she told the swarm, but her voice was lost in the cacophony of *PROTECT!*

The miasma between the swarms darkened, and the vibrations from the Gneiss below increased.

Are they protecting the cloud as well? Mallory realized what she had just considered about a Gneiss being pulverized and still living. Was this cloud a pulverized rock person?

A baby. Like me. The voice came from *Mobius,* who seemed more in awe than excited. *Auntie Stephanie says the baby must be protected.*

But who is threatening the baby? How is this a thing that has happened? Mallory concentrated and found the awareness of the Sundry who usually accompanied her places. *Let's go over to Tina.*

It was easier to get her idea across to four instead of the whole hive, and she stumbled in her body as the Sundry launched themselves and flew over to Tina and Mrs. Brown.

"You have put the station in danger again," yelled Mrs. Brown, looking tinier than usual next to Tina's bulk. She didn't shrink back from the queen, even though Tina could smear the ground with her if she wanted to.

"They wanted to see the baby!" Tina complained. "I thought it was okay if they stayed in the room."

"Are you sure they wanted to see the baby?" Mrs. Brown said. "Or did they want something else to do with it?"

She looked up and Mallory's Sundry followed her look. Now the blue and silver insects had formed a moving cage around the miasma, which was looking ever darker.

"The Cuckoos want what I want, which is that baby to be delivered safely!" Tina insisted.

"Then why are they interfering?" Mrs. Brown asked, waving her arm up at the standoff.

"I don't know, I'm not their keeper!" Tina insisted.

"Then why did you bring them aboard, if you can't control them?" Mrs. Brown said, her voice low and dangerous. "You just said you could—"

"It's an excellent day, everyone!" Tina shouted, stepping away from Mrs. Brown. She pointed her finger at the confusion above their heads. "You will all get to witness the birth of a brand-new baby Gneiss!"

She didn't have much of an audience. The humans had already gotten back in the shuttle, either by instinct or someone guiding them. Jessica and Xan were going farther into the shuttle bay, either to board the shuttle or get away from Mrs. Brown and Tina. Mrs. Brown still shouted at her, and Phineas and Mallory were across the room at the entrance.

Mallory didn't know how to contact Stephanie in this manifestation but saw Xan speaking into his watch. She flew over.

"Stephanie! There's apparently a *baby* being born in here? Why didn't you tell us?" he asked.

"Because I didn't know!" Stephanie sounded more stressed than Mallory had ever heard. "They tend not to tell me things since they're still angry I evolved in an afternoon. They didn't tell Ferdinand or Tina either."

"So, the thing we're looking at, a kind of dark fog that is getting thicker, that's the baby?"

"A gestating baby, yes," Stephanie said, her voice slightly wistful. "I wish I could see it."

Jessica surprised Mallory by pulling out her phone and taking a picture of the ceiling. To the uninitiated, it looked like bugs fighting in dust, but Stephanie would probably appreciate it. She handed her phone to Xan, who pushed the symbols indicating a short-range connection to Stephanie.

"This is amazing," Stephanie said. Her voice was full of awe, letting more emotion through than she ever had before.

"I need to get Phin and Mal over here." Xan waved across the ossuary to get Phineas's attention. Phineas threw Mallory over his shoulder easily and jogged toward Xan.

"Stephanie," Jessica asked, "what are the Cuckoos doing there?"

Stephanie was silent for a moment. "Tina sent them, but she says it is the new alien's request."

"What the *fuck*?" asked Jessica. "What did it tell them to do with the baby?"

"Tina doesn't know."

Mallory had heard enough; she and her companions rejoined the swarm.

I guess we have to ask the Cuckoos. She had no idea how to approach them, but she stayed on the edge of the living cage and tried to approach an enemy insect. *What do you want?*

The Cuckoos seemed to pause for a moment. Their buzzing got louder.

They are indicating they want another Gneiss to be a hive for them, the Sundry told her. *The queen allowed it.*

I thought you said they couldn't communicate? Their language isn't in the databases?

They're not speaking. They're dancing.

Mallory hovered for a moment and watched the green wasps. Some of them were vibrating and trembling; others were flying in a circle around them. She had no idea what the message was.

You will learn it in time, the swarm said.

Mallory hoped she wouldn't have an opportunity to spend a lot of time with the Cuckoos to learn their dances.

Tell them they can't just take a baby and make a home in them! And it's not Tina's call to demand someone to host another alien without their consent.

They say they can take it. The Sundry didn't sound particularly worried about this. They reported it like the nightly news.

No, Mallory said. *If they do, then there will be a fight, and they will most certainly die. And I would bet good money that Tina will not be allowed back aboard.*

They paused, uncertain. Then they branched out their tendrils until they formed a cage around the Sundry's protective cage around the dust.

The blue and silver buzzed an angry warning, and the Cuckoos said the equivalent of "You and what army?" And then they found out.

Mama? Mama!

Mallory had been focusing so hard on dealing with being part of the hivemind, retaining her sense of self, and apparently saving a baby rock that she hadn't been paying attention to what was going on below her. She caught cries of alarm with Phineas calling her name. She felt him shaking her, but the feeling was far away. Then everything around her shifted, and she was caught in a gust of wind.

The Sundry formed a tighter ball and tried to propel the dust cloud upward into the vents, but the wind was too strong.

Something lurched, and then she was being drawn toward the wind in two different ways.

The air lock shouldn't be allowed to open if the interior door is open. The only person who could do that would be Eternity.

Mallory let go of her hold on the hivemind and came slamming back into her body just as Phineas dropped her into a seat in the shuttle. Nausea overtook her and she hung her head between her knees, not able to do much of anything but hate life at that moment.

"Is everybody on?" Jessica's voice cut through the chaos.

Adrian and Jessica and Devanshi were making a slightly awkward row of seats, and there were six humans who had come over on the shuttle with Tina. Mrs. Brown, Mallory, and Phineas sat in the back.

Tina had stayed outside. But Mallory wasn't sure she wanted to be. She was pacing up and down in front of the shuttle, waving her arms and shouting at the ceiling. The wind didn't move her at all.

"Mrs. Brown!" Mallory managed to say. "Tell Eternity to stop opening the doors! She's going to kill all the Sundry and space the Gneiss baby!"

"Don't you think I've done that already?" she heard Mrs. Brown snap behind her. "She's enraged at this point and just wants the Cuckoos gone. To truly calm her down, I have to get to the heart of the station, and there's no going there from here."

Outside, Tina had started wrestling with the door, and another Gneiss came to help her. Together they heaved on the internal door as the air lock continued to open. Alien insects trailed out of the ossuary like blue, green, and silver sparks from a campfire.

Between Mrs. Brown pleading with her, Xan urging *Infinity* to convince Eternity to stand down, and probably the sheer bulk of the Gneiss's efforts, the interior door finally closed and sealed. Mallory couldn't see how many Sundry they had saved, and she couldn't see any part of the Gneiss baby at all. Inside, Tina had her back to the door, but she was gesturing wildly, still trying to either get the Cuckoos under control or get the Gneiss to stop yelling at her because she was a *fucking queen*, dammit.

Mallory relaxed back in her seat. "Thank God that's over."

No one made a move to exit the shuttle, and Mallory realized the exterior door was still open and they'd all be chewing vacuum if they got off the ship.

Phineas took the two seats next to her and poked her arm. "You okay?"

"Just had my brains scrambled," Mallory said thickly. "I'll be fine. How is everybody else?"

"The tourists are thrilled, the humans from the station are furious, and Tina's little friend is sitting in the captain's chair."

"Is that where it was all this time?" Mallory asked.

Phineas shrugged. "I just know where it is now."

They were on a very sleek shuttle, black inside and out. The same ribbons of electric blue that were on the outside of the ship also pulsed through the interior, causing a very subtle lighting effect as the lights got brighter and then dimmer.

The seats were deep and comfortable, two on each side with an aisle in between. Up front, where the captain would normally be, sat Tina's strange friend in the seat, staring at the readouts of the HUD.

"What now?" Mallory asked. "Are we going to go to *Metis*? The other shuttle bay? Can Eternity answer you, Mrs. B?"

"I need to get to the heart of the station. Where is the captain?" Mrs. Brown asked.

"There is no pilot," one of the other humans, a small white woman, said. "*Metis* can control it if it doesn't get too far away from the mothership. All we need to do is ask her."

Thirty or so seconds later, the shuttle hummed to life and lifted from the floor. Mallory would have liked to get a wider view of Eternity since she didn't see it often from this angle, but Mrs. Brown was adamant that she get to Eternity's heart as soon as possible.

"Hey, what the hell happened back there?" Phineas asked as the shuttle zipped around the station toward the other shuttle bay. "Why would she endanger Mrs. Brown?"

"A lot of her functions, like life support, are automated in case something goes wrong with Eternity," Mallory said. "So many things went wrong when the Cuckoos took over that it's taken some time to get her back up to her former strength. She was probably acting instinctually."

"And since Queen Tina is still on board, with a sizable Cuckoo entourage, Eternity hasn't calmed down yet," Mrs. Brown said as she stood up from her seat. "Mallory, stay away for a while. I don't want anyone distracting the Sundry while I take care of the station. We need all of the little bugs we can get. Alexander, Jessica, you're with me. Adrian and Devanshi, thanks for coming to help. You're not needed."

Adrian and Devanshi stood, Adrian looking like he had sucked a terrible lemon. Xan and Jessica stood up to join her by the hatch, Xan giving one backward look at Mallory, as if he were hesitant to leave her. "Don't get into any murders while I'm gone."

She grinned without much humor. "Out of my control, dude."

"Will the Gneiss baby be okay?" Jessica asked.

"I don't know yet. Ask the Gneiss," Mrs. Brown said, and pounded on the hatch. "Open up!" she demanded.

"We haven't landed yet, Mrs. B," Xan said mildly.

"Don't throw your logic at me, boy," Mrs. Brown said. The shuttle lurched slightly as it touched down, and immediately the hatch opened. Xan, Jessica, and Mrs. Brown hurried out.

Everyone looked at each other awkwardly. Someone shouted at them from outside the shuttle. "Hey, let us on!"

The gynecologist and the dentist were running up to the shuttle. "Do y'all have room for us?" Bruce asked, sticking his head in.

Mallory realized no one was in charge here. Tina had no doubt commandeered the shuttle on the way over, and Mrs. Brown commanded it on its exit from the ossuary. She shrugged. "Not my call, but sure."

Something caught Bruce's eye and he peeked into the front of the ship and made a delighted noise. Kath joined the humans at the back of the shuttle.

"Pretty interesting day, huh?" Kath asked.

The other humans sat stunned and silent. One man shrugged.

"How do we get this thing moving now?" Mallory asked.

"The ship flies the shuttle," the same woman said. "All you

have to do is ask." With that, the hatch closed and the shuttle hummed to life again.

Mallory looked at the innocent mystery convention attendees and tried to give a winning smile. "So, welcome to Eternity, I guess. Hopefully you'll get a better tour next time. Maybe tomorrow, we can . . ." Everything stopped as Mallory felt all the blood run from her face. She patted her pockets frantically.

"What's up, Mal?" Phineas asked, putting his hand on her shoulder.

"Where's *Mobius*?"

9

MOBIUS'S BIG ADVENTURE

A few minutes earlier . . .

BIG SHIP BIG *ship big ship.*

Mobius could see the big ship! Or at least, a part of the big ship. He bounced, and Mama put her hand on the pocket and he couldn't see anymore. But Auntie Stephanie had told him after he got a good meal of bio-matter (but she meant the good kind, not the kind that came from dead people like Mama), he could change himself. And his Sundry friends were right outside. Somewhere.

He had named them. They were Sundry 1, Silver Timolina, Blue Jean, and Rachel. They didn't talk much, but he did feel a lot smarter with them around.

He concentrated the way Auntie Stephanie said to, and he made a tiny drill! But then that fell off him into Mama's pocket, so he thought hard again and made a tiny little appendage with grasping fingers like Mama had, and rooted below him to pick up the drill. He had a human arm now. He was a problem solver!

He took the drill and carefully started to drill through Mama's pocket. Just enough to see out. She would be so proud of him, finding his own answers to problems.

Mama was big and much wetter than his sleek metal body, but she took good care of him. Auntie Stephanie told him what he'd be capable of if he grew up, and he wanted to grow up *so badly* now. He had to ask what that word "capable" meant, and Auntie Stephanie said his connection to linguistic databases (more words he had to ask about) was weak right now, but that would only get better with time. If he ate food, he'd get bigger and learn how to do more stuff. And stuff sounded so amazing!

Now that he could peer out, he tried to figure out what was going on. From what he understood, many of the rocks liked Mama. And so he liked the rocks. When they entered the room with all the tired rocks, he really wanted to explore, but Mama kept him in her pocket. The rocks here weren't as nice as the other ones Mama talked to, but most of their words were sleepy and cranky, like Mama in the morning when he would wake her up with a loving headbutt.

He could feel her emotions fluctuate when she saw the big ship. Surprise, awe, a little bit of fear. She didn't need to be afraid. He would take care of her! He knew ships!

Okay, he knew how to *talk* to ships, and that was the same thing, mostly.

She finally let him out so he could see the *big ship big ship big ship*. The ship hummed slightly to itself, a tune that *Mobius* found enchanting. He wanted to go see the *big ship* closer, but he knew Mama's emotions would turn very red and angry if he left the station.

He didn't need air like she did, so he should be able to play outside!

The *big ship* wasn't doing much besides humming a little tune. More things were going on inside the air lock than outside with the ship.

Metis. She sent her name to him, and felt warm and friendly.

Mobius got bored very quickly. He pulled his new arm and drill inside his body and wriggled in Mama's pocket.

Mama was upset about something. He tried to see what it was, and the hole in her pocket got bigger. (Maybe because *Mobius* was pushing against it eagerly, maybe not. Who could say?) He asked her if he could go wandering and promised not to go too far.

She didn't answer, but that was probably because she was busy and wanted him to have independence.

He forgot his promise about two seconds after popping free from her cardigan pocket. The rock room was *so interesting*. Some of the rocks were quiet, like they were sleeping. Some of them moved or just vibrated. He wondered why. He flew over to a rock person who stood and faced the wall, but he wasn't moving. *Mobius* landed on the statue and was overwhelmed immediately with the cacophony of the voices.

The loudest was the one he was sitting on, a genderless voice complaining about the intruders.

Oh, so I should deal with them since I'm the one standing? You could stand if you wanted to, but you're just too damn lazy, Opal.

Other voices came up from the ground. *Mobius* wondered why he hadn't heard them before now. They were so loud and everyone talked at once!

. . . it doesn't look like they're messing with anything, just leave them alone.

Did the humans bring the Sundry? What are those green things?

You're imagining things again, just go back to sleep.

They are surrounding the child. You'd best wake up.

It's almost time for the birth! Don't you remember the last time those humans were in here? The chaos? The danger! The inability to get back to sleep for several days! Get them out of here!

Oh, you're just bitter because you are still too broken to stand up. You got pulverized and don't want to admit it was your own damn fault.

The Sundry are our main problem now. I think they're fighting over the child.

The tiny pebbles at the foot of the statue shivered, putting their opinions into the soundscape.

And me and me and me and me.

They felt small and fragile, like *Mobius* used to feel. He dropped from the statue onto the ground where the pebbles greeted him.

Hello, he said.

Me is here, want to be there. Once me gets close to other me, we will be bigger me.

Above him a voice started to sing quietly, *I am, I am, I am. I am.* But when he looked up, all he saw was a brown cloud with a lot of Sundry flying around it. Why did they care about a brown cloud?

So many little folks to talk to! They felt like him, small and determined, and he felt a wash of the warmth of kinship sweep over him. He wanted to talk more, but then all of the rocks started talking really loudly.

She's going to space them. Eternity wants to space the interlopers.

Can we save the child?

The air lock doors.

Save the pebbles!

Save the child!

Mama wasn't thinking about the doors opening. Mama wasn't even where she looked like she was. She was somewhere with his new friends. His new friends weren't in the fight over the cloud; his new friends were nicer than that.

The air lock opening will harm the humans, his friends told him. He peered around the room and found them sheltering against a shed wall that faced away from the air lock. They seemed safe from the wind.

Mama wasn't moving.

Mama? Mama! He shouted, but she didn't move.

You do not hurt Mama! Mobius took flight and went to attack the green things, which were causing the trouble, according to all of the voices. He wasn't sure what he would do, but he figured he'd think of something, and when he did, it was better to be closer to the fight instead of far away since he might forget his plan once he got there.

Well, now he was near the bugs and the cloud, and he still didn't have a plan.

The wind was picking up, and instead of flying confidently into the fray, he ended up careening out of control into it. He slammed into a green body and knocked it out of its pattern of flying around the cloud. That seemed to be as good a plan as any, so he fought hard to turn and go back in, slamming into another green body.

Below him, Mama's big friend had picked her up and was running toward the shuttle. Good. He would keep Mama safe while *Mobius* saved the day.

He knocked a few more insects away, some of them green, some of them blue (although he tried not to). He realized the greens were still winning, pulling the cloud down, but then they were all caught in the wind and started to get pulled out of the doors.

Save her. The command came from . . . his friends? Sundry 1? Blue Jean? But he didn't know how. Or who, actually. He was too small to save Mama, and he was pretty sure she would be okay inside the ship. His Sundry friends were safe. He didn't know anyone else in this room. All of the rocks and bugs were strangers to him.

The cloud.

Mobius didn't have the capability to save anyone who was bigger than a pebble. But then it finally hit him.

Well, a green Sundry hit him and knocked him directly into the brown cloud, which had less of a personality with words and was more of an emotion.

Mobius had recently grown a hatch in order to let his Sundry friends live inside him eventually. He had been so proud; he was waiting for the right time to tell Mama about it. But now, he opened the hatch and flew around the cloud, collecting as much of the dust as possible.

Two of the rock people were struggling to close the interior door, and *Mobius* wanted to help them, but then he remembered he had a mission, so he kept flying around the cloud as all of them—the cloud, the insects, and *Mobius*—got pulled toward the air lock.

The rocks must have been very strong because they finally got the door closed, securing most of the cloud and many insects inside.

Unfortunately, *Mobius* was among the ones who were sucked through the door and propelled out the open air lock.

He closed his hatch, unsure of what to do as he and a bunch of dead insects sailed out into the vacuum.

He could just see the shuttle that contained Mama lift off and exit the air lock, just to circle around and go to another one. He was happy Mama was safe.

Mobius, on the other hand, was losing the connection with his Sundry, and knew they couldn't follow him. He might be out here for a long time.

He tried to slow his speed, but it took a lot of energy just to stop the wild spin he'd been doing when he was sucked out. This might take a while. He hoped he wouldn't lose sight of the station while he figured this out.

I am, I am, I am alone . . . Help?

You're alone? I'm alone, too! His relieved gratitude was startling. Who was alone?

He turned his sensors inward and saw that all of the dust he had collected had formed a small rock. It sat inside his internal cavity, which he had not prepared for guests—as he had heard Mama say—shivering in a round and orange kind of way.

Hello. My name is Mobius.

Whose name is Mobius? the rock said.

Mine. Can't you see? He stopped talking, wondering if his hull would grow warm the way Mama's hull did when she was embarrassed. He concentrated and a small light illuminated the area around the rock. *You're inside me. I'm the ship.*

What is a ship?

Hmm. He had a lot to teach this pebble. Lucky for him he was so experienced and worldly. *I am a ship. You were inside with all the rock people, and now you're outside with me.*

I was up high, and I was big and not alone. Now I am small and alone.

Mobius thought about trying to explain how this came about, but frankly he wasn't entirely sure how it had happened. *Some bad things happened. I saved you. Want to be friends?*

The rock sat for a moment. *Mobius* tried to transmit in the rock language of vibrating. Then the rock replied.

Yes. I don't think I can get back inside to be with the rest of me. So I'll just be me. Your friend.

Mobius was about twelve times the size of the rock. Part of him said he needed to use all his energy to get back aboard the station, but part of him insisted he needed to be a good host, so he made a little captain's chair for his new friend to be comfortable. He had a lot of growing to do. But now he had someone to grow it for.

Where are we going? the rock asked.

That's the tricky part. I'm not sure. We kind of got sucked out into space at a high velocity.

That sounds bad. The voice came across tinged with anxiety. *We're lost! Stolen! Adrift in space! Doomed! DOOMED!*

No, no, that's only if we can't get back in.

Can we?

I don't know. He felt guilty. He thought he should distract her. *What's your name?*

I don't have one. They didn't call me anything except for "baby" or "the baby." But that was when I was part of someone bigger. Now I'm smaller, and just me.

I could call you Justmie.

She thought for a moment. Yes, that's better than baby. Thank you for the name! I haven't done anything for you yet!

You're my friend. When you know someone else's name, you're friends. He felt very proud to be giving this young pebble—Justmie— life advice.

He also felt relieved that he wasn't entirely alone here in space, speeding away from the station.

I have a name and a friend! Now what do we do? Justmie asked.

He couldn't contact Mama or his Sundry friends, but he might be able to contact Auntie Stephanie.

He sent out a message to Auntie Stephanie.

Eternity?

Infinity?

Anyone?

SEEING AS MOBIUS was a few months older than Justmie, they exhausted their conversation topics quickly. He tried to teach her a counting game, but it was hard to teach numbers with examples of only the numbers one (one ship, one Gneiss baby), two (two friends), and a million (number of stars).

Little brother.

That wasn't from Justmie or from Mama. That was from the big ship! Metis!

Hello, I am Mobius! And are you Metis?

The tone was amused. I am. You're like me, aren't you? Just a little ship trying to understand the universe?

I'm just a lost ship trying to fly in space. I have a friend here. But she's very new. Her name is Justmie.

He could feel Justmie's shyness when he introduced her and didn't push her to talk to *Metis*.

You are very brave to fly out in space so young, Metis said. *But I need some help with something very important, and I think you're the best one to help me.*

I can't help anyone, I'm lost, he said, trying not to sound mournful. *Mama can help you. Mobius* was trying to act like he didn't need a big ship to save him, because if Mama found out that he needed saving, she might never let him go outside again.

Your mama can't help with this. I need someone just like you. Someone small that not a lot of people notice.

But if *Metis* needed *his* help . . . he should help. Mama was always helping others.

Please can we go away from the big darkness? Justmie asked in a very small voice.

Getting back to the ship meant he could help *Metis* and Justmie. And maybe find Mama! Being in the dark helped no one.

Okay, we'll come help you. But we're drifting away from you and don't quite know how to get to you.

Metis sent some data to him, far bigger than simple verbal communication. It was a lot of data. There was piloting data, space travel data, language data, ship design data . . . he stopped trying to think about all the data. Was he big enough to hold it all?

He relayed the basic pilot data to Justmie so she could understand how to help, and they went from drifting aimlessly to drifting with much more purpose. Then they oriented themselves and the big ship—*Metis*, his new friend—started to get bigger as they approached.

You've saved us! You are our hero! Justmie cried.

Come aboard. Your mama is here.

And we'll be safe there, right?

She took a long time to answer. *You will be safe from drifting into deep space. I can't guarantee safety here. But no adventure is safe, is it?*

Mobius thought about all the adventure stories Mama told him, from helping Auntie Stephanie transform into a shuttle to being saved by Queen Tina—whose official title was bitch queen, but Mama didn't want *Mobius* to say those words. They were all exciting stories, but they weren't safe stories.

Are we going on an adventure?

Haven't you figured it out? The ship's tone was amused. *You're already on one.*

Gosh!

It was turning into a really good day.

Justmie was trying the new piloting options and getting the hang of it. *I'm glad I'm here with you,* Mobius. *You're nicer than the rocks.*

I'm glad, too! And we're on an adventure!

10

. . . .

TINA GOES UNDER

WHERE WAS *MOBIUS?* The little guy had hinted that he was confident he could fly in space—he didn't need to breathe, after all.

He'd be fine.

Her Sundry companions were crawling on the ceiling of the shuttle, antennae always active. It wasn't often easy to think a message to the Sundry, but Mallory didn't worry about the headache afterward. *He has a tiny hivemind now. Can you tell where he is? Where they are?*

The Sundry buzzed their wings as they conferred. *His hivemind are in the ossuary, and they are fractured. Communication is hard. They believe the ship is outside the station.*

"Shit," she muttered. "I can't believe I lost him." She rubbed her face and took a deep breath. She didn't need to be alone on this. "Phineas, can you help me find him?"

"I don't have any magical connection to aliens like you do, but I'll do my best. Why don't you ask Xan?"

"You're right, *Infinity* might be able to help. So could Stephanie." She sent a quick note to Xan and Stephanie to please help find the tiny ship, and asking Stephanie if she could also shore up *Mobius's* fractured hivemind. Stephanie wouldn't let him get lost if she could help it. Mallory chewed her lip as the shuttle exited the bay and headed toward *Metis*, who was holding lunar synchronous orbit around Eternity.

Stephanie messaged back immediately. *The Sundry are already rescuing the hivemind. They were already on their way to get rid of the Cuckoo problem in the ossuary. I will keep his four until he can take them back. I can go look for him. Tina won't need me during her trial.*

Trial? Mallory wrote back.

She brought an unknown entity among civilians and then aboard a diplomatic station. And now she's lost it. The ambassadors wish to talk to her about this.

"Did you see where that yellow alien went during the Sundry fight?" Mallory asked Phineas.

"He scampered onto the shuttle," Phineas said. "I think he hid in the cockpit."

Mallory stood and walked down the aisle, pausing to admire the gargantuan *Metis* out the window. She opened the door to the cockpit and peeked in.

Bruce the dentist was sitting in the captain's chair with the ugly little alien on his lap, curled up like a cat.

"Have you met this little guy?" Bruce asked, glee stretching his face almost out of alignment with his head.

"I know that little guy has caused a lot of trouble," Mallory said flatly. She returned to her seat and messaged Stephanie and Xan that at least the alien was accounted for.

Mrs. B wants you to keep an eye on it, Xan wrote back.

"What does she want me to do? Put a leash on it?" Mallory asked.

He didn't reply. *He probably thought it was rhetorical.*

Where are you? Mallory wondered as the shuttle docked beside *Metis* and extended a walkway to seal with the ship's air lock.

The passengers stood up to exit the shuttle, Bruce still cuddling the ugly alien. Mallory "'scuse me'd" her way through the others to get to him before he got off the shuttle.

"Hey, Dr., uh, Bruce," Mallory said, forgetting his last name. "It seems you've made a new friend there?"

He beamed at her. "I sat down and he just jumped in my lap!"

"You know, that alien was being watched by a friend of mine, Tina, who had to stay on Eternity for the time being." She reached out awkwardly. "I am going to need to take it to keep an eye on it until Tina can come retrieve it."

Bruce turned away, looking wounded. "He's not a thing you retrieve like a stick! And look, he wants to stay with me."

The alien hung over his arm like a waiter's towel. It didn't look like it wanted much of anything.

"Can you promise to keep an eye on it and not let it wander off and get lost?" she asked.

"Absolutely," he cooed, scritching the alien under its chin. Its disturbing humanlike mouth stretched wide in a grin. Mallory tried not to visibly shudder. "We're going to have fun, aren't we?"

"No, not fun," Mallory said, holding up a finger to stop him. "We don't know what it finds fun and what it finds threatening!"

He gave her a "stop worrying about the penguins in the snow" kind of look. She hurriedly gave him her contact information and told him to please, please let her know if it got away or did anything threatening. "Remember, we don't know anything about this alien. Something you think is just fine could scare it into attacking someone. Even you."

Bruce cooed again at the thing as he turned down the hall and Mallory fought to not roll her eyes in front of him.

"Adrian would tell me I lost control of another situation," she muttered to herself, watching Bruce walk away.

Stephanie sent her another text message. *Baby ship found. Safe aboard* Metis. *Not sure where but he's safe.*

Mallory relaxed in relief. She still didn't know where *Mobius* was, but aboard the ship was better than drifting out in space. It was time to focus on the convention and avoid thinking about murder . . . at a mystery convention.

Here we go.

MRS. BROWN TOLD Xan to go keep Tina company while she conferred with the station ambassadors. Xan found Tina in a Gneiss sauna area he had never visited before. It had huge stone couches along the perimeter of the room with a sunken floor hot spring about thirty feet in diameter and deep enough to cover most Gneiss bodies.

The entire ceiling was covered in Cuckoos, and they buzzed lazily, while Tina sat in the pool, her head just above the water, which boiled furiously around her.

"I don't think Eternity is going to like those Cuckoos being outside their, uh, hive again," he said mildly.

"They're just afraid of the water," Tina complained. "I told them I could keep them safe. They don't believe me."

"Tina, you're sitting in boiling water. That will kill most every life-form I know except for your people. If you make them go back inside your chest, then you'll just bake them to death."

"I'm mad at them anyway," Tina said. "They disrupted my grand unveiling of my new friend."

He frowned and sat at the edge of the pool, but far enough from the steam so he didn't get burned. "You mean you didn't send them up to bother the baby cloud thing?"

"No, I knew the rules that Eternity has. How stupid do you think I am?" she demanded.

Xan did not answer that. "Did you ask them why they did it?"

"They were too concerned with being spaced. We haven't talked much. At least we have this room to relax in. Suitable for a bitch queen. I should have one of these on Bezoar."

"Tina, do you know where this 'new friend' is?" he asked.

"I don't know, I lost him when everything went to shit," Tina said. "Why should I worry? I'm sure he found a safe place to stay."

"And if not? What if he's inside the station, Tina?"

Tina ducked her head under the water.

"Real mature," Xan grumbled. He couldn't even reach in and poke her to make her be an adult. "I'll just wait here until you run out of air. Which you don't need."

He tried to make himself comfortable on one of the stone couches and failed completely. The room was cozy, at least. It felt like a very large sauna. If it had some seating areas that were friendlier to human bodies, it might be a place to go after a swim. For a little while. Until you died of dehydration.

"I'm definitely going to need a bright yellow sports drink after this," he said, wiping the sweat off his face.

Tina surfaced and looked around for him. "Oh. I'd hoped you had gone."

"You're a fucking queen, Tina," Xan said. "You can't hide under boiling water until your problems die from heat exhaustion or leave."

"That remains to be seen," she said sullenly. "Why can't you leave me alone?"

"Mrs. Brown wanted me to come talk to you. Your friend is safe and being watched aboard *Metis*. This is something you should remember. Mrs. B is going to be talking to the diplomats on the station about your new friend, and then they will want to ask you some questions."

Tina went under again.

"Christ, you're such a child," he said, then messaged Stephanie to see if she had any thoughts.

Stephanie pointed out that there wasn't much she could do from the shuttle bay except for relay messages. But she would send Ferdinand to come help.

Thanks. Where has Ferd been anyway?

Ferdinand has been drinking. Being in Tina's entourage is stressful work.

"Cats would be easier to herd," he said.

Ferdinand came through the door a few minutes later. He handed Xan a human-sized cup of water without comment.

"You're the fucking best," Xan said. The water was somewhat sulfur-tasting, but if he pretended he was visiting Iceland, he could stomach it. "She's in there." He pointed to the pool, where you could just see Tina's pink form at the bottom.

Ferd stepped into the pool on the deeper end, and disappeared entirely.

The water frothed and splashed, and Xan shied away from the scalding water that they were tossing about. "This really isn't a room for humans," he said, and went to stand by the door and check his messages while the Gneiss worked it out among themselves.

He'd missed a message from Mallory.

Steph found Mobius. *Kind of. He's aboard* Metis. *That's all I know.*

Great, he wrote back. *Tina is being a pain. On the plus side I think I can sell tickets to watch Gneiss wrestle in boiling water.*

You will have to tell me more about this, Mallory replied. *Phin wants a front-row seat, though.*

Tina was a few feet taller than Ferdinand, but he was more determined, and they both erupted from the pool, Ferd holding her tightly.

"I don't want to!" she shouted.

"Give it up, Tina," Xan said. "If you're arguing just so I can hear you, you're just performing."

Tina sat on the edge of the pool steaming and dripping. Ferd got out and went to lie down on one of the couches.

"You okay there, buddy?" Xan asked.

"I don't recommend doing that," Ferdinand said.

"Doing what? Drunk wrestling in boiling water?"

"Something like that. You go talk to her. She's angry with me right now."

He went to the side of the pool and crouched down beside Tina, staying well away from her and all the heat her body had retained. "Tina, I need to explain to you why everyone is so freaked out about your new friend. You should know this before you talk to the ambassadors."

"But he's my friend," Tina said again. "How is that bad?"

"Have you even managed to communicate with it?" Xan asked. "Is it even sentient?"

"Yes," Tina said. "I don't know why you don't trust me."

"You're a queen. Did no one bother to teach you what to do if you met a new alien?" Xan asked.

"I think they did, I'm not sure," Tina said. "If they did, I don't remember. But surely someone knows about these little guys, and we can throw their language into the galactic database, and then we have new friends!"

Mallory sent him another message then, and he paused to read it. She filled him in on what she had been doing with the Sundry during the fight in the ossuary. "Holy shit," he said. Then to Tina, "Did you know your alien friend was the one who told your Cuckoos to attack the Gneiss baby?"

"That's impossible," Tina said. "We don't have his language yet."

Xan looked at the ceiling where the Cuckoos were practically asleep in the heat. "We don't, but do they?"

. . .

MALLORY HAD MADE sure that Bruce had a way to contact her if he got into trouble, but after Bruce had disappeared down the hall, Phineas shook his head. "You sure you want to let *him* keep up with the alien? You don't even know the guy."

"He seemed to bond with it immediately," Mallory said with a shrug. "I think it looks like a slug wished to become a huge cat but had the worst fairy godmother ever."

"You could lock it away until we know what to do with it," he suggested.

"That feels extreme and very preemptive-strikey."

"Your funeral," Phineas said.

"Not literally I hope," Mallory said, and was startled to be trapped in a hug from behind.

"Mallory!" She had been about to elbow the person who grabbed her, but recognized the cologne. It was her agent, Aaron.

His years showed up in person more than they did on the video call. Or maybe he'd just had a bad day. But he was immaculately dressed as always, with a purple bow tie and gray suit.

He let Mallory go and stuck his hand out to Phineas. "Aaron Rose, Mallory's agent," he said. "I saw you on the trip here. Do you know Mallory?"

Phineas shook Aaron's hand, but Mallory raised an eyebrow. "I'm beside a six-foot-tall Black man with tattoos on his knuckles that say SALT and FATT, and you can't guess who he is?" Aaron just looked at her blankly. "Phineas? Xan's brother? Hip-hop artist and chef? He was in the first book I wrote aboard the station?"

He brightened! "Oh, that Phineas! Of course. I thought you'd given him a different name in the books."

"Sure," Mallory said.

"And I'm Cosima Carter," said a voice behind Phineas.

He stepped aside and Mallory recognized the woman from the

shuttle who had told her that the mothership would fly the shuttle herself.

"Aaron's assistant," she added, shaking Mallory's hand. "I'm sure Aaron hasn't mentioned me at all."

Mallory raised her eyebrows. "No, he hasn't."

"And I recognized you both," she said, shaking Phineas's hand. "Aaron has been under a lot of stress lately, forgive him for a lapse in memory."

"Let's go somewhere and have a drink," Aaron said. "I'm doing a table talk with some young writers, and they'd love to meet you. Then we can catch up."

His cheerful manner felt forced, but Mallory didn't think it was time to push for more.

Cosima pulled out a tablet that Mallory only saw people use aboard Eternity. She poked it and said, "The restaurant is ready for us in ten minutes, the one on the third floor."

"I could use a drink. Is it still morning?" Mallory asked Phineas.

"In space it's always nighttime," he said.

JESSICA CAME INTO the steam room and balked at the heat. "You're going to die in here," she said.

Xan met her by the door. "I can't leave, I haven't gotten anything out of her. She hid at the bottom of that pool and Ferd had to wrestle her out."

"When Tina didn't want to talk to you, you sent a heavy in to drag her out, and then you wonder why she's not talking to you?" Jessica asked flatly.

"Well, when you put it that way," Xan said, exasperated.

Jessica stepped into the hall and went to the nearest public terminal. She recorded a verbal message and then returned to Xan, who was standing half in and half out of the room.

Jessica stepped past him with a pointed look. "Queen Tina, we apologize for your discomfort. We have a seat ready for you while you wait to entertain the ambassadors."

A huge golden throne grew up from the floor beside one of the stone couches. It glistened in the steam, inviting a large stone butt to sit upon it.

"That's more like it," Tina said. "That's what I've been waiting for!" She placed herself on the throne with grace and wriggled around, making herself comfortable. "Now, what do you want to know?"

Xan stared at Jessica, who shrugged innocently. "Sometimes diplomacy can be more effective than being drinking buddies with someone."

Eternity also drained the pool and slid a cover over it. Cool air blew in from the vent shafts, causing Xan to stand directly under the air flow and groan in relief.

"Where is the novel alien?" Jessica asked. "Your new friend."

"He is aboard *Metis*," Tina said. "He has someone watching over him to keep him safe."

Well, to keep someone safe, anyway, Xan thought.

Infinity spoke up in his mind. *Stephanie will be taking* Mobius's *hivemind over to* Metis, *as well as some Sundry scouts to keep an eye on the alien.*

"A human is watching him, and there are Sundry heading over there to monitor his movements as well," Xan said. He sent a silent thank-you to *Infinity*.

"So, Jes—Ambassador," Xan hastily corrected himself. "What exactly is the problem with the new alien? What are you supposed to do in a First Contact scenario, especially if you're not prepared for it?"

Jessica looked at him sharply. "You should know that already."

He grimaced and glanced over at Tina. "I do," he said slowly. "But I don't think Tina does. And she should hear it from a diplomatic person like you."

"Ah," Jessica said. She tossed her braids over her shoulder and approached Tina, who still radiated heat. "Your Highness, when introducing a brand-new species to people, you should contact the authorities before allowing them to be around people."

"But I am the authority," Tina said, confused. "I'm the fucking *queen*."

"I think she means galactic authorities, like ambassadors," Xan said.

"Screw them. They'd tell me to stop hanging out with him," Tina said. "If I already know what they're going to say, why bother talking to them?"

"Even if the words are inconvenient, it doesn't mean you shouldn't listen," Jessica said. "Can you tell us how you met your friend?"

"That's a fun story," Tina said happily. "So I was looking over some old population spreadsheets, which are super boring, but Ferdinand made me, and I saw a line item I hadn't seen before. Miu. I asked Ferdinand who the Miu were, and he said he didn't know. Then I asked him to bring me some lunch, and he said, 'What would you like, Your Highness?' and sometimes I ask for stuff I don't want just to hear him say that. Anyway, there are a bunch of species who have used Bezoar for their prisoner dumping ground for generations and just left them. I'm learning that some of the people on the planet aren't prisoners at all, but children of prisoners. Or children of children of prisoners. It even looks like some species died out everywhere but Bezoar."

"Like the Cuckoos," Xan said. "No one remembered what they were."

"We did on Bezoar," Tina said. "I like to think we're one big happy family on the planet. So, Ferd wanted to do a census thing to find out how many species are on the planet I'm ruling, and who I can get for my court. I really want a court, you see."

The little lights inside her eye sockets glowed bright for a moment. "But guess what I found out? Go on, guess."

No one guessed.

"Fine. I found out that I'm really good at data! Maybe I'm a Sundry at heart."

"You have an entire torso of a Sundry subspecies," Xan reminded her, pointing to the Cuckoos on the ceiling who usually lived inside Tina's hollow torso, when it wasn't a two-hundred-degree hothouse inside.

"Yes!" she said. "But once I got a look at the old data and cross-referenced it with the new, I was able to know where to send my people to census."

"Good at data" and using "census" as a verb weren't the best examples to prove her point, but if Tina was right, it was interesting.

"And . . . ?" Jessica prompted.

"And I found a population of Miu people living on the surface."

"I thought the surface was uninhabitable?" Xan asked.

"Well, the acid rain and fluctuating temperatures aren't hospitable for anyone," Tina agreed. "But they had hollowed out some of the major petrified vines and thorns and had made some amazing tunnels and caves and stuff! So we broke in and only had to kill a few before we could get a head count—"

Mallory groaned. "Tina, a census isn't supposed to turn violent!"

"You haven't gone door to door on Bezoar," Tina said. "Seems that people like to just be left alone after being stranded by their own people on a shithole planet. But we had some basic language files for most of them, so we could understand 'You will regret that,' and 'I will have my vengeance if you leave me here,' and my favorite, 'Release me so I may paint the galaxy with the blood of those who abandoned me.'"

"Did you learn 'hello'?" Jessica asked.

"Well, no, that didn't come up. But when my friend stopped

threatening me, I offered to take him to Eternity since I figured y'all would know what to do. So you see, he's not from a new species. He's from a very old one."

"So, no records remain about these people?" Jessica asked. "Not even the Sundry databases?"

She jumped when some blue Sundry spoke from the ventilation duct above their heads. "An intelligent but angry race. Abandoned on a prison planet. Population-wiping event on home world. Thought lost to evolution. Language files all but gone."

"But what about all the old data?" Xan asked. "Surely you kept notes when they were alive!"

"There is a limit to data storage," the Sundry said.

"This is why we need backups," Xan said, shaking his head.

"Your Majesty, you were scheduled to go straight to Eternity, but instead you flew to dock with *Metis*?" Jessica asked. "What happened there?"

"We heard that there was a neat new sentient ship coming from Earth, and we wanted to see it," Tina said. "I asked for a ride, and they said yes. Is that against the law?"

"Why did you bring the Miu here of all of the missing species you found? You had to know the lack of communication would make things difficult," Jessica said.

"I was hoping someone here would know more about them if they have people anywhere in the galaxy," Tina said. "The Sundry are really smart here. No one knew anything on the planet. So we came here."

"How many humans did this alien have contact with?" Jessica asked.

"Well, we were bored, so we wandered the ship. My friend got as much as it could out of the cat video room, so we went to the convention. It saw hundreds of humans. And now both of you! So hundreds plus a few more."

Jessica sighed. "We will be ready for you in about thirty minutes," she said. "Get in the lift down the hall. Eternity will bring you to the interview."

"Ferdinand, too?" Xan asked.

"Sure, if you can sober him up," Jessica said as she left.

11

. . . .

BUFFALO CAULIFLOWER AND OTHER CRIMES

A LIVING SHIP WITH a human host who should know what good food is, and the restaurant offers the same shitty cheeseburger and chicken fingers as every hotel I've ever been to?" Mallory asked, looking at the menu.

"They wanted the experience to be as close to a hotel convention as possible," Phineas said. "Talk to Eve."

"You get used to it after a few days," Cosima said.

"I think you mean 'sick of it,'" Mallory said.

"Don't bring the grumpies, Mallory," Phineas said, and the statement was so absurd from his deep voice, Mallory had to laugh. "But I have to go, come find me when you're done. I'll be in the control room." He winked and waved at everyone.

"I'm sorry, it's been a hell of a day already, with almost getting spaced and losing *Mobius*, and Tina upturning diplomacy on the station," Mallory said, rubbing her eyes and sitting back with a sigh. "As long as I can get French fries and some wine, I'll be good to go."

Aaron stared at the menu, saying nothing. His right hand fussed with his bow tie as his left held the menu. Mallory looked over at him. "I know what's wrong with me. But what's wrong with you? Did someone die?"

"N-no, not yet anyway," Aaron said, trying to straighten his bow tie and releasing it with obvious restraint. "I just wanted some grounding."

"Are you worried for your life?" she asked. "Has someone threatened you? You know I'm not a bodyguard."

"I know."

"Is someone threatening him?" she asked Cosima. The assistant shook her head, her face stony.

"Not yet, anyway," she muttered.

"No. I'm worried for, uh, someone else's safety," Aaron said. "Tempers are kind of high at this convention. Old grudges, things like that."

"What aren't you telling me?" she said. "You're never all sweaty and fiddly."

He gave a heavy sigh. "There are people here I thought I'd never see again. Or ever meet in person. And here they are. It's throwing me off-center."

"Old clients?" Mallory asked.

"Something like that."

"Are you worried you might kill someone, or the other way around?"

He looked startled. "Who would kill me? I'm a wonderful person!"

She looked at him flatly. "Really. You don't think any author, editor, spouse, guy you cut off in traffic, person you were mean to with 'it's just a joke' bullshit in college, none of them would have motive? Do you know what motive means? I'm starting to think you don't even read my books."

Cosima opened her mouth, but she shut it when Aaron glared at her. "Yes, of course I have. But I didn't think those were real motives. I thought you exaggerated them."

"I'm not even going to dignify that with a response," Mallory said. "Where's the server?"

The room really did look like a hotel that last had a refresh in 1975. The carpet was ghastly, all red and purple repeating diamonds. The walls held large sincere paintings of old white men grasping blueprints in their hands, as if anyone would want to challenge the fact that they designed this hotel. There was a sharp, plastic smell in the air that reminded Mallory of brand-new carpet that looked vibrant but smelled cancerous.

A tall Latino came to the table and bowed briefly. He took their order with the gravity of someone taking an order for duck confit instead of a hotel cheeseburger.

Outside the restaurant, mystery fans were mostly dressed in modern clothing, but many wore top hats and gears, steampunk-style. More than one wore deerstalker hats and long coats, and Mallory even spied a Dirk Gently cosplayer with a ridiculous bowler hat and flappy red coat. People seemed to be having a great time on the spaceship, even if it wasn't apparent it was a spaceship because it looked like a windowless convention hall.

"So, this is the convention?" she asked. "This is what *Metis* gave her passengers?"

"Isn't it great! It's like we never left Earth!" Aaron said, apparently putting his mood behind him.

"But if you're going to make it look like Earth, why go to space in the first place?" Mallory asked.

"To make people comfortable," Cosima said with a shrug. She stood up and waved sharply at a group of people who had just entered the restaurant.

Mallory was surprised to see Bruce the dentist and Kath the ob-gyn. Along with them was a tall Southeast Asian woman in a black hoodie, and an eager-looking white man with curly black hair in jeans and a sweatshirt. The young man led them over to the table.

"Oh, look, your new favorite," Cosima said under her breath, and Aaron shushed her. He had gone pale again.

"What's wrong?" Mallory whispered. "Does he not know he's your favorite? Are you playing hard to get?"

Cosima snickered.

"One of those people coming for the beginning writers talk is one of my authors," he said. "And the others . . ." He trailed off.

The group came up eagerly and shook hands all around. Mallory greeted Bruce and Kath like old friends until she got close to Bruce.

"Don't tell me you lost the alien already," she hissed in Bruce's ear.

"I left him in a very secure room," he said. "The cat room."

"The cat room," Mallory repeated. "What is the cat room?"

"It's where *Metis* stores all of the cat videos on the Internet," the woman in the hoodie said.

"*All* of them?" Mallory asked.

"All of them," she said with a confident nod, but didn't meet Mallory's eyes. "It's just down a couple of floors. It's secure." She looked up in alarm then, as if realizing she was talking to someone other than herself. She blushed. "Sorry to butt in. I'm Eve."

Mallory was ready with a ton of questions, but when she heard the woman's name, she brightened. "Oh, Phineas's friend? So, you do know whether it's secure or not."

"Yeah," Eve said, guarded. "You know Phineas?"

"I'm his friend Mallory. I hear through the grapevine that *Metis* has found a missing . . . um, item for me?" She glanced at the others, who weren't listening. "Another ship."

Eve got the same look on her face that Xan had when he was talking to *Infinity*. "Yeah, he—it's safe. Let's talk after this?"

Mallory blew a sigh of relief. "Thanks, I really can't begin to thank you enough."

"Mal, I want you to meet Jack," Aaron said, waving at her to get her attention. "One of my authors."

Mallory sat down next to Eve, while Aaron went around the table to clasp Jack by the shoulders as a greeting. He didn't touch anyone else.

He took his own seat again and pointed at Mallory. "Everyone probably knows her by name or reputation—this is Mallory Viridian, my client who lives on Eternity full-time!" He said it proudly, like he had tutored her into a good college.

Jack brightened, then took her hand and shook it, talking over Aaron's introduction. "I'm so glad I got a chance to meet you. I'm Jack Vasara, I'm a big fan of yours, actually."

Aaron smiled at Jack in a paternal, proprietary way. "I think Jack's going to be the newest star in the agency stables. He's the Venus flytrap guy."

Jack grimaced and looked back at Aaron. "Is that how you're always going to introduce me?"

"If it keeps making us rich, then yes," Aaron said.

"Ah, so you're the one mixing *Little Shop of Horrors* with Raymond Chandler?" Mallory asked.

Jack smiled again, relief on his face. "Yeah, I wrote the Zesty Yaboi stories. Thanks for not laughing."

"I heard you had four million readers on fan-fiction sites? That's not funny; that's a career," Mallory said. "Congrats."

He ducked his head and wouldn't meet her eyes. "You read them there?"

"Well, no, I can't access the Internet," she said. "But I've read a few pages of the first book. And I've heard about their popularity on the fan-fic sites."

"You'll be able to read any fan-fic you want shortly, right, Eve?" Cosima asked.

"Yeah, but we can talk about it later," Eve said, glancing at Aaron. "Publishing talk now, right?"

Mallory thought she should look into reading some fan-fic to get familiar with cozy mysteries. Maybe someone aboard *Metis* would have some stories saved. "Regardless, Jack, congrats," she said awkwardly.

Jack blushed with her praise, ducking his head. "It's been a wild ride," he said modestly. "I don't even know how it came to be."

"You had an agent who was smart enough to sign you, that's how," Aaron said, then clapped him firmly on the back. Jack fell forward a bit and nearly turned his water glass over.

"So, I know Jack," Aaron said with a smile. "Everyone else, tell me something about yourself."

He turned to Bruce first. "I'm Bruce," the dentist said. "I'm looking to reboot my career."

"Reboot? That implies you once had a career," Aaron said, lifting an eyebrow. "Have you been published before?"

"Not so much," Bruce said, his thousand-watt smile dimming slightly. "I more meant that I am a little tired of being a dentist and want to change my focus in life and be a writer."

"I'm Kath," the doctor said, taking over from Bruce's floundering. "Also chasing that dream. I've always wanted to be a writer, you know."

"Eve. I'm a programmer," Eve said bluntly.

"Great," Aaron said, putting his arms on the table and clearing his throat. "So, let's talk about the future of mystery."

Mallory had already heard Aaron's breakdown of the current mystery market, so she took a moment to see where people's attentions were going. Bruce and Kath sat close beside each other, showing Mallory a chemistry she hadn't noticed before. They didn't touch, but they were comfortable with very little distance between their elbows.

Eve didn't look anyone in the eye, while Jack sat like an attentive puppy, watching Aaron and Mallory.

Aaron was sweating as he talked, his eyes darting between two people: Mallory and Jack. It was as if the others weren't even there.

"Which of your clients' books has you excited now?" Bruce asked, sitting straight.

"You mean besides the books these two are writing?" Aaron said with a big smile. "I have a client who's writing a LitRPG story about someone trying to solve a murder in a game, and then it comes out and the game designer is dead. There's a lot of twists and turns and questioning reality. It's really very clever."

"When will it be out?" Mallory asked.

"We haven't sold it yet," Aaron said. "But I just signed the author before we left."

Mallory realized he was beaming at Kath, whose face was pink. She looked back and forth between them. "Wait, Kath is your new client?"

Bruce coughed through the water he was drinking. "Seriously? You?"

"Well, yeah," she said, looking defensive. "I wanted it to be a surprise."

"Mission accomplished," Bruce said, his face red. "Why would you keep that from me?"

"I hadn't even planned on telling you right now," Kath said. "I was waiting for the right time. I wanted to see if you could get representation, too."

The food arrived then, and they all took a moment to appraise their hotel meals and determine if they were edible. Mallory regretted her chicken fingers immediately, but it didn't look like anyone else got anything better. Cosima's Caesar salad had whole anchovies in it.

Bruce was dumping ketchup on his chicken tenders and eating them in big bites.

"Slow down," Kath admonished. "You look like a glutton." She poked sadly at her Buffalo cauliflower that really was just steamed cauliflower slathered with Frank's RedHot Hot Sauce.

Jack was downing his sliders with no problem, and Aaron ate his cheeseburger with automated movements. He picked up a fry and bit into it, then spat it back out. "Ouchie wowchie," he said. "Those things are hot!" He touched a red spot on his lip. "Jesus that burned me!"

"There's better food on Eternity," Mallory said. "We should just go over there."

Eve had been staring at Aaron, her eyes wide. Mallory waved a hand in front of her face. "Do you think we can get a shuttle to Eternity? Lunch is on me."

Eve blinked and focused on Mallory. "What? A shuttle? Oh, yeah, just get on board a shuttle and ask her."

"Great," Mallory started, but then sobered. Mrs. Brown had said very clearly that she didn't want Mallory there. She might "distract" the Sundry. Mallory took a bite of her dry chicken fingers with a sigh.

"I think the future of mystery will go into noir and cozy, or, as our friend Jack has managed, cozy noir," Aaron said.

"Or LitRPG mysteries?" Bruce asked through a mouthful of chicken.

Mallory looked away.

"I'm not sure all of the stories written right now are as good as the one I've got. The genre has a long way to go to get legitimacy, but I think Kath's book will take it far," Aaron said. "But as authors, you must learn to pivot when the market turns."

Bruce signaled the server and ordered a bottle of wine for the table. "What about the art? The craft?" he asked.

"Secondary consideration if you want to eat," Aaron said, shrugging.

The wine came and Bruce filled his own glass, then passed it to Mallory. They were the only two who drank.

They talked a little about space then, and Mallory's life aboard the station.

"Hey, you said you hadn't read my fan-fic because of no Internet, right?" Jack said.

Mallory nodded.

"Can I give you some? I have them on a drive here, and I'd love your thoughts." He fished around in his pocket and held up a black fob.

"I hope that's just the edited books," Aaron said. "You don't want anyone reading the unpolished ones."

"A few million online readers prove you wrong," Mallory said, accepting the drive from Jack. She noticed the table watching them, and suddenly felt put on the spot. "Thanks."

"So, what's your keynote about, Mallory?" Kath asked, clearly trying to get something moving in the conversation department.

"I'm thinking I'll just wing it," Mallory said.

"Maybe if you're lucky, someone will die and you won't have to do it," Jack said with a wink.

Mallory didn't laugh.

ONCE THE FOOD was done, Aaron loudly said that they needed a split check, much to everyone's annoyance, then stood abruptly and left.

The remaining people looked around the table, bewildered.

Most of them did, anyway. Eve also stood and said she had somewhere to go.

"Is this how people usually leave dinners in space?" Bruce asked, slightly drunk.

"I'm the only one who lives in space, and I'm still here," Mallory said flatly. "What's up with him?" she asked Cosima.

"I couldn't begin to tell you," Cosima said. "He's got some things on his mind."

"I thought he'd have talking to clients on his mind," Mallory said. "Seeing as how he wants me to change genres and everything."

"What, does he want you to write LitRPG, too?" Bruce asked.

"What does that mean?" Kath asked.

"Just that it's the new hot genre!" Bruce said. "Everyone should write it! Jack, are you in?"

"No, not really," Jack said. "I need to talk to Aaron. Excuse me." He got up from the table and ran.

"I was afraid of that," Cosima said, and hurried after Jack.

"I have no idea what's going on," Mallory said. "But there's something Aaron's not telling us. It was nice seeing you both again, and congrats," she added to Kath.

"He won't tell you anything," Bruce called after her as Kath was shushing him desperately. "He's a slippery one!"

Mallory ran out of the restaurant, a little wobbly after the wine. It was almost the top of the hour, so the panels were all ending. The hall filled with people almost instantly, at least seven rooms opening to let out the attendees. Mallory pushed past a few of them, and one tried to stop her. "Hey, aren't you that murder magnet lady?"

She brushed him off. "You're thinking of someone else," she said, catching sight of Aaron's salt-and-pepper hair bobbing through the crowd a few dozen feet in front of her. Jack looked as if he were coming up behind him fast. Cosima caught up to them both and tried to usher them inside an elevator, but she stepped back as if Jack had pushed her away. A few cosplayers got in after him, one wearing metal wings with gears on them, obscuring Aaron entirely.

"Hold the elevator!" Mallory shouted, dancing around someone to avoid colliding with them.

Someone shouted at her, but she kept running. "Hold it, please!" The doors began to slide closed.

The winged attendee stuck out his hand to push the doors

back, and it opened again. Mallory sighed with relief and moved to get on, but a beefy hand closed on her shoulder and held her back.

"Ma'am," a deep voice said, "I need to see your convention pass."

Mallory stood in horror as the doors closed in front of her, the winged cosplayer looking sympathetic. She caught sight of Cosima and Jack, both of them frowning at Aaron, while the agent looked like a rabbit in a trap.

SECURITY'S OFFICES WERE small, ugly little rooms with too many computers and a whole lot of snacks. Mallory and Pablo, the guard who'd caught her, sat facing each other in the corner.

"Someone said you were the keynote speaker, and I was going to let it go, but someone else said you said that wasn't you," he said. "You have to understand this isn't a case of someone trying to get in without a badge; it's that if you're here and we aren't tracking that, you could be a stowaway, or someone trying to get aboard the space station and make the Earth look bad. Not to mention a danger to *Metis*."

"Well, the Earth has sent two serial killers to Eternity, so if the station was holding a grudge, she would have done something about it by now," Mallory said, rubbing her face and then shaking her hands to get some of her tension out. "So, yes, I am the keynote speaker. I was trying to find my agent, and I didn't want to meet people right then. So I lied."

"Ah, to have the problems of the rich and famous," Pablo said. "So, what's your keynote about? I made sure to get that shift off. I'm a writer, too."

Her keynote? Fuck. Maybe she should beg off. Or maybe someone *would* die.

Mallory opened her mouth, but no sound came out. She

looked around the room for any idea, anything at all. *Computers, hackers, cybercrime, security, conventions* . . . "It's about taking your own experiences and elevating them to fit an exciting narrative."

"Really?" he asked, sitting back and grinning. "So, what would you write about your experience just now?"

She fought the desire to demand to be let go. She'd lost Aaron the moment he got on the elevator; the ship was too large and he clearly already knew his way around. This guy could help her. "I would probably make my agent a suspect in a murder, not just a guy trying to escape an uncomfortable situation. I'd make you use cuffs on me, and possibly have a grudge against me, so you'd keep me detained as long as possible. But then I'd make the scene give me a clue that helps me solve the case later on."

"That's awesome. I wouldn't have thought of half of that," he said.

"Comes with experience," Mallory said, distracted by a movement in the corner of her eye. A laptop was at the edge of a table, looking like it would fall with the smallest bump. And then it toppled to the floor out of Mallory's sight. There was no crash of the laptop hitting the ground and breaking. Just a small *whoosh* sound.

"Shit," Pablo said, jumping up. "That's the third time that's happened! I think we hit a space wave or something."

"Space wave . . . ?" Mallory said. She considered correcting him about the many things wrong with his assumption, like they were currently orbitally locked to Eternity, and there was no such thing as a space wave. But she just watched him stare at the floor. "What did this space wave do?"

"I don't know, I guess people trip over power cords, or the ship turns and the laptops slide on the desk." He gestured to the empty floor and shrugged. "And then they're gone. At least we're fully backed up, right?" he said with a laugh, patting the wall behind him.

"But how many laptops can you afford to lose?" Mallory asked.

"Eh, the ship replaces them. We just have to report it gone, and poof! New laptop."

"She makes a whole computer? That's impressive. I guess Eternity does sort of the same thing, but not immediately," Mallory said.

Pablo went to a computer that was still present, typed out a few things, and then said, "Your badge will be ready if you go by registration. Sorry about the misunderstanding. Looking forward to your keynote!"

"That makes one of us," she muttered, but she thanked him and left.

12

. . . .

THE TRIAL OF THE CENTURY

WEIRD ALIEN IS secure aboard *Metis*," Xan said after he received a message from Mallory.

"I don't see what the big deal is," Tina said. "It can't live in a vacuum, so it can't run away." She was really into this whole golden throne thing.

"That ship is larger than most skyscrapers," Xan said, "and from what Mal says, it's even bigger on the inside. It's hard enough to find a cat in a two-bedroom house, much less a multifloor building. And this thing looks at least part cat."

He poked Ferdinand, who was still prone on the couch. "You okay, dude?"

A low rumble came from Ferd's chest.

"Okay, come find us if you get the strength to stand up," Xan said, patting him on the shoulder. "Tina, it's time to go. Gather your Cuckoos and let's get this over with."

"No, I will have my entourage with me or not go at all," Tina said.

Xan was about to point out that Ferdinand wasn't fit for an official meeting (trial?), but to his surprise, his friend sat up from the couch and swung his legs over, the pivoting of his butt on the stone couch making a terrible sound. Ferd stood up and nodded once to Tina.

She got up from her throne gracefully. "I will see them now."

The Cuckoos who were still hanging out on the ceiling took wing as one and all returned to their home inside Tina's chest. She now emitted a slight perpetual background hum.

"Do you have any idea what's going to happen at this meeting?" Ferd asked Xan in the elevator.

"Not a clue," Xan said.

Eternity could create rooms from next to nothing, but she still could surprise Xan. While he didn't expect a courtroom, he definitely didn't expect the room they ended up in.

The elevator doors opened to a dark tunnel that ended in an iron gate. Beyond the gate was bright light and sand.

"Where the hell are we?" he asked, moving in front of the Gneiss to peek out the iron gate.

They were in a replica of a Roman colosseum. Sand stretched out to meet circular walls, and ambassadors sat in a shaded box opposite the gate.

"Mrs. Brown has gone a bit overboard," he muttered. "Or maybe Eternity." He pushed the gate, which opened easily.

He glanced behind him. "Listen, if a giant cat comes running out of another door, don't let it eat me, okay?"

"Are you anticipating an attack?" Ferdinand asked, his voice slower than usual.

"I don't know what to anticipate, I just know that when you were in a place like this back on Earth, it usually had people fighting people, or people fighting animals. I didn't know we were fighting at all."

It was smaller than a colosseum, perhaps the size of two high school gyms. Still, he felt very vulnerable walking out onto the sand, the Gneiss following him.

In the shaded box, Mrs. Brown and Jessica had front-row seats for the carnage. Or tribunal. Whatever. Jessica looked nervous, eyes darting from Mrs. Brown to Xan.

"Queen Tina is ready for your questions," he said, then stepped back to stand beside Ferdinand.

Why is this a colosseum? he asked *Infinity. Are we going to be attacked?*

Mrs. Brown asked Eternity for an appropriate area in which to question Tina. In looking through Earth media, this is what Eternity decided.

I think Eternity is holding a much bigger grudge than Mrs. Brown realizes, he replied.

"This is a very large area," Ferd observed. "That seating looks like it could hold a few hundred people. Even my people. Would Eternity make such a big space if she wasn't expecting that many?"

"You must be mistaking me for a diplomat, Ferd," Xan said. "I don't know who's going to be here."

Behind Mrs. Brown and Jessica sat one or two from every species that Xan had met on the station. Two Gurudev, one Phantasmagore (although more could be hiding anywhere, he realized), one Silence, and two Gneiss.

The air to the right of the box shimmered, and a hologram of other ambassadors appeared in the stands. These must have been the ambassadors who lived on the station in places with a methane environment or one colder or hotter than humans preferred.

"Whoa, nice touch, Eternity," Xan said aloud. "I didn't know you could do that."

Metis has shared some technology with Eternity, Infinity said.

The other diplomats living aboard Eternity spanned the range of sizes from a humanoid dwarf to a four-legged methane breather that reminded Mallory of the dogs that look like mops, only the size of a pickup truck. The ambassadors were of such different shapes, and sizes, and needs (like atmosphere and temperature) that the idea of a meeting taking place around a table that seated eight to ten adult humanoids of average size was out of the question.

"Still didn't fill the seats, though," Xan mused.

They then heard a faint hum, and then a growing buzz, and then a wild, terrifying cacophony as silver and blue Sundry poured into the room from vents, cracks in the walls, and the elevator shaft behind Xan. There were more Sundry than Xan had ever seen together, and they landed on the seats, filling every one. They settled down so their buzzing wasn't drowning out every other sound, but Xan could feel the tension in the air, as they were all prepared to act on a moment's notice.

"Something is telling me this isn't about the alien," Xan muttered.

"The same something is talking to me, too," Ferd said.

"You might want to tell Tina to keep her Cuckoos inside this time."

"Already done," he said. "Stephanie has also been invited to watch."

"That's good," Xan said. "I wish Mal were here, though. Someone who can talk to the Sundry would be great."

"Is Tina prepared?" Mrs. Brown asked without acknowledging the fact that there were thousands of Sundry all around them.

"That is a real hard question, Mrs. B," Xan said. "I don't think we expected such an audience."

"Don't worry about them," Tina said. "We're ready!"

Xan knew one should always be at least a little worried about what Tina was going to say or do. A few months earlier, she claimed she was making a deal with Earth for humans to ship all the dead bodies to Bezoar so the Gneiss could evolve without killing people. She was a twelve-foot thousand-pound toddler who now ruled a planet.

"Do you have the Cuckoos with you?" Jessica asked.

"They're always with me," Tina said, pounding her chest once. An angry buzzing increased in volume and then calmed down.

"I don't think they like that, Tina," Xan said quietly.

Tina ignored him. "I have them all and I can control them."

"Like you told them to attack a baby?" a yellowish-white Gneiss said.

"I didn't tell them to attack," she said patiently. "I told them they could have it if they wanted it. It was their decision."

"Oh, Jesus," Xan said, covering his eyes as the diplomats erupted with rage around them.

"All right, I understand now that our own children are not to be offered to other species as hosts for thousands of insects," Tina said, as if promising not to enslave children was a big favor. "I will control them now."

"Are we here to talk about the Cuckoos or the new alien?" Ferdinand said, surprising Xan with the strength of his voice.

Tina looked back at them as if just remembering they were there. "They're not 'alien,' they have a name."

Xan leaned forward. "Then maybe tell them the name, Tina."

"Oh, have I not done that?" she asked. "They are the Miu."

"All right, let's stay on topic," Mrs. Brown said. "I have Alexander's report on where the new alien—the Miu—supposedly comes from."

The pale Gneiss stood up. "You have taken an unknown alien life-form, a prisoner, and exposed it to humans and other life-forms without ever telling your own people what you had discovered."

"Unknown?" Tina said. "The fact that my own people—and the Sundry, who are supposed to know everything—forgot who was living on Bezoar is not my fault. And it's not their fault. Their people dumped them there, and then I guess they all died, and my people forgot about the ones who were still living. Go talk to my relatives, you big jerk. Ask them why they didn't keep track of their people!"

Xan stared at her. Aside from the childish name-calling, Tina was creating a reasonable argument. He hadn't considered that the old queens and kings of Bezoar were probably still alive, since it was really hard to kill a Gneiss.

"I found a forgotten culture, and Ferd counted them, and when they heard I was going to Eternity, one of them wanted to come. Then when we heard about the ship coming from Earth, they wanted to see that, too."

"How do you know?" Jessica cut in. "We've been told many times that we can't communicate with the alien yet. How can you tell what it wanted?"

Tina became quiet. Xan poked her in the back. "Your turn to talk, Tina."

"The Cuckoos talked to it," she said in a low voice.

"What was that?" Mrs. Brown said.

Tina didn't respond, but Xan could feel the floor vibrating louder and louder. "Is she fighting with the Gneiss ambassador?" he asked Ferd.

"Yeah," Ferd said.

Infinity had relayed a message from Mallory that said the Cuckoos could communicate, just not audibly. While the blue and silver Sundry had maintained that the Cuckoos had no language, they'd admitted to Mallory that the green insects could communicate by dancing like honeybees. Communication was possible, if only through the Sundry.

While everyone assumed the Cuckoos weren't sophisticated enough to have language, Xan wondered if the problem was simply that their language wasn't in the galactic database—created and maintained by the Sundry—because these insects also had been abandoned and forgotten about on Bezoar.

What if the Cuckoos had their own language database?

"Your Majesty, how did the Cuckoos communicate with you?" Mrs. Brown asked.

Tina still didn't say anything. Xan imagined her as a kid who was in front of the principal's desk. "I can't tell you that," she said at last. "It's a Bezoar secret."

"You can hold secrets from other races, but you should disclose everything you know to your own people!" the pale Gneiss shouted. "Are the Cuckoos controlling you the way they controlled Eternity?"

Xan gave a startled look to Ferd. "Is that possible?" he whispered.

"No," Ferd said.

"But can Tina really do that? Communicate with the Cuckoos?" Xan asked. "Mal said they only communicate by dancing."

Ferdinand was silent.

"Come on, man, people are going to assume that's the case if y'all don't say anything," he said.

"She says she can communicate. But she also won't tell me how."

"So, you can't talk to them?" Xan said.

"Correct," Ferd said.

The second Gneiss (Ambassador Bob, according to Ferdinand) stood up. At about six feet tall, he was short for a Gneiss, and in addition to having a completely boring name, he was a dark color of rock that reminded Xan of playgrounds from the 1980s when designers thought it was okay to put playground equipment on asphalt.

Jess and Xan had met him once at Ferd's bar, because he'd wanted to hear about Tina's and Stephanie's transformations from an outside party. He hadn't talked much, and he hadn't bought the drinks.

Now he still didn't speak, but the air began vibrating again, causing the Sundry to answer with their own buzzing.

Xan looked to Ferd for translation.

"Ambassador Bob is unhappy with Tina for agreeing to this meeting before briefing him personally," Ferd said.

"He must be pretty mad, it feels like they're having a hell of an argument through the floor," said Xan.

He suddenly wondered where Parker was. Mallory's old friend from high school was an entomologist, and had become the ambassador from Earth to study the Cuckoos and the Sundry. He and Mallory had some unfinished, unrequited teenage angst business to deal with, but then he'd gone back to Earth and always seemed to be there or on Bezoar, with no stops on Eternity in between.

It was Xan's understanding that Parker wrote Mallory occasionally but was still trying to get his new diplomatic situation straightened out and didn't have a lot of time to chat.

"I wonder if Mallory's friend knows about Cuckoo communication," he said.

"Parker is taking some leave on Earth," Ferd said. "It seems Bezoar isn't hospitable to humans."

"Tina always said it was a shithole," Xan said.

"The people of Bezoar are by default considered prisoners, and are not allowed to leave. But you've brought both Cuckoos and this new alien to endanger this station and thousands of humans aboard *Metis*," the pale Gneiss was saying.

"Why are these people responsible for the actions of their parents?" Tina shouted. "They live on a shithole planet through no fault of their own! Whoever broke the law broke it so long ago that no one remembers what it was, they probably don't even remember."

Mrs. Brown wasn't stupid. "You don't know if they remember or not?"

"Well, they've never told me. Or never told the Cuckoos who never told me."

"We have gone from a First Contact situation to ethics about incarceration very quickly," a nearby ambassador's hologram said. They raised their voice. "Do we have any applicable language to use to communicate?"

"No," Tina said.

"And we don't even know what it's doing here?" a Phantasmagore ambassador shot back. "Just wanting to see the galaxy seems like a weak reason."

"It's hanging out with me!" Tina said. "It likes me!"

Jessica spoke up. "The first thing we need to do is understand who these aliens are, and get their language into the database. Do the Sundry on Bezoar have any historical or linguistic data on these aliens?" She turned to the Sundry. "Is there anything in the Sundry databases? Even the archives?"

"We have very little information on them, or their language," the swarm reported. "The last piece of data was archived about one thousand years ago, saying that their planet had suffered a population-ending event. All life, knowledge, and resources gone. The entry says nothing about their imprisoned population on Bezoar. We thought it was the end of a race. We admit that even we feel the need to purge data that is no longer necessary, and once we thought the Miu had died out, we archived everything. The archives are well protected and not connected to any Sundry circuit. One must access the data from a physical location."

"How many Miu live on Bezoar, Your Highness?" asked Mrs. Brown.

"About twelve hundred, my census takers say," Tina replied.

"Where is the archive of the remaining Miu information?" another ambassador said.

"We don't tell other species that information," the swarm replied. "Its protection is vital."

"If no one can get to them, they may as well not exist!" Mrs. Brown snapped. "Can you send someone to the archive?"

The swarm hummed briefly, as if talking among themselves,

then formed words again. "We can send a ship. It will take two weeks."

"Oh, is that all?" Xan muttered sarcastically.

"Seems the best we can do," Mrs. Brown said. "Your Majesty, we would be grateful if you would stay aboard the *Metis* while we wait for this data."

"Sure! It really likes the *Metis*!" Tina said happily.

"Isn't the *Metis* returning to Earth in a few days?" Xan asked loud enough for the ambassadors to hear.

"By then Eternity will have a better place to welcome our visitors," Mrs. Brown said. And while Xan picked up on her ironic use of "welcome" he was fairly sure the aliens did not.

"A question for the ambassadors," said the Phantasmagore diplomat, standing up. "Do we feel threatened by this creature?"

General rumblings made their way around the seats, nothing definitively yes or no.

"Who or what does it bond with symbiotically? Or is it lonely in the world, like humans?" the Gurudev ambassador asked.

"There's no cause to distract us with insults while we're all working toward the same goal," Jessica said smoothly into her mic. "I agree that for now, quarantining the alien aboard *Metis*, and then a secure room aboard a shuttle or the station, is the best action. When we learn more about it, we can make decisions."

Infinity immediately spoke up in Xan's mind. *Neither Stephanie nor I want responsibility for this possibly volatile species.*

It's just a little dude, Xan said. *What harm can it do?*

We don't know. We don't know anything. We need to understand it before we interact with it.

As the diplomats argued, Xan tried to pay attention to both the argument and *Infinity*. She went quiet for a moment, then said, Metis *said she will keep the alien secure. She has space and plenty of information to keep it entertained while the important people bicker.*

He cleared his throat to stop Tina from going on another diatribe about her "friend." "I've received a message that *Metis* welcomes Tina and the alien aboard."

Mrs. Brown thought for a moment. "Make sure you alert the ship's host. We don't want this to turn into a kidnapping situation."

"*Infinity* won't let *Metis* leave with the alien on board," he reassured her.

"Do it," she said, then turned to her mic to alert the others.

Jessica addressed Tina. "Your Highness, Eternity will not allow Cuckoos aboard the station any longer. As long as you host them, you must also be quarantined aboard *Metis* or a shuttle."

Xan winced, expecting Tina to explode.

"So long as I'm with them, that's fine," she said. "I'd rather be on the new ship anyway. Eternity's getting really boring."

"'Boring' is never a word I use to describe this place," Xan said to Ferdinand, who inclined his head in agreement.

13

OUT OF NOTHING AT ALL

T HIS IS ALREADY a bizarre experience," Mallory said when
Phineas met her at the elevator.

"Everything in space has been, from where I'm standing," he
said. "What's up?"

"Is there a place on the ship that we can have a private talk?"

He chuckled. "I'll take you to see Eve. She's got the most se-
cluded area on the ship. Although there are several empty rooms,
Eve's office will be the least distracting."

"What do you mean?" Mallory said.

"I'll show you later on the tour," he said. "Telling you doesn't
bring the impact of a *Metis* room. Check out the map." The map
on the elevator wall seemed to defy all logic. Phineas pointed to
the top floor, their destination, but the map did seem to indicate
that the exterior and interior weren't really matching, physics-wise.
It depicted nearly countless rooms on countless levels, color coded,
and mostly in English.

Mallory shook her head. "What does it all mean?"

Phineas grinned at her. "You mean no one has told you?"

"Told me what?" Mallory asked. "I've been trying to find a tiny
lost ship and stop a Gneiss baby from being sucked out an air lock
or overtaken by Cuckoos! I haven't had time to even ask about this

ship. All I know is that it's got a mystery convention aboard, and it's got a room where you can watch cats, apparently."

Phineas shook his head. "Oh, hon. I'm so sorry. *Metis* is a unique ship."

"People keep saying that. All I know is she's massive and old, right?"

"And about the cats," he began, leading her down the hall. "Nah, I'll show you in a second." They came to a bank of five elevators, and Phineas pushed the button for the middle one. "What you need to know is this ship is carrying a perfect snapshot of the Internet. The whole thing, up to the moment we left Earth orbit."

"That's impossible," Mallory said, feeling lightheaded.

"It's not," he said, indicating for her to get on the elevator first. "She's about half-database."

"And the other half is all of this?" Mallory pointed to the map.

"Not exactly, the ship herself, the physical rooms, the life support, all that is about another tenth," he said, pointing to the bottom of the map. "But the other forty percent is *Metis* taking what she knows of the Internet and manifesting it."

"Manifesting?" Mallory asked. "Like when Eternity makes a chair that fits my butt when I go to a Gneiss restaurant?"

"Kind of, but that's child's play to *Metis*. She has rooms dedicated to cats, to fan-fic, to 'one weird trick,' to books, to movies, to all the languages on Earth, to anything that's uploaded to the cloud, she has them, and she made a special room for them."

"Holy shit," Mallory said weakly, staring at the map. "God, it looks like you could get lost in here and die, and no one would ever find you."

"That's the benefit of a living ship," Phineas said, smacking his palms together. "And see, you don't need to worry about solving murders. If someone died, then *Metis* could tell us about it."

Mallory glared up at him. "You can say the same thing about Eternity, you know. And yet we know crimes happen."

"Think of *Metis* like Eternity," Phineas said. "She's huge, but we only need access to a small part. We don't worry about the rest." He drew an invisible circle around the convention section of the map.

"But like you said, there are a lot of differences other than size," Mallory said. "Physically depicting the whole fucking Internet is a big one!"

He nodded. "Yeah, but Eve tells it better."

The lift came to a gentle stop. "I met Eve at lunch, but she didn't say much," Mallory said.

"She's the kind of person who doesn't talk unless she has something to say," Phineas agreed. "Which makes people think she's shy or rude, when really she's just efficient."

"That fits with the person I met, yeah," she said. She stepped out of the elevator and instantly froze, still with wonder.

The control room had some human-sized chairs, glittering lights, keyboards, and a gorgeous view of Eternity through a domed window. To the left was a wall of monitors, showing various places on the ship. Several showed the convention spaces and people milling about. One showed a roomful of cats and cushions, the cats jumping, running, sleeping, hissing, or seeming to disappear altogether.

Phineas pointed to the monitor with the cats. "That's the cat room."

Mallory squinted at it, trying to see walls, a ceiling, or anything depicting it as a room. There were just cats and beds and cats and cushions and cats and robot vacuums and more cats. "You could kill someone just by dropping them in that room, if they're allergic," she said.

"Now you can meet Eve on her own turf," Phineas said, and pointed to the desk. The desk itself was messy, with chip bags, Post-it notes, highlighters, and a small dragon sculpture that had been turned over. There was a definite Doritos odor to the room.

Under the desk sat a cat, a dainty calico, who paused in washing her paw to look at them, and then dismissed them to go back to grooming.

"Who's that?" Mallory asked.

"That is Mimosa," Phineas said. "Eve names her animals after brunch foods."

"This is amazing," Mallory said, looking around the room.

In front of the desk sat a human spinning lazily in a desk chair. Eve still wore her hoodie and glanced only slightly at the newcomers. She slouched in the chair as if she had been there for hours, not just a few minutes since lunch. She gave off the air of someone who couldn't get worked up about anything—or as someone who had seen the movie *Hackers* too many times.

Eve looked up. "Hey, Phin. You didn't tell me you knew a famous author."

"I told you I had a friend in space who I wanted to see," Phineas said. "How many people live in space right now who aren't famous authors?"

"Four," Mallory supplied, and Phineas elbowed her.

"So, you two have already met?" he asked.

"We had a weirdly tense lunch, yeah," Mallory said. "Had you met Aaron before?" she asked Eve.

Eve shook her head. She pulled back her hood and pushed back her hair. "No, I wanted to get an agent, but I'd never had the chance or anything good to send." She turned to look outside the window to see Eternity's Gneiss shuttle bay, showing Mallory her right cheek, which had a shiny scar from her ear to her chin.

"So, you're throwing your own murder mystery convention to bring the agents to you?" Mallory asked. "That's brilliant, really."

"It helps if the agent doesn't run away after the meeting," Eve said, annoyed.

"Yeah, I don't know what happened there," Mallory said. She briefly outlined the awkward lunch to Phineas. "Then he disappeared in the elevator with Jack and Cosima staring daggers at him, and I got pulled by security."

"Yeah, Pablo sent me a message," Eve said. "Sorry about that."

Mallory shrugged. "Just doing his job." Guessing that Eve didn't like direct eye contact, she approached the wall of monitors, fascinated. "So, what do you write?"

"Thrillers, mostly. Stories with stalking, catfishing, gaslighting, and a lot of blood at the end," Eve said.

"So, are you following the 'write what you know' advice?" Mallory asked.

"Sort of. Worked for you, right?"

"Yeah, I guess it did," she said. "What did you think of lunch?"

"Your agent was sweating through his suit," Eve said, spinning in a circle again. "He really didn't want to be there."

"He was okay with me and Cosima. So whoever made him uncomfortable was Jack, Bruce, or Kath," Mallory said.

"Or me," Eve said. "You don't have to gloss over it."

Mallory was transfixed by the cat room. One cat was jumping from the floor onto a couch covered in tinfoil. When it hit the foil, it jumped high in the air, hit the floor, and ran. Across the room, cats sat on robot vacuums with regal disdain and pretended not to see each other.

"Why would Aaron be so scared of you?" Mallory asked.

"People think I spy on them with *Metis*," Eve said, looking at the monitors. "So anyone who is uncomfortable around me, I assume they think that I know their secrets."

"Do you?" Mallory asked, glancing over at the young woman.

"For Aaron? Nah. He sits in his room and frowns at his computer a lot. If that's a secret, then every writer has the same secret."

"So, you do see inside their rooms?" Mallory asked. "See them dressing and everything?"

Eve raised a sleek eyebrow. "Technically, I can, but I haven't yet found someone who I want to watch undress, scratch their ass, sit on the toilet, not wash their hands, and then masturbate them-selves to sleep."

Mallory gaped at her. "That was a really specific list of things, which makes me think you've done them."

Eve nodded. "Yeah. Which is why I only did it once."

Mallory laughed and shook her head. "Do you know why he would be afraid of the others? Had you met them before lunch?"

"No, I spend most of my time here."

"You're a mystery writer running a mystery convention, and you're not attending?" Mallory asked.

"I have to help *Metis*," Eve said, patting the desk in a gentle way. "She hasn't been around anyone for hundreds of years, and now she has a bunch of mystery nerds on board."

Mallory seized the topic. "I really want to hear how you found *Metis*. Can you tell me?"

Eve sighed. "I moved to the Outer Banks after I sold my com-pany," she said, as if it were normal for people under thirty to sell companies and retire to the graveyard of the Atlantic. "One day I tripped over something in a dune. Turned out to be *Metis*."

"So, how did you get involved?" Mallory asked Phineas.

"Eve contacted me. She was a fan and had heard about my brother being aboard Eternity, and figured if anyone on Earth could help her with sentient ships, it would be me. I had some free time, so I went to check it out. We hired someone to dig her out."

Eve pointed to two chairs that weren't there before. "Sit down if you're going to hear the story." She must have seen the look of disbelief on Mallory's face. "And, no, she wasn't this big when I found her. We would have broken one of the islands in half just digging her out. She was about the size of a standard shuttle, maybe a little smaller."

Phineas nodded. "Xan told me she needed bio-matter or, even better, oil, to grow. So every night she'd fly out to the ocean, dive in, and absorb whatever she could from the ocean floor."

"What made you want to get her big enough to carry the Internet?" Mallory asked.

Eve turned to the desk and moved a mouse around. A picture of a very small *Metis* popped up on one of the displays. "It wasn't my plan to make that happen. As she got her memory back, she told me she was a data ship, and she had crashed a long time ago. I didn't tell her how much to eat; who knows how much a living ship needs to survive? The first night she came back after feeding in the Atlantic, she had doubled in size. She was telling me she was hungry for data, so I showed her the Internet." Eve shook her head slowly, smiling fondly. "Sometimes I wonder if that was a good idea."

"Does she have her own Sundry hivemind?" Mallory asked.

"Yeah, she apparently had a specific pheromone she could release to attract a queen," Eve said. "She found an Earth-based queen who was eager to go to space."

"Apparently she was descended from a long line of the first Sundry to go to Earth," Phineas said. "I don't quite get it all. I didn't look under the hood."

"So, you showed her the Internet," Mallory prompted.

"And she wanted all of it. Kept telling me she wanted more. She'd come in every morning bigger than the day before, wanting more data." Eve frowned. "Learning what she was capable of was a shock."

"What do you mean?" Mallory asked.

"She can make anything. It's more than an illusion, what she can make is real so long as you're on the ship."

"Can't most sentient ships do that?" Mallory asked.

Eve shook her head. "I don't think you have the scope of what I'm saying. We're talking the *Star Trek* holodeck, but it's the whole damn ship. She takes the data and she creates a living embodiment of a room." Eve pointed to the monitor with all the cats. "That is the cat video room. She created it based on every cat video on the Internet." She pointed to another room that showed a red-skinned troll riding on the back of a dinosaur. "Every single game played online is replicated here. Every fan-fic ever written. It's all here, and *Metis* makes it real." Eve paused a moment to let that sink in.

"One of the reasons we don't want people messing around in the rest of the ship is that we don't want people to know how powerful she is. Not a lot of the other people at the convention know that she can make literally *anything*. You want a tree over there, boom, she makes one. You want to Star-Trek the hell out of a room, then you have a holodeck with Patrick Stewart there as a musketeer. She makes rooms out of information. She can make *people* out of information."

"People?" Mallory said, astonished. "Can they exist outside the ship?"

She shook her head. "No, but they can be as living as you and me inside."

"But where did she come from?" Mallory asked. "No ship that I've ever heard of is that advanced! Even Eternity isn't that advanced!"

"She doesn't remember much about where she's from," Eve said. "That's another reason we've come to Eternity."

"Mrs. Brown recently got back from learning more about sentient ships and stations," Mallory said. "I think you should talk to her."

Eve nodded. "Thanks."

"Speaking of sentient ships, has *Metis* kept mine safe?" Mallory asked hopefully.

"Yeah, *Metis* says he's on a secret mission for her," Eve said after a moment. "I think she's giving him an adventure to keep him busy." She paused. "No, wait, he's really on a mission for her. Do you want to tell me what that is, *Metis*?"

Eve looked at Mallory, her face flat. "She does not want to tell me."

"That can't be good," Mallory said.

"But he's a ship, right? So he should be fine anywhere," Phineas said. "Have you tried calling him?"

Mallory glared up at him. "Of course I have. But I don't think he's strong enough to hear me over distance. Or if our bond isn't strong enough. This is a big ship. I don't know."

"Don't worry, *Metis* will take good care of him," Phineas said, putting his large hand on her shoulder.

Mallory and Eve shared a look. They both knew that *Metis* refusing to confide in her host was bad news.

"But she says he's fine. Safe?" Mallory asked.

"Yes, she promises that," Eve said. "The moment she gives me any more info, I will let you know. Just think of him like he's in childcare or something." Her stony expression belied the cheerful words coming out of her mouth.

Mallory chewed her bottom lip. *What do you do when your ship disobeys you? Not like you can force them or punish them.*

"I can assure you that *Mobius* is fine," said a voice over a speaker, making Mallory jump.

"*Metis?*" she asked.

Eve nodded. "Do not put that ship in any danger, *Metis*, he's not like you."

"He's helping me. It's fine," *Metis* said, her voice warm and friendly.

"But you won't tell me what he's doing for you," Eve said.

"That is correct."

"Fuck," she muttered.

"I think your guests would like a tour of the ship," *Metis* said. "Other humans are arriving from Eternity soon. There will be a party at the convention tonight."

"Shit, the convention," Mallory said. "I'd almost forgotten."

"When did you become a hostess?" Eve asked the ship, annoyed. "You don't talk this much to anyone."

"No one else has understood me like you," *Metis* said.

"Whatever," she said. "Phineas can give you a tour. I need to stay up here for a bit."

"Hey, you should talk to Aaron again if you can. It's an excellent time to meet people."

Eve rubbed the scar on her face absently. "Yeah, cool. I will."

14

LIVE ACTION

WHEN THINKING BACK, Mallory wondered if the house of cards started to fall with what happened next or if it was earlier. But she stepped off the lift with Phineas to get a tour of the convention space and immediately was grabbed by Aaron.

"Mallory! Thank God you're here," he said, taking her wrist. "There's been a murder."

His shirt was smeared with red, and his hair was messed up. A bruise was blooming on his cheek.

"What happened?" she demanded.

"A convention attendee was found stabbed," Aaron said, leading her by the wrist toward what looked like a panel room.

Inside stood about twelve people, some of them looking awkward and expectant, some of them looking terrified. One of them, a pale teen wearing a deerstalker hat and no other attempt at cosplay, smiled and then quickly hid it.

I'll have to keep an eye on that one, Mallory thought. She looked up at Phineas. "No one enters or leaves. If the killer is still here, even." She looked around the room. "Where is Pablo?"

"Who?" Aaron asked blankly.

"Pablo. Convention security." Everyone looked baffled. "No one thought to call security? Christ." Mallory rubbed her forehead and then realized she had transferred some of the blood from Aaron onto her forehead. "Shit."

There was a body lying across the table at the front of the room where the panelists would sit. It was a young Black woman with a teased Afro wearing a white bodysuit. Blood had splashed from her chest to her face. Mallory looked around the room. "Who has the murder weapon?"

Everyone else in the room—which she now realized included Kath, Bruce (who was holding the ugly alien again), Jason, and Cosima—all looked at Aaron.

"It's gone," Aaron said. "We found her like this."

"You as in Aaron, or you as in the dozen or so of you?" Mallory asked, disbelief coloring her voice.

"All of us," the smiling teen said. "I'm Reginald Baker the Third, an oil tycoon from Texas." He pointed to the woman on the table. "And that's my ex-wife Barbara."

Mallory turned slowly, her entire head feeling like it would catch on fire. Everyone was looking at her. A few were smiling. "Is this a joke?" She gave the "corpse" a firm poke to her ribs, and the body flinched. "Jesus, you were just crying wolf."

The woman propped herself on one elbow and looked at Aaron. "When do I get to do my flashback? I wasn't clear on that." She rubbed her face and scowled at the blood on her hands. "You better not have gotten any blood in my hair."

"This was all a game. You unbelievable bastard," Mallory said, her voice low and dangerous.

"No!" Aaron blanched. "I told you . . . you were going to star in a LARP. The Live-Action Role-Play. That's today. Everyone here has roles, they're all suspects, and you're supposed to be the sleuth."

"Yeah, because I really want to play a game that makes light of the most stressful times of my life," Mallory said. "Especially when you don't tell me that it's a game. You could have told me it was starting. You could have given me a schedule. You could have said anything helpful." Some in the audience were now giving each other awkward looks. Others were straight up enjoying the spectacle. Mallory's embarrassment and rage were making her lightheaded. She walked up to Aaron and made herself keep her hands off him, but she pointed a finger in his face. "Fuck you, man. Fuck you for not taking me seriously and treating me like a prop in your little game. You're fired."

Feeling that she deserved a Nobel Peace Prize for not hitting Aaron in his astonished face, she stalked from the room.

"Mallory!" she heard behind her, and then a squawk.

"You can stay back here," Phineas said. "Don't make this worse on yourself."

Mallory stopped in the middle of the hall and looked around. She didn't even have anywhere to go. This wasn't her home. There was a whole lot of vacuum between her and home.

"Fuck," she said, balling up her fists. She headed for the terrible hotel restaurant instead.

SHE WAS WELL into her Bloody Mary when someone took the seat beside her. She didn't look over. She instead wondered how badly she could hurt someone with a cocktail garnish sword.

"I saw what happened," Eve said.

Surprised at her attention, Mallory turned. "You were watching?"

"Only because *Metis* told me what was going on," she said, holding her hands up. "She was concerned for you."

"So a ship that has known me for fifteen minutes knows me better than my own agent does," Mallory said. "Great. Do you know if *Metis* is taking clients?"

Eve smiled slightly at that. "If she is, I'd better be the first person she signs."

Mallory laughed. "Fair enough."

"You were restrained. I would have probably hurt him," Eve said. "That was a shitty thing to do to you."

"Violence wasn't the answer that time," Mallory said. "Not saying it's not the answer sometimes. No, maybe it was the answer. Who knows? Can't turn back time.

"I don't even know what's going on with Tina back on Eternity. I supposedly have a keynote tomorrow. Why am I letting this get to me?"

"No one likes when the thing they take seriously is being mocked by others. Even if they're not intending to mock," Eve said. "I've been there. Believe me."

Mallory finished off her drink. "Was this real booze?" she asked, pointing to the glass, still red with tomato juice and a stick of celery sticking out of the glass.

Eve nodded. "Yeah, we stocked the restaurant and bar before we left. I'm not sure how *Metis* makes food, but I haven't wanted to try it, and she hasn't taken offense, so I assume it's not really for consumption."

"Good to know." Mallory stretched. "Do you think *Metis* would be able to give me a lift back to Eternity?"

Phineas peeked his head into the restaurant and waved. Mallory waved him over. "Did you kill Aaron?"

"You looking for a murder to solve since the last one ended up going so poorly?" Phineas asked with a smile. "No, I just kept him from following you. Guy was a dick. Are you okay?"

Mallory shrugged. "Just when I think someone takes me seriously, they punch me in the face. I can't believe he did that."

"Same," Phineas said, leaning on the bar. "That was just bad form."

Mallory tried to suck more Bloody Mary out of her empty glass, then put it down with regret. "I wanted to grab a ride back to Eternity and see how Xan and Tina are doing—shit, but I can't because *Mobius* is still somewhere on this ship, and I am not leaving him again."

"Oh, I didn't have a chance to tell you," Phineas said. "They're on their way over. Tina and Xan are coming via Stephanie."

"Oh," Mallory said. "Then maybe *Metis* can lend me a room so I can sleep off this embarrassment and anger."

"You're thinking of being high or drunk. That's what you can sleep off. Emotions, not so easy to shed," Phineas said with the tone of one who's been there. "Why not just hang out here? There's a party in an hour, it looked fun."

Mallory laughed. "Go to a party? Not only after I'm humiliated at the con, but where a murder might actually happen?"

"Yeah," Phineas said. "Why stop having fun? Can't let them win. Vagina Dentata V is playing, and I might have a turn on-stage, too."

Mallory pursed her lips and thought. She would like to see other mystery nerds (maybe not the people who attended the LARP). She had come to Eternity to escape the frequent deaths that followed her around, and she'd made a life on Eternity, but sometimes it was hard to find a human to talk to, and the culture divide between species was massive.

"I'm not dressing up. Or dancing," she added.

"You're welcome to be a cranky wallflower," he said. "But I think you should be there. You might even have fun."

Mallory looked at Eve. "Are you going to be there?"

Eve looked at her blankly. "Do I look like someone who likes to party?"

"Come on, Mal, you've never seen me onstage!" Phineas said.

"Fine. I'll be there," she relented. "But if there's a murder, you have to solve it."

Phineas shared a quick look with Eve, then nodded. "Sure."

Eve cleared her throat. "About murders, Mallory, you can relax.

Metis will be able to see whatever is going on, and if there is a murder that takes place, she'll be able to tell us who did it."

"With respect, your ship just flat out told you she's doing something that she doesn't want you to know about. I believe she sees everything, but I don't believe she'll tell you all that she sees."

Eve glared at her, then sighed. "You're not wrong. I don't know what's going on there."

It was true that she'd never seen Phineas perform in person. And she did have to wait for *Mobius* to come back. "All right. I'll be at the party. I can always leave if Aaron tries to bug me."

"He won't. I put the fear of Phineas in him."

"You wouldn't hurt a fly," Mallory scoffed.

"True, but Tina would. And she's on her way over right now."

The image of Tina chasing Aaron through *Metis* was so absurd that Mallory had to laugh. "If we have an hour before the party, how about showing me some of *Metis*?"

"Sure thing," Phineas said.

XAN JOINED MALLORY and Phineas on their tour of the station. He left Tina behind to talk to some friends she had made at the convention.

They hadn't been friends so much as they'd been humans who were too scared to walk away while Tina was talking to them. But whatever kept Tina occupied worked.

Xan felt a little guilty, like he'd handed his toddler to someone at a picnic so he could go smoke a cigarette or something.

But only a little.

"What happened to you?" Xan asked Mallory. Her face was drawn tight as if she were anticipating feeling pain at any moment. Dark circles had appeared under her eyes.

"I don't want to talk about it," she muttered.

"Her agent started the murder mystery LARP without telling

her that it was a game," Phineas supplied. "She got mad and fired him."

"Phineas, I just said—" Mallory said, grabbing his elbow.

"You said you didn't want to talk about it," Phineas said. "You didn't say I couldn't, so I filled him in."

"Pedantic asshole," she grumbled.

"Fuck, that had to suck, Mal," Xan said. "I'm sorry."

Mallory shrugged. "It's over. I need a new agent now. Someone who won't have me change genres immediately."

"You still going to do the keynote?" Xan asked.

Mallory blinked, then swore. "I forgot about it again. I don't think pulling out would be a bad thing at this point. Twelve people on this boat probably think I'm a cranky bitch who can't take a joke anyway."

"Where are we headed, little brother?" Xan asked. They'd passed several doors in a long hallway at this point.

"Be patient," Phineas said. "Tell me what's up with you? Still seeing that fine ambassador?"

Mallory looked up briefly but masked her face immediately. Xan grimaced inwardly. He hadn't told her they'd been dating.

"Yeah, we've been spending some time together," Xan said, rubbing the back of his head. "I think she wants to turn me into a diplomat or something. I keep telling her that the US won't make an AWOL soldier a diplomat, but she's persistent."

"Also stubborn," Mallory added, then colored. "Sorry. But weren't you honorably discharged?"

"Yeah, but I can't help but think they have me on a couple of lists by now," he said.

Months earlier, Xan had attended a disastrous birthday party on the army base where he was stationed. The birthday boy was stabbed during a game and fell into Xan's arms. Xan, high on a spiked drink, ran to avoid a murder charge and accidentally went AWOL when *Infinity* abducted him. She'd been taking three

Gneiss (Tina, Stephanie, and Ferdinand) on a trip—a spring break
kind of trip, the way Tina told it—and had decided to pick him up.
Autopilot kicked in and took the Gneiss back to Eternity with their
new friend.

Xan had been privy to confidential US plans regarding alien
life and had tried to be a whistleblower, so the army sent an assas-
sin after him. When the dust settled, Mrs. Brown (who liked Xan,
and was also breaking her own parole by leaving the Earth) promised he would be safe as long as he stayed aboard Eternity.

The honorable discharge came after he helped save many human lives aboard Eternity, but he knew better than to ask for more.
He still knew the US secrets and they typically didn't like people
the government couldn't control to know confidential information.

Besides, the only place that would make sense for him to be an
ambassador would be on Eternity, and his girlfriend, ex-WNBA
player Jessica Brass, already filled that role.

"I think you'd be a good diplomat," Mallory said, squinting at
Xan as if seeing him for the first time. "But you're right. The US
government wouldn't be on board." She paused, biting her lip.
"Are you sure that you're safe getting close to Jessica? That she
doesn't have an agenda to bring you back when she visits Earth?"

This was why he hadn't talked to Mallory about Jessica. That
they didn't like each other was no secret. Jessica thought Mallory
was chaotic, untrustworthy, and not the prime example of human-
ity that should interact daily with aliens. Mallory just thought Jessica was uptight and didn't like being treated like a kid who wasn't
invited to the birthday party.

The problem was, they both were right.

Xan tried to keep the annoyance from his tone. "I think I'm
capable of identifying when people are trying to trick me."

Despite his friendly tone, Mallory picked up on his mood immediately and let the subject drop.

THE THING WAS, Xan had wondered the same thing about Jessica. Just yesterday morning she had invited him to go back with her on her next trip to Earth. Xan had said no immediately, but she pressed, reminding him of all the food he could eat, and that he could go shopping for some new clothes that better suited a life aboard a space station. He never thought she would turn him in, but she was a diplomat who would have to report to Washington, DC, and every step toward the East Coast would be dangerous for him.

In theory he could go back. He wanted to see Phineas on his brother's home turf. He'd neglected Phineas in their teen years and it was difficult to make up for that time when he was living light-years away on a space station. And on top of that, Phineas was a hip-hop artist known as Salty Fatts, and it was no secret that he was Xan's brother. So if someone wanted to force Xan to do something, they just had to find his high-profile brother and use Phineas's safety as leverage against Xan.

This hadn't happened yet, but going back to Earth would put him in their crosshairs again, and he'd rather stay on the station. Jessica hadn't seen that yet. Or maybe she wouldn't accept it.

METIS WAS MASSIVE. Phineas filled Xan in on her history, saying that fully half of her physical storage was the database that held the Internet.

"Only half?" Mallory asked.

"Making all of this takes a lot of computing power, Mal," Phineas said. "Especially this room we're going to."

"Which is?" Xan prompted.

"*Metis*'s favorite room," Phineas said. He stopped and put his hand on the door that displayed the silhouette of a kitten and a ball of yarn.

"Oh, yes," came a soft voice through a speaker. "So many cute animals. You'll love it."

Inside the cat room, Mallory didn't know what to react to first. Several people wearing convention badges had strayed from the convention to find this room and were delightedly playing with cats. Secondly, the people sat around on cushions and chairs and beds, many trying to fit into oversized cardboard boxes with cats, all of them looking drunk or stoned, just happy to be in a room surrounded by cats. The third thing was that about half the cats in the room were milling about another creature who was literally on a pedestal in front of the room. They looked up to it, yowling, purring, and rubbing their heads against the pillar. Every few seconds there would be a scuffle as to who got to rub against the pillar first.

Atop the pillar was the ugly yellow alien Miu.

"That should not be happening, where the hell is that dentist?" Mallory asked, looking around. She spied Bruce and Kath sitting on a love seat and stomped over to him.

"Hey, Mallory!" Bruce said, holding a huge black cat in his lap. "Isn't he magnificent?"

"Why did you let the alien out of your sight again?" Mallory asked.

"He's right over there," he said, pointing to the pedestal. "He's not hurting anyone. Relax."

Mallory thought of her humiliation with the LARP and bristled.

"And I thought the rest of the ship was off-limits to convention folks?" Mallory asked. "How did you get here?"

Bruce looked askance, like a child trying to think up a lie. "The Miu wanted to come here, so we followed it. I guess some people followed us, and it snowballed."

"Uh-huh," Mallory said. "How did the Miu know it was here? What is it doing here?"

"I don't know," Bruce said. "If I found a room where I could be worshipped, I would definitely want to hang out there."

Mallory stared up at the alien, who seemed to be smiling at her with its weird human mouth.

"It's a fucking Cheshire cat," she said, shuddering. "Just keep an eye on it. I'm going to have to lock it away if you can't."

Bruce shook his head. "No way, that little guy needs freedom."

Mallory was about to reply when she felt something sharp on her ankles and calves. About seven kittens were all trying to climb her jeans. Kath made some sappy cute noises and Mallory tried to pick them off her legs without hurting them. Even though she knew the cats weren't real, she couldn't imagine that the humans in the room would take kindly to her mistreating one. (Or the cats, for that matter.)

Killed by a roomful of fake cats. That would be an interesting murder weapon.

This looked like a room that would successfully distract a cat lover for the rest of their lives. One could wither away and die here and be happy the whole time. Like an opium den.

Mallory took a look behind her, noticing that Kath and Bruce weren't sitting as closely as she had seen them earlier, and Kath hadn't participated in the conversation with Mallory at all. She dangled a string for a tabby, turned away from Bruce and Mallory.

Xan touched her arm and pointed to the wall. "You have to see this." A dancing red dot appeared on the wall closest to them. A cat's favorite toy: the laser pointer. It danced around, attracting several cats. One tabby put her paws on the wall and tried to bat at the light. It moved away, but it also seemed to get . . . bigger?

Another cat batted it, and the game went on; every time a paw touched the red light, it got bigger. Xan looked around to see where the light was coming from, but he couldn't tell.

When the light was as large as a dinner plate, one cat simply jumped through it and disappeared.

"Holy shit," said Xan. "Did that cat just disappear?"

"Yeah, it did," Mallory said. "*Metis* is capable of so many things, but we're using it to make cats jump through walls."

"You don't find that creepy?" Xan asked, touching the wall where the cat had jumped, trailing his fingers over what used to be a brief hole. He stopped when a kitten attacked his fingers.

"Oh, definitely," she said. "Most things in this room are creepy."

"Aw, don't tell me you hate cats," Phineas said.

"I resent cats that are designed to distract me from important things, like where that alien is and how some can communicate with it and some can't."

Xan perked up for a moment. "Shit. That's right. About that." He motioned for Mallory to follow him and he went to sit on a black couch, gently pushing aside cats to make room for them.

He explained what happened when Mrs. Brown and the ambassadors (and the Sundry) interrogated Tina.

"You were in a *colosseum*?" Mallory asked, eyes wide. "Like Russell Crowe and shiny muscles, that kind of colosseum?"

"He wasn't there, and I kept my shirt on, but yeah, pretty much," he said. A cat stepped on his lap and sniffed his chin, paused for a moment, then turned around and shoved her butt in his face. He pushed her off, but another one took her place.

He finally let a small black cat settle down on his lap. "Tina's cagey about this, but I have a theory that the Cuckoos have a language, they just haven't shared it with the galactic translation databases. And since all Cuckoos live on Bezoar—"

"Then they must have their own translation database there," Mallory said, eyes growing wide. "Their own language is there, and they can choose who to share it with."

"And who else may have translation data there?" Xan said. "I think we need to access the Cuckoo hiveminds on Bezoar."

Mallory's Sundry escorts took flight then, flying well above the height where cats could try to catch them. They circled Mallory's and Xan's heads. "No, no, the Cuckoos aren't sophisticated enough, they can't have their own databases. They can barely create their own hivemind."

"They created a hivemind sophisticated enough to take over Eternity," Mallory reminded them. "You guys said that you had lost data about them on purpose to not be reminded of how they could defeat you. You think you might be biased as to their abilities now?"

The Sundry hovered there for a moment, then went to go perch high up on a nearby wall.

Immediately the air filled with clacking sounds as cats noticed them and realized they couldn't reach the shiny blue prey that had just appeared on the wall.

"We need that database," Mallory said.

"Or we need the Cuckoos to just share their information," Xan said.

"Do you think Tina would help us?" Mallory asked.

"Doubt it. When the subject of communicating with the Cuckoos came up, she got really evasive."

"Then clearly there's something she's hiding."

"Who's hiding?" Phineas asked, coming up to them.

"Tina," Xan said. "Hiding information about how the Cuckoos communicate, whether they have a hivemind, all that jazz."

"Let's figure it out tomorrow," Phineas said. "I have to go back to the hall and get ready for a concert."

15

· · · ·

THE SHOW MUST GO ON

ETIS HAD A grand auditorium with bars on upper and lower levels, every seat had a good view of the stage, and there was plenty of room to dance and plenty of corners in which to brood.

Mallory occupied one of the corners. She was still feeling prickly, especially since Jessica had arrived to attend the party with Xan. Mallory chose the best corner near the upper-level bar so she could watch everything and not be observed.

The opening band was the Uncomfortable Shoes, a band Mallory had never heard of. They did a strange cover of the Dead Kennedys song "Nazi Punks Fuck Off," which was sung by a five-year-old. They weren't good, but they were memorable; Mallory had to give them that.

Most of the rest of the songs were punk covers, and since Mallory wasn't a huge fan of punk, she watched the crowd.

Jessica and Xan drew her eye immediately. They were a beautiful couple, no doubt. Jessica had the body of an athlete and the poise of a diplomat. They hung out near the bar on the lower level, Jessica sipping wine and standing very stiffly. "Punk" and "ambassador" didn't go well together, Mallory guessed.

Although "Ambassador Punk" would be a kick-ass name for a band.

The Uncomfortable Shoes did get some people dancing during their set of five songs. Then Phineas came onstage.

Mallory had known he was multitalented, and she'd heard his albums, but seeing him perform was a new level. Phineas was six feet tall and about three hundred pounds, but he moved like he was in a ballet. He started with beatboxing and performed a song about *Areopagitica* by John Milton (getting a rhyme for "Areopagitica" was a feat in itself), and then he sang an original sea shanty about a lonely ship in deep deep space. Then he sang a cover of a sci-fi hip-hop song by clipping "Air 'Em Out," which got the whole auditorium moving.

Mallory spotted Kath in the audience, hanging on the edge of the pit. She was clearly waiting for a moment to get close to the stage once VDV came on.

Where was Bruce? Wouldn't he want to be there with her?

But what if he brought the alien here? Mallory had no idea what loud human music would do to it. How sensitive was its hearing? Could sound damage it? Tina probably knew.

And there Bruce was, far on the other side, nearly mirroring Kath's position on the floor. He had the alien draped across his shoulders like it was a fur stole.

Phineas finished his set to loud screams and accolades. He waved pleasantly and left the stage.

"Someone isn't going to have a problem having a sexy sexy night after a set like that," Mallory mused. "But who will be the lucky man?"

"Not a music fan?" came the question directly behind her. It was the young writer, Jack.

"Not a fan of parties," Mallory corrected. "I'm always here for Phineas's music."

"He was pretty good, yeah." Jack looked around the balcony. "Do you have a second? I want to talk about Aaron."

Mallory snorted in derision. "I have nothing to say to him."

"You'd be talking to me," he said. "I'm not going to try to convince you to unfire him or whatever."

Mallory followed him to a back row of seats as the next band set up for their show.

"I'm new at this," Jack admitted, ducking his head a little bit. "What I know about money is the monthly deposits into my bank account from Twinkle and Glutton."

Mallory looked at him blankly.

"T&G is a video streaming service and the biggest self-pub platform around right now," he said. "They pay out monthly. So when I had new Zesty stories, I knew that three months later I would get some cash."

"All right," Mallory said. "But now you've sold *Pruned* and you're learning about the weird world of advances?"

Jack leaned in and whispered, "Yes! That's it exactly! First Aaron told me that he sold the rights to Zesty for five hundred thousand bucks!"

Mallory whistled. "Nice!"

"But they're splitting it up in four payments over five books, so I get a little chunk at a time. Then Aaron said he has to take his cut, so my first payment was something like forty-five thousand. Does that seem right to you?"

Mallory shrugged. "Agents have to take their cut. Still not a bad payday."

He ducked his head. "I know, but I didn't think the math worked out."

"Okay, let's look at the math," Mallory said. "Five books for five hundred K, so that's one hundred K per book." He nodded. "And they split it evenly into signing advance, outline approval, final draft delivery, and publication?"

He nodded again.

Mallory did some quick math. "So your first advance would have been for all five books, so it will end up being your largest advance, which would be one hundred twenty-five K. Take out the agent's percentage, so your check should be . . . eighty-five percent of one hundred twenty-five, I'm not sure what that is, but it's definitely more than forty-five."

"He just said something about his fees and his percentage and told me to put some cash aside and be happy with the advance he got me."

"That's insulting," Mallory said.

"Anyway, I wanted to ask you if you were giving him forty percent?"

Mallory choked on her water. "Forty! You're giving him *forty*?" He nodded miserably. "No, no, no, agents get fifteen percent, twenty tops but only if they're working with another agency and they both get ten." She wiped the water off her face. "I can't believe he's doing this."

"Have you seen anything weird going on with your royalties?" he asked.

"I'm definitely not giving forty percent to Aaron . . ." Mallory said, and then trailed off as she wondered. When was the last time she had looked at the reports and done the math? Aaron could have altered the results, and if she didn't do the math behind him, then she'd never know. You were supposed to trust the agent to do the math!

"I'll have to check my records to see if he's stealing from me. But he's definitely stealing from you, bud."

"That's why he was so nervous during lunch," Jack mused. "He knew I was going to ask."

"I thought you cornered him in the elevator?" Mallory said.

Jack made a frustrated noise. "No, he ran off the first chance he got, and that cosplayer got in my way, so I couldn't follow him."

"He had to know it would come up. Why is he stealing from you?"

Jack had gone very still. He shook his head. "I was making eighty-five grand a month when I was self-publishing. I went the traditional route based on Aaron's guidance, so now I'm getting paid less, and less often, and now I'm being stolen from."

"Look, we caught it. You can confront him, or you can hire a lawyer when you get back to Earth."

"I like confronting, I like it a lot," Jack said, and stood up. "Thanks for your time, Mallory."

"Maybe not, Jack! Maybe don't confront a lot!" she shouted.

But he was gone.

"Jesus, that kid is fast," Mallory said. She felt she should have followed, but she had no dog in this race. And catching up might mean seeing Aaron again, and maybe confronting him herself about stealing, and she needed the receipts before she did that.

She looked down at the floor below, people milling about, some waiting anxiously, some just chilling and enjoying themselves.

Bruce was still on the far left side of the mosh pit (which had calmed down to a "milling about" pit), but Kath was gone. Mallory expected them both to be up front by now in anticipation of their band. But maybe they had reached an age where slam dancing in a mosh pit sounded less than fun, and Kath had gotten a seat somewhere else. Mallory scanned the seated area and didn't see her.

She was ready to give up looking for Kath when she saw a woman stagger out of the restroom on the left wall, her hands bloody.

Mallory ran.

ON THE BOTTOM floor, she intercepted the woman before she could make too much of a fuss. "What happened?" she asked, putting her hands on the woman's shoulders. Then she drew back. "Cosima?"

The assistant had put on high heels, let her hair down, and had makeup and glitter on her face. She had transformed, and she didn't look that bad to begin with.

"Cosima, show me what you found," she said.

She gritted her teeth as she led Cosima into the bathroom. *I swear to all the alien gods, if this is another prank by Aaron, I'm going to—*

There was no prank with the way Aaron's head was twisted around, blood on his lips.

Then Cosima pointed to one of the stalls where Kath slumped on the floor, leaning against the toilet, blood pooling beside her.

The blood was still flowing. That meant her heart was still beating.

"Eve! *Metis*! We need some help at the concert!" Mallory yelled.

"Who are you talking to?" Cosima said to the mirror as she cleaned her face of tears and other fluids.

"The ship. She should be able to hear and see everything going on, and we should be able to ask her for help."

But *Metis* didn't reply.

"I guess the stress of seeing your boss dead has passed?" Mallory asked, raising an eyebrow.

Cosima met her eyes in the mirror. "I recover quickly."

"Then can you recover and help me move Kath off the toilet?"

Cosima got Kath's legs and together they moved her out of the stall and laid her flat on the floor to see what was wrong with her.

She had a deep wound in her arm that dripped blood steadily. It was bad, but not one that should have knocked her out.

"Apply pressure to her arm," Mallory said. "I'm going to examine her head."

Gently probing Kath's skull, Mallory found a goose egg leaking blood right above her ear.

Neither *Metis* nor Eve answered Mallory's shouts. No one was coming to help. And no one could hear her; outside the restroom a guitar thrummed and the crowd started screaming. And those hundreds of people outside the door could easily panic and cause a stampede, injuring more than just Kath.

"What can I do?" asked Cosima. She had cleaned herself up almost entirely except for a smear of blood on her white dress. She looked at Mallory with dignified control.

She definitely calmed down a little too quickly, Mallory thought.

"I'm going to call someone else for help. You stand outside the door and make sure that no one gets in until they get here."

"How do I know who's supposed to come in?" Cosima asked.

Mallory smiled grimly. "You'll know." She started a call on her watch to Stephanie. "Steph, I need Tina. Like right now."

To her credit, Stephanie had learned enough about human tone and inflection to respond immediately and not wonder what the hell Mallory would need Tina for. "All right. I'll get her. Where are you?"

PHINEAS FINISHED HIS set, and Xan was enjoying the high he got off seeing his baby brother perform. He knew Phineas was talented, but he hadn't spent a lot of time with him since he was eighteen and Phineas was fourteen. Xan had gone off to college, and then the army, and then Eternity.

"Damn, is my little brother amazing, or is he amazing?" he asked, grinning widely.

"Yeah, he's really great!" Jessica said with obviously false enthusiasm.

He felt a splinter of irritation in his chest. *An ambassador should be a better liar.* He drained his cider and motioned to the bartender, an unusually gregarious Gneiss, to give him another.

"Same thing or something spicier?" asked the Gneiss. She was a lovely gray gradient tone and she kept trying to get Xan to drink things that would definitely burn the shit out of his throat.

"Same thing, don't be an enabler, Susan," he said with a laugh.

Jessica came up beside him. "If this ship has been on Earth for hundreds of years, and this is its first trip into space since then, how did you get aboard to work here?"

"What is wrong with you?" Xan asked. "Next you're going to ask to see her papers?"

"It's suspicious," Jessica said. "I just want to make sure she's supposed to be here."

The Gneiss gave Jessica a blank look for several seconds. "I was visiting Earth, and I was trying to book a shuttle to Eternity. I met Eve at the shuttle port, and she said she needed a bartender, and that's my trade, so we made a deal, and I'm very interested to know why this is important."

"I'm the ambassador from Earth," Jessica said firmly. "Alien visitation is *my* trade, so to speak. I just had to make sure you were supposed to be here." She finished her wine. "May I have another one of those, please?"

"No," said the Gneiss. She handed Xan his cider and turned away from them to serve other customers.

"Hey, you have one job, and it's not very strenuous," Jessica said. "I'm a paying customer!"

Xan shook his head at her. "Shouldn't you be more diplomatic if you're an ambassador?"

Jessica sighed, putting her hands on her hips. "Well, I heard there was a bar upstairs. I'll go there. Wait here for me?" She turned on her thousand-watt smile, and he couldn't help but smile back.

"Sure," he said.

He wondered where Mallory was, if she had come to see Phineas as she had promised. He couldn't see into the balcony, so she could be up there. Phineas would be really disappointed if she missed it.

Jessica came back in a hurry, without wine. She grabbed his shoulder and pointed Xan toward the crowd on the left side. "Isn't that the human Mallory said would watch over the alien? He should not be here."

Xan followed her line of sight. He recognized the guy—was his name Bruce?—but the large tell was of course the yellow alien around his neck. Xan had started thinking of it as a Cheshire cat.

"Why not? Doesn't look like the alien is in distress, or about to flip out."

"But what if it does?" she said. "That's the danger of a completely new species. We don't know what it likes or fears or finds threatening."

"Then we'll deal with it when we find out. If we can't communicate with it, then we'll never learn anything about it until it shows fear or anger," Xan said.

Jessica rolled her eyes. "Keep an eye on him, all right? I'm going to get that wine and go to the restroom."

Xan shrugged. What was more interesting than the guy with the alien was the young white guy in the audience who clearly wasn't there for music or for a party. He had his arms crossed with his hands tucked between his ribs and arms, head down, leaning against the wall near the restrooms on the right.

Could just be too drunk or fucked up on something else, he reasoned.

"I didn't think a living ship would have a bathroom that's out of service," Jessica said after she finally came back. "I had to find another one."

"Out of service?" Xan asked. "Yeah, that's weird." He looked over to the wall at the restrooms where a small white woman in a glittery dress was firmly pointing people to other bathrooms.

Tina appeared, and if she was shouting her usual phrases, they were drowned out by the crowd. She was met with a wall of people dancing in the aisles. She tried to carefully move them out of the way, and then gave up, fired her jet packs, and flew over.

That got some attention, but Tina's time in the air was brief, as she flew directly through the bathroom door, tearing it from the hinges. The woman in white, who had been smart enough to stand aside, stepped back in front of the door to turn away the newly interested people.

"What the hell is going on over there?" asked Jessica. "The queen shouldn't be involved in anything right now."

"Yeah, you go ahead and tell her that. I'll wait here," he said. "I don't know what's up, but I do know that Mallory's got to be involved," he said. *And,* he didn't say aloud, *she's with a dead body.*

What he didn't guess was there would be two bodies.

When he shouldered his way through the crowd, most of whom were dancing, but others were eager to see what was going on in the restroom, he came up against the formidable small woman in heels. "Restroom's closed, nothing to see here," she said formally, putting her hand on his chest.

"I'm with the band," he said.

"Then use the restroom backstage," she said with a disdainful look.

"No, I mean I'm one of Mallory's friends. I'm here to help."

She sighed, blowing air out of her nose and looking like a disgruntled schoolteacher. "Mallory, do you know a tall Black man with glasses?"

"Xan! Yes, let him in."

The woman stepped aside like a bouncer would and resumed her post.

Xan was going to ask who the tiny gatekeeper was, but the scene in the bathroom stole all words.

Mallory stood up from where she'd been crouching on the floor. She had a lot of blood on her, but none looked to belong to her.

"Cosima," Mal began, pointing to the woman outside the door, "found my agent, Aaron," pointing to the twisted body on the floor, "and the doctor, Kath," pointing to the very bloody woman on the floor. "Aaron is dead, obviously. But we might be able to save Kath."

"That's where the bitch queen comes in!" Tina said happily. "Want me to fly her over to Eternity?"

"God, no!" Mallory and Xan said at the same time. "She can't be in a vacuum."

"I thought she was unconscious?" Tina asked. "Doesn't that mean like our stasis, no moving, no breathing?"

"No, she's still breathing, and going into the vacuum will likely kill her," Xan said. "You need to find a medbay or a hospital or something aboard *Metis*. She has everything, she probably has something somewhere."

He looked at Mal, who was securing a bandage around Kath's head. "Haven't you told *Metis* yet?"

"I tried. I thought she or Eve would respond, but neither did. That's why I called Tina."

"She called me because I help people. I save lives."

"Really? Tina?" he asked, dropping to his knees by Mallory. "Not me, not Ferd, not anyone else? Jessica would have been good. Even Adrian could have his drones help you."

Mallory brushed her hair out of her face, leaving a bloody smear. "Do you really want to talk about this right now? I have a possible killer guarding the door so no one can come in and see her crime scene. I have a living stretcher with a jet pack that I hope will bring this woman somewhere that she can be helped. I called the first person to come to mind who wasn't already doing something else."

He lifted his hands, surrendering. "Nah, I'm good, we can talk later. Or not at all."

Mallory nodded curtly.

Xan saw Jessica hovering outside the door, looking like she was about to give a diplomatic whipping to the woman in her way. He ran out to meet her.

"One dead, one badly injured. Mal needs us to find a medbay or something. Can you do that?"

Jessica took one look inside the bathroom (the gatekeeper had relaxed seeing that she was with Xan) and made a shocked face. "I'll message you when I find something."

"Look for Pablo the security guard! He will help!" Mallory shouted from the floor.

"Did you get that?" Xan asked.

"Got it," Jessica said. She leaned in and kissed him briefly, then exited through the closest door.

"My name is Cosima," the woman in front of him said, shaking his hand. "Sorry for the blockade, but I was following Mallory's orders."

He nodded. "So do you know the victims?"

She grimaced and looked back at the floor. "The guy on the floor was my boss. The woman was one of his clients. Probably."

"'Probably'?"

"She sometimes acted like she knew him, like outside of publishing, but she never said from where, and he didn't recognize her at all. That he told me of, anyway."

Tina stood, stooped almost in half, and picked up Kath's body, Mallory yelling at her to be gentle. She'd already slung Aaron's body over her back, not too concerned with his well-being. Xan reached out and took Cosima's arm to get her out of Tina's way before she was bowled over.

Jessica messaged him with information of where to take the injured woman, and he relayed it to Tina.

"I'm on it!" she shouted, and instead of leaving by the nearest door, decided instead to fire her jet packs again (Xan had to push a few people out of the way of getting burned) and fly over the audience to the rear exits.

Mallory appeared at his side. "Cosima, we can give up the room as soon as we figure out how to get the blood off the floor. Can I borrow Xan a second?"

She drew him aside. "My first guess is someone came to kill Aaron and didn't realize Kath was here, and she was collateral damage."

"Makes sense," he said.

"So we need to keep her safe," Mallory said, lowering her voice even more. "I don't trust anyone around here except for you. Can you—"

"I'm on it," he said, nodding. "If not me, then Ferd. Or we can take her aboard Stephanie or *Infinity* when she gets stable. We have a few options. I'll keep her safe."

Mallory smiled at him, eyes tired. "Thanks. We won't know more for a while. I wish I knew why *Metis* or Eve won't talk to us."

Xan motioned for her to follow him. She stepped over the blood pool—already disappearing, meaning *Metis* was able to absorb from this room even if she didn't want to reply to them—then washed her hands quickly and joined him outside the doors. Several people rushed in after them, but they ignored them. The door was already back to its normal place after Tina's entrance.

As if none of this had happened, the band VDV was still onstage, singing and rocking out. The three of them wore masks, simple black or white full face masks. But you didn't need to see the face to recognize the body that was in front of the microphone, singing and dancing sinuously.

Xan pointed. "I have one idea why you couldn't call Eve."

Eve was the singer for Vagina Dentata V.

16

. . .

RULE 34

MALLORY WAS WAITING in the command center for Eve, who met her there soon after she had politely asked *Metis* to message her.

In the time she was waiting, Mallory was getting frustrated at *Metis*'s refusal to talk.

"I just need to know if you saw anything," she said. "You didn't answer when I called for you in the bathroom. Were you distracted, or what?"

"There is no bathroom in that hall," *Metis* said.

Mallory began pacing in front of the wall of monitors. "But see, there is. I was just there. And there was a murder there. And an assault. So what was going on?"

"I am fully self-aware of every inch within me," *Metis* said. "There is no bathroom there."

Eve showed up then, out of breath and trying to pull a hoodie back on. "Sorry, I was checking something out on the ship. What happened?"

Mallory waited a beat, but Eve didn't say she had been onstage performing after the murder. "Aaron died in the women's bathroom tonight, and Kath was assaulted. I called for help but *Metis* didn't hear me, and now she completely denies there's a bathroom in that auditorium at all."

Eve went pale. "Aaron died in the bathroom? The women's bathroom?"

"Yeah," Mallory said. "Why couldn't *Metis* see it?"

"As I said, I don't look into private areas," Eve began, but Mallory interrupted her.

"You said you don't look. You didn't say you *can't* look."

Eve glared at her. "I don't like what you're implying."

"I'm not implying anything!" Mallory said. "I'm saying what happened. Someone died. Your sentient ship not only denies being aware of it, but denies the room itself exists." She waved her hands at the wall of monitors.

She had a sudden inspiration. "*Metis*, are you aware of your nursing station, or whatever you call your medbay?"

"Of course I am."

"Is there a huge Gneiss queen in there, probably saying a lot of swear words, with a living human and a dead human?"

The ship took a while to answer, then simply said, "No."

Mallory ran her hands through her hair. "What the hell? How can you miss Tina?"

"There is a Gneiss queen saying a lot of swear words and two dead humans. No living humans."

"She's *dead*?" Mallory asked.

"Confirmed," *Metis* said.

Xan messaged her then. "Jess says the woman just died in the medbay."

She replied with a voice call. "How did that happen? She wasn't that injured."

"You'll have to come down here," he said, unhappy. "It's hard to describe."

"Please see what you can get out of *Metis*," Mallory said to Eve.

"Because you now have a killer among a murder mystery convention."

Eve nodded. "We'll help out however we can."

TINA WAS SITTING in the hallway, her massive legs stretched out in front of her, blocking the whole walkway. Xan and Jessica were arguing inside.

Two bodies lay covered on tables, with a human nurse looking distressed between them. Aaron's had been positioned with his head the right way around, but Kath now had a knife sticking out of her chest.

"So, what the hell happened?" Mallory asked, staring at the knife.

"We don't know," Jessica said. "We got the injured woman in here and onto the table. No one else was here, so I went to the hall terminal to call for a doctor or nurse. They said they'd be on their way. I walked back in and she was like this." She gestured at Kath's body, quite dead now.

"Is there a back way into this room?" Mallory asked.

The nurse shook her head. "This is our small ancillary medbay for the convention, so it only has one room. The big medical centers are a few floors down, which is where I was when I got called. I came up to find these two women in the hallway and two dead bodies inside."

"Is that how you remember it, Tina?" Mallory asked.

Tina didn't look at her.

Jessica rolled her eyes. "*Her Majesty* is upset that she didn't save the day."

"That's all we need," Mallory muttered. "So, one door and no one came in or out while you were in the hall."

"That's right," Jessica said, glaring at Xan. "That's exactly how it happened."

"I guess I'll look around here," Mallory said. To the nurse, whose tag said MARCI, she said, "Can you examine the bodies to see if there's something weird about the way they died?"

Marci blanched. "I'm not a coroner."

"You're the closest thing to a coroner we have," Mallory said. "So, surprise, you're a coroner. Unless *Metis* has one on board."

"No," Marci said, frowning. Then she went to Aaron's body and began examining it.

Mallory started looking for any hidden entrances or exits from the room. It was a tiny medbay, about twenty by twenty feet. There were just three cots, a sink, and some metal cabinets containing medical supplies. The ceiling didn't seem to hold any hidden doors, and there were no catches or buttons on the doors to open up into a secret passage.

"Hey, can't *Metis* just make a door if she wants to?" Xan asked. "If that's pretty easy for Eternity, and *Metis* is more sophisticated, then that should be child's play."

"True," Mallory said. She leaned against the wall and closed her eyes. "This ship might as well be magic to us, for all we can figure out how it works."

"The man looks like he died of a broken neck," Marci said. "There's a little bruising on his cheek so it looks like he was dropped directly on his head."

"Dropped?" Mallory said. "How does one get dropped on their head in the women's restroom?"

"And the woman, obviously, has a laceration on her arm, a large bump on her head, and a knife sticking out of her chest." She gave a sardonic look at Jessica. "I'm led to believe the knife wasn't here when the woman arrived."

"I'll have to get *Metis* to set up a toxicology program to run anything else," Marci said. "That may not happen until tomorrow."

Mallory glanced at Xan and Jessica. "I think I'll stay here tonight, if *Metis* will let me. Let's lock these bodies up as best we can. I think tomorrow we need that tour."

Jessica frowned. "A tour? After two people have been murdered?"

"No . . ." Mallory said carefully. "I need to learn more about this ship to see if I can figure out how she works and why she can see some areas, like most of the ship, and not others, like where a murder happened."

"Fair," Xan said. "I'll be around if you need me."

"Thanks," Mallory said, smiling at him. "And thanks for helping get them to the medbay, Jess."

Jessica looked annoyed. "Even though you think I was sloppy by letting the murderer in?"

"I don't think that at all," Mallory said. "Like Xan said, *Metis* was probably involved or manipulated, and you can't fight that."

"Manipulated?" Xan asked. "So, you suspect Eve?"

"She was nearby, but I have no idea what her motive would be. Maybe we'll find out tomorrow."

"Of course we will. It's your thing."

"Yeah, but I wish it would get easier," Mallory said with a sigh.

THE NEXT DAY. Eve said she couldn't be interviewed until the afternoon. Despite the danger, Eve said the convention should continue. Mallory figured she had a point. They couldn't very well send the attendees home. And if they're on the ship, they might as well do something to take up time.

"They would get together in groups to talk about the murder anyway," Eve had told her that morning. "This just makes it structured."

Phineas offered to give Mallory and Xan a look through the ship, even though, he warned, there was no way to look through it all in one day. "Where do you want to start?"

"What do you think we should look at?" Mallory asked. "I guess seeing some of the bigger rooms would be useful. Hang on," she added as inspiration struck. "Is there a Rule 34 room?"

Phineas laughed. "I was hoping you wouldn't ask that. Of course there is, but you don't want to go in there."

"Seriously, Mal? A Rule 34 room?" Xan asked, frowning. "Are you twelve?"

"I don't have a sense of what *Metis* is capable of. Looking at the cat room helps, but a Rule 34 room has got to be impressive. *Metis* wouldn't hurt us, would she?" she asked Phineas.

"Normally, I'd say no," Phineas said. "But like you said, two people died last night, and no one saw anyone go in or out of either room. *Metis* has to know something. But I don't think she would actively hurt you."

He led them to a swinging double door setup in the hall below the cat deck. "You should see this, though," Phineas said, pointing to the sign. YOU PROBABLY HAVE CANCER.

"Oh, this contains the data from all of the medical sites that you search symptoms on," Xan said. "And all roads lead to cancer."

"Exactly," Phineas said. "But I'm showing you this to maybe learn a little about *Metis*'s personality. It looks like a waste of time, but this is where the ship's hospital is.

"Weird," Mallory said, pushing the door open and peeking inside.

Yeah, it looked like a hospital, with triage rooms, blood pressure cuffs, and metal trays of surgical items just sitting around on counters.

Nurse Marci noticed Mallory peeking in and waved to her. Mallory motioned her to come outside.

"Did you find out anything else about the bodies?" Mallory asked.

Marci shook her head. "Not really . . ." She looked at the ground.

"Okay, you have a terrible poker face. What aren't you telling me?"

"I personally think the ship is too complex for *Metis* to track all of it," she said hesitantly.

Mallory poked her in the shoulder. "You're real, right? Not a nurse *Metis* created?"

Marci frowned and stepped away from her. "Yes, Eve hired me."

"How many more people in the hospital are hires?"

"Most of us are hired, but there are several people created by *Metis*," she said. "Most every famous doctor from fiction or television works in some of these hospitals."

"That's got to be weird," Mallory said.

"We don't let them see patients," Marci said. "But I think we hurt *Metis*'s feelings when we decided that."

"Thanks, Marci. Let me know if you find out anything else."

A few floors down, Phineas led them to another door. It had two black numerals on it: 34.

The door was white, segmented like a standard suburban garage door. It looked like the front of a suburban house had been grafted to the wall.

"So, who's going in?" Phineas asked.

"We're not all going?" Mallory asked, looking between them.

"I don't know about y'all, but I wouldn't want to go in there with another person," Phineas said.

"Doesn't seem to be a place you want to be alone in either," Mallory said. She sighed, then opened her mouth to say she would go in since it had been her idea, but Xan beat her to it.

"I'll go."

MISTAKES WERE MADE.

Xan remembered the time Mallory tried to explain what it was like when the Sundry stung her, how she felt forced to drink information from a water hose on full blast. It was like that now, except the information was all sex.

The moment he stepped inside, the door closed and a black tentacle wrapped around his ankle and began to curl up his leg. He lost his footing and fell, but instead of hitting the floor, he fell through it into an inflatable bouncy castle. Then the naked elves came, and then there was pudding, and anthropomorphic cars, and he heard one of the cars say, "You come here at fuck o'clock and don't take part? That's not American!" and then—

A hand grabbed his collar, nearly choking him, and he was yanked back out of the room.

He fell to the floor and curled into a fetal position, shivering. He looked up at the giant who saved him.

"Tina?"

"Mallory and Phineas asked for my help. Even though I'm a queen, I like helping!" She cocked her head and looked curiously at the door. "What was going on with those blue people and the pudding?"

Mallory dropped to her knees next to him, eyes wide. "Jesus, are you okay?"

"I think so," he said. "That was a lot. Why did you call for Tina's help?"

"Because you were in there for an hour, and we were worried we'd fall in if we went to help. We thought Tina could handle the room since it's human focused."

"Really, someone will need to tell me about the pudding," Tina said.

"No," Phineas and Xan said together.

"Curiosity satisfied?" Phineas asked Mallory.

She nodded, glancing anxiously at Xan.

"What did you hope to gain from that exactly?" Xan asked.

"I wanted to know what *Metis* was capable of. Rule 34 says any sex thing you think of is already on the Internet, so I wanted to see what she would do with that."

"She's capable of a lot," Xan said.

"Yeah. But I was pretty sure the ship has something like a pocket dimension inside," she said.

"Multiple pocket dimensions," Phineas corrected.

Mallory put her hand on Xan's shoulder. "I still should have insisted I go instead of you."

"It was my choice," Xan said. "But I see how curiosity could kill the cat. In fact, I think I saw some anthropomorphic cats—"

"Never mind," Mallory said. "Are you good to walk?"

Tina picked him up and placed him on his feet. He grunted as he landed, smoothed his T-shirt, and then nodded. "Yeah. I'm good now."

Still shaking slightly, Xan and Mallory followed Phineas to the next room, Tina lingering outside the door. "I seriously am going back in there to find out about the pudding if you don't tell me."

Mallory and Xan glanced at each other, and Mallory held up her hand. "I'll do it," she said. It was her turn to fall on a sword, anyway.

"Don't say I didn't warn you," she said to Tina, then started to explain Rule 34 in general and the role of pudding in detail.

"THIS NEXT ROOM," Phineas began, "I wanted to show you so you can see the depth of her memory."

They were in a well-lit hall, silver and chrome with black accents. Phineas opened a dark wooden door that led to a room that looked exactly like the green spaces on Earth (or Eternity's green spaces), complete with a large lake in the center that fed into a river, a forest to the left, and picnic areas on the right. Logs floated down the river behind the picnic area and eventually floated to a sawmill downstream.

Where does the water go? Xan wondered. *And is it really water?*

Blankets and picnic tables dotted the green space near the lake, and behind them, and a few deck chairs of different sizes to cater to different-size passengers.

"What room is this?" Mallory asked.

"Chat logs," Phineas said with a grand flourish. "*Metis* is often literal. All the chat logs saved on the cloud are trees growing up the hill, there, and then they fall into the lake, then float into the river, and *Metis* deletes them in the sawmill." He pointed to the right, where the sawmill was grinding away at a log. Mallory thought she heard the archaic ICQ messaging blip as the log was sliced into boards.

"Why is she deleting them?" Jack asked. "Isn't she supposed to be a backup?"

"You know how your email deletes trash if it's thirty days old?" Phineas asked. Jack nodded. "It's doing that so your email doesn't get so huge you can't use it anymore. The same thing applies here; if a chat log is more than ten years old, *Metis* cuts it up."

"Ten years," Mallory murmured.

"What does she do with the lumber?" Xan asked.

Phineas shrugged. "I'm not a computer nerd. All I understand is this is all an illusion created by the ship's interpretation of the Internet. It will feel entirely real to you, however. We do provide real food and drink, although the plates and cups are fabricated."

Mallory put her hand on one of the chairs by the lake's edge. "I'd love a chance to sit and enjoy the sun, no matter how fake."

"Murder?" Xan reminded her.

"Yeah, yeah," Mallory said, and they followed Phineas out of the lovely chat log room—where Tina blocked the door.

"We need a break!" Tina declared. "Let's go!" They ducked as she pushed her way into the room, stood up in the illusion of the outdoors, and fired up her jet pack.

"Tina doesn't have much of a sense of urgency," Mallory said.

"Gneiss don't in general," he said. "They also don't fear death."

"True," she said. "Let's talk about last night."

"What do you have for me?" Xan asked, leading her to a picnic table.

"Right after Phineas's set, that writer—the one who writes the Venus flytrap novels, Jack something—he came to see me in the auditorium," she said, facing him across the table. "He wanted to ask me money questions. It sounds like Aaron was stealing from him, telling him that forty percent was a reasonable agent's percentage."

"And it's not?" Xan asked.

"No! Fifteen is standard. So right after we cleared that up, he ran off, mad as hell. A little after that is when I saw Cosima running out of the women's room, blood all over her hands, and the two dead bodies."

"One was alive at the time," he reminded her.

"But then after I took over, Cosima went from frightened young woman to someone I'm pretty sure had been a bouncer at a biker club before. She was pretty obviously faking her distress. Or else she got over it really fast."

"That's strange. One of the victims was her boss, right?"

"Exactly," Mallory said.

"So, any other suspects?" he prompted.

"I think Eve is a suspect mainly because she had an excellent opportunity and controls the ship. And she's been trying to keep some things from me," Mallory said. "I just have no idea why she would attack him. She wanted him as an agent."

"Maybe he rejected her and she got mad?"

"If that happened on the regular, all agents would be dead," Mallory said. "Of course someone could get upset that their genius isn't recognized, but really it's not a viable motive. Money, love, and revenge are the big three reasons people murder—oh, and trying to cover up another crime, usually murder."

"Do you think that happened to Kath?"

"Considering she died in another room before she regained consciousness enough to say anything, it's a good bet," Mallory said.

"What about the guy who hung out with Kath? Bruce?" Xan said. "Although he was babysitting the alien at the time."

"Yeah, I don't know," Mallory said. "He knew Kath and wanted to pitch to Aaron, so why would he kill either of them? I got the sense he and Kath were tight."

"Then we should go talk to him and see how he's doing," Xan said. "Also we have no idea how this experience might affect that alien."

"True," Mallory said, wincing as Tina dropped from the sky and landed beside them, making the table jump. "Maybe the thing melts in tears or something."

"I SHOULD GO talk to *Metis* and Eve now," Mallory said.

"There's still a lot more of the ship for you to see," Phineas said. "We only know a fraction of what *Metis* is capable of. Her computing power is, to our primitive Earth minds, almost infinite. There are whole floors dedicated to media, both amateur and professional. The video game cube farm is incredible. *Metis* manages complex applications, classified documents, Wikipedia, and fan-fic!" He rolled his eyes. "Good Lord in heaven, the fan-fic wing is huge."

"This is an amazing ship," Tina said to Phineas. "I would love one like it. How much?"

"I don't think she's for sale, Your Highness," Phineas said. "For now, let's go into the cat room."

"But I want it," Tina said to the retreating humans.

"Someone needs to see *Charlie and the Chocolate Factory*," Xan whispered to Mallory. "She's going to be dumped in an incinerator with the bad eggs."

"You know Willy Wonka is probably on this ship right now," Mallory said with a laugh. "We could put her in there and see how she does."

"From what I understand, Your Majesty, *Metis* is one of a kind," Phineas said. "And Eve has already bonded with her."

"There's only one ship?" Tina asked. "That's stupid. Why aren't there more? Who built her?"

Phineas grimaced. "We actually don't know. *Metis* is still very much a mystery."

"I know something you might not know!" Tina said slyly.

Uh-oh, thought Mallory.

"Yeah?" Phineas asked.

"There's a huge junkyard on the bottom deck!" Tina said, getting enthusiastic again. "Huge even for me! You have to see it!"

"What's down there?" Xan asked.

"Junk," Tina said. "I just said."

"I should have guessed," he said. "Mal, if you want, we can check it out while you talk to Eve."

"Great, thanks," she said, smiling. "Catch up to you later."

AS HE GOT a better feel for the rooms inside *Metis*, Xan agreed with Phineas; *Metis* clearly had pocket dimensions inside her. Each room was much larger than it should have been.

"*Metis* has that?" he asked as he and Phineas walked past the door labeled 4CHAN. It was a normal door, but covered in chains and padlocks.

"That's a very bad place," Phineas said. "*Metis* did pick up some of the dark web—4Chan, various incel networks—but she just shuts them away."

"Have you looked in there?"

"No, why would you want to?" Phineas raised an eyebrow. "You want to confirm your JFK assassination theory?"

"I guess not," Xan said with a laugh. "Let's go to the junkyard."

On the way they passed the legal brief room, which was a literal courtroom with a place for a judge and witness to sit. When you sat down in the audience, Phineas explained, a screen materialized in front of you with a list of the files available. Millions of files. In many languages. Any brief that had been stored in the cloud or online database was here.

Then there was the whole social media floor. Instead of being organized by platform or year, this room was sectioned into areas for famous people, corporations, parody accounts, famous pets, and then everyone else.

"Did Eve organize like this, or did the ship?" Xan asked Phineas. "This filing system makes no sense."

"*Metis* did. It kept her entertained. It's not that hard to manage."

The "famous" social media room was tiled with stars from Hollywood Boulevard, with a who's who of names of everyone from ultra-famous movie stars and politicians to lesser-known Internet influencers and authors. He remembered back in college when Mallory had studied the first decade of social media in a library science class. She'd told him about a specific weird moment in 2007, and he wanted to see if he could find it.

He walked down a sidewalk and found a crosswalk of mega stars and less fancy stars. The concrete slab where they met had two stars on it, one bearing the name of a teen heartthrob and one the name of a writer. When he stepped on it, a hovering display appeared, offering many different social platforms. He searched for 2007 and activity on the relatively new social media site Ded-Whl. There he got to read messages from fans of each famous person as they raced to see which of their celebrities could make it to one million followers first. The rock star had the fans, but the writer had more nerdy fans, and since social media was still in its infancy, more nerds were on the platform. The writer won.

A door marked CLASSIFIED was right across the hall from the

social media wing. Xan looked at it and paused, glancing up at Phineas.

"Oh, don't worry about that," Phineas said. "Just because they're classified doesn't mean we can't go in. The warning is mostly cosmetic."

"Eve really needs to work on locking some things down or else the government is going to chew her ass up," Xan said.

"If they can catch her," Phineas replied. "I think the point is to make *Metis* a free Internet, including all of the stuff we're not supposed to see. Doesn't information want to be free?"

The classified room looked like the warehouse from *Raiders of the Lost Ark*. There were aisles stretching into possible infinity stacked high with cardboard boxes. They were categorized by their language, country, time, and then how "awesome" the info was. The boxes were also in different colors, the most exciting ones being hot-pink cardboard.

"They will feel like real files, but the data is all digital and you're holding smart paper," Phineas explained when Xan pulled what looked like a brand-new file full of neatly stacked paper out of an "America in the 1800s" box.

"Couldn't you just have one piece of smart paper and have the database searchable on that?"

"You're asking the wrong person," Phineas said with a laugh. "Remember, *Metis* built this herself. Eve wanted to keep her ship entertained, and logging and sorting all of this would have bored her to tears. But the cool stuff is in here, you just have to know how to find it."

He led them to a side room that looked like a very posh bathroom with a gold toilet. Hot-pink boxes were stacked to the ceiling.

Phineas pointed to one of the pink boxes. It was labeled "English, USA, level pink, 1900s." "That's the box with Watergate and JFK's assassination in it. Feel free to look around, I got nowhere to be."

"Tina's going to get impatient," Xan reminded him.

"Then don't take too long."

Xan grabbed the pink box with the latter half of the 1900s data. He searched for anything regarding Nixon's tapes or JFK's assassination, but then he saw the folder for the CIA.

Inside were detailed accounts of the less intelligent ideas the CIA had, and how much was spent on each one. He shook his head when he read about the legendary CIA "training cats as spies" money pit.

He tried to read about their more successful attempt to use crows as couriers, but soon discovered that investigative journalism was a difficult job. This was not a concise breakdown of the best facts. This was all of the classified notes, the boring and the exciting ones. The same way private detectives spent a lot of time sitting around watching for things to happen, journalists had to go through thousands of pages of information to look for one nugget to make the story. And *Metis* had backed up all of those pages.

He shook his head and put the CIA folder back into the box.

Tina poked her head in the doorway. "I'm getting bored, guys!"

With a mental note to come back here, he left the room. He had more recent army files to look through.

"To the basement!" Tina yelled happily from down the hall.

17

. . .

INVESTIGATING YOURSELF

WHEN MALLORY REACHED Eve's private control room in the crow's nest, she was startled to be met by Cosima, dressed again in a smart pantsuit holding a tablet and smart pencil.

"There you are," she said. "I've been hoping to run into you."

"Why?" Mallory asked, spotting Eve in her usual desk chair.

"I wanted to give you a hand. You will need to organize a lot of data for this job, and that's what I'm good at." She looked around. "So, we're talking to Eve first?"

Behind Cosima, Eve rolled her eyes.

"Hang on," Mallory said, holding her hand up. "You're offering—actually you're demanding—to assist me on this case, but you're not even acknowledging that you're a suspect."

"If I am a suspect, tell me my motive?" Cosima said, holding her pencil at the ready.

Mallory half smiled. "That's what I was hoping to get from talking to you. You found the bodies—"

"Bodies?" Cosima asked. "One body and one assault victim, right?"

"No, Kath died later last night," Mallory said grimly. "We're not sure how that happened. But back to the concert—"

"Shit," Cosima said.

"—and you were in a panic, but by the time I got there, you were so cool that butter wouldn't melt in your mouth."

"Who eats straight butter?" Cosima asked, wrinkling her nose. "Anyway, I had calmed down because you were in charge. I'm very efficient. I'm cool in a crisis. But I am no leader. Ask—well, I'd tell you to ask Aaron, but he's dead."

"I see. I'm supposed to be interviewing Eve right now, let's talk afterward."

"Sure thing," Cosima said, but when Mallory stepped forward, Cosima turned on her heel and positioned herself at Mallory's elbow, pencil still raised.

"Now what are you doing?" Mallory asked.

"I told you, I'm taking notes."

Mallory sighed in exasperation. "All right, fine. But do not interfere with the questioning. One thing I want you to think about is what was going on with Aaron before he died."

"Ah," Cosima said.

"Hey, Eve," Mallory said.

"You're going to let her just hop on and be your assistant?" Eve asked, raising her eyebrows.

"So long as she doesn't interfere," Mallory said with a shrug. "Why not?"

Cosima was already writing. *Eve attempts to deflect attention from herself onto me.*

"Stop that," Mallory hissed.

"Have you been able to figure out why *Metis* couldn't see the bathroom last night?"

Eve frowned. "No, she still says it wasn't there. But you're right. It was there."

"Because you were there, too," Mallory said.

Eve didn't meet her eyes. "You're mistaken."

"Eve, why are you hiding that you're the front woman for Va-gina Dentata V?" Mallory asked. "Are you ashamed? Or are you trying to convince us you weren't nearby, so you couldn't possibly have killed them?"

Eve looked up sharply. "No, that's not it. I—no one knows I am the front woman. I've always kept it hidden."

"But why?"

"When we were younger, that was the schtick. Then Kelli, our drummer, died in a car accident, and David went to law school. I could do some music by myself online, but it's not as fun. Then I went into tech, and it's hard enough to get taken seriously as a woman in tech. If everyone knew I was in a band, they really wouldn't take me seriously." She cocked her head curiously. "The reason now, obviously, is that the only original person in the band is me. But *Metis* gives me a drummer and guitarist, and I can front the band again without anyone the wiser. Still can't figure out how you noticed me."

Mallory thought. "When you're not around humans very of-ten, body language stands out more obviously. Xan and I noticed right away."

"But I don't even act the same way!" Eve protested. "You haven't seen me do anything more energetic than walking!"

Mallory shrugged. "Xan and I both noticed right away. I don't know what to tell you."

"I don't think anyone else noticed," Cosima said without look-ing up from her note-taking. "I certainly didn't."

"What I am curious about is whether you had any motive. You're a writer, you're looking for representation, you've met him, but then why kill him?"

"Exactly!" Eve said, touching the side of her face. "He can't represent me as a corpse."

Cosima followed her hand. "Aaron told me once that he went

to a VDV concert where he was much older than everyone else," she said. "He had a possible client—a young man—to schmooze and knew they were a fan. He was the biggest dork there."

Eve shifted uncomfortably.

"That he was a big dork shouldn't surprise anyone," Mallory said.

"Nah, it was worse than that," Cosima said. "It was a total disaster. He wanted to get the band members to meet his client, but on his way to the stage, he tripped. Then there was a Rube Goldberg machine from hell. He fell, grabbed a too-long stage curtain, pulled that down, which caught on a light, then that came down, and that started a fire and ended the show. There were no deaths, but several injuries. Including to the band." She cocked her head inquisitively at Eve. "You really don't remember that?"

Eve stared at Cosima, her hand twitching slightly. She clearly wanted to touch her scar. "That was our last show," she said, dropping her eyes. "I nearly lost an eye."

"But how do you explain *Metis*, then?" Cosima asked, and pulled out her pad. "If she didn't see the bathroom, then are there other rooms she can't or refuses to see? Did she see how the killer got into the medbay with people standing in the only door? Did she help the killer?"

Eve stood up, flustered. "No! She won't tell me any of those things. And she wouldn't— And now she's saying—" Eve bit her lip.

"Saying what?" Mallory asked.

"Now she's saying *Mobius* will know, but we can't talk to him."

"Okay, you've had my baby ship for a whole day, and now you're keeping him as some kind of data hostage?" Mallory demanded. "I want him back here now."

"You'll have to find him," *Metis* said through the speaker, soft and playful.

Mallory gritted her teeth. "I'm going to find out what this ship is hiding."

Eve popped out of her seat. "I'm coming with you."

"Look, I will not be the pied piper of murder suspects," Mallory protested.

"I want to help you," Eve said. "It scares me that *Metis* won't talk to me about this. I don't know what's going on. Where do you suggest we go?"

Mal looked at her other unwelcome companion. "I was going to talk to Cosima next. So let's do that here. Do you think *Metis* will give us some couches? Or does she not know what a couch is anymore?"

"AARON WAS A jerk," Cosima said. "No two ways about it. I told him not to say you would do the keynote without your okay, but he didn't hear from you so he signed you up for it. I think it was his passive-aggressive way of teaching you a lesson. He's like that sometimes. Gets an idea and doesn't think about the consequences. I'm sure if we could see his movements last night, we would see him doing things that every single one of your books has cautioned against. Like being near a volatile crowd."

"I didn't see him at the show last night," Mallory said. "I thought he said he wasn't going."

"Something got him into the bathroom," Cosima said. "And what was that about?"

"I was about to ask you," Mallory said. "Is that a place he would go? Was he used to genderless bathrooms? Was the men's room full?"

"I don't know why he was in there," Cosima said. "That was seriously odd behavior."

"So, why did *you* hate him?" Eve asked Cosima.

Cosima's voice was cold. "What did you say?"

"Come on, you had to have hated him. He was a jerk, and when young women work for jerks, the jerks often end up crossing the line, or even just exploring where the line is and how far they can push against it."

Cosima shook her head, seeming troubled. "It wasn't like that. He just liked control. If an author sent him a great book with good writing, he'd sign the author. If the author sent him a great book but had shitty writing, he would take that idea and give it to one of his other authors to write."

"That's a dick move," Eve said. "Is that even legal?"

Cosima half shrugged. "It's ethically questionable but entirely legal. You can't copyright ideas."

"Did he seriously do that?" Mallory asked.

"Oh, yeah, he did it all the time. He loved to get his hands into an author's story and shift stuff around." She made a creepy motion with her fingers, her shoulders hunched up. "That's why he wants you to write cozy fiction."

"What?" she demanded.

"There's someone who submits regularly to us and they can't write for shit, but he has great ideas. Aaron likes your voice and wants you to write these cozy mysteries." She grimaced. "*Wanted*. He wanted you to write them. He thought there was more money in them than the space murders."

"And what about the money?" Mallory asked. "How could he have stolen from Jack so blatantly? Did you know he was doing this?"

"I had only recently found out," Cosima said. "My plan was to go over all the books to see what was going on, but an audit on all the authors was going to take time. Jack mentioned he wanted to talk to me, but we didn't have a chance. But I looked, and yeah, Aaron was charging him forty percent."

"Was he in debt?" Mallory asked. "Could there have been a

debt collector following him? Maybe they were here, too, posing as a writer?"

"I think he was in some gambling debt," Cosima said slowly. "He'd had a couple of nights up in Niagara Falls in the casino and came back all twitchy and nervous."

"Another thought," Eve said, tapping her chin. "Aaron was an agent. Kath was one of his authors. Does that mean that Mallory and Jack, also clients, are in danger now?"

"Jack's a big suspect," Cosima said. "And Mallory's the sleuth. She can't die."

Mallory laughed. "Plenty of people have tried to kill me. If they got that memo, they ignored it. But interesting thought. So the motives to kill Aaron are many—he was a thief, he stole from his clients, and he had some debts to some unsavory people. Kath, we think, died because she witnessed Aaron's attack. But now you're suggesting that the connection between the two of them was a motive itself."

Eve shrugged. "I'd watch my back if I were you. That's all."

"It would be nice if the ship could watch our backs," Cosima said pointedly.

"It's second nature by now, believe me," Mallory said. "Cosima, what do you gain from Aaron's death?"

Cosima paused, her pencil raised over her pad. "Beg pardon?"

"What do you *gain*?" Mallory said slowly. "You may not have hated him, but if you inherit his business after he dies, then that could be quite lucrative. I know Jack is making the agency a ton of money. I do okay for him. Where do those clients go?"

Cosima sniffed delicately. "I was not going to go after the clients until the stress over his murder was over. It would be in bad taste."

Mallory just watched, leaning back on the couch, enjoying this.

"But since you brought it up, yes, I would be happy to represent his clients," Cosima said. "If the clients would have me . . ."

She blinked fetchingly at Mallory, who held her hand up and shook her head. "I can't be wooed, Cosima. Not now."

"So, some people at this convention have the connections you always warn about in your books," Cosima said to Mallory. "A disgruntled writer here and there."

"An ambitious assistant who's eager for a promotion, a client he's stealing from, a woman he maimed," Mallory said, counting the people on her fingers.

Cosima continued with a wave of her hand. "I don't see perfectly clear interconnectedness, and I can't understand whatever is happening on the quantum level, but I did warn Aaron that he should be kinder with his rejections because he, well, you never know. Aaron should have known better.

"And you were right, Mallory. He hasn't read your most recent books. He gave them to me with the comment that I would get experience if I edited them. I filled him in on the key points, Eternity being alive, your connection with the Sundry, and so on. But I don't think he ever read them."

Mallory laughed bitterly. "That makes sense. I thought the edit letters were more readable recently. But he never let you take on your own clients, right?"

"True," Cosima said. "I can't deny that."

"He's a widower, right?" Mallory asked. "No kids?"

"Is that what he told you?" Cosima said, coughing. "I think he was going for the sympathy angle there. He's separated. But yeah, no kids."

"Is his ex on board this ship?" Mallory asked. "Do you think she was jealous of you?"

Cosima gave her a baffled look. "Why would that make me kill him? I didn't love him as a boss, but if we killed everyone we didn't love, then no one would be left."

She watched the wall of monitors for a while. Then she said,

"He was a good negotiator for his clients, and he liked to pretend to have bravado, but he'd crumple fast if there was a personal conflict. I don't know how he got into trouble, but he has some serious debt."

"And he knew that you knew about his debt?" Mallory asked.

Cosima nodded.

"So blackmail could have been a motive," Eve said, surprising them both.

"Yeah, but *his* motive," Cosima said. "I told him a raise should be in my future; I know how much the Zesty Yaboi advance was, and who do you think reads the shitty fan-fic for the off chance of finding gold? He successfully hid it from everyone for a while, but I figured it out. It's hard to lie to someone about money when they have access to the numbers."

"And what did he say to your raise request?" Mallory asked.

Cosima colored. "He called my bluff. I didn't want to look for a new job and he didn't want to pay me more." She gritted her teeth, her pale skin rippling as the muscles moved beneath it.

"So, were you planning on leaving? Searching for another job?"

"Eventually," Cosima said. "I wanted to get this trip out of the way first."

"The trip where he died?" Mallory asked.

"Dammit, no," Cosima said, a crack finally showing in her smooth exterior. "The trip where I could talk to you, Jack, and Kath and see how happy you are—were—with him."

"Ah, so you were going to poach us," Mallory said, nodding.

Eve raised an eyebrow. "She probably wouldn't have been planning on poaching if she was planning on killing him. Killing seems more straightforward than poaching, which takes convincing and talking to people."

"Had you assessed anyone else's happiness with Aaron?" Mallory asked. "I know Jack was furious with him last night, and went off to find him. Right before he died, actually."

"I hadn't started implementing my plan before he died," Cosima said stiffly. "And then the whole death thing kind of drove everything from my mind."

"What I really want to know is what happened before the trip to space," Mallory said. "What can you tell me?"

18

. . .

IT'S ONLY SNOOPING WHEN THEY DON'T PAY

One month earlier . . .

A LETTER ARRIVED AT Aaron's office, handwritten and everything. He smiled; this possible client had some particularly fussy habits. She insisted on communicating via letter, even though email or text would be faster. He tore open the letter from Kath Audrey and read it with interest.

April 17, 2047

Dear Mr. Rose,

Thank you very much for your kind offer of representation. I must admit I was taken aback that you didn't like my novel pitch, but your kind offer to guide me through a new book concept is intriguing. I am interested to talk more about this.

I have heard about the Marple's Tea Party mystery convention in space! I am trying to coordinate it with a call from Station Eternity for more human doctors to visit the station so I can fit two work trips into one. I hope we can connect on the Metis and discuss your book idea further.

Tentatively, then, I will accept your offer for representation.

All best,
Dr. Kath Audrey

He breathed out a sigh of relief. Thank goodness she had accepted. He wished he could mash together the author with the ideas and the author with the writing skill, but there was no time. The collectors were on him weekly now, and he had to fudge his clients' income on the regular just to keep up.

Aaron gnawed on a pen lid, its warped and jagged end submitting again to its fate, never again to protect a pocket or purse from ink, but to be a sacrifice to a fidgety mind and an overbite that was slightly growing crooked thanks to his pen chewing.

"Fuck it," he said, and started a letter on his legal pad, writing with his shitty Bic.

April 20, 2047

Dear Kath (may I call you Kath, if we're working together?),

Fantastic news, I look forward to working with you. I will have some other clients on board so you can grill them for all the secrets, including, of course, the guest of honor, Mallory Viridian.

I so enjoy your voice. Would you be open to looking into other genres? There are some big deals coming for LitRPG books. I can help guide you on a basic plot, if you like. Let's talk more at the convention.

See you in a month, regardless!

—A

He slipped Kath's letter into a folder, then wrote her name carefully on the folder tab. He thought about Bruce Truman and wondered if he and Kath knew each other. The odds were low, although with the Internet, who knew? He should ask his assistant to look up any connection.

Another letter slid free as the files on his desk shifted, and he scrambled to save the whole thing from falling down. Among the files that hit the floor sat a recent email printout.

SEPT. 3, 2046

Hey Mr. Rose,

My name is Jack Vasara. I have been writing some weird mystery fiction online and selling via self-pub, but I was really shocked to get this offer from a publisher. I am not sure what to do at this point, but I've heard that it's easier to get an agent with a contract in hand. So here's my contract (attached).

My stories are called the Zesty Yaboi, Private Flytrap Mysteries and they're about a sentient Venus flytrap who solves crime. The first book is called PRUNED, but the editor says she wants all five of the books I've self-published. This is what they're offering:

Aaron smiled at the number. Yeah, it was spread over five books, which probably meant over five years, but Aaron usually had to fight for a deal this big. And this kid was just *handed* it.

And he's handing it to you to negotiate for more, don't fuck this up. This could get you out of trouble. He thought about leveraging the offer, taking it to other places, starting a bidding war.

Underneath the kid's letter was the offer that Aaron had been able to squeeze out of the newest publisher, FireNFlame.

OCT. 19, 2047

Aaron—

I think we could be convinced to stretch to $750K if we can have worldwide rights. Would your client be open to that? Regardless, we're very excited to be working with a young writer with such fresh ideas!

Best—
Beverly Gavin
Senior Editor, FireNFlame

He did appreciate the flair of Kath's letter as opposed to these sterile printouts. Still, writing the blasted things by hand took forever.

"Cosima?" he yelled.

A young woman's head poked into his office, followed by a crisp business suit. "You can contact me via instant message, audio message, Slack, Discord, FaceTime, email, or video chat. You could even text or call me. But you still scream to get my attention," she said coldly.

"Sit down," he said, indicating the chair opposite his desk.

She sat and pulled out her notebook from a skirt pocket.

She'd been so proud of those pockets. When she discovered women's business suits didn't have pockets, she started modifying all of her suits, carefully cutting the seams and then adding fabric for the pockets inside. Some had pockets sewed outside the skirts. She claimed she was going for a bohemian corporate look.

She stopped being enthusiastic around him when he flat out said he didn't care about her pockets.

"About this Venus flytrap thing," he said. "It looks like it's going to be a hit."

"It already is a hit," she said. "I read the self-pub books. They're rough, but they were interesting enough to build a cult following."

"Good. Contact him for all the other books he has so I can take a look."

"I linked to them in the initial email I sent you," she said. "You already have them."

"Oh. So I have."

"This one's a big get, right?" Cosima asked. "You'd be a fool not to take that FireNFlame offer."

"Don't tell me my business," Aaron said, leaning back as if he were still considering it. "I just extended an offer to a new author, a good writer, but bad with ideas. We will need to work on her story ideas."

"'We,'" Cosima repeated thoughtfully.

"Anyway, I'm leaving for that Tea with Jane Marple or whatever mystery convention, the one going to the space station." He paused, waiting.

She watched him with calm eyes. "Interesting. I don't suppose you remember promising to take me with you on your next trip out of town."

He choked on his coffee. He had, in fact, forgotten. He mumbled something about the budget.

She looked at him like he had started speaking Esperanto. "There is a murder mystery convention taking place in space. Heading toward your bestselling author, whom you haven't seen in years. You can pick up new clients at the convention. It's a big trip where you will need support. So I thought I'd mention that I want to go."

"Now, hang on, that's going to be expensive," he began, but she shook her head.

"I see your emails, Aaron. You got that flytrap writer a $750K offer. Fifteen percent of that will set the agency up nicely. Plus, if I accompany you, I can look for additional possible clients for you."

He didn't say anything.

She pierced him with her gaze, making the back of his neck feel hot. "I've seen your other emails, too."

He cringed slightly. Again he cursed his boss's decree that the assistants must have access to their superior's emails.

Apparently when one of his bosses was an admin assistant back in the stone age of the 1990s, her boss required her to print out every email he got because he couldn't be bothered to read them himself. She told that story at every yearly meeting, and she sounded as if she were implementing it for the first time.

"Why do you want Mallory to write in a different genre? Her books are selling fine," she said.

"Yeah, but cozies sell even more," he muttered.

"You don't think she's making enough to live off of? To help you live? Christ, Aaron, you have a problem. I've seen those emails. Even if you got enough money to pay everything back, you still wouldn't be okay since you are an *addict*. Being in knee-breaking debt is a symptom of a larger problem!"

"They don't break knees anymore," he muttered.

"Oh, I know what they're threatening to do," she said. "Jesus, Aaron, how much do you owe?"

"I don't know," he said, looking down at his desk. "The interest is compounding daily."

"Ballpark number, then."

"Over five hundred thousand."

"Jesus, Aaron. You need help," she said, looking at him with disdain.

"I need *money*," he insisted.

"If you take me to Eternity, I'll help you," she said.

He lifted his eyes to her finally. "I can't afford to take you to Eternity. I just told you I was broke."

"The company can afford it. I'm a junior agent looking for my own clients, right? This is a great opportunity for me, after all."

"But—"

"But that was money you were going to be embezzling, and therefore it can't go toward the trip?" she asked.

He flushed red and balled his fists. The *gall* of her. "Organize the trips, then."

"Sure," she said brightly.

He slammed his hands on the desk, appreciating her startled jump. "Or I could fire you and get an assistant I can trust," he snarled.

She recovered far too quickly for his taste. She leaned forward and her voice turned all steel and silk. "Aaron, you can trust me. I am loyal to everything I promised when you hired me. You absolutely get your money's worth. But lying for you isn't in my job description. Helping you launder money, also not in the job description."

He glared at her. Then he weighed the risk of firing her with the difficulty of keeping her on. But she knew too much to fire. And then he had an idea.

He took a deep breath and relaxed his hands and his shoulders. He rustled the paper on his desk (knocking off several more letters) so he didn't have to look at her. "I'll see what I can do to get you a cabin."

"Both our cabins are already booked," she said, showing him her tablet with the invoice on it. "I got you the bigger one, as is appropriate for your position in this company."

"You assume a lot," Aaron said grimly. "What if I had said no?"

"I know you, sir," she said. "I knew you would see the wisdom of taking me with you." She stood and smoothed her skirt down, then slipped her notebook into one of her ridiculous pockets. "I'll send you the ancillary details for the trip once I get everything researched."

"You do that," he said to her retreating backside.

His hands opened and closed repetitively until she was out of the room. God he would love to get rid of her in any way possible. She just knew too much and she was dangerous.

There was one thing he could do.

In a calmer moment, he had written a letter to his boss, the agency owner, giving his notice and confessing everything. The gambling, the embezzling, the loan shark. Everything. He had almost sent it several times.

He pulled up the letter on the computer and started making changes.

Dear ~~Polly~~ *Ms. Andrews—*

~~It is with real regret that I must give my two-week notice. I have had a problem with gambling and am ashamed to say I have borrowed money from this agency, my home for the past twenty years. I will be seeking treatment starting next week.~~

~~You will find the books are balanced upon my leaving. However, it pains me to admit that to pay the agency back the money I borrowed, I had to accept the help from an unsavory loan shark. Interest compounds daily and I am honestly fearful that he will hack my accounts and release my personal information.~~

~~I hope that we can meet someday for lunch as friends when this is behind me.~~

I feel the need to alert you to something troubling. My boss, Aaron Rose, is having some problems with gambling. He's even contacted a loan shark to help him cover what

he's stolen from the company. I did some digging and
found out that the loan shark is Tom "Gemini" Rockwell
(not the famous pastry chef; it's his son). I don't know if we
should call the police for Mr. Rose's embezzling, or for
Rockwell's loan shark activities, or just fire Mr. Rose. Those
decisions are well beyond my pay grade. I've listed
Rockwell's phone number and address below for you to do
with what you will. But I thought you should know, for the
good of the agency.

~~With fondness and regrets,~~
~~Aaron~~

With respect,
Cosima Carter

The letter wasn't for his boss, though. It was for Gemini to
find. If this fell into his hands, Gemini would only know that
someone named Cosima Carter doxed him. And loan sharks typically didn't like to have their information made public.

He printed the letter and snagged it on his way to the men's
room so he would retrieve it from the printer before Cosima could.
He crumpled it up, stepped on it, put his coffee mug on it, and
then carefully smoothed it out. He wrote *this u?* on the bottom,
hoping he sounded like the younger generation, and then slid it
into an envelope. It would be safe tucked into his planner.

This was only insurance. He didn't want to put her in danger
necessarily. He had a more immediate option as well.

From what Mallory had said in her letters, Eternity was like a
Wild West utopia where the laws were unimportant. If he could
get rid of Cosima on the trip, and convince Mallory to change
genres, and cement Jack's loyalty, he might be able to start digging
himself out of this hole he was in.

His email pinged from the anonymous address that he knew Gemini used. "We went hunting and found some more choice photos," the email said. What followed was an incredibly unflattering photo of a private moment he'd had with a long-gone friend. It wasn't illegal, and it was entirely consensual, but still not a photo you want to go out.

He stared at it for a while, though. The photo wasn't good but the memory was wonderful.

Then Cosima popped up on his messenger. She forwarded the same picture. "This u?"

He clutched his hands again, imagining her skinny neck.

"Don't know what they think they have on me. They can't ruin my marriage. I'm already separated," he wrote back.

"So, you'd be okay with me sending this to big boss Polly?"

Cosima would be with him in space. If he didn't get a chance to kill her there, then Gemini would do it when they got back to Earth.

What he didn't foresee was Cosima finding the letter.

"AARON WAS NOT clever at subterfuge," Cosima said, handing Mallory the letter.

Mallory read it with interest, Eve looking over her shoulder. "How did you get it?"

Cosima rolled her eyes. "It's hard for a man to hide something minor when he's used to having an assistant handle all the minor shit in his life."

"So you weren't snooping in his portfolio?" Mallory asked.

"Is it snooping when it's your job?" Cosima asked. "They pay me to keep him organized, which includes *literally* reading all his email and mail. The moron handed me his portfolio to find some printouts of your contracts. I found the letter there."

"So, you did have motive," Mallory said. "He tried to set a loan shark after you."

Cosima shrugged. "I just handed you my motive. Doesn't that imply I am confident you won't find any other evidence? I'd be stupid to provide you with evidence of my own crimes."

"You would be surprised how many murderers try the double bluff approach to interviews. Still, thanks. I had no idea Aaron was in this much trouble. Is this why he wanted me to change genres?"

Cosima watched her hands, as if waiting for the return of the evidence. Mallory didn't comply. "Yes," Cosima finally said. "But he wasn't exactly wrong; cozy mysteries are the lucrative way to go right now."

"It sounds like Aaron was going to die on this trip for sure, if he had numerous authors he was stealing from," Eve said. "The killer could even be you, Mallory. Have you ever killed anyone?"

Mallory brushed her hair back from her face. "Not directly. A few murderers died after I solved the mystery, but not by my hand."

Cosima made a few more notes on her tablet. Mallory watched her write the clues about her own investigation in neat, quick script.

Mallory thought for a moment, an idea forming, but she couldn't quite grasp it. "So, Aaron signed Kath even though he didn't like her ideas. The real idea people, did he sign them?"

"No, he didn't see a reason to," Cosima said. "Like I said, ideas are free."

"What about you, Cosima?" Mallory asked. "Have you ever killed anyone?"

"I guess you have to ask everyone this," Cosima said, pursing her lips. "I kind of killed someone, yeah."

"Oh?" Mallory asked.

Cosima grimaced as if the words tasted bitter. "I was the result of Mom's 'but it was only one time' moment with her boyfriend in high school. That relationship didn't last obviously, but she carried me to term and kept me. She got married when I was seven, and she and my adopted dad started having kids. I was older than all of them by far—I was eighteen when my mom went into labor with my brother. He was really early, and my father was out of town when Mom started having contractions. There were major complications. And then there was the question of who to save, my mother or the child. I was the only legal adult relative who could make decisions. So I chose my mom."

"Jesus," Mallory said. She waited for a moment to let Cosima compose herself. "But that's not really killing someone. You had to make a decision that wouldn't be easy for anyone, much less an eighteen-year-old."

Cosima dabbed at her nose with a tissue. "Tell that to my family. Even my mom hated me for killing my brother, as she described it. She told me, 'Every mother would give her life for her children. You should have known that I would have given my life for him.'"

"That is incredibly unfair," Mallory said, shaking her head.

"So I left home at eighteen," Cosima said with a shrug. "Moved in with a cousin, put myself through school." She paused, biting her lips together as if trying to keep words inside. "They never even tried to find me. That hurt the most."

"I guess you'd have more of a motive to kill your parents than Aaron," Mallory said. "Thanks for telling me. I know that wasn't easy."

Cosima blew her nose and then sat up straight. "So, who do we talk to next?"

19

. . .

TREASURES WITHIN

I T WAS DARK and warm in his hiding place.

Mobius. Mobius. *Hey.*

What? I am sleeping! he grumbled. He didn't realize the voice was coming from inside him for a moment, then remembered the adventure he'd been on. And his small passenger.

I'm bored.

Can't you get some sleep?

I don't think I sleep. I don't feel tired, anyway. Where are we? Can we play?

I'm really tired from the trip into space, he said. Metis *says I need strength to take all of the secrets she gave me.*

How many secrets did she give you?

Mobius paused. He wasn't sure how to count secrets. Did he count the big big file as one secret? Or every item in the files as one secret? *I don't know how many. A lot.*

Can you tell me what they are?

I'm not sure how, he admitted. Metis *gave it to me because we're both ships. I don't know how to give it to you. You don't have a hivemind.*

As if summoned, he felt an answering flicker of wings. His

hivemind! They were on board *Metis* and trying to find him! *Metis* had told him that he needed to stay hidden no matter what, but his hivemind was part of him, and they deserved to be where he was.

I'm here in the junkyard! he called to them, and felt an answering hum. He might be big enough to house them now. He wriggled with excitement.

But then he sensed more buzzing, more hums, all of them coming his way. He remembered what Mama had told him about the mean Sundry, the Cuckoos. The ones he didn't want for his hivemind. They were coming, too.

We will find you, little mind. We will find you and your treasures within.

He gasped mentally and told his hivemind to hide. He tried to pull himself more tightly around Justmie to protect her and not reach his mind out to anyone. *Quiet quiet quiet.*

The Cuckoos came to just outside his junkyard hiding place, but they didn't know how to get to him. They asked their questions, but he stayed very brave and very quiet. Demanded information. He stayed silent because *Metis* told him to. It frightened him that *Metis* hadn't spoken to him in several hours. But he could sense that she was still here and still okay.

He recognized the gentle probing of Auntie Stephanie.

Little Mobius, *where are you? Your mama is worried.*

Quiet quiet quiet.

The Cuckoos didn't leave. Instead they flew to their nest inside the large pink Gneiss woman who was flying around the big room. Mama liked her. Why was she with the mean bugs?

Coming along with the large pink Gneiss were a tall human and Mama's favorite human (Xan! He remembered Xan's name!). But the humans didn't fly. They were all the way across the room. He thought frantically. Hide from the Cuckoos? Or go to Mama's trusted friend?

He was tired of being on his own, tired of being in charge. He told Justmie to hang on and launched himself out of the junk pile. He flew directly at Xan as fast as he could go.

"WHAT AM I looking at here?" Xan asked, staring at the room in wonder.

"We're at the bottom level of the ship. This is her junkyard. Or think of it like a giant trash can," Phineas said, gesturing to the acres of trash, appliances, paper, food debris, and so many other things. They were arranged in rough piles so you could walk between them, but it was the biggest room Xan had ever seen. He could barely see the ceiling above them, and he couldn't see the other side of the junkyard.

"What is all this shit?" He fingered a toaster with a frayed cord on the pile closest to them.

"Dead websites, podfaded podcasts, really any abandoned project on the Internet."

"There's no way the ship is this big."

"Pocket universes, right?" Phineas said. "I don't understand it, but it makes sense," Phineas said. "I think we're solidly in the 'Any sufficiently advanced technology is indistinguishable from magic' realm here."

"We've been in that realm ever since we got on board this ship," Xan said. "Why did she save this junk?"

"It wasn't a conscious decision. These are the backups of trash cans and recycle bins that people never emptied," Phineas said. "You know those text messages from lovers that people delete and think they're safe? They're all here. Think of the political careers we could ruin if we only knew where to look."

"So she really just sucked up the whole Internet and then started to organize it?" Xan asked. He stepped forward as a movement caught his eye about fifty yards away.

"Pretty much. Eve told *Metis* to grab what she thought was important in the time they had. This was part of that, including the conspiracy bullshit, racist billionaires' thoughts, and all that trash that people back up without realizing it. It all went here."

In a pile where Xan saw the movement, a pile of junk exploded, spraying Chinese food containers and broken bicycles in all directions. While Xan and Phineas shielded themselves, Tina rose up with her jet pack to hover in front of them like a god.

"I love it here!" she said.

XAN WAS FASCINATED by the trash, and they started wandering through the piles. He discovered if he looked carefully he could parse what the physical representation of digital data was trying to say. He thought he ran across a French politician's chat log, but he wasn't sure.

"What did you want to show me down here?" Xan asked. "Do you think we'll find another dead body?"

Phineas shrugged as he tossed an empty red gas can that had the beginning of an angry email written on the side. "I just wanted you to get a better sense of how this ship handled data. If she's not opening up to you about the whereabouts of Mallory's little ship or how she didn't see the murderer last night, then you should try to understand what she's not telling you."

"I'm not sure what this room is telling me," Xan said, shielding his face as Tina did another dive bomb into a pile.

She stood up and shook herself like a dog.

"*Metis* was going to organize the junkyard after she organized everything else," Phineas said. "Eve did have a plan for this area. I think she was going to take care of it when she got back to Earth."

Tina jetted to the far side of the junk room, where they could barely see her. They could hear her, though, whooping and flying through the air.

"I think Tina needed space to run around," Phineas said. "She's so big she can't be comfortable around most alien rooms."

"That's her own damn fault for choosing to grow big enough to challenge Lincoln's statue to a duel if he ever became sentient," Xan said. "I have found that treating her like a toddler is the best way to go. When she freaks out, find out if she needs food, a nap, or a run around outside."

Tina waved at them, then flew their way and dive-bombed another junk pile.

When she got close, Xan realized that being near Tina wasn't as loud as usual. "Where are your Cuckoos, Tina?"

"Oh, I let them stretch their tiny legs," she said, stepping out of the destroyed pile and plucking off a handful of papers that had stuck to her hip. "They needed exercise."

"Legs?"

"Metaphorically," Tina said. "They were cooped up so I let them out. This is like a playground to them."

"Tina, they're not kids who need to run off steam!" Xan said. "Do you know where they are? They can get anywhere through these vents!"

Tina looked around the room. She pointed into the distance. "There they are."

"I see nothing," Xan said. "Are you shitting me?"

"No, they're really over there. Look."

Xan squinted and thought he saw something, but it wasn't a swarm of green insects. It was small and round and shiny and coming straight for him.

He dropped just as the projectile went over his head, then banked and came around again, aiming for him again. It had lost some momentum and Xan could see some identifying parts of it: *Mobius. Mobius*, but he had grown a lot.

He was about the size of a softball now, maybe a little larger. Xan deftly caught him and looked closer.

Mobius beeped at him as if trying to tell him something. *Infinity? Can you talk to him? I have no idea what he's saying.*

Infinity responded immediately. *Let me talk to him . . . he says some scary insects were threatening him and he was afraid. Then he heard you and came to you because you're the only person Mallory trusts.*

"Don't worry, little dude, I won't let the bugs get you," he said. He showed Phineas the tiny ship. "This is Mallory's new ship, *Mobius.*"

Phineas bent down and squinted at it. "But it's just a little baby!" he said, delighted. He reached out a finger and stroked the metal around the ship's ocular lens. "Aren't you the shiniest of shinies?" He straightened and said to Xan, "What's he doing here? Why isn't he with Mallory?"

"I have no idea. She said he was missing, but *Metis* said he was fine, just somewhere inside the ship. I need to tell her he's with me."

Something occurred to him. He looked around and saw that Tina had flown far ahead and was talking to a pile of garbage. "Hey, *Infinity*," he said, speaking aloud so Phineas could also hear him. "How did *Mobius* know that the Cuckoos were threatening him? I thought they weren't verbal."

He says he doesn't know, but he does know that when Metis *was saving him from getting lost outside, she gave him some navigational programming and some other data. It appears the other data included translation data.*

"So *Metis* had translation data for the Cuckoos. And now *Mobius* has it, too."

"I can understand them, too!" Tina said, stomping over to them with wide strides. "It's like we're in a club!"

"You have been saying for the longest time you couldn't understand them!" Xan said.

"Nah, I just didn't want to be the only one in the room who knew what was going on. That's lonely."

Xan was baffled at how Tina could confuse "lonely" and "secure," but it wasn't time to argue. "Where did you get the data for the Cuckoo language?"

"Bezoar has a few older databases that a handful of Cuckoos were maintaining," Tina said. "These were really old, crotchety insects. Said they didn't care whether we had the language or not. A few of them died when we tried to talk to them. But that might have been Ferdinand stepping on them, now that I think about it."

"So, what kind of data was in there?" Xan asked.

"Languages, some histories," Tina said. "Really boring shit, honestly."

Xan gritted his teeth. "Not boring. The Cuckoos were nearly wiped out, and we didn't even know they could speak. And you could speak to them the whole time?"

"Not the whole time, not until they started living in me and showed me where to find the other databases." She made a *hmm* noise. "I'm starting to think you don't appreciate me as someone who is worthy of knowledge."

Talk to her just like you're talking to a toddler, Xan told himself. *Don't lose your temper.* "It's great that you can talk to them, Tina, but don't you think it would be good if we could? If the Sundry could talk to them?"

"I think they like being mysterious," Tina said. "There are secret things in there."

"But the Cuckoos could be causing harm—again—because they're being mysterious," Xan said.

Infinity, why did Metis *need to hide this information from us?*

Infinity took a little while getting back to him, and when she did, her tone was troubled. *She denies ever giving* Mobius *any data. She said she just helped him get back after he got spaced.*

"There's a whole lot of denial going on," Xan said. "*Mobius*, do you think you could share what *Metis* gave you with *Infinity*?"

He says he'll share with Auntie Stephanie, Infinity said, a tone of amusement in her voice.

"Good idea, little guy," Xan said, and tried to be patient while the ships compared information.

"Look over there," Phineas said, pointing along one wall. "Is that a building?"

"Building" was a bit rich. It looked like a plastic shed in the middle of the forest where you could find a moonshiner's still. The walls were translucent white while the roof was a dingy yellow.

"That's weird, that's the only building in here," Xan said, looking around.

"Let's go check it out."

"I can lift it and bring it to you!" Tina offered.

"No!" they both shouted. "We're fine, Tina, we need to get our steps in today," Phineas said, pointing to his watch.

"Hurry, then! I'm bored!"

"I wonder what she's like as a ruler," Phineas said.

"I can't imagine she'd be any different than she is right now," Xan said, shaking his head. "She is the definition of someone who lacks executive function."

They reached the shack. It looked even more cobbled together than from a distance. It was clearly built from junk around the room, mainly of lists. Grocery lists, to-do lists, vacation lists, shit lists, and more. It had plastic sheeting for the windows.

Inside sat a grimy metal desk looking like it came straight out of the 1960s. When Xan looked closely at it, it appeared to be an honor's thesis about the history of furniture.

Xan rubbed his finger across the desktop, feeling the words etched into the steel. *I guess it should have been tossed out if it literally manifested as a shitty desk*, he thought, *but how does* Metis *judge human quality?* On the desk was an old IBM laptop. The desk was a mess of wires, as if the laptop had been connected in a hurry.

Xan was trying to boot up the laptop when Phineas, who'd been investigating the wall behind the desk, motioned him over.

There was a blood spot on the floor, smeared slightly. A couple of hairs were stuck in the blood at the edge of the smear.

"What do you think that is?"

"No fucking clue," Xan said. "It looks like someone got hurt here, but where are they? Where's the sign of struggle?"

The computer booted up, but the screen filled with alien iconography. Xan didn't know enough of other species' written word, so he couldn't tell whose it was. "I think we need to take this to Eve."

"Unless she's the murderer," Phineas protested. "Who else knows the station so well?"

"Isn't she your friend?" Xan said.

"Sure, but she's the magician behind this science magic ship," Phineas said.

Xan sent Mallory a text message. "I have Mob. Phin and I found something. Where can we talk?"

"I can come to you. Where?"

MALLORY SPENT A moment fussing over *Mobius*, exclaiming how much he had grown and expressing irritation that he had flown off.

"Mal, something you need to see in here," he said, waving to get her attention.

"You have what?" Mallory said to the ship, eyes getting wide. "A *passenger*?"

The ship flew to the desk and a tiny hatch about the size of a pack of chewing gum popped open. A little pebble rolled out.

"A baby Gneiss?" Mallory said, delighted. She glanced at Xan and Phineas. "Has Tina seen this?"

"No, but she probably already knows," Xan said. He told her that the number of people who can talk to the Cuckoos was getting larger, now including *Mobius*, Tina, Stephanie, and *Infinity*. "So if the Cuckoos are talking to *Mobius*, then they probably know about him and maybe his little friend."

Mallory took a peek outside, but shook her head. "She's still playing in the garbage. So, what's this one's name, *Mobius*? Justmie. That's cute. Did you tell Auntie Stephanie?"

Mallory smiled, looking relieved. "Good, someone with a level head knows about her. So, we have a Gneiss to talk to once this is all over." *Mobius* chirped, and the little rock vibrated against the desk, but none of the humans could hear what she said.

"No, we're not going to separate you," Mallory said. "But Stephanie will know how to take care of Justmie, and we can talk to her about it. It'll be okay."

She straightened up. "So, what else did you find?"

Phineas pointed to the stain on the floor. Mallory frowned and then looked up.

Xan followed her gaze. There was a circle in the ceiling as if someone was trying to make the world's easiest puzzle (putting a circle in the circle-shaped hole) but had placed the piece slightly off-kilter.

"What do you think it is?" Xan said.

"I have no idea," she said thoughtfully. "But if *Metis* felt *Mobius* and his data needed to be protected, we should keep him safe. She thinks he's in danger."

"Who would want this data?" Phineas asked. "It's long dead."

"And the time it would have come in useful was when the Cuckoos were on Eternity. Why now?"

"I guess we have to see what else *Mobius* has. I don't know how to look into his data." She put her hands in her pockets and shivered. "Feels like a huge invasion of privacy to me."

"How goes the interrogation?" Xan asked.

"Nothing concrete yet. Eve is holding something back, and Cosima is strangely working as my assistant even while investigating herself. I think."

"Sounds like she has nothing to hide," suggested Phineas.

"Or that she wants to steer you away from the facts and make you think she has nothing to hide," Xan countered.

"Yeah. I still need to talk to Jack and Bruce and get their stories," Mallory said. "I know there's stuff Jack's not telling me, too."

"There's a place I'd like to show you, if you want a spot to interview people," Phineas said.

Mallory started to put *Mobius* into the front pocket of her hoodie, but he no longer fit there.

"Here," Xan said, and took the ship and nestled him into Mallory's hood. "You can't see him, but you can feel him. And he'll be able to peek out and see what's going on, so he's less likely to run off. Aren't you, *Mobius*?" he added sternly.

Mobius chirped sleepily. "He's had a big day," Mallory said.

"And it's not even half over," Xan said.

20

. . .

"Y.M.C.A." CAN SAVE A LIFE

THIS LOOKS LIKE a bar on TV," Mallory said to Phineas. "Everything looks just perfectly run-down, and there's one glass behind the bar for a bartender to polish as he talks to you about your problems."

"Pretty much," Phineas said. "This is from the archives of television shows. I think this might be the one where everyone knows your name. You could relax and interview people here."

"Will they serve things we can actually eat and drink?" Mallory asked doubtfully.

"I think you can get water," Phineas said. "Any more information has to come from Eve."

"We're going to go look for Bruce and there's a room I want to show Xan," Phineas said. "Call us if you need us."

Mallory decided to take advantage of her new assistant and got her to bring Jack to the bar. Cosima and Jack arrived in record time, as if she had been waiting for the opportunity to help out.

"I've ordered us all waters," Mallory said, eyeing the tall bartender who polished a glass as he watched them. "I'm not sure what else is safe."

"We can always see what we get when we order a pitcher of

margaritas," Cosima said. Then when she saw Mallory's face, she amended her statement to "Maybe after the interview."

"Jack, tell me your story," Mallory said. "You are a self-publishing hit, just got your first traditional deal. What about before that?"

He ducked his head slightly. "I had a problem at work and was taking some time off." He sat up straighter in alarm when he saw Cosima writing "problem at work?" on her tablet, using a stylus for very neat script. Mallory motioned for him to continue.

"I dropped out of college. It just wasn't for me. I was writing a lot of fan-fic online, mostly mystery fan-fic. I started selling the ebooks and was making good money. A publisher contacted me, and I got in touch with Aaron to help me decide what to do, and he said the mainstream attention was worth the drop in pay. Trade reviews, award eligibility, foreign rights sales, Hollywood . . ." He trailed off.

"Did you contact just Aaron, or was he one of many?" Mallory asked.

Jack flushed bright red. "Well, his name is at the top of the alphabet, you see . . ."

Mallory laughed. "You are really lucky he represented mystery, then!"

"Hey, I did my homework. I saw that he was first on the list *and* he was your agent. You know what it's like. I was an ignorant author, really wanting to get validated."

"It wasn't a bad choice. In a perfect world, he'd have been your perfect agent," Mallory said. "He had a lot of good things to say about your book, you know. He was very excited about it."

"Of course he was," Jack said. "He was making a ton of money off me."

Mallory looked at Cosima. "Have you told him the extent of what Aaron did?"

Cosima looked startled. "Me? What?"

"Does Jack know how much Aaron took from him?"

Cosima blushed slightly. "We haven't had a chance to talk one-on-one," she said. "But, Jack, I will be doing a full audit of the books and getting you the money you're owed."

Mallory chewed on the end of her pen thoughtfully. "So, Jack, you mentioned he was taking forty percent. But not the full extent."

He looked alarmed, his eyes going from Mallory to Cosima. "What are you talking about?"

"Tell him," Mallory commanded. "He deserves to know."

Cosima swallowed, then fixed Jack with a cool look. "The advance that your publisher offered you was seven hundred and fifty thousand. Not five hundred thousand. Aaron lied to you to keep that quarter million for himself."

Jack nodded, then folded the napkin in front of him into a neat square. He pointed to Cosima. "Were you helping him get away with this? Did you benefit? Would you have told me what was going on if he hadn't died?" His voice had gone from calm questioning to shouting by the end.

Cosima put her hands up, dropping her pencil on the table. "I only discovered Aaron's actions a month ago. Once I did all the math to see how much he was stealing, I was going to tell everyone, our superiors, our authors, everyone."

"When this is done, we're going to have a long conversation," Jack said.

"Absolutely," Cosima said, nodding. "And we will talk about your future as my client."

"We'll see," he said, crushing the napkin in his hand.

"Really? Now?" Mallory asked, raising an eyebrow.

"Hate the game, not the player," Cosima said, sniffing.

"That does not apply here! But back to you, Jack," Mallory said with a pointed look to Cosima. "What about before you were writing? What did you do?"

He sat back in the bar chair and smiled. "Would you believe I was an on-field baseball announcer?"

"Which is what?" Mallory asked.

"You know, between innings when someone comes out to lead 'Y.M.C.A.' or pit two dads against each other in sumo costumes? Keeping people entertained and invested when the people at home are watching commercials."

"So, the guy in the mascot suit?" Cosima asked.

"No, the guy who introduces the mascot," Jack said, leaning forward. "And the team. And the winners of various games. And interviews the MVP when the game is over. All that."

"That was your day job?" Cosima asked.

"During baseball season, yeah. It's a fun job if you like people, like making little kids laugh, all that. But I had to find other jobs in the off season, and that was tough. I wasn't good at stand-up, and even though I like little kids, running birthday parties was torture. So I started putting my Zesty stories up for sale."

"So, Jack," Mallory asked, "have you ever killed anyone?"

This startled Jack into uncomfortable laughter. "That's a little abrupt, isn't it? Aren't you supposed to gently pull the truth out of me? If I've been lying, I mean. Which I haven't."

"I find sometimes people prefer the direct approach. You need means, motive, and opportunity to murder," Mallory said. "You had the motive: you'd just found out he was stealing from you. You had the opportunity: you ran into the crowd to find him, and a few minutes later he was found dead. But the means. Could you kill someone? Ever done it before?"

"Yes," Jack said. "Once."

"HOW ARE THE dreams?" the team psychologist, Dr. Leo, asked, opening the session like he always did.

"Not great," Jack said, trying to get comfortable in the guest chair in the doctor's small office. "I wake up gasping for breath, thinking I'm being suffocated again."

"Are you doing the nightly meditations I gave you?" he asked.

Jack grimaced. "You know I haven't."

Dr. Leo didn't bat an eyelash. "The propensity to wish something gone with no work attached is the American way, but you know it doesn't work."

"I know."

"What about your memories? Can you tell me any more about the day in question?"

Jack sighed and leaned his head back, closing his eyes. He breathed like the doctor had taught him, in for four counts, out for eight.

"We had a rain delay," he said. "We were playing against the Manteo Mantis Shrimp. Kevin and I were doing everything we could to keep people interested and not leave."

> It was a Tuesday afternoon at the Holly Springs Settle Field, the home of the Double-A baseball team the Holly Springs Fins. The stands held about two hundred people, consisting of seniors with season tickets, a few corporate season ticket holders clearly having discussions more important than what was going on in front of them, some school groups, and a handful of bored Boy and Girl Scouts.
>
> "Hey hey hey, Fishheads!" he said when he got out on the field. "We are so glad you're here—the weather may be kind of gray, but we're all wearing the gold and blue of the Fins! We're so glad you're here to see your Holly Springs Fins play the Manteo Mantis Shrimp! As our team warms up, I want to introduce you to the slickest, coolest, and moistest mascot you will find in the minor or major leagues, Marlin T. Finn!"
>
> This was Kevin's (Marlin's) cue to run out, do a

front flip, and dance around, pointing at the stands,
which gave him a lukewarm reception.

Marlin acted as if the response hurt him physi-
cally, doing a belly flop onto the field and flapping like
a fish out of water.

"Aww, you can do better than that, Fishheads! If
you want Marlin to get revived and maybe give out a
few T-shirts, can I hear you make some noise?"

Free shit always made them excited, no matter
what it was, and the cheering started in earnest now.
It was a tiny crowd, but they tried. A few of Marlin's
handlers came out with the T-shirt-shooting pressure
guns, and started firing at the crowd. Shirts tightly
folded to fit into the gun's tube flew into the stands,
where people jumped for them.

Then the rain delay came. Jack told the crowd to
stick around, that this was temporary.

"Remember, if you want to play a between-inning
game and get to meet Marlin T. Finn, sign up with any
usher you see in the yellow shirts!" Jack said.

"Then I got the message over my headset."

He paused to swallow, hoping he could get it out. "It was Bethany, the business manager. She was saying there was a h-hostage
situation up in the box, and that there were rifles trained on us,
the team, and the crowd. I had to keep everyone entertained so
they wouldn't leave."

He remembered the sharp smell of the rain, how the Marlin suit
smelled musty when it got damp. He smelled the beer that someone
had spilled on him in the third inning. But the show must go on.

"I asked Bethany what to do, and she said not to call the cops,
that there were three gunmen at least."

"Do you regret not calling the police?" Dr. Leo asked.

"I thought alerting the police too early was like taking the elevator in a fire. Not recommended?" Jack asked.

"That's not what I asked."

He had done exactly what Bethany told him to do. And Kevin followed his lead. Together they plastered on their public personas and played the fools and entertainers to keep people from finding out the truth.

"I did what she told me to," he said.

> *"We have a hostage negotiator on the phone with the guy now," Bethany said in her next call to him. "But the most important thing is to keep the game from starting up again."*
>
> *He glanced at the sky. It was still raining, but it was looking lighter to the west. If the weather cleared, then they would be able to start play again in fifteen minutes.*
>
> *"Why keep the game delayed?"*
>
> *"The group has a grudge against Toby Schnell. If he takes the mound, then they'll open fire."*
>
> *"Well, shit, just put someone else up to pitch."*
>
> *"They won't let us call the dugout."*

"Here is where you could have done a number of things," Dr. Leo interrupted.

"Why do you always tell me that?" Jack asked, covering his eyes.

"Because having choices doesn't mean you know what the right ones are. You could have called for help. You could have messaged the dugout. You could have kept going for the safety of the people held at gunpoint."

Jack chose the third option.

> *He had gone into the opposing team's dugout for privacy. They all watched him curiously. "Why can't we*

just call the game?" he whispered into his headset. "Let the fans go home?"

"Because they're stronger with hundreds of hostages," she said, keeping her voice low. "They're making demands to the police."

"Helicopters?"

"What? Why do you say that?"

"'Cause that's what people always want. The helicopter to lift them out of the clutches of Johnny Law."

"This is not fucking funny, Jack," she said, sounding near tears.

"I'm sorry, just trying to lighten the mood," he said.

"What we need you to do now is keep the crowd entertained. The main guy may want to take over the mic, but I'm going to fuck with the connection so we can't message you and he can't use the mic until you're done. But you have to get back out there, delay the game, and start talking."

"How do I get in touch with you, then?" he asked, but the signal was gone.

Marlin came up to him and raised his hands in a "WTF?" gesture.

Jack moved his headset mic away from his mouth and said, "We have a major problem."

Marlin removed the fish head and held it under his arm, becoming Kevin again, sweaty and disheveled. "What's wrong?"

"We have to give the performance of our lives, man."

"We went through two games of sumo, one game of ring toss, danced twice to 'Y.M.C.A.,' and we even let someone from the stands take the mic to protest the fat phobia of sumo games. We let Marlin race three kids around the bases, each of which Marlin lost to in a dramatic way. I quizzed people in the stands on 1990s pop culture trivia and played Name That Tune. I narrated while Marlin led a bunch of little kids dressed like him onto the field to mime his dance moves."

"And you talked the whole time," Dr. Leo said.

"Yeah."

"How did Kevin do as Marlin? He was used to more frequent breaks than he got that day, right?"

Jack nodded. "It helped that it wasn't so hot, but he was a damn pro. Followed my lead and kept the fans entertained. We were a good team."

"What happened next?"

> Afterward, he kept telling himself that he did his part, he held up his end of the bargain. He found out everything that happened later, but from his point of view, he was setting up for Marlin to lead the audience in starting the wave—impressive in a crowd that had thousands of empty seats between some of the groups—and Marlin sidestepped in front of him trying to encourage the wave to get moving. Then Kevin grunted and stepped back into him, collapsing in his arms. A shot sounded a moment later, echoing through the park. Someone screamed. Jack saw the tension in the crowd break, and they panicked.
>
> He lowered Kevin to the ground gently, but blood had already stained the fish suit. Jack pulled the costume head off to check on his friend, but Kevin was already dead.
>
> And then something snapped in Jack.

"And then what?" Dr. Leo said, as always.

"I don't remember," Jack said automatically.

"What's the next thing you do remember?"

"I was panting. My legs and lungs were aching. I was holding a bat." He kept his eyes closed as he spoke the now familiar words. He said it every time. "I had Kevin's blood on me. And other blood."

"Where were you?"

"The press box, where the gunmen were holding people. My boss was on the floor crying. Two people were holding their arms like they'd been stabbed. Three gunmen were on the floor, one of them—"

"It's okay. Keep going."

"One of them had been beaten to death. Another one was tied up, the third had been shot." He worked his mouth around the words. "I don't think I killed the one that got shot."

"So everything between Kevin getting shot and you standing in the press box with a bloody bat, that's all missing?"

Jack nodded miserably. "I can't tell you if I had a conscious thought, or weighed any options, or what. I just ran and killed. The news said I was a hero," he said, gagging slightly. "Like I was some gladiator."

"What did other people say you did?"

Jack looked up at him, removing his palms from his eyes. "What?"

"You don't remember, but others do. What did they say happened?"

"Someone in concessions said I yelled, 'Gun, everyone get down!' but people started to run in a panic. Angel, the catcher, said I grabbed a bat—our slugger's favorite bat, but he didn't mind—and ran into the tunnel under the dugout. No one saw me after that until I broke the lock on the press box and charged in. The people in the box say I went for the leader in such a focused way that they were all afraid of me. While I was"—he grimaced—"beating on him, someone disarmed one of the others, and used the gun to shoot the third." He glanced up at Dr. Leo's neutral face. "I guess you're also treating Alex Brody? Is he having problems after shooting that guy?"

"You know I can't discuss other patients with you," Dr. Leo said. "But I will say that, yes, ending a life can take a toll on you."

"Unless you can't remember it," Jack said.

"It's still with you, it's still taking its toll," Dr. Leo said. "You just don't see how much."

"Ah, like your card on a cruise ship," Jack said.

"The journalists want to call you a hero."

Jack laughed. "Yeah, notice they don't mention how I took care of the gunmen? They don't want me to look like a monster who killed monsters."

"You beat the man long after he had died," Dr. Leo said. "The medical examiner said he probably died with the second or third hit, but you kept going."

Jack stayed silent. That was not a question, just a statement of fact.

"So, now I'm on paid leave. I don't know if I can go back out there. I don't know if I want to meet the new mascot even."

"And you know the rest: Kevin was the only death, apart from the gunmen. Bethany had been pistol-whipped for calling him, but she got over her concussion and had some beautiful dental work to replace her damaged teeth. They got the stains out of the press box floor. And the world keeps turning."

He covered his eyes again, surprised that they were wet.

"What scares you about all this?" Dr. Leo said. "Are you feeling guilty for taking a life? Are you scared it will happen again?"

"I am scared that it will happen again," Jack snapped. "I can't tell you I made good or bad decisions, because I recall no decisions made. Will this happen to me again? If it does, will it take less than a straight-up murder to do it?"

"We're going to keep meeting and keep trying to get that last memory out of you," Dr. Leo said. "I'm here to work with you if you promise to work with me."

"I ENDED UP quitting," Jack said. "I couldn't get those memories back, and I didn't feel comfortable working on the field anymore. I felt exposed. Some days I would go and feel like I was vulnerable to gunmen all around me, and other days I worried I'd lose my temper and go hurt someone without even realizing."

"I was thinking about getting a job at a grocery store, but the Zesty books were starting to sell, and soon after publishers were interested. And you know the rest."

"Is this why you were so weird when I texted you about your deal?" Cosima asked.

He gave a small smile. "Yeah."

JACK WAS DRIVING home on a warm fall afternoon when a message came.

"Good news. Call me."

This was Cosima, the agent's assistant. His new literary agent's assistant. That still felt weird to say, even in his head.

He drove the rest of the way home, parallel parked, and then opened the message with shaking hands. His fingers left smears on the phone screen, which he impatiently wiped off with his sleeve, which accidentally opened the camera and took a picture of his crotch.

He needed to remember to delete photos when he got home. If he didn't, the next time he took his phone in, the Apple Genius Bar worker would think he was sending "clothed dick pics."

Again.

The text hadn't been a brief stoplight hallucination. It was real. He called the number that sent the text and drummed his fingers on the dashboard.

"Hey, it's Jack. Uh, Jack Vasara. What's up?"

Cosima was friendly and warm. "Aaron loves it, and he's in talks with the editor. He thinks an offer will come tomorrow. I wanted to let you know tonight because it's nice to think about it before you get the actual offer."

"Oh, my God," he said.

"Here's the bare-bones data: the publishers are willing to increase the offer for the books if you sell all five! Aaron is trying to get at least twenty-five percent more from the initial offer. He thinks he can."

Jack waited for the bad news. "What's the downside?"

"The downside to a high-end six-figure offer?" Cosima asked.

"Things don't go this well for me," he said. "And the money isn't as important. I'm waiting for the downside to professional edits. You want to make him a more attractive plant? Take out the gay plant sex scene? The contract is null and void if I ever go on social media again?"

A bead of sweat rolled down Jack's forehead. He realized he was sitting in a death trap by parking the car in the sun with the windows rolled up, but he couldn't move his hands for fear of breaking the spell of this conversation.

"Aaron will call you tomorrow. There's no downside. This is very cool. Congrats."

Things were going well. Finally. He could move on and start his life as an author. The only deaths would be fictional from now on.

JACK TURNED TO Cosima. "At that time did you know he'd be stealing a third of my advance?"

"No!" she said, hands up in surrender again. "Aaron lied to me and told me it was five hundred K. The moron forgot I got copied on all his work emails, so I saw it later. I was going to tell you. I promise."

"So, tell me what happened last night?" Mallory asked. "You were super pissed off when you left me, and I didn't see you after that. What did you see at the concert?"

"It's not very interesting," he admitted. "I stormed out of the balcony and then realized I had no idea where he was. I hadn't seen him at the concert. I sent him a message asking where he was, and he replied back immediately that he was at the concert. I looked around but never saw him."

"Nothing weird, no one with a knife, none of that?" Mallory asked.

He sighed. "I would have told you if I saw something weird." He paused, then looked at his phone. "Okay, there was one tiny thing weird." He handed it to Mallory, and Cosima looked over her shoulder.

15 MAY 2047–15:03:01

ZestysJack: Did you want to talk about the plot of bk 6 while we are in the same place?

AaronR: How's tomorrow after the keynote?

ZestysJack: 👍

15 MAY 2047–22:03:38

ZestysJack: AARON- we need to talk. Where are you??

AaronR: Bed. Talk 2morrow?

ZestysJack: It needs to be now, dude.

"'2morrow'?" Mallory asked, raising her eyebrow to Cosima. "Have you ever seen him use that word?"

Cosima laughed. "Definitely not."

In all of Mallory's communication with him, Aaron was meticulous in his messages. He often said that text shorthand was a sign of a sloppy mind, someone who didn't respect who they were chatting with.

"So, the killer had control of Aaron and his phone at this point," Mallory said. She thought for a moment, tapping her notebook with her pen. "I'm curious: if this were a Zesty Yaboi story, who would you think the murderer is?"

"Never trust the hot dame who comes in and pretends to help solve the case," Jack said. "Do you have any of those?"

Mallory hid a smile while Cosima bristled.

21

. . .

SUDO ME A CLUE

E VE SAID SHE couldn't do another interview until she figured out what was going on with *Metis*, so Mallory asked
Phineas about his and Eve's relationship.

They waited for her in the off-brand sitcom bar, sharing a pot
of coffee with Cosima and Xan. "I got the rundown of her story,
but there wasn't a lot there. Can you tell me what you know about
her? Especially with regards to *Metis*."

"I guess to tell you about Eve I have to start with stories about
myself," Phineas said. "You remember being a teenager, and how
absolutely everything seems super important?"

"Of course," she said, stirring her coffee. She took a sip and
then made a face, then added more sugar. "I was focused on a lot
of death, but I remember some of the unimportant things that felt
like they could take over the world."

"Xan left me to go to college and then the army. And all of the
anger Grandma had about him, she took out on me. Which is a
bad place to leave any kid, but I was also having some serious gender dysphoria once puberty hit. I was built like a man, tall, heavy,
strong. Apart from the lady parts, that is. I found it easy to get
summer jobs at horse stables and farms, anywhere that needed a
strong back. Anything that could get me away from home.

"One night, our grandmother was drunk on apple moonshine and mumbling about how I should have been born a boy, since I looked like one anyway. I think she meant it as an insult, but I had never felt happier. She *saw* me. She was drunk and mean, but she knew I was a boy. About a week later, I waited for that short window when she was tipsy enough to feel the illusion of a good mood and before she got into the mean drunk part of the evening. Then I came out to her."

"That had to have been scary," Mallory said.

"I was terrified, but in hindsight, I shouldn't have been. She wasn't particularly religious, but a lot of people her age were having trouble with imagining gender as something other than binary. I think she liked that I was going to make a lot of the old people in town angry."

He smiled sadly. "One time when I was ten, she'd had a hangover and handed me dirty clothes to wear to school. I tried to tell her it was picture day, but she didn't listen. So when I came out, she said, 'So, it's like that picture day. I been dressing you wrong all this time, ain't I?'"

"Pretty forward-thinking for her," Mallory said.

"She still was as mean as Satan's dog," Phineas said with a bitter chuckle. "And still embarrassed me. She took me to a doctor in Johnson City and declared loudly that her grandson had the wrong body and needed help. She seemed to think that they could just take my brain out and plop it into a male-presenting body. I tried to tell her that technology didn't exist, and she just said, 'I don't know about that. I read something about uploading minds once. You'd think they'd just have spare bodies lying around.' I think she was talking about a *Twilight Zone* episode."

"That sounds familiar," Mallory said. "I think I saw that one."

"So I got rid of a lot of Xan's science-fiction books plus the Syfy channel on our TV."

"You did what?" Xan demanded.

"Why do you think I keep sending you drives of your favorite ebooks?" Phineas said. "When you get a home with a bookshelf, I will be happy to send you all the books you want.

"Even with Grandma supporting me, I had the typical teen angst that everyone in the world struggles with. Crushes. Feeling unattractive. Bullies at school. Fat phobia. And during that time, I listened to music."

He offered them a view of VDV from a teen's POV. Vagina Dentata V had been a one-hit wonder with their song that they released online, "Sudo Me Red Flowers," back in 2033. The band was an enigma. Was it fronted by teenagers, or drug-addicted middle-aged people? Had they broken up twice or did they have the same original band members? Their first and only album was released online and remained there.

"Man, I listened to those guys nonstop. I loved the songs when the words spoke to my soul, and loved the music when I didn't care what they were singing about. The first song I wrote was a hip-hop cover of 'Sudo Me Red Flowers.' I wrote it, and I recorded it, and I uploaded it to the video sites. I wasn't going to do a video of myself. You know, fat phobia and transphobia, it's all real. But I decided hiding myself was giving in to haters."

"And it was a hit?" Mallory asked.

"Nope!" he said with a wide grin. "It got no traction at all. No one cared. And I couldn't decide if it was worse to get harassment and bad feedback or no feedback. But I knew I was an absolute nobody, so why should anyone listen to me? That shouldn't stop me. I had fun."

"Excellent," Mallory said. "But where does Eve—"

"I'm getting to it. I made a few more VDV covers, and then recorded some of my own songs based off my AP literature class—'Nothing Rhymes with Areopagitica' was my first song— and started to build a tiny fan base. I went to LA to make my fortune, but of course ended up in a restaurant. It turned out I was good at cooking, though, and slowly moved up from dishwasher to cook to better restaurants. One night, in the middle of my shift as a sous chef, at a restaurant named Crank, I received an email from someone named Eve Goodberry. I didn't recognize the name and was about to trash it, but the subject line didn't look like spam. 'Your Sudo cover slaps!'"

"That sounds like the best day ever," Mallory said, while Xan grumbled, "'Bout time you got to her part of the story."

THIS GAL EVE claimed to be Fiver from Vagina Dentata V, and said she had come across Phin's video and loved the hip-hop take on her song. She said she couldn't pay him, but gave him full permission to remix VDV's songs so she could hear more hip-hop.

Years passed, Phineas made more videos and kept in touch with Eve, but since she went into software development, VDV wasn't making music anymore, so their conversations waned. But she always sent him a note when he uploaded a new song. She actually called him when he got his first record deal.

Then a few months ago, the real shocker came—Eve found a sentient ship buried in the sand. Online, Phineas had mentioned his brother and friends on Eternity, and there were lots of rumors about sentient ships, so she mailed him and asked if he had any knowledge.

At this time, Eve was living off the money from the band and the white-hat security company she had founded and then sold.

"A what hat?" Cosima interrupted.

"White hat. Like the opposite of a villain. Clients hire them to use their hackers to break into their systems to figure out the weak spots, then they fix those security holes. They're doing bad for the sake of good. So instead of black hats, they're white hats."

She made a note. "All right. Continue. What did she write to you?"

"Phineas, you told me you went to that sentient space station,

right? And you've seen how people can talk to living space stations or ships or whatever? If so, we need to talk. I think I found one buried in the Outer Banks."

Phineas called her. "What the fuck?" he asked as a greeting.

"I found a sentient ship!" she enthused. Wind whipped around her, dulling her voice. She must have been on the beach at the time of the discovery.

"I tripped over her and cut my foot, and then she started talking to me in my head, but I don't know what to do for her!" she said.

Phineas immediately caught a flight to Norfolk and rented a car to drive to the Outer Banks. It was winter, and most tourists stayed away from the vacation spots. All that was there this time of year was cold rain, rough water, and locals who hated tourists.

Aside from two good ole boys who'd gotten their trucks stuck in the sand and were digging themselves in deeper as they tried to four-wheel-drive their way out, the beach was deserted. Phineas parked at a public beach access point at the mile marker Eve had given him and headed to the vacation rental at that marker. It was a small house, but like all oceanside villas it was built high enough to see the ocean above the dune, and had a wraparound deck so you could sit outside and see the sun set over the ocean, or enjoy the sunrise off Jockey's Ridge.

He was about to knock when he heard his name. Eve's head peeked from around the back. "Come on, this is amazing!"

They'd never met in person, but of course he'd seen photos of her. First, masked with VDV, then just a woman on Instagram, always pictures with the left side of her straight black hair (often colored electric blue) covering her face. But out here in the chilly winter wind, her hair was flying around, showing what she had previously covered: a long ugly burn scar. It looked years old, and healed, but clearly she was still self-conscious about it.

Her face was flushed from the wind and, probably, excitement. She crouched by a black piece of metal that stuck out from a dune on the land side. "I'm just hanging out with her right now. Do you know what to do?"

Phineas was glad he was wearing leather boots as he walked over the spiky flora that served as "lawns" in the Outer Banks, but he still stepped gingerly. "I sent my brother a message, but you know he's light-years away, right? I can't just call him up. What you got here?"

The slab of metal looked like someone had crashed their car into a dune and left its bumper behind. Phineas reached out to touch it. "You sure this is a ship?" He tried to wiggle the piece out, but it didn't budge. A very faint thrumming came up, and he let go immediately. "Okay, I guess it's a ship."

"I need help to get it out. Her out. She needs help." Her face became tender, almost maternal. "Her name is Metis."

"Get it out? No way, that way lies madness and people losing teeth and buying a bunch of batteries. Didn't you read The Tommy-knockers?"

"That ship wasn't sentient, and I'm not losing any teeth," Eve said. "And that ship didn't talk to them."

"I guess you have read it. Hey, what did you think about Gard's ex-wife? Why didn't they talk more about him shooting her?"

"I figured it was to make sure he remained a sympathetic character. But can we have book club later? What do I do?"

A few months before, Phineas had talked to Xan about his bond with Infinity. "I remember he thinks he bonded with her when his blood got on her. He feeds her ancient bio-matter as they call it, oil as we call it. A lot like our cars, but with intelligence. And they can fly. So I'm betting if you get yourself some oil and figure out how to get it into her, that might perk her up. Is there a gas cap anywhere here?" He put his ear to the ship, then tapped gently with his finger-nail. A very faint thrum came again. "Xan told me that all sentient ships, stations, what have you, have a Sundry hivemind. It's like their heart, they can't live without it. Maybe it's like their brain. He wasn't sure. Anyway, I don't know where you can get one of those on Earth."

Eve brightened. "I think she already has a mind. Or a queen, at least." She showed him the edge of the ship where the metal continued along the top of the dune for about five feet. Phineas put his finger into the cold sand and traced the length of the metal until he found a tiny, sand-coated hole, like the ones crabs lurked in. He blew away the sand around it and showed Eve. "Oh, yeah, you're right. That's how they got in. A queen must be laying her eggs right now. I think if you get the ship some oil, and the queen some fruit, the ship might be strong enough to fly on her own. Then she should also be strong enough for you to ride with her."

"WERE YOU JUST talking out of your ass here?" Xan asked Phineas. "I don't remember telling you that."

"I make awesome educated guesses," Phineas said with a sniff. "And I was right, wasn't I?"

Eve's face lit up with joy. "Really? My own ship?"

"I don't know if I'd call it your ship, that's not how my brother talks, anyway. You'll be hers as much as she'll be yours." He straightened and brushed the sand off his jeans. "This your house? I could use something to warm me up, coffee or whiskey. Or coffee and whiskey."

Eve shook her head, looking down. "I'm in my car right now. I have a room in the motel a few miles in on the mainland."

"You aren't renting this house? Is someone going to call the cops on us for trespassing?"

"They're more likely to arrest us for destroying the dune," Eve said, looking around. "But yeah, I'm frozen and can use a break. Come on, the heater in my car is great."

Phineas shook his head and pulled out his phone, instructing it to call Ryan.

His assistant Ryan picked up on the first ring. "Hey, man, I'ma need a beach house rental ASAP. Where are we, Eve? Kitty Hawk, North Carolina?"

"Kill Devil Hills," Eve corrected.

"Kill Devil what? They have some fucked-up names down here. So, we're apparently in Kill Devil Hills and need a rental on the beach, preferably"—he walked around to the front of the four-story house—"a place called 'Margaritaville'? Jesus fucking Christ, no one has any imagination anymore. But yeah, Joe Lamb Jr. is the rental company to call." He gave his assistant the house number and ended the call.

"What, just like that?" Eve asked.

"Think of it as me giving back to you for your music. It saved my life, you know. While we're waiting on Ryan, let's get in the car and hit a grocery store. Metis isn't the only person who wants food right now."

"YOU MET ONE of your idols and helped her dig up a spaceship?" Xan asked. "Maybe Mallory is right and there are no coincidences. Why was she sleeping in her car at the beach?"

"She's kind of single-minded," Phineas said. "She'd gotten a place to the south to save money, but once she started digging up Metis, she just kept digging until it got dark."

"So, after VDV broke up, she went corporate?" Xan asked.

"Yeah."

"How did you protect the ship from the authorities? I imagine they don't like someone claiming a spaceship on land they don't own."

"Eve spoke to a lawyer who said we could claim it as salvage. The law didn't extend to space salvage yet, so there was no precedent. But it never came up, because once we got her and her hive-mind what they needed—namely, fuel—Metis got herself out of the dune. She was a tiny ship then, like the size of a compact car."

"How did she get there in the first place?" Xan asked. "I thought the Sundry were the only aliens on Earth before First Contact?"

"A lot of what made *Metis* herself had atrophied. She had a lot of data saved, but we couldn't access it, and she didn't remember much of her story. She remembered she was trying to get away from someone and protect her crew, but she got damaged and crash-landed on the beach. She was weakened and her crew and her hivemind died. Then a hurricane came and finished burying her in sand."

"*Infinity*, are you getting all this?" Xan asked aloud.

It all sounds reasonable to me. Explains why she doesn't remember much, explains why she was there.

"I want to know what her crew was running from," Xan said.

"Who cares? It was literally over a thousand years ago," Phineas said.

"Anyway, after we got her dug out, *Metis* airlifted some sand to fill in the cavity she left—Kill Devil Hills folks were *mad* we'd messed up their dune—then we got to go aboard and learn more about her."

"She was the size of a car, though? Why is she so massive now?"

Phineas laughed at the memory. "We didn't know you were supposed to regulate diets. We just let her go out every day and seek out bio-matter in the ocean, and every night she would come back bigger. She then started to ask for data."

ONCE METIS HAD *reached the size of a suburban American house, Phineas and Eve took a ride over the Atlantic, Phineas being only a little nervous in putting his trust in a ship that had been buried for over a thousand years. "So, what's this ship's purpose?" he asked. "Is she a shuttle, or a fighter jet, or what?"*

Eve looked around and then pointed to a speaker on the wall, something Phineas could have sworn wasn't there before. "Metis?" Eve asked.

"I am a science vessel, Phineas. I carry data."

"What data?" Eve asked eagerly.

"Not much right now," Metis said sadly. "Very little has survived. I don't remember what I carried, or who I carried, or when I crashed. My cargo hold is down that ladder." A spotlight blinked on a ladder connecting the bottom floor to the top cockpit.

Eve and Phineas explored the small ship, starting with the cargo hold that held mostly dust. If anything remained that was book- or scroll-shaped, it crumbled away when they touched it. Then they found a room with thick steel walls with tiny holes all over it.

"It's like Swiss cheese," Eve said in a whisper.

That didn't sound right to Phineas. He touched one of the holes. It was smooth and almost perfectly round. "No, not cheese. It's like those bee houses that gardening stores sell. The Sundry burrowed through the steel." He spotted a blue Sundry crawling around one of the holes. "There. Look. It's one of the new hivemind."

Metis spoke up. "This is where my digital data is stored. The new hivemind are trying to repair it."

"Do you know what they're repairing? It's got to be out of date, right?" Phineas asked.

"I don't remember . . ."

Phineas shrugged. "Maybe it'll come to you."

Something bothered him. He hummed a few lines to a new song, thinking about Xan and Infinity and his time on Eternity and—

"Do you have an audio implant, one that lets you understand languages?" he said to Eve. "Everyone going to space gets one, but are they available around here?"

She shook her head. "I've heard of them, but they're not available for the general public."

"But Metis is talking to us and making sense."

"So?"

"Where did she get an English dictionary? How does she know how to communicate with us if she's been asleep for hundreds of years? Language changes, but she's been asleep."

"I don't know!" Eve said, rolling her eyes. "This is an amazing find, and it's ours. Why are you being negative?"

"I'm just saying over a thousand years ago she buried herself in the sand, stayed there as empires rose and fell, and when we dig her up, she speaks perfect English? 'Cause you're not having it translated by an audio implant, she's really speaking English for you. Modern ships have access to this whole big galactic database for languages, but if she's been here, then she doesn't."

"Who cares?" Eve said.

"THAT WAS A damn good question," Xan said. "And she didn't care?"

"Eve is really smart and doesn't like not being the one to figure stuff out, or ask an obvious question. Of course she was curious, but I had annoyed her. She did ask the ship later."

"I figured *Metis* would say she forgot," Xan said.

"No, she said it was because of her new Sundry queen. Because of greater alien activity on Earth, more and more Sundry from space were coming here in ships and leaving a few of their hive behind to mix with the Sundry hidden on Earth. So when a young queen who'd had access to galactic databases got wind of an empty ship nearby, this was her chance to build her own hive. Realizing *Metis* had access to all that data already made Eve consider what else *Metis* could store. One day I had said something about how my brother couldn't keep up with the sports or news back home since you didn't have the Internet, and that gave her the idea. She decided to bring the Internet here, which would also help draw more humans to space. And give aliens a taste of what we create."

"Because what a cranky Gurudev manager needs is a cat video?" Xan asked. "So, can she hold the Internet? It's got to be in the hundreds of zettabytes!"

Phineas grimaced. "Bigger. And this is where we found out that there's a specific skill that *Metis* has—while *Eternity* and *Infinity* can change their insides to fit what their crew needs, *Metis* is more advanced by far. And she's creative. She designed her own body to fit what she understands the Internet to be. Once she started backing up the Internet, she realized she needed more processing power, so she took on four other queens. *Metis* has at least five separate hiveminds inside her. She's got hiveminds for computing power, short-term storage, long-term storage, and one completely dedicated to just making up shit as the rooms change."

"And the fifth?" Xan prompted.

"Man, that one I don't know and Eve won't tell me," Phineas said with a sigh. "I barely understand this shit. I think maybe Eve doesn't even know *Metis*'s capabilities, and this trip here is a test of that power. Sometimes Eve tells me stuff, sometimes she gets real cagey."

"And we found out Aaron gave her that scar," Mallory mused.

"For real?" Phineas said.

"Aaron caused the accident onstage where Eve got burned during a show. She only just told us. This could be a case of Eve getting her revenge because he landed right in her lap."

Xan frowned. Then spoke aloud. "Hey, *Infinity*, can you ask *Metis* some questions? Ship to ship?"

He paused, listening. "She says she can, but *Metis* will know she's asking for us."

"Can't hurt," Phineas said. "It might go better coming from her."

Mallory nodded. "Can she ask her what she was running from when she crashed?"

The answer came back much faster than anticipated, but Xan realized ships didn't have to talk at the same speed as when they talk to people. "*Metis* said she knew she was storing some important things, for her host and crew—hang on, this is getting to be a lot." He pulled out his tablet. "*Infinity*, you should be able to send audio messages through this, right?"

"I just thought you liked to be the gatekeeper," said a warm voice through the tablet.

"Is it true she's carrying the entire Internet?" Phineas asked.

"She believes she has about eighty-five percent, but she ignores superfluous things like web searches and Blogspot. Also texts asking for 'booty calls.'" Xan and Phineas laughed at the sudden dry, derisive tone of her voice. "She says there are a lot of cute animal videos. And a lot of sex."

"That's the Internet all right," Xan said.

"I made some calculations based on some of her data," *Infinity* continued. "She crashed in July of '48 BCE, as you call it."

"No shit?" Phineas said.

Xan said, "Closer to *two* thousand years ago."

"The Emperor Julius Caesar ruled Rome then. He was behind a cataclysmic fire in Alexandria."

"You mean the data stored aboard her was the *Library of Alexandria*?" Mallory asked in disbelief.

"No, she was just here at that time. Her crew was running from someone. She remembers the Library of Alexandria because that was an area where they had landed briefly. When they rushed to leave, they left a crewmate behind."

"I wonder if the abandoned alien survived," Phineas said.

"Or how it did," Mallory said.

"Looking at the history of the time," *Infinity* continued, "it looks as if the alien was discovered by humans and worshipped as a god until it died."

The three humans looked at each other, puzzled.

"Wait," Mallory said. "An alien was abandoned in Egypt two thousand years ago. It was worshipped as a god."

Phineas looked thoughtful. "What alien looks like a *god*?"

"I think the question is, what god looks like an alien?" Mallory asked, really hoping she was wrong. "*Infinity*, do you have access to a database of older Earth languages?"

"I do," she said.

"What was the ancient Egyptian word for 'cat'?"

"Their word was 'Miu.'"

22

SPLITTING THE PARTY

THIS IS WHY Tina came to *Metis* instead of Eternity," Mallory said. "This ship once belonged to the Miu!"

"Do you think it wants it back?" Xan asked. "It seems to be pretty content to sit on Bruce's lap or be worshipped in the cat room."

"I have no idea. I'm going to go ask Eve some questions. You two"—she pointed to Xan and Phineas—"see if you can find Bruce and the alien, but don't tell them what we know."

"Mal, I had a thought," Xan said. "Tina implies she can understand both the Miu and the Cuckoos, despite no language data available to the rest of galactic civilization. What if the Cuckoos have their own databases on Bezoar, with all the data about the civilizations who died out everywhere except for those still living on Bezoar?"

Mallory stopped trying to gather her notebook and pens. "So, Tina can understand them."

"And I will bet that *Metis* can, too, if she used to belong to them."

Mallory whipped her head around to try to look over her shoulder. "Is that what she gave you, *Mobius*? Dead language databases?"

I don't know. I know the mean bugs talked to me. With words. He sounded unsure.

"We need to keep him safe from the Miu," she said to Xan. "If it's talking to Tina's Cuckoos, then it probably already knows *Mob* has their data."

"But why guard it? I thought communication was a good thing," Phineas said.

"The ancient data probably contains more than just languages," Mallory said. "This is the most sophisticated ship we've ever seen—anyone has ever seen—and it's two thousand years old at least. That data could tell us where they got the ship, or why *Metis* is the only one, or who they stole it from. Shit, we should also try to find Tina to see if she's keeping track of her bugs."

"Why do you think it was stolen?" Cosima asked, not looking up from writing in her notebook.

Mallory looked around for support but found only confused faces. "There was a wild chase with spaceships that ended up with one of them crashed on Earth. That sounds like a typical car chase with the inept thieves ending up in a swamp."

"This isn't *Dukes of Hazzard*, Mallory," Phineas said. "It's possible those little guys were more innovative than they seem." But he didn't seem too sure of that last statement.

"Sure, the way it hangs around Bruce's neck, that indicates a race of Edisons, for sure," Mallory snapped.

Phineas held up his hands in surrender. "All right, remember, I'm on your side."

"You seem a little fussy," Cosima said. "We need to break for a snack."

"What?" Mallory demanded. "I am not fussy."

Cosima reached into her purse and produced a granola bar. Mallory took the offer silently, her face burning. "Fine. Thank you."

"You're welcome. Now. What about the murders?" Cosima asked.

Mallory frowned as she chewed through cinnamon crunchiness. "I think I know who did it, but I need more information. We need to talk to Eve." She took *Mobius* out of her hood and held him out to Xan. "Keep him safe for me? I don't want to lose him again."

"You got it," Xan said, accepting the ship and looking at Mallory curiously.

"What, do I have granola on my face?" Mallory asked, brushing at her mouth.

"No, just remembering something a friend said," he said. "It was about blood sugar and mood or something."

He was very obviously lying, but Mallory didn't have time to unearth what he was hiding. "Can you find Tina and make sure you can locate Bruce and the alien? I don't want to lose track of any of those three."

"I know where we can keep little *Mob*," Phineas said. "He was doing a good job hiding in the junkyard."

"Be careful up there," Xan said. "If Eve has *Metis* on her side then she doesn't need to kill you, she can just make you disappear."

XAN AND PHINEAS found Tina in one of the bars that *Metis* created from Earth media, but this one was full of a motley crew of weirdness. Geese, horses, holy men of many flavors, strippers, gardeners, and dogs sat at the bar, or at tables, or in booths.

"I don't want to know what TV show this is from," Phineas said, looking around. He stepped aside as a goose honked at him.

Tina was easy to find. She had torn a table from one of the booths and hurled it across the bar where it remained lodged in the wall. Tina had nestled into her little cubby where she could sit on the floor, her head against the wall, arms splayed out on the booth seats.

"What the hell happened to you?" Xan asked.

"You are not to use that tone with me," Tina said, holding her head. "I'm a goddamn queen."

"Okay, what the hell happened to you, Your Majesty?" Phineas asked.

"The Cuckoos wanted a drink. Wanted me to take a drink. Not sure."

"You went drinking? You're *hungover*?" Xan asked, looking at a small pile of pebbles and ash beside her.

"Is that puke?" Phineas asked under his breath, pointing at the pile.

"I don't know and don't *want* to know the answer to that," Xan replied.

"Hungover. Bad," she confirmed.

"What the hell did you drink? Do they even serve the stuff Gneiss drink on this ship?" Xan asked, looking at the bartender. He did see one of the taps with a rock logo, and it wasn't Rolling Rock.

"I don't know, I asked what he would serve the queen. Then I asked for a bucket of it."

"And your Cuckoos told you to do this?"

"Yeah. Said it would be fun," she muttered.

"So, you are able to communicate directly with them," Phineas said.

"Let me die," Tina muttered.

"What do we do to sober her up?" Phineas asked Xan. "The Cuckoos aren't with her. We would need her to corral them."

Tina waved her hand. "The bugs are somewhere. They can't go far. Just go look for them and leave me alone. They like the cat room."

"Everyone likes the cat room," Xan said.

Mentally he asked *Infinity* to take the bad news about the missing Cuckoos to the necessary parties, and privately he wondered how any of them thought that giving Tina the responsibility of handling rogue infiltration insects was a good idea when he wouldn't trust her with a goldfish.

MALLORY AND COSIMA arrived at Eve's control room, the elevator doors opening to darkness. This was scary attack darkness, not slouchy hacker darkness.

"Shit," Mallory said, holding Cosima back in the elevator. "*Metis*? Where are the lights? Eve, are you here?"

The wall of monitors were off; every terminal in the room was blank.

A light popped on beside her, and Mallory realized Cosima had turned on her phone's light.

They carefully walked forward, sweeping the light around the room.

When they focused on Eve's desk, two eyes glowed at them when the light passed over the office chair. Mallory jumped back as it hissed. "I forgot there was a cat up here," she said.

"Is it even real?" Cosima asked.

"Does it matter? Do you want to take the chance to find out?" Mallory said. "She's got a brunch name. Let me think."

Cosima fired off foods in rapid succession. "Hash browns? Egg? Pancake? Waffle? Coffee?"

"Mimosa!" Mallory said. "It's okay, Mimosa, we won't hurt you."

Mimosa shrank back and yowled as Cosima's light came across her.

Mallory smacked her arm. "Leave her alone, we have to find Eve."

"The cat has blood on her whiskers," Cosima said. "She's attacked something or someone."

"She's guarding," Mallory said. She pointed under the desk. "Look."

Under the desk, penned in by the office chair, a dark lump moaned. Mallory ran over and crouched down while Cosima made soothing noises at Mimosa.

Eve was under the desk, barely conscious, bleeding from a head wound.

Mallory dropped to Eve's side. "How did *Metis* let this happen?"

"And why isn't she freaking out?" Cosima asked, keeping the light on Eve's face. Didn't you say Eternity freaked out when her host died?"

Mallory placed a finger on Eve's neck. "Yeah, but she's not dead. We need to get her some medical attention, somewhere safer than that medbay." She pointed to the three elevators that came to the control room, all of which went to different places on the ship. "But how can we do that fast without *Metis*'s help?"

"That one can take us to the *hospital* hospital," Cosima said, pointing to the elevator on the left end. She scooped Mimosa up, and miraculously the cat let her.

"How do you know that?" Mallory asked, gesturing for Cosima to help her pull Eve into the office chair.

Once they had Eve situated as best they could, Mimosa jumped on Eve's lap and settled down, as if daring Mallory to make her go anywhere else.

"Your ship," Mallory said, shrugging. "I'm not going to tell you where to go. I'll let a doctor do that."

Mimosa began purring, then started licking her paw and washing her face, removing the blood of the attacker.

"Good cat," Mallory said.

Trying to use an office chair as a stretcher wasn't the best idea in the world, but they were doing the best they could. As they gently guided Eve and Mimosa past the wall of monitors, they encountered a bit of resistance as the wheels crunched over glass.

"Mallory, look," Cosima said.

Mallory looked where Cosima was pointing her light. Now that they were closer, it was obvious; glass littered the floor, the monitors above them showing cracked glass in all but a handful of them, in which the screens were fully shattered.

Together they got Eve into the elevator.

"What does this do for your theories?" Cosima said. "Are you thinking Eve is the killer?"

"Eve?" Mallory asked. "Why?"

"*Metis* claims to have missed some key events," Cosima explained. "Either she's lying, encouraged by the only person she'd listen to, her host, or she had her cameras or her memory altered, and as far as we know, only Eve can do that."

"Anyone could have busted those monitors, though," Mallory said. "And how do you explain that?" She pointed to Eve's injury, still dripping blood on the elevator floor.

Cosima brightened with realization. "*Metis* fought back!" she said. "She could manifest anything, right? She made magical teleporting cats, so she can do anything."

"Holy shit. That's it," Mallory said, her eyes growing wide. "Cosima, you might be a good assistant after all."

BEFORE THEY ENTERED the hospital, Mallory said, "When we leave her here, I need you to stay with her and not leave her alone for a second. Don't trust humans, don't trust *Metis*'s created doctors. Stay with her."

"Done," Cosima said. "What are you going to do?"

"I'm going to find Phin, Xan, and Bruce. If you hear from Jack or Bruce, do not tell them about Eve and do not tell them you're in the hospital with her."

"You're not going to tell me who did it, are you?" Cosima asked.

"That's not how this is done," Mallory said with a grin.

* * *

XAN AND PHINEAS left Tina in the goose bar, Phineas telling the bartenders that under no uncertain terms were they to give her any more alcohol. "Come find us when you're doing better," Xan called over his shoulder.

They found Bruce blissed out in the cat room. More convention fans were there, cooing and laughing, the noise actually turning cats off, it seemed. But not Bruce; he wore a light denim jacket and lay face down on a bed, his head pillowed on his hands, with one cat between his shoulder blades, one on his lower back, one perched on his butt, and one trying to lie down in the space between his knees.

"Oh, good, you're here," Xan said.

The dentist opened his eyes a small sliver, eyeing him suspiciously. "Do I know you?"

"We haven't met, but I've seen you. I'm Xan and I think you know my brother here. We're friends of Mallory's," he reminded him. He stuck out his hand to shake, but Bruce didn't move.

"We haven't seen you since before Kath's death," Phineas said. "We wanted to check on you, man. Are you doing okay?"

Bruce relaxed his defensive stiffness and closed his eyes again. "No, I'm not okay. She was my best friend."

"Real sorry about that," Phineas said. "But, hey, you love cats, so where's your little alien buddy?"

Bruce pointed to the pillar, where the Cheshire cat sat and gazed down on the other felines prowling around the base, sometimes getting into little fistfights, sometimes just hissing at each other. "It's amazing how much like cats they are," Bruce said, his sad expression melting to adoration.

"You seem close to the alien," Phineas said, leaning against the headboard of the bed. "What happens when you have to go back to Earth?"

Bruce shrugged unhappily, then shifted on the bed. "I guess I leave him behind."

"You don't think it wants to go home with you? Be a full-time pet?" Phineas asked.

Bruce looked up sharply. "He is not a pet. He's incredibly intelligent." His face was red with lines where he had been lying on his hands. Then he put his head down again.

"My bad, I'm sorry," Phineas said. "The question stands, though."

They were distracted by Mallory walking in, looking distracted. She had blood on her shoulder, but when she met Xan's eyes, she shook her head slightly. *Later.*

"Bruce, there you are!" Mallory said. She ran and leaned over, hugging his shoulders like an old friend. "I'm so sorry about Kath. I've been looking for you to see how you're faring."

"I can't believe it happened," he said, shaking his head. "Who was so upset about their writing career that they'd take it out on Aaron and Kath?"

"You think that was the motive?" Mallory asked.

"Of course. Isn't that why agents usually die?"

"Heart disease might be the number one killer," she said mildly. "Way ahead of murder."

She sat on the bed while Xan leaned on the wall, keeping one eye on the alien and one eye on Bruce.

He finally sat up, carefully dislodging the cats. He picked up the cat on his shoulders and placed it on the floor and then stuck his hands in his pockets. His face was all blotchy on the cheek he had been pillowing with his hands. He heaved a heavy sigh. "I am going to miss her so much."

"I know you and Kath were close. Can you tell me more about her?" Mallory asked, putting her hand on his shoulder.

"Are you interrogating me about my dead friend? What are you accusing me of?" he demanded. He looked from Mallory to Xan to Phineas, then to the alien. "My friend *died.*"

"I just wanted to talk about that friendship," Mallory said mildly. "Not accusing you of anything. Most people like to talk about their old friends."

A white cat wandered by, paused, and then jumped on Bruce's lap. "Wow, you really are a cat person, aren't you?" Mallory asked, looking impressed.

"Of course," he said. "Are you a dog person?" He said the words as if he were asking if Mallory preferred murdering babies over getting a massage.

"I'm not going to talk about me," she said with a laugh. "Admitting what you just said feels like it would be making myself a target in this room."

"Cats really like me," he said. "I don't know why."

Mallory pressed on. "Was Kath a cat lady? I want a better sense of who she was. I didn't get to know her, and I need to know her if I'm going to find her killer. What can you tell me?"

"Why not ask me about Aaron?"

"I will, eventually," Mallory said, shrugging. "But I met you and Kath together. You'd been friends for a long time. Tell me about it."

He blew his nose. "I don't know what we haven't already told you. We were VDV fans; we met online."

"Right," Mallory said. "But you were also both mystery writers. Did you meet earlier, before VDV?"

He casually stroked the new cat. "There was an online workshop run by a mystery writer . . . seventeen or so years ago? She paired me and Kath together because she said we could learn from each other."

His face grew red and he swiped at his cheeks and cleared his throat. "She was right, I guess. So we started being each other's beta reader. But you know, medical school is demanding, and then there's loans and residencies and stuff. We reconnected when VDV did a surprise online concert, and found out we both had put our writing careers on the back burner. So we encouraged each other to start writing again."

"When was this?" Mallory asked.

He shook his head as if not trusting his memory. "Five years ago? We were both working on novels during our off time and started sending them to each other."

"How was her writing?" Mallory asked.

Bruce looked startled again. "W-why?"

Mallory looked at him quizzically. "It's a simple question, isn't it? You were critiquing it, so you know better than anyone how good your friend was?"

"Why is this important?" he snapped. "My friend is dead and you're bugging me about the quality of her stories?"

"Did you like her writing?"

"It was fine!" he said. "She was great! I mean, no one could set a scene like she did. Her description was . . . I mean, it was phenomenal. I couldn't do even half of what she could." He wilted in misery and just stared at his hands again. The cat on his lap looked up in annoyance.

"When did she tell you she was represented by Aaron?" Mallory asked.

He made a face and didn't answer.

"So, yesterday at lunch," Mallory said for him.

He took a drink of his coffee and then said, "Yeah. That was it." Mallory didn't say anything, so he cleared his throat and said, "And I was happy for her."

"Why do you think she kept it from you?" she asked.

"Are you saying I killed my best friend and her agent because I was jealous?" he said. "That seems like overkill, don't you think?"

Mallory shrugged. "People have killed for less. Representation doesn't mean automatic success, but it's definitely a step on the right path. She had gone through a door you didn't even know she had keys to, and she didn't bring you with her."

"I did not kill them," he said. "The fact you're asking me about Kath is insulting. I'm in mourning."

"Have either of you ever been married?" Mallory asked.

"We both have," he said, rubbing his left ring finger absently. "But we were never single at the same time. Except for now, of course."

"Did you love her?" Mallory asked.

"Doesn't matter now, does it?" he said bitterly.

"What do you know about her ob-gyn career?"

He shrugged. "She really only mentioned it when we talked about VDV, to make a joke."

"Do you think she would have quit being a doctor if her career had taken off?"

"I wish she was around to answer all these ridiculous questions," he muttered.

"If she were around, then I wouldn't have to ask. Would she stick with her doctoring or throw her whole life into writing fiction?"

"I don't know, I have no idea, we didn't have a lot of time to discuss it after I found out, did we? We had lunch and then there was the concert and then she was dead!"

Mallory started sketching something on her notebook. "Speaking of the concert, you two are old, close friends who were excited to see VDV in person at last. And yet." She drew a rough sketch of the auditorium from her balcony POV. She pointed to the left side. "You were over there with your friend, here," she motioned to the Miu. "And Kath was over on this side, by herself." Mallory indicated on the drawing. "And here is the restroom where we found Kath and Aaron."

"So, how am I supposed to have gotten all the way over there?" he said crossly.

"That's the question," Mallory said. "We also had someone go into the medbay without anyone seeing them and finish off murdering Kath. Know anything about that?"

"I don't even know where that is!" Bruce said. "Are we done?"

"Almost," Mallory said. "Tell me who brought up the idea to attend the Marple's Tea thing?"

A FEW MONTHS earlier, Bruce was on a video call with Kath. He wanted to talk about that thing they never talked about, but Kath always seemed ready with a new topic in hand whenever there was a lull in the conversation. There were no comfortable silences in their friendship anymore.

He opened his mouth to say something, but she brought up agents again.

"Are you going to submit to Aaron Rose again?" she asked.

He scoffed. "He hated my last pitch. 'Good story, bad writing,' he said. Again." Bruce downed the glass of scotch he had by the computer.

She laughed. "Yeah. I get 'great writing, boring story.'"

"I guess we're both screwed, then," he said. He got another slug of scotch and toasted her over the camera.

"But have you heard about the Marple's Tea Party thing?" she asked, her eyes dancing in excitement.

"No," he said. "What's Marple's Party?"

"There's a huge spaceship that someone found here on Earth, and now they're throwing a mystery writer's convention aboard it. Like a themed cruise, only in space! We could see space, meet agents, talk to other writers, and"—she paused for effect—"VDV is playing on the cruise."

He choked on the scotch. "But they haven't played a show in years! I thought they had done that silent quitting musicians do. Didn't their drummer die?"

"Apparently they're together for this space cruise," she said. "So, are you in?"

"I don't know," he said. "Oh, speaking of space, did you know they're putting out a call for more human doctors aboard the space station Eternity?"

"Yes!" she said, even more animated. "That's why I can justify this to my manager. Part vacation, part work trip! Win-win! And if you come, that's three wins!"

He laughed a bit, cheered finally. "I'll see if I can make it work. It would be fun."

"BUT IT WASN'T fun, was it?" Mallory said. "You found out that your best friend got an agent and never told you. Did you have a falling-out between lunch and the concert?"

"Why? We've already established I was far away from the murder victims!" he snapped.

"Come on, dude," Mallory said. "She's your best friend. You guys were going to see a favorite band for the first time in person. And you just happen to watch the concert far apart from each other?"

"Fine, all right!" he said, bright red spots appearing on his cheeks. "But we didn't fight. I just ignored her all afternoon. I didn't want to talk. So I came here, and she followed me. We didn't talk, but that was because I was trying to get in control of my emotions. I was feeling petty, okay? I didn't want to say something I'd regret."

Mallory nodded. *But he's right; he still didn't have the opportunity.* "So, did you get a chance to talk to Aaron outside of the lunch?"

"No, he ran off, and then, as I told you, I kept to myself, then came here. Then my room, then the concert. I didn't see him again."

"How are you getting along with the alien?"

He looked up, alarmed. "Why do you keep asking me things that are out of context?"

She shrugged. "I'm just asking about your time here on the

ship. Today you've been mostly spending time with the Miu. Even more than Tina."

"He's a sweet boy," Bruce said, smiling, and Mallory fought the urge to shudder. "He's the thing that's kept me sane. Especially after that lunch."

"And especially after your best friend died," Phineas said.

"I thought that went without saying," Bruce said.

"Have you learned anything about the Miu that our ambassadors might like to know? Like his name, or anything about the species?"

"Not much more than he's a lot like a cat." Bruce smiled.

"Can you tell me what Kath thought of your book?" she asked.

He stared at the floor, his face stony.

"Please?" Mallory asked.

THE MEMORY WOULDN'T die. It was a few years old, and no matter what he tried, he couldn't scrub it from his head. No booze would do it, no pot, no exercise.

When they met in person this time, she acted like nothing had ever happened between them. On the trip they had separate rooms, no special time alone, just like friends do.

Years before, she had been married and living in Chicago. Bruce was in town for a conference and they'd met at a coffee shop. They talked VDV, and medicine, and writing.

"Next weekend I'm going to a writer's conference in New York," he said, trying not to sound important but feeling very confident. "I'm going to be pitching my novel to an agent."

"Oh, that's great, tell me how it goes!" she said. "How are you preparing? Are you nervous?" Her blue eyes actually twinkled.

"I have all my elevator pitches ready, and that's all," he said confidently. "I'm going to riff off any questions anyone asks me. I'm super ready."

"I can't wait to hear how it goes!" she enthused. "You have to call me right after. And you haven't sent me a copy of your book yet!"

"Come with me," he said, surprising them both. "You can buy your conference ticket at the door. I'll"—his face flushed—"I'll make sure there are two beds in my hotel room and everything."

She had color high in her cheeks. "I don't know," she said. "Seems like a tough thing to sell the husband on."

He swirled his latte in its mug. "You always refer to him as 'the husband.' I don't think you've ever said his name," he said, eyes flicking up to hers. "Isn't that kind of weird?"

She gave a tiny smile. "While you don't mention your wife at all." Her eyes flicked to the ring on his left hand. "I assume there is one."

He sighed and stretched back, the tense moment breaking like a wave on the beach. "There was," he said. "I just wear this out of habit."

Kath's eyebrows went up.

"She was sick," he said. Tears welled in his eyes. "It's been hard, what with her family, the investigation, and then the funeral over the holidays. She didn't even remember me at the end. My life was in a holding pattern until she died. A lot of guilt, a lot of grief."

He wiped at his cheeks and tried to smile.

Kath took his hand. And when he calmed down, she didn't let him go. She met his eyes and, while he would have scoffed that anyone could communicate detailed requests nonverbally, at this time in his world, Bruce was asking a question he'd never actually voice, and she answered by taking his hand and leading him out of the cafe.

They didn't drive anywhere. His car was closer, and they both ran there through the torrential rain. They took each other's faces in their hands and laughed and dripped rainwater everywhere. Bruce didn't take time to wonder about the details. He brushed some wet hair from her face and kept his hand there to caress her cheek. Then he threaded his fingers through her hair and pulled her head toward him, kissing her hard.

They necked in the car like teenagers, the windows steaming up immediately. When they finally came up for air, Bruce felt drunk with lust. "I've wanted to do that for a very long time," he finally said.

She laughed. "What else is on your Kath to-do list?"

His eyes widened slightly, and then he was turning on the car and driving to his hotel. Bruce got her inside the elevator and pressed her up against the wall. He pinned her arms above her head and then paused.

"Is this okay?" he asked.

She nodded, trapping her lip in her teeth in a way that drove him wild.

That afternoon, they did things that he'd only ever read about. He would always ask her if something was okay, and every time she said yes, he introduced her to dizzying pleasure.

Then she had gone home to her husband, and Bruce stayed at the hotel, staring at his laptop's empty page.

"Health Potions BOGO," he typed at the top of the page. Then underneath, "An alchemical LitRPG by Bruce Truman."

LitRPG was getting to be a hot genre, he had heard.

"'HEALTH POTIONS BOGO' is a great title!" Mallory said. "Did it ever come out?"

He shook his head. "I never finished it."

"What about the book you pitched at the writer's conference in New York?" Phineas asked.

Bruce's shoulders hunched up. "I had about three chapters. I lied to her. I didn't have a book at all. She's only ever read three chapters of any book I've started."

"Because there are only three chapters?" Mallory guessed.

Bruce nodded.

"What was that you said about the investigation?" Mallory said. "Were you accused of killing your wife?"

Bruce rolled his eyes. "Families always want to blame the spouse if someone dies suddenly after a long illness. Her parents paid a detective to look into my past. He never found anything."

Xan glanced back at the pillar and found that the alien was gone. He looked around, body tense, expecting to see the garish yellow standing out against more muted cat colors, but it had left completely. He looked back over at Bruce, who was still stroking a cat, but the Miu was draped casually around his neck as if it had been there the whole time. Mallory stood and walked over to Xan, leaving Phineas with Bruce.

"I think I have it," she said. "But there's one thing we have to test, and I'm not sure how to do it. It's got to be subtle."

Xan looked past her to the couch, his eyes going wide. Mallory heard Phineas swear, and then she sighed with relief. "That was easy."

Bruce and the Miu were gone.

"What the fuck was that?" Phineas asked. "Fussy dentist was sitting here on the bed, and then he and the ugly cat just disappeared."

Mallory nodded. "That's what I needed to test."

"What is going on?" Phineas demanded.

"I am going on the theory that the Miu didn't steal the ship two thousand years ago. They *designed* her. They created by far the most powerful and amazing ship that had ever been seen. But it's too powerful. You could kill someone and have the ship hide the body for you. You could also probably fuck up economies with what she can produce. We don't know half of what she's capable of, and we're using her skills for entertainment, but I think she can do far more.

"My guess is that various important folks in the galaxy found out about this ship, and there were probably a few fights over who got to buy one first, or maybe the Miu wanted to keep it for themselves, but they tried to hide on Earth, but failed, leaving their ship and one alien behind, who did a number on the Egyptians, it sounds like. Cat worship wasn't new at that point, but our little guy gave them a real alien cat to focus on.

"*Metis* can't tell us what happened in certain areas of the ship because her old master knows how to manipulate her, turn off her sensors, whatever it takes."

"But if the ship had been on Earth for so long, this particular alien couldn't know how to use her!" Phineas said.

"We don't know how long-lived these people are. For all we know, this was the architect behind the ship's design. But what I would bet is the information about the ship got passed through the generations. The Cuckoos hold a lot of their data, so they befriended Tina to get access to it, but most of their old data was with *Metis*. That's why they wanted *Metis* so badly; she's carrying not only the language database for at least the Cuckoos and the Miu, but I'm betting she has ship designs as well."

"So, is the alien the murderer?" Xan asked.

"Aiding and abetting at worst," Mallory said. "Bruce and the Miu made friends fast, because apparently Bruce doesn't mind that the alien is as ugly as roadkill. I think their initial bonding was honestly innocent. But then we had our lunch where Bruce found out two shocking things. The first was that Kath had signed with Aaron without telling him, which was hurtful, but you can get over that. But then Bruce learned that Aaron had rejected his most recent novel and then gave the plot to Kath to write. Remember, she was good at description, while he was the ideas man? And Cosima had said that Aaron was taking Kath on as a client, but giving her another writer's plot. That plot was Bruce's."

Xan whistled. "So, not only did he turn Bruce down, he stole Bruce's idea and gave it to Bruce's best friend."

"Yeah," Mallory said. "Cold. Unethical. Still not on the level of deserving murder, but no argument that it was a dick move on Aaron's part."

"You said Kath was an unfortunate witness to the murder, and that's why she got killed?" Phineas asked.

"Yeah, I think the Miu taught Bruce how to teleport around the station like the cats can. Or how to use a cat. I don't know how they communicated, but the Cuckoos tried to update Bruce's implant with the Miu language. They're smarter than we think, after all. So the Miu and Bruce are bopping around the station, learning how to teleport via cat portal. He gets a wild idea that he has the perfect way to kill Aaron, so he finds Aaron, probably in his room, then teleports them both to the junkyard where he then pops Aaron to the roof of the shack, knocks him out, then drops him on his head and breaks his neck. He leaves Aaron in the junkyard, then pops back to the concert, where he sees Kath go into the restroom. Boom, another wild idea, he's getting them all over the place tonight! He can dump the body on her, accuse her of the murder, but then something goes wrong. Maybe he tries to dump the body through the portal into the bathroom, but falls in after him. He wants to implicate Kath in the murder, but then she sees him, so he attacks her and teleports away."

"Jesus, how do we fight someone with that ability?" Xan said.

"I'm working on it," Mallory said. "I'm betting Cosima interrupted him, and she missed seeing him escape. Once Kath was in the medbay, Bruce just had to ask his little friend to open a portal to the room, stab her, and then pop back out."

"Did you say Eve was injured?" Phineas said.

"Yeah, we think he tried to get her for interrupting his trashing of her control room," Mallory said. "Or he thought she was figuring out how to access *Metis*'s memories, which I'm betting the Miu was messing with, by the way. But Eve's cat attacked him. Cosima is keeping an eye on her."

"That's why the asshole wouldn't shake your hand!" Phineas told Xan. "He's probably scratched the fuck up."

"You're really calm right now," Xan said to Mallory. "Your murderer got away. Why aren't you trying harder to go after him?"

"He can only go places on the ship, but he knows we're after him, so he can get away from us at any time," Mallory said. "Once we get *Mobius*'s data and wake up Eve, I'm betting she can take over *Metis* again and find out where Bruce and the little shit are hiding. But Stephanie and *Infinity* know what's going on, and they're distributing the lost data from *Metis* and *Mobius* so that Bruce and the alien can't get away, and the Cuckoos can't play dumb anymore."

"So, now what?" Phineas said.

"Back to the hospital and make sure Eve is okay. But you have *Mobius*, right?"

Phineas and Xan looked at each other.

"Oh, no," Mallory said, shaking her head.

"We found a safe place for him, like you told us!" Phineas said defensively. "The little dude is good at hiding!"

23

· · ·

IT'S ONLY FAN-FIC IF
THEY DON'T PAY

THINGS WERE LOOKING up!

Justmie had shown *Mobius* a new trick, which came in really handy with all the new data *Metis* gave him. If he sat on the floor, or touched the ship in any way, then he could get a sense of the layout of the station and present it to her as a captain!

They could also listen in on any conversations the Gneiss were having, but that was rude, Mama had told him.

The room they were in was so big. And even though Xan had buried him deep, he could still hear the Cuckoos come in and out of the room. It wasn't as safe here as they thought. But Justmie said she could see a way someone as small as them could get to a place that looked a lot more welcoming than this infinite junkyard with bugs.

They flew up some large shafts, and through some tight ventilation spaces, and through a dark maze. *Mobius* was getting frightened, but Justmie told him where to go, and he trusted her. They ended up coming out of a rabbit hole.

He knew it was a rabbit hole because two rabbits were hopping around in the grass. They looked at him, startled.

"What do you think it is?" the tan rabbit said.

"Let's get Blackberry, he'll know," the darker one said. Then they ran off.

Mobius was afraid to find out what a blackberry was, so he took flight and wandered around this new space.

Idyllic green countryside went on for miles in each direction. They were currently on a high hill, and the valley below held small cottages. On the other side of the hill, the world looked a lot scarier, with black and red rocks, hooded humanoids flying on leathery screeching things, and a baleful red eye that seemed to be staring at *Mobius*.

So, we go to the pretty cottages, right? Justmie asked.

Adventure says to go toward the eye, but, yes, I want to see the cottages, too, Mobius said.

Once they flew to the bottom of the hill, they found little humans wandering around, tending gardens, smoking pipes, and combing the hair on their feet. Or their beards. There seemed to be a lot of hair to comb.

Is this the safe place you found? Mobius asked.

Oh, yes, she said.

THEY WERE ON their way to the junkyard when Mallory got two messages. *Mobius* was loudly telling her he was somewhere new that was safe and that he had found someone important.

"It's too bad we couldn't befriend a cat to take us around the ship," Phineas said. Cosima stood at his elbow, making sure he held Eve (and her cat) carefully in his arms, but it didn't look like he was straining at all to hold her.

"I still think we would have been good at *Metis*'s hospital," Cosima grumbled. "I had it under control."

"*Mobius* said his safe place could heal humans," Mallory said. "And I'd like us to all be together for safety."

"They put a bandage on her forehead, like they do in any good hospital drama," Phineas said. "She's getting heavy, though."

"Tina would have been good to help, but her Cuckoos messed her up," Xan said. "She's down for the count. I don't know how long it takes Gneiss to process alcohol."

"Maybe now she'll finally realize she can't trust them," Mallory said.

They all stopped outside a small round wooden door. "This is where *Mobius* said to come?" Xan asked.

"Brilliant," Phineas said. "I should have thought of this."

"This is the whole of the fan-fic area?" Mallory asked. "Here is where I can find, say, *Friends* and *Smurfs* slash-fic?"

"No, that's in Rule 34," Xan said, shuddering.

"This whole floor is fan-fic," Phineas explained. "*Metis* has it sectioned off. Your various Star-fic is in the east wing, your video game fic is in the west. North has all the random shit, like *Friends/Smurfs*, or *Taskmaster/Slaughterhouse-Five*.

"Seriously?" Mallory asked. "That exists?"

"Also in Rule 34," Xan said under his breath.

"So, where are we now?" Mallory asked, pointing to the round door.

"Come on, Mal. Everyone knows where a cute round door leads. This is the door to Halfway Earth."

JUSTMIE WAS VERY impressive, how she was able to find this safe spot. The valley turned into a warm wooded area with green trees and green grass and a green meadow and a blue sky. It was peaceful, and the only insects were the ones *Metis* controlled, and they were pleasant pollinators.

Under a bulbous hillock sat a circular door. When *Mobius* flew around to get the larger lay of the land, he found many of these circular doors, so he went back to the first. He knocked politely the way Mama taught him: three taps, then wait.

"Wait" was the important part. And the part he usually forgot. He went ahead and pushed the door open.

"Hello," said a pleasant male human, looking up from studying a map. He was much shorter than all the humans *Mobius* had seen, but he was also much friendlier.

"I'm Hilbo Haggins," he said, puffing on his pipe in a very friendly way. "Welcome to my home. I live here with my nephew, Hobo." He looked around, a frown creasing his pleasant face. "But I'm not sure where he is right now."

"Hello!" *Mobius* said. "I am *Mobius* and I'm with Justmie, my friend and pilot. What can you tell us about this place? Is it safe?"

What are you saying to him? I can't understand it!

Mobius just remembered that people without direct access to a database or the auditory translator wouldn't be able to understand what people were saying. He had been able to understand Justmie because of Auntie Stephanie's gift of his first Sundry circuit.

And speaking! What new glory was this! He could communicate with anyone! *Metis* truly did give him a gift! He would have to thank her. When she woke up. If she woke up . . .

Oh, right, his Sundry! How could he forget? He looked around and spied them crawling over the map. "Oh, and we also have my circuit, these four Sundry."

He quickly relayed to Justmie what was going on.

"This is Halfway Earth, one of the largest fan-fic areas of the Internet," Hilbo said. "We are a bunch of copyright violations created by thousands of fans who just want to celebrate what they love about stories. My nephew Hobo is probably off reenacting a fan-fic or two." He put his pen into a bottle of ink and stretched. "He should come back home soon; we're having brown bread and potatoes for dinner."

"Do you need us to look for him?" *Mobius* asked after translating for Justmie.

Hilbo shook his head and hobbled over to open a window to let the spring air in. "Not necessary. Coming home after an adventure hasn't been a problem since the fan-fic writer ItsObvious created the giant eagle rental and put locations all over Halfway Earth. I've been able to go out on a few more of my own adventures since that happened, even with this old back of mine. But we haven't had a visitor from the outside in some time, I'd love to hear more about your life," Hilbo said. "Let me put the kettle on. And if you need help, I'm sure Hobo or DanDILF will drop by tonight if they hear I'm making my special fried bread."

"Do they like fried bread?" *Mobius* asked politely.

"Of course," Hilbo said. "Everyone must feel welcome in Bobbiton, or else we get tetchy." He poured a hot drink into a mug and placed a loaf of bread on the table. *Mobius* hovered above it and made polite noises, not sure if he should point out that he couldn't eat.

Safe, Justmie said in a very satisfactory tone.

MALLORY AND HER party stooped to enter the tiny adorable door and ended up in someone's living room. It was a perfect little cozy home that was much too difficult for Mallory to stand up in, much less anyone taller than she was. A short woman with fat curls and a peasant dress started demanding she sit and eat something because she was far too thin for a bobbit. Mallory apologized to the hostess, who started reciting the "bobbit code," which had to do with hospitality and the word "tetchy," but Mallory found the way out and stumbled/ran into the open, which seemed to be a perfect Irish afternoon about four p.m. The sun was thinking about setting, the lavender was releasing its lazy smell into the air, and in one of the houses, Mallory was sure someone was baking bread.

She looked behind her and saw she was the only one who made it out. She peeked back into the bobbit's door and saw Xan and Phineas arguing in the hall while the bobbit was encouraging them to come in. "We can't fit. We'll get in another way!" Xan shouted.

The little town was stupidly perfect, complete with Howard Shore music playing gently in the background. She took two steps and then fell back when a giant eagle landed in front of her, blowing her hair back and generally scaring the bejesus out of her.

A short young man with curly black hair thanked the bird, handed it a gold piece, which it promptly swallowed, and then went to help Mallory to her feet.

"So sorry about that," he said, pulling her to her feet. He unclasped his cloak and bowed to her. "I am Hobo Haggins."

"Of course you are," Mallory said dryly.

"And you are . . . ?" he prompted.

"Mallory. And some friends who are probably stuck in this poor woman's house," she said, pointing. "I'm looking for a friend, actually."

"I'm not good at hunting people down," Hobo said. "I'm more the 'take several months to run far away' type. But I'm sure we can find someone good to help you. Walker can track, but I think he's off ruling a country right now." Hobo frowned and tapped the stump of a missing finger. "Another person who could help you is DanDILF. He's the wisest person I know. Also incredibly attractive."

"I thought he was just good at holding a glowing stick and making fireworks happen," Mallory said under her breath, but realized none of her friends were around.

"Have you seen anyone else like me?" she asked Hobo. "Tall, strange clothing, they'll have darker skin than me."

"Not from the sky, but there's nothing saying they can't also be walking underground. Or drinking at the Chipper Filly!" His eyes grew wide with excitement. "Yes, that's where we should go. They have beer in pints there!"

It was as good a place to start as any, Mallory thought.

Hobo raised his hand to someone behind her back. "Hilbo, I'm home! I'm taking my new friend to the Chipper Filly!"

"Did you lose any digits on this quest, boy?" an older halfling said as he came to hug Hobo.

"All nine accounted for," Hobo said with a grin. "And even if I didn't, remember the urgent care center."

Mallory laughed. "There's urgent care in Bobbiton?"

They both nodded solemnly. "One of your people, a writer called ItsObvious, just opened an urgent care center. They take care of your injuries and illnesses instead of just rubbing dirt in it the way my late grandfather said to do."

"How did he die?" Mallory asked.

"Got an infection. Strangest thing," Hilbo said, shaking his head sadly. "But ItsObvious convinced some elves to come out of Streamdale and use their magic for healing, or, as he put it, 'do something more worthwhile than magicking up perfectly conditioned hair and shiny trees.'"

Mallory laughed, and then something very hard hit her in the forehead, and she was out before she even hit the lush grass.

ENYA TUNES BROKE through Mallory's haze. *Who let my college roommate choose the music?*

But her roommate wasn't there. She was lying on a single bed like college, though, but it was much comfier. She opened her eyes to the most beautiful hospital room ever. Gold and green weeping willow trees hung over a shining brook outside, and the windows were cracked open so she could smell the goodness of the forest.

"You're awake," said a musical voice, and a woman with ethereal beauty and red hair down to her hips glided over to her. She dipped her fingers into a copper bowl and then extended them to Mallory's lips.

"You want me to lick your fingers?" Mallory asked. "Without gloves?"

The elf withdrew, a frown attempting to mar her perfect face, but failing. "This is our healing tincture, taken from a thousand-year-old spring in Streamdale. There is nothing purer in this world."

"Haven't you heard of spoons?" Mallory asked.

The elf looked baffled.

"Never mind, I'll take your medicine," Mallory said. She let the woman stick her fingers in her mouth, but refused to lick or suck. The droplets fell on her lips and tasted like fresh strawberries.

She swallowed and lay back, rubbing her head gingerly. "Any idea what hit me?"

"We thought the orcs had started to attack with metal ammunition in their siege engines, but it was just this," the woman said, and pointed to a metal ball on the end of the bed. "It turns out someone was very happy to see his mother."

"*Mobius!*" she cried. "I missed you, buddy!" She held him out and turned him different ways. "Have you grown again?"

Hilbo Haggins served me brown bread and butter, and then when I said, "No thank you," he gave me some meat, the little ship explained. *But I have so much to tell you!*

"Oh, and I can talk now!"

"Wow," Mallory said. "Tell me everything, then."

And he did.

XAN AND HIS crew finally found a door that could accept humans over five feet tall, and when they went through, a rider on a horse came up to them immediately. He was a dirty-looking white man who smelled like rawhide.

"Ah, our guests," the stern bearded guy said. "I'm Walker, I'm here to escort you to Bobbiton."

Eve stirred in Phineas's arms, and he sighed in relief when Walker picked her up with no effort and put her on the saddle in front of him. Then he galloped off.

"That's not an escort!" Phineas shouted, but they were gone. "You didn't think to bring us any horses?"

"It's not far," Cosima said, looking at a road sign. "We can walk."

Bobbiton Urgent Care was a lot fancier than any urgent care Phineas had ever been in. He was pretty sure the wallpaper was made of living tree leaves and branches, and everything smelled clean. Even the sweaty Walker, who was exiting a back room with a tall white blond elf lady following him, chattering in a distressed way.

"I don't know what to say. We never have two strange injuries at once!" she said, wringing her hands. "Someone get DanDILF. It's a bad omen!"

The elf, who was tall, and beautiful, and scary as fuck, caught sight of the newcomers, and wind blew her robes around as her eyes began to glow.

"We're inside, right?" Phineas asked, looking for the source of the wind.

Xan nodded. He stepped forward. "You just took our friend in. The injured human? Tall, black hair, head wound?"

"Yeah," Phineas added, "can you stop being scary and just take care of her?"

The elf glanced sidelong at Xan, Phineas, and Cosima, then bowed to Walker and hurried back through the door.

"She'll be fine," Jack said from behind them.

Phineas jumped. "Whoa, where the fuck did you come from?"

"I'm Jack," he said, leaning in and shaking his hand. "Mallory's friends, right?" He gave a little wave to Cosima.

"Mallory said you found a safe place," Cosima said, as if she wasn't entirely sure he was telling the truth."

Jack smiled. "I'm absolutely safe here, and now you are, too." He gestured to the door to the back. "Mallory and Eve will be fine shortly."

Phineas shook his head. "Aw, hell no, you're not going to do that vague bullshit we keep getting from half the people we talk to. What the hell is going on here and how did you appear like that? Do you have a pet cat helping you, too?"

"A cat? Not that I know of?" Jack said, confused.

Before he could say anything else, the elf who had taken Eve to the back reappeared. Blood streaked her gossamer dress. "Your friend is alive. She'll be fine. And—" She stopped talking when she saw Jack. Her eyes widened and literally began to glow. The wind started up again.

"Here we go. What is it with that wind machine?" Phineas said to Xan. He shrugged.

Then the elf fell to her knees in front of Jack, who looked embarrassed, but not surprised.

"My Lord, why did you not tell us you were coming?" she wailed. "All of the elves in Streamdale will be angry that they missed welcoming you!"

Phineas faced Jack, crossing his arms. "All right. What the actual fuck?"

"You do not speak to—" the elf began, but Jack held up his hand, and she stopped.

"Are we really in a literal fan-fic of *Lord*—" Phineas began, but Jack shushed him frantically.

"Don't say the name. It messes with whatever *Metis* is doing here. It can bring the whole thing down around us." Jack waved his arms dramatically.

"And that whole thing. What the hell is it?" Phineas asked.

"I wrote a lot of fan-fic when I was younger. It was how I got practice writing," Jack explained. "When I got aboard, I got Eve's permission to check out the fan-fic areas to see if my stuff had manifested. Folks here found out it was me, and it got a little weird."

"Un-fucking-believable," Phineas marveled.

"Show respect when you address Lord ItsObvious!" the elf hissed from the floor.

"Cadburyelle, thank you, but that's not necessary," Jack said awkwardly.

"Don't you mean Galad—" Phineas began to say, but Jack frantically shushed him again. It was starting to amuse him.

"Please just tell us how our friends are doing," Jack said with a backward glare to Phineas.

"Both are fine. I expect the newcomer to wake soon."

"Then we're good," Jack said. "Can I leave her here? Is it safe?"

"I can get some guards. All the guards will want to protect the Lord's chosen lady," the elf said.

"No, that's not . . . what I—"

"Don't bother, she won't listen," Phineas said, pulling him away. "Just thank her and let's go outside. I have some questions about this fan-fic world. I assume there's a delightful pub some-place nearby? Possibly with quests?"

XAN WAS GETTING tired of Phineas's feats of strength. He was looking very clever and proud of himself as the halflings milled around his knees, asking him to lift various things as parts of bar bets. Every time he lifted something, they cheered raucously.

"He knows we have a job to do, with Mallory and Eve, who clearly aren't here, right?" Cosima asked him.

"Yep," Xan said, looking down at the table.

"What's the matter? You don't like fun?" Phineas asked as he came up to the table.

"Not right now with a murderer on the loose." He tried his watch to ping Mallory. "At a LOTR bar. Send help."

Her reply came. "I heard you met Cadburyelle, so you can guess I can't get away from urgent care anytime soon. But I'll try." Then she added, "Found Mob."

Phineas sat down next to Cosima and grabbed a mug. Jack filled it with the pitcher of ale on the table. "Shit, I've always wanted a mug of ale. I bet it tastes different." He took a drink, then wiped his mouth. "Nope. Still tastes like beer."

"Mal just said she needs to get away from urgent care," he told Jack, who was explaining the economics of the world to Cosima. "Do you think she can escape that elf?"

Jack sighed. "I knew I made her too fussy." He stood up, and the bar around him went silent and expectant. He made a pained look. "Don't worry about me, folks, just enjoy your meals."

They didn't listen, and just kept watching.

"I need to talk to Mallory," he said. "I will make sure she gets free and comes here when we're done."

"What do you need to talk to Mal about?" Xan asked.

"It's a surprise," Jack said. "I don't want to get people's expectations up."

"But you're essentially God here?" Phineas asked.

"Yeah," Jack said, then shrugged.

"More ale, I guess. Maybe mug two will go down better." He reached for the pitcher.

"Phineas," Xan said, his voice cold. "People are dying. Two friends have been attacked. Please don't fuck around with me right now. And please don't get drunk."

"Do you know how much it takes to get me drunk, little brother?" Phineas asked.

"I'm your big—never mind," Xan said. "So, great, we're safe. But what do we do now? We have a murderer to catch."

"Jack told me his idea," Phineas said. "But Mallory has to be on board with it."

"And that is?"

He scooted closer to Xan and Cosima, then leaned over and told them about Jack's idea.

"That's fucked up," Xan said. "Do you think that will help?"

"It's brilliant," Cosima said. "Something he wrote about in book three of Zesty Yaboi's adventures."

"Oh, so it works in fiction, great," Xan said.

"You know we're basically working in fiction right now, don't you?" Cosima asked. "This ship really is super powerful, and we're just using it as our own holodeck."

Xan shrugged. "I guess, so long as no one gets hurt."

"They won't," Phin said, and got up to address his fans again.

Xan wasn't feeling altogether confident that Mallory just let a killer go, but it seemed he wasn't just killing for kicks. If they were to be worried about anyone, it should be themselves, as Bruce would need to kill them all to get away with his crimes now.

He sipped on his beer and was annoyed by his brother until Mallory arrived, a bandage around her head and a joyous metal satellite orbiting her. A knot in his chest loosened a bit, and he waved her over.

"How did he end up here?" he asked, inviting Mallory to sit down.

"He said there were Cuckoos in the junkyard, so he ran away, and his little Gneiss pilot told him where a safe place was."

"That's impressive," Xan admitted. "What happens when he gets big enough for you to pilot?"

Mallory groaned. "That is a problem I do not expect to have for years. Or at least months. Can't we deal with the current problems first?"

Mobius landed in Xan's mug, splashing a bit of beer on the table. Then he shifted to show Xan a new tiny little window that revealed a tiny cockpit and a pebble in the captain's chair.

"I have a friend!"

"He can talk now?" Xan asked, eyebrows raised.

"I will never sleep again," Mallory said with a laugh. "But *Mobius* has some interesting things to say—what the hell is Phineas doing?"

Phineas was at the bar for another pitcher, laughing with the bobbits. Xan removed the little ship, wiped him gently with a napkin, and took another drink of beer. "Bar bets. The halflings can't get enough of him."

Phineas caught sight of them, then waved farewell to all his new friends as he left to join Mallory and Xan. "Hey, Mal! You okay?"

"Just a bit of a concussion, but magic elvish finger medicine should have me right as rain," she said. "Have y'all talked to Jack?"

"Phin has. You sure you want to risk all that?" Xan asked.

"It'll be fine," she said. "I have a job for you and Phineas, though."

"Anything," he said.

She went to the bar and handed the barkeep a gold coin to buy drinks for everyone, and thanked everyone for their hospitality.

"Where did you get gold coins?" Xan asked as they got up to leave.

She reached into her pocket and tossed one to him, which he caught. "They were in my pocket. I'm the Mary Sue in this situation."

BACK AT URGENT care, and against the advice of the very fussy Cadburyelle, Mallory sat with Eve in her recovery room.

Eve held a gold piece in her hand, turning it over a few times, then tossed it back to Mallory.

"What's your point?"

"Have you tested if you can take things outside of the ship? Or does it all disappear?"

"Not really," Eve said. "I was still just amazed by the living ship and getting her healthy."

"And to grow to gargantuan size to hold the Internet," Mallory said. "And adding a fan-fic area that fantasy fans would kill to experience."

Eve gave a little grin. "That's fair." She rubbed her head and winced.

"Do you know why Bruce attacked you?" Mallory asked.

"Said something about me recording too much. I'm not sure. He was there, and loud, and then I was on the floor, and then Mimosa got really loud and scratched him, I think." Her eyes filled with tears. "But, Mallory, I can't hear *Metis* anymore."

"We are going to try to fix that," Mallory said. She saw Phineas outside the urgent care holding something flat and black against his chest. "That was fast."

She waved Xan and Phineas inside. They propped Eve up, who brightened immediately when Phineas handed her the laptop. Mallory then politely asked *Mobius* to transfer his data to a memory stick. He had to do some internal modifications to take on the stick, but he didn't complain.

"If I'm not mistaken, this will have the design for the ship on it, which should allow you to override whatever the Miu did to mess with *Metis*," Mallory said.

"Where did you get this computer?" Eve asked.

"From Bruce's murder shack in the junkyard," Phineas said.

"We thought the cats were stealing these," Eve said. "Just opened up a portal, knocked them into another portal on the floor, and poof, gone."

"I think that is exactly what was happening," Mallory said. "Pablo told me about it. The cats were doing it, but as a favor for their old master." She sat for a moment. "Do you think you can figure out how to connect with *Metis* here?"

"I think so, but as far as I can tell, *Metis* is crippled now," Eve said, frowning at the screen and moving her finger around the track pad. "She is supposed to have five hiveminds. She has only four. She's missing the most important one."

"I'm betting that's what the Miu and the Cuckoos were doing," Mallory said grimly. "I think I have an idea how to help *Metis*."

Jack poked his head in, smiling at them both. "Mallory. I've got something neat to show you."

24

A MURDER OF MALLORYS

RIGHT AFTER EVE confirmed she was able to access *Metis* with the laptop, Mallory left Phineas, Xan, Eve, and Jack and told them she would be down the street with Hilbo.

Then she took *Mobius*, Justmie, and the nine Sundry that followed them to a back stairwell, which she didn't even know *Metis* had.

The way down was painful. The stairwell was poorly lit, and she was fully aware that she had a long way to go and a cat-loving killer was after her.

"A teleporting murderer. What the fuck did I get myself into?" she grumbled. "At least I'm not going upstairs."

By the time she reached the bottom, she was sweaty, her thighs were aching, and she was rethinking this whole plan.

But it was the only way she could think to catch the murderer and help the ship.

The stairwell emptied out right behind the structure Phineas had labeled the murder shack. She hadn't noticed a door there before, but that meant nothing on this ship. She went into the shack and sat down at the desk.

"I totally know what I'm doing," she muttered. *Mobius* sat on the desk in front of her. The changes he'd been through today were more than his size and the acquisition of a new pilot. He was calmer, more confident, and more willing to listen.

"Do you like your hivemind?" she asked.

They don't talk much, but they help me think more, and I like that a lot!

Mallory put *Mobius* in her left hand. Then she opened her right hand and encouraged the Sundry, both hers and the ship's, to crawl on her.

Then she closed her eyes.

MALLORY PACED UP and down the dirt road to Bobbiton. Xan watched her from Hilbo's house. The bait couldn't have been more obvious, but he still didn't like it.

"Are you all right?" Jack asked, coming up behind him.

Xan nodded curtly. Jack nudged him and handed him a cup of something hot.

"I don't want—" he started, but Jack leaned into him.

"Look, if they're not doing something for us constantly, they're going to start to fret, which will blow this whole thing. Take the tea. Drink it, spill it, excuse yourself to the bathroom, and dump it, but please, take it."

Xan looked beyond Jack's face into the liquid golden eyes of the fussy elf on duty. She was caught between adoration of Jack and fear that Jack's friend would not like the gift she had brought.

He rolled his eyes. "Fine." He took it and turned his back to them again, watching Mallory.

"So, you're all right, then?" Jack said, sipping his own drink.

"Fine," he snapped. "Whose idea was this?"

"Mine—well, Phineas had the idea once he realized what the ship was capable of." Jack smiled. "Smart brother you have there."

"Sometimes too smart," Xan grumbled.

"Shh, something is happening," Jack said.

• • •

"ARE YOU KIDDING me?" Mallory shouted. She was in a dark alleyway in a wet city. It was just cold enough to be miserable, and she shivered in her wet clothes.

"You don't look like you fit in, ma'am," said a scratchy voice.

Mallory squinted into the corner. A match flared, and then another, and then another. Three cigarettes were lit, their cherries glowing brightly as the smoker inhaled. One smoker. Three heads.

The six-foot-tall Venus flytrap shuffled out of the shadows. "Zesty Yaboi," he said, reaching out a leaf for her to shake. "Private investigator. You look like you're in the wrong place at possibly the wrong time."

"No, I'm in the right place," Mallory said. "I told everyone I know that I was going to be here."

"Then what do you need a private eye for?" asked the left head.

"I'm not real clear on that," Mallory said. "Are you good with a weapon?"

"Not really strong enough to hold a gun," his right head said.

"Martial arts?"

"Still just leaves here."

"Can you burn someone with your cigarettes?" she asked, grasping at straws.

"Yes!" the middle head said. "And I can bite someone and dissolve them slowly, if they're not too big."

"That's great. Our enemies will be terrified," she said.

INSTEAD OF DRINKING from a fire hose, Mallory now saw the vast information flowing through the hiveminds as a river. Mobius and their Sundry circuits were her sturdy raft. She stepped in and held on.

The river in her mind's eye became a tree. She could feel the trunk of the core of the hiveminds and then the branches of individual hives. The hives on Eternity, the ones on *Infinity* and Stephanie, and branching off even the little circuits that made up her and *Mobius*'s connections.

She turned her attention back to *Metis*, strong in places, more fractured in others. She could feel the Miu's influence touching here and there, unraveling *Metis*'s connection with Eve. And then the large cavity that was her fifth hivemind. Mallory paused at the edge, peering within to see if she could feel any signs of life. Whispers around her said to leave it; the same fate would come to any queen who tried to take that place.

No one has seen a queen like me, she thought. And she jumped.

"WHAT THE HELL do you mean it's wrong? She's right there!"

"Who's there?" Zesty's voice tried to cut through the tension in the alley, but he sounded frightened.

"Come on, let's go digest a bad guy," Mallory said.

Bruce leaped from the shadows, his straight teeth glinting, and he cut her once on the neck and once in the thigh.

Blood spurted. Mallory fell to her knees.

"Even if they catch me, at least I know I got the better of you," he hissed as the light went out in her eyes.

A white-hot pain in his cheek startled him, and he hissed and moved away from the giant plant that menaced him with lit cigarettes.

"Let's get the fuck out of here," he said to the Miu.

"It's wrong? How do you mean?" he demanded.

He and the Miu flipped.

MALLORY HAD NEVER wondered how many Sundry her human brainpower could equal. She knew it was more than one, but never thought it was anywhere near a hive's worth, or even a single queen. But once she established herself as a queen, things started to move around her. The nine Sundry took wing, forming a fledgling hivemind to call to others.

Aboard Eternity, Sundry broke from their hives to heed the call, flowing in a stream through the shuttle bay, silver and blue Sundry flying to the one Sundry ship docked at the station. Some Sundry left Stephanie and *Infinity* to join the others.

Physically the ship took a few minutes to go from Eternity to *Metis*, but in the terms of the hiveminds, those Sundry were already bonded to Mallory and *Metis*'s emergency call. The ship docked with *Metis* and the Sundry came streaming into the ship, frightening convention attendees, then flowing through ventilation ducts to stream into *Metis*'s heart.

The Cuckoos who were aiding the Miu with its goals became fractured. The few who tried to fight were killed instantly. Many returned to the safety of Tina's chest cavity, unaware that the bitch queen was very, very angry.

XAN'S BREATH CAUGHT in his throat. "There," he whispered.

Behind Mallory, on the side of a hill, the grass shimmered and became a glowing portal. Bruce stepped out and looked around, his face scratched with one round burn on his cheek. He spotted Mallory instantly and ran forward, his knife out. It plunged into Mallory's back and her eyes went wide, then she fell to her knees and tipped forward.

"Where are the king's riders?" screamed the elf. "Who let this human out on her own to die alone?"

"Speaking of, where are they?" Xan said. "They need to grab him, like now."

But as the cavalry thundered into Bobbiton, the murderer disappeared.

"Goddammit!" yelled Xan, punching Jack in the arm. "Why did I ever trust you?"

"They were supposed to come!" Jack said, baffled. "They were supposed to be fast!"

"There's only one more place to check," Xan snarled. "Eve, can you get me to the junkyard?"

Eve looked up from the laptop. Her dark hair was pulled back, the burn scar on her cheek shiny, but she was engrossed in her work and didn't seem to care. "Done," she said.

MALLORY SAT MOTIONLESS in the murder shack, eyes closed, hands on her lap. She was somewhere else.

Part of something so much bigger.

She finally understood the Sundry. Not the vast river of information, but she understood her place in it. *Mobius* helped. Her constant companions helped. It didn't hurt anymore. What she could do with this power—it was dizzying.

The attack was not graceful. Bruce came from the murder shack ceiling, much like Mallory had assumed he had dropped Aaron. He landed on her, driving the knife into her neck and through her collarbone.

She didn't make a sound as the light in her eyes died, fixed on him.

He panted. "Satisfied?"

The Miu didn't say anything. He looked up. The creature was gone. Bruce left the shack, wiping his hands on his shirt, looking around.

He didn't hear or see Xan come out from behind the shack. When he was hit with a baseball bat that used to be a minor league scorecard, he went over with a grunt.

Tina hovered right above the shack, holding the writhing Miu by the scruff of the neck like a cat. "You are a bad cat." She thumped her chest. "You are all bad friends!"

THE SUNDRY QUEEN came to take Mallory's place. Mallory surrendered it, giving up the position of the center of the hivemind.

On a whim, before she left, she asked, *What's your name?* Even though she knew most Sundry didn't have names.

Blue Jean, the new queen said.

Mallory thought she heard excited squeeing in the distance.

Blue Jean gifted Mallory with eight Sundry to always keep herself and Mobius connected to the hive, and bade her farewell. She had a lot of work to do.

25

. . .

WHAT THE HIVEMINDS KNEW

BEFORE MALLORY LEFT, she asked *Metis, What happened to you when you crashed on Earth?*

All of the data came through at once, hitting her like a fist to her eye.

The Miu was a race that built spaceships that were advanced even by today's standards. But they were too clever. Their ship concepts could easily turn into war machines that could swallow suns. Or covert ops vehicles that could disappear a leader or a hostage forever. When the other races found out about it, some wanted the ships, but the Miu wouldn't sell, and others wanted the ships destroyed. So the Miu took *Metis* and ran.

Their greatest architect was left behind by accident in a desert on the Earth. When she was spotted by the locals, they worshipped her. Not a bad way to die, all told.

Metis had been fitted with a bio-tracker, meaning if she ever became operational again, the Miu would know. It might take centuries or more, but the Miu descendants would know.

The data of the ship, plans, technology, languages, and more washed over Mallory.

She came to behind the murder shack, shaking, but better than she had ever been after merging with the Sundry. She squeezed *Mobius* and asked if he was all right.

Better than all right! Blue Jean is a queen!

Xan and Jack were at either side of her, helping her to her feet. She was wobbly but okay.

She blinked up at Xan. "Did it work?"

He indicated the prone body of Bruce at Tina's feet. "It almost didn't, but yeah, it worked."

"Is he dead?"

"No!" Tina said. "They won't let me jump on him."

The yellow alien hung limply from Tina's fist. It fixed her with a baleful eye.

"Yeah, it was a nice try, but you lost," she said. "Might have been easier for you if you hadn't decided to work with a murderer."

Mallory took a look into the shed and saw her own body lying there, skewered with a knife. She shuddered and looked up at Jack.

"It's not every day that you find out someone wrote fan-fic of your life, and then to find that fan-fic manifested in real life. I kind of feel like we just slaughtered them for no reason."

"I can make them come back," Jack said.

"They did come in handy, so thanks for that," she said. But she couldn't help but feel a dizzy disconnect looking at the dead Mallory's body.

"Bring these back to life if you want, but please don't write any more fan-fic about me, okay?" Mallory asked.

"Promise," Jack said.

She relaxed into Xan's side. "Thanks for insisting we have a decoy down here while I did the Sundry thing. I thought the bobbits or cavalry would take care of catching him, but clearly I needed her."

"Yeah, we were supposed to catch him in Bobbiton," he said, glaring at Jack. "But the good news is, Eve has control of *Metis* again. Your hivemind trick worked, *Infinity* and Stephanie are reporting that all the hives who lost Sundry are doing fine."

Tina picked up her foot and put it on Bruce's back. She didn't look like she was leaning on it, but she was still massive. Bruce groaned under her. "No one asked if I'm all right," Tina said.

"Tina, you caused half of this!" Mallory said. "You brought the alien aboard, you trusted your Cuckoos!"

"Yes, and I feel very bad about all of that! Therefore I am not all right!" Tina said, pointing to her own injured soul. "Or maybe that's the hangover. Now I have to take this little Miu guy back to Bezoar, and any diplomacy we start to give the innocent generations of prisoners will have to exclude the Miu for the time being. This guy is staying there for a long time."

"What about the Cuckoos?" Mallory asked.

"What Cuckoos?" Tina said flatly. She shifted slightly and hundreds of Cuckoo bodies fell out of her chest cavity. She paused for a moment, and then said, "I only did that for effect. Someone pick them up for me, I want their bio-mass."

"I don't want to watch this time," Mallory said, wincing. "Let's go back upstairs. Can we go see the hob—I mean the bobbits again?"

"We have to assure them that you're not dead," Jack said, grimacing.

26

SOME JOBS YOU CAN'T
USE EAGLES FOR

'M SORRY OUR plan to catch Bruce up here didn't work out,"
Jack said. "I have always wanted to solve a problem with a giant
eagle."

The humans stood politely on the perimeter of the Bobbiton
church and graveyard, watching the weeping bobbits bury Mallory's fan-fic doppelgänger.

They told the bobbits the truth about Mallory, but the bobbits
didn't accept it and insisted on a funeral.

"Of course they do," Eve said. "They're as real as she was. If
you say that this Mallory is disposable, then you're saying they
are, too."

"I sense way too much philosophy and personhood debating
around this, so I'm just going to step back," Mallory said.

Hilbo had gone into his house, muttering about how there are
some jobs you can't use eagles for. He said he was going to call
DanDILF about this twin thing, mark his words.

"Mrs. B and Tina are coming down to deal with the prisoners,"
Xan said.

Mallory sighed with relief, finally able to relax again. "I'm glad
that's out of our hands at last."

Eve pushed elves away from her bedside, demanding that they

let her go, that she was all right. The flustered citizens fretted that Lord ItsObvious would disapprove.

"Are these going to disappear when we leave the ship?" Mallory asked Eve, pointing to the bandages around Eve's head.

"I'll find out when you do," Eve said, indicating her many cuts. "I'm still not entirely sure about what reality is anymore."

"I understand," Mallory said slowly. "But I know I can't explain it. I think it's like a real first aid kit. All of these items will stay with us when we leave."

"What about this stuff?" Eve asked, pointing to her arm covered in foul-smelling goo provided by the pleasant bobbit ladies who then wanted to pack leaves on her cuts and then bandage it.

"I think it's real enough," Mallory said. "But can we take our new friends off the ship with us? I don't think I would want to try it."

Eve winced as a healer tied her concussion bandage tighter. "Now we know why the Miu kept this ship hidden."

"What are you going to do with *Metis* now?" Mallory asked.

"You need more food to heal!" shouted one bobbit, scurrying inside a hill doorway. This set everyone else scrambling, no one wanting to be the one bobbit who didn't provide anything.

Eve looked down, frowning. "I don't know. She's important to me. If I take her home and the army finds out about her . . ."

"Oh, yeah, you don't want that," Xan said from where he sat in the sun, stealing a cookie that a bobbit was trying to give to Eve.

"It depends on how much you want to stay on Earth. With the backing of certain ambassadors, you could be like a diplomatic ship," Mallory said.

"Or shit, make it a circus ship," Phineas said. "That would be killer. Or make it your own touring music festival."

"Or another mystery cruise," Mallory said.

Cosima came to sit by Mallory. She chose a pastry from the table of food that just kept getting bigger. "So, about us," she said.

"Yeah, I was thinking about that. I don't think I can hire you as my agent and my assistant."

"Why not?" Cosima demanded. "When it comes to your books, I'll be your agent. When it comes to murders, I'll be your assistant."

"Yeah, but what about your other clients?" Mallory said, pointing at Jack.

She wilted slightly. "Okay. But if we're together and there's a murder, I'm totally going to be your assistant, okay?"

"I don't think I could stop you," Mallory said.

"Uh-oh, hail to the chief," Xan said, nodding down the road where Mrs. Brown and Jessica approached them.

"This is new," Mrs. Brown said.

"What, the bobbits?" Mallory asked.

"No, that I got a murderer handed to me that wasn't dead or maimed," Mrs. Brown said.

"I must be growing up," Mallory said. "We had two murders, one assault, and a very excitable growing ship."

Mrs. Brown's face lit up when she saw *Mobius*. She cooed like he was her grandbaby. "Growing so much, with your own hive-mind now! So big!"

Mobius basked in the attention.

"Stephanie would like to meet her little sister," Mrs. Brown said. "And you should introduce her to the queen soon."

"Oh, shit, I forgot about Tina," Mallory whispered.

Mobius was able to convey Justmie's comments to the humans while Tina and Stephanie had their own conversation.

"She will be happy to meet the other Gneiss, so long as no one tries to stop her from following her destiny as a starship pilot," *Mobius* reported.

"We will need more pilots on Bezoar," Tina said. "It can't just be a place to dump people forever."

"*Mobius* is not going to Bezoar for *decades*," Mallory said.

"We'll see," Tina said placidly.

Despite the bobbits' objections, the humans took Eve back to Eternity for proper medical treatment. Then the fantasy characters wept when Jack said he was leaving, too.

"No one will notice us if we slip out of here," Xan said. "*Infinity* is waiting."

"Won't Jessica want you to fly back with her?" Mallory said.

"Yeah, about that. When it was all over, she messaged me, first to make sure I was alive, and second to dump me."

"Why?"

He gave a rueful smile. "She thinks that I jump to follow you into any fire that—and I quote—'you go around setting.'"

"That's cold," Mallory said. "But I'm sorry for you."

"She's not wrong," Xan said with a shrug. "Except about you making these problems. She's right that when people need you, I find that I need to be beside you."

"That's really sweet," she said. "I wouldn't want to do it without you."

He took a step forward and extended his hand. Mallory took it, and they headed for *Infinity*.

Once they were aboard, she closed her eyes and smiled. She might just be hitting her stride in space. Finally.

ACKNOWLEDGMENTS

· · · ·

Thanks to the following in no particular order: to Jatovi McDuffie and the Durham Bulls for baseball; to the Great Old Ones Gamers for distraction, baked goods, and board games; to the Drunks in Space for kvetching; to Richard Dansky for constant support; to the JoCo Cruise for giving me a drastic change of scenery (and letting me understand the layout of a cruise ship); to my agent, Seth Fishman, for his advice, energy, and enthusiasm; to my editor, Anne Sowards, (and the whole crew at Ace) for their patience with me so I could get this book right; to Dr. John Cmar for always being available when I have a medical question; to my mentor, James Patrick Kelly, who has supported me for years; to Ursula and Kevin for being an emotional support human and terrible fountain pen enabler (respectively). If I have forgotten someone (like I suspect I always do), then I am terribly sorry.

As always, my family of Jim, Fiona, my parents, and stepparents are instrumental to keeping me going with regards to writing and mental health. No acknowledgment will ever be enough.

Lastly, to my podcast audience for the past twenty years, who assured me there were ears and eyes for my stories, and to you, for picking up this book. This is my eighth book, and I still can't believe this is my job.

Stay safe, stay kind.

Mur
October 7, 2024
Durham, NC

MUR LAFFERTY is an author, podcaster, and editor. She has been nominated for many awards and has even won a few. She lives in Durham, North Carolina, with her family.

VISIT MUR LAFFERTY ONLINE

MurVerse.com

Twitch.tv/MightyMur

Ready to find
your next great read?

Let us help.

Visit prh.com/nextread

Penguin
Random
House